"This may be the best news of the summer—T. R. Pearson is back...giving us an invitation to remember what life and literature is essentially about. How he can bring that off amidst such hilarity is something like a miracle....Neely, N.C. should be as well lodged in the American literary mind as Faulkner's Yoknapatawpha."

The Atlanta Journal Constitution

"Good news for fans of Pearson's *A Short History of a Small Place*. This second novel is even funnier and more inspired, with scenes (especially sex scenes) that will make readers laugh out loud."

Publishers Weekly

"That his narratives are more often attempts at narratives, proposing to tell a story but veering helplessly at every fork in the road to scoop up other stories that strike him as equally worthwhile, is partly what makes them so funny. Like one of his own characters, Pearson can't present the simplest occurrence without a preliminary 'two or three dozen laps all roundabout the dilemma.'"

The New York Times Book Review

(more...)

Also by T. R. Pearson
Published by Ballantine Books:

A SHORT HISTORY OF A SMALL PLACE

OFF
FOR
THE
SWEET
HEREAFTER

T. R. PEARSON

BALLANTINE BOOKS • NEW YORK

Library of Congress Catalog Card Number: 85-30027

ISBN 0-345-34369-7

This edition published by arrangement with Simon & Schuster, Inc.

Manufactured in the United States of America

First Ballantine Books Edition: June 1987

For
J. Nelson Hathcock
himself

One

THAT WAS the summer we lost the bald Jeeter who was not even mostly Jeeter anymore but was probably mostly Throckmorton or anyway was probably considered mostly Throckmorton which was an appreciable step up from being considered mostly Jeeter since Jeeters hadn't ever been anything much while Throckmortons had in fact been something once previously before the money got gone and the prestige fell away leaving merely the bluster and the taint and the general Throckmorton aroma all of which taken together hardly made for a legacy worth getting stirred up over but any one of which taken singly still outstripped the entire bulk of advancements ever attempted and realized by Jeeters who had scratched around in the dirt but were not much accomplished at farming and who had speculated in herds of cattle but were not much accomplished at speculating either and who at last had turned their energies to the construction of a henhouse which commenced ramshackle and got worse but became nonetheless the chief Jeeter advancement along with the hens and the little speckled brown eggs and the localized ammonia cloud which was itself most probably the primary Jeeter success though no particular Jeeter or group of Jeeters together actually contributed to it or could prevent it either so when the bald Jeeter, with the fat Jeeter as her maid of honor, exchanged vows with Braxton Porter Throckmorton III in the sanctuary of the Methodist church on Saturday

June the twelfth, 1942, and afterwards set up house in Neely proper she got away from the hens and the hen-house and out from under the ammonia cloud which was most likely beginning to expand in June of 1942 since it set in to expanding most every June and swelled straight through August and on into September, especially this past August and especially this past September when it was bearing down on the town limits and posing some threat to the icehouse which was regular and ordinary for the season, particularly in August and particularly in September, so we were having what had come to be our usual summer straight up to the moment Mr. Derwood Bridger laid his ladder against the Throckmorton clapboard and climbed to the upper story where he pressed his nose to the bedroom windowscreen and shaded his eyes and called and hollered and shrieked at the bald Jeeter until he was satisfied that she was gone from us for good.

Mrs. Askew's front gutter had been troubling her some of late. It was not living up to its responsibilities as far as Mrs. Askew was concerned, and though she did not to any degree consider herself an authority on guttering she did hold to her personal conviction that downspouts were intended to serve more than a purely ornamental function which Mrs. Askew believed to be the solitary function her downspouts were serving since they did not seem to get involved much with rainwater when the opportunity presented itself. Instead whatever the front gutter happened to catch off the roof did not flow to the right or the left but proceeded direct over the lip into Mrs. Askew's jonquil bed and onto her front stoop where it puddled up nicely for the newsboy, Bill Ed Myrick jr., who could throw a *Chronicle* almost anywhere that was wet or out of reach or otherwise excessively inconvenient and what part of the puddle the paper didn't sop up eventually seeped off through the foundation to Mrs. Askew's cellar floor where it did what it could to con-

tribute to the mustiness roundabout. Of course Mrs.
Askew's downspouts had lapsed in obsolescence long
before Mrs. Askew got sufficiently worked up to cure
them of it. Ever since Mr. Askew passed away in 1967
the dilapidation of the Askew house had proceeded
unchecked and with some serious velocity since Mrs.
Askew was not nearly so adroit and handy as Mr.
Askew who had not in any real sense been adroit and
handy himself but ever could successfully manipulate
the telephone so as to introduce a proper expert into
whatever situation might be ripe for one; as a rule Mr.
Askew, who prepared the weekly payroll at the cotton
mill, did not take a personal interest in any manner of
degenerated household item unless it could be added,
subtracted, multiplied, or divided into good repair.
But Mr. Askew had not put his dialing finger to much
use or even wiggled it for that matter since October of
1967 and Mrs. Askew had never come to develop any
sort of purposeful relationship with the Neely yellow
pages, so season in and season out for very likely a half
dozen years or more rainwater dripped off the roof
and overflowed the front gutter into the jonquil bed
and onto the stoop without ever venturing towards the
downspout to the left or the one to the right either,
each of which hung at an opposite corner of the house
and both of which together enlivened the general
aspect with their presence.

There's no reason to believe Mrs. Askew would
have ever repaired, replaced, or otherwise unduly
bothered herself with the front gutter if Bill Ed Myrick
jr. had not landed Mrs. Askew's brother's child full
into the heart of a fully developed stoop puddle. Mrs.
Askew's niece, Miss Belinda Heather Sewell, had
come out at the country club on a Friday evening in
late July and a picture of her and her father was to
appear in the Saturday *Chronicle*, a picture Mrs.
Askew intended to clip and hold for a keepsake since
what girls got the chance to come out were not gener-

ally allowed to do it more than once. However, along about two o'clock Saturday afternoon a tremendous rainstorm kicked up out of the southeast and while Mrs. Askew's runoff was still beating back the jonquils and pooling up against the threshold Bill Ed Myrick jr. came round with the paper and delivered Mrs. Askew's copy by way of a sharp overhand toss from the curbing. Bill Ed did not see it necessary or fitting to squander the time it would take to walk the twenty-five feet up to Mrs. Askew's door and back again or up to anybody else's door and back again either since Bill Ed was not one to meander until he got onto the boulevard where he could do some meaningful loitering under Marcia Satterwhite's bedroom window. So Bill Ed threw Mrs. Askew's *Chronicle* from the curbing, with his wrist mostly, and like usual fired it square against the bottom portion of Mrs. Askew's aluminum stormdoor and thereby produced a severe dose of flutters and palpitations in Mrs. Askew who was momentarily too preoccupied with regulating her breathing to figure out that the racket had to be made by what it was made by. Consequently, Mrs. Askew could not manage to fetch in the paper until it had already sopped up all the stoop puddle it could hold, and even though she peeled the society page off from the rest and dried it in the oven the photograph of Mrs. Askew's brother and Mrs. Askew's brother's daughter had bled into and been ruined by a sizable rectangular advertisement for Dr. Norma Talton's Clinic of Chiropractic on the Richardson Road. And in a fit of matchless and highly uncharacteristic pique, and with Bill Ed Myrick jr. already gone off down the boulevard to Marcia Satterwhite's bedroom window, Mrs. Askew snatched up the phone and more than held up her end of a passionate exchange with a gentleman at Sears and Roebuck.

They sent Mr. Mountcastle on the Wednesday following the Saturday of the photograph of Mrs.

Askew's brother and Mrs. Askew's brother's daughter at the Friday night coming out. Mr. Mountcastle was one of the Eden Mountcastles and though he had his own business he did most all the Sears and Roebuck gutter work roundabout. As a rule, Mountcastles are by nature excruciatingly conscientious and Mr. Mountcastle the gutterman was not any exception. In fact not any of all the dozens of Eden Mountcastles was any exception except for one, that being Watt Mountcastle of the homeplace who had somehow or another got burdened with all of the sloth and sorriness that the rest of the Mountcastles had neglected to take on for themselves. But even Watt Mountcastle was a joy to the family and all of the rest of the Mountcastles clamored to do for him because, with the exception of Watt himself, Mountcastles are excruciatingly considerate also, and Mrs. Askew's Mr. Mountcastle was probably one of the most excruciating Mountcastles to be had anywhere. Mr. Mountcastle told Mrs. Askew that he would come by at ten o'clock on Wednesday and he did which should have given Mrs. Askew some indication of what she was in for. Then he climbed up on the roof straightaway and studied Mrs. Askew's front gutter from all over and poked at it and tapped at it and scrutinized the downspouts with a flashlight, and the thing of it was Mrs. Askew did not want him to study the front gutter or poke it or tap it or even begin to scrutinize the downspouts. She simply wanted him to take the whole business down off the house and replace it with some of Sears's best seamless aluminum guttering which she knew to be on sale on account of the most recent of the supplementary catalogs which still came to Mr. Askew through the mail though he was not inclined to do much shopping any longer. But after Mr. Mountcastle had concluded his studying and poking and tapping and scrutinizing and had come down off the roof, he did not find himself disposed to sell Mrs. Askew even the first seamless foot of Sears's

best aluminum guttering because he had brought all
his native excruciatingness to bear on the subject and
could not get comfortable with the notion that seamless aluminum guttering was what the situation called
for. And Mr. Mountcastle screwed the toe of his right
shoe into Mrs. Askew's front lawn as he commenced to
endeavor to make an observation which he persisted in
commencing to endeavor to make for a measurable
span of time, since Eden Mountcastles are extraordinarily slow-tongued on top of everything else, until at
last he did manage to say, "Ma'm, have you tended to
your guttering lately? Cleaned it, I mean, cleared it of
leaves and pine needles and such rubbish as that?"

And Mrs. Askew, who figured herself to be slam in
the middle of tending to her guttering, crossed her
arms over her chest and told Mr. Mountcastle she'd
had no occasion to be up on the roof anytime lately, to
which Mr. Mountcastle did not reply and did not screw
his toe into the lawn either but instead simply smiled
much like the way Jesus smiles in those pictures of him
on the walls of the Methodist fellowship hall.

"Let's just you and me tidy this thing up some," Mr.
Mountcastle said and helped himself to Mrs. Askew's
garden hose which was rolled up behind a camellia
bush at the corner of the house. He hauled it up onto
the roof with him, squatted on the shingles, and told
Mrs. Askew if she'd just step over to the faucet and
give it a turn he'd wash her gutter down for her.

But Mrs. Askew did not want her gutter washed
down or tended to or tidied up or otherwise fooled
with. She wanted it hauled off. So Mrs. Askew did not
leap directly into the shrubbery to the watertap, did
not go much of anywhere at all, but instead stayed
where she was, laid her head back a little, and aired
out some rather emphatic sentiments on the subject of
seamless aluminum guttering which was a rare display
for Mrs. Askew since neither Askews nor Sewells either are known to be particularly emphatic people by
nature.

From where she was there on the front lawn Mrs. Askew probably could not see that Mr. Mountcastle was smiling like Jesus again. She watched him stick the nozzle of the hose into the near downspout, descend the ladder, cross into the shrubbery to the watertap and back out again, and then up towards the roof once more, and though she did not ever not watch him from the time he came down off the house to the time he went back up onto it, Mrs. Askew still probably did not notice that Mr. Mountcastle was smiling like Jesus since she seemed to be looking at him a little too hard to actually be seeing anything. And Mr. Mountcastle sat on his heels all the way across the roof and plucked the serious debris out from the gutter and tossed it onto the lawn and washed most everything else into the downspouts until at last he was satisfied that the water was going where it ought to or anyway that most all of the water was going where it ought to except for the drips and droplets that fell through the various rust holes in the galvanized metal, holes which Mr. Mountcastle told Mrs. Askew he could patch as good as ever.

But Mrs. Askew had not wanted her gutter washed out or tidied up or tended to and did not care to have it patched either. She wanted it hauled off. So before Mr. Mountcastle could begin to spread his lips even a quarter of the way out across his face, Mrs. Askew said to him, "I do believe aluminum gutters would be the thing," and while she remained excessively emphatic for an Askew or a Sewell, she had fallen off some from her previous showing.

"Yes ma'm," Mr. Mountcastle said and swung around onto the ladder.

"I mean I do believe they are just what I need," Mrs. Askew told Mr. Mountcastle, told his backside mostly.

And Mr. Mountcastle paused in front of Mrs. Askew and replied, "Yes ma'm," before continuing on across the lawn to his truck and fetching from it a tube of plumber's dope.

"They would be a refreshing change," Mrs. Askew insisted.

"Yes ma'm," Mr. Mountcastle said, "they probably would," and back up the ladder he went with his tube of plumber's dope and squatted all across the roof dabbing a little of it into each of the rust holes. And when he'd replaced the cap on the tube and when he'd removed the tube to his pocket, Mrs. Mountcastle stood stark upright and asked Mrs. Askew, "What about the backside?"

"Everything's fine there," Mrs. Askew told him, "no trouble at all, not a leak or a drip or a puddle anywhere ever."

"Yes ma'm," Mr. Mountcastle said, and then him and the nozzle end of the hose disappeared over the rooftop.

Mr. Mountcastle suggested that Mrs. Askew have the insides of her gutters painted with a sealer within the month and he wrote down Mr. Derwood Bridger's name and number on the back of the bill, for all of which Mrs. Askew did not exactly let on to be so exceedingly grateful but earned herself one of Mr. Mountcastle's most accomplished Nazarene grins anyway. And in fact Mrs. Askew intended to follow Mr. Mountcastle's advice and call Mr. Bridger straight off. She intended to call him directly after Mr. Mountcastle departed but somehow she only continued to intend to call Mr. Bridger on through the third week in July and the fourth week and the first and second weeks in August and into the middle of the third one simply because it was far more convenient for Mrs. Askew to perpetually intend to do a thing than it was for her to actually set out and do it. Anyway after Mr. Mountcastle brought the garden hose down off the roof and carried his ladder to his truck Mrs. Askew discovered she was not plagued with a runoff problem anymore or a stoop puddle either and could not convince herself to feel plagued or troubled or even the slightest bit bothered by the insides of her gutters since that was not anything she could stand on the front lawn and get annoyed over. So Mrs. Askew could not seem to get beyond intending to call Mr. Bridger until midmorning of Friday August the eighteenth which was significant to Mrs. Askew only because it followed the afternoon of Thurdsay August the seventeenth which was truly the crucial time on account of it was Thursday the seventeenth previous to Friday the eighteenth that Bill Ed Myrick jr. cocked his wrist from the curbing and launched Mrs. Askew's afternoon *Chronicle* clean up onto the roof where it settled against the toilet vent, and while Mrs. Askew believed herself a touch niggardly for leaving her gutter troughs unpainted she could not begin to abide the sight of a newspaper on the roof of her house since of all the things a woman who can stand most anything cannot stand, trashiness is probably at the top of the pile. So Mrs. Askew slipped the Sears and Roebuck bill out from under the magnet on the refrigerator door, snatched up the telephone, and became somewhat passionately emphatic all over again.

Mr. Bridger could not possible come by on Friday the nineteenth or Saturday the twentieth or Sunday the twenty-first or Monday the twenty-second and Wednesday was more likely than Tuesday though Thursday was probably the best he could do unless it rained. As a primary occupation Mr. Bridger drove the backend of the hook and ladder out of the Omega firehouse and he was on four days and off three days during the weeks he was not on three days and off four days. As it turned out, Mr. Bridger had duty from Friday the nineteenth through Monday the twenty-second and he figured he would need Tuesday the twenty-third to rest himself from the rigors of his occupation which in Neely consisted of eating and playing ping pong and eating and playing canasta and eating and watching television and eating and sleeping in the up-

stairs barracks so as to slide down the pole hungry
again. There was not much call for firefighting roundabout and there was not any call for a hook and ladder
or a driver of the backend of it or the frontend either
unless in some unlikely happenstance the topnotch of a
yellow pine managed to burst into flames on its own.
So Mr. Bridger did not do much of anything in the way
of work on his on days and let himself out as a house-
painter and general fixit man on his off days when he
did not do much of anything in the way of work also.
Not that Mr. Bridger was a lazy man or a slackard, he
was just what people call steady and earnest, like a
glacier is steady and earnest. Consequently, when Mr.
Bridger told Mrs. Askew he'd come by on Thursday if
it didn't rain and then it didn't rain and he came by on
Friday, Mrs. Askew did not lay any particular blame
with Mr. Bridger because she understood that Mr.
Bridger had in fact been coming on Thursday but simply had never arrived. It was like the world spun
around faster than Mr. Bridger could bring himself to
spin with it.

But he did come by on Friday along about the middle of the afternoon and that was only one full day and
four hours later than he'd said he would come which
would have been unforgivable in most people but was
very nearly early for Mr. Bridger. However, even on
Friday and even four hours later on Friday than he'd
promised to come on Thursday, Mr. Bridger did not
make anything in the way of feverish progress on Mrs.
Askew's gutters. Initially, him and Mrs. Askew stood
together on the front lawn and considered the gutter
and considered the downspouts and considered the
Thursday *Chronicle* next to the toilet vent, and then
Mr. Bridger asked after Mrs. Askew's well-being and
Mrs. Askew obliged him with a fairly interminable and
lamentatious account of her lack thereof, and Mrs.
Askew, being as she was a widowwoman of considerable complaints with no regular ear to pour them into,

did not leave off lamentating or contemplate leaving off lamentating until she had run up a sizable catalog of annoyances, afflictions, and general torments. Mr. Bridger, through no particular fault of his own in this instance, lagged near about twenty-five years behind Mrs. Askew and so had become only partially as annoyed and afflicted and tormented as Mrs. Askew was, but Mr. Bridger did recollect he had an aunt down with the piles and since Mr. Askew had been a pile sufferer, Mr. Bridger and Mrs. Askew landed upon some common territory and carried on from there for an appreciable spell. They did get on to the topic of gutters eventually, not because the topic of piles wore out but mostly on account of Mrs. Askew who felt that the discussion was heading in an indelicate direction and who believed that there were some things a woman of standing did not speak of with her gutter-painter. However, even once they left off with the piles and set in with the gutters, Mrs. Askew and Mr. Bridger did not go to the trouble at hand straightaway but instead commenced with gutters as a general item and wandered some to the theory of the downspout before coming full around to Mrs. Askew's specific run of freshly cleaned, plumber's doped, galvanized trough. And Mr. Bridger took ahold of his chin and surveyed the underside of Mrs. Askew's front guttering and Mrs. Askew surveyed it along with him until she finally suggested that Mr. Bridger would probably have to get his ladder and climb up onto the roof since it was not the underside of the gutter that needed any attention, and Mr. Bridger blew a breath overtop of his knuckles and told Mrs. Askew he did not see any way around it himself.

So Mr. Bridger unstrapped his aluminum extension ladder from off the top of his Country Squire station wagon, ran it up several rungs past the front guttering, and climbed onto Mrs. Askew's roof. Now Mrs. Askew's neighbors all roundabout had been watching

through their windowsheers Mrs. Askew and Mr.
Bridger on Mrs. Askew's front lawn discussing whatever it was they were discussing which not any one of
them even remotely imagined had anything whatsoever to do with piles but which they had each speculated upon and wondered at until they were all fairly
much thoroughly eaten up with curiosity. But while
peeking through sheer draperies had developed locally
into a kind of sport on a par with bowling or miniature
golf so that hardly a promiment windowlight in the
town limits did not bear a noseprint on some part or
another of it, outright gawking in the open air was not
nearly so stylish unless of course the outright gawkee
could be construed to be engaged in some form of active labor which automatically forgave any onlookers
since watching other people work enjoyed considerable favor throughout the county and on into the far
reaches of the state. So Mr. Bridger had not put shoe-
leather to shingle when the clatter and rattle of dead-
bolts and screendoor hooks kicked up around him like
a hailstorm. One house down the street the widow
Mrs. Jennings W. Hayes stepped out onto her frontporch blinking in the sun and one house up the street
the bald Jeeter Throckmorton make a great show of
peering into her mailbox before hooting at Mrs.
Askew as if she was verily astounded to see her.
Across the way Miss Bernice Fay Frazier and her sister, Mrs. Estelle Frazier Singletary, left off haggling
with and snapping at each other long enough to poke
their heads out the sidedoor, and Mr. Tiny Aaron enjoyed the great good fortune of having turned off the
boulevard onto Mrs. Askew's street in his stark white
Impala just as Mr. Bridger was hunkering down into
his initial squat on the roof, and Mr. Aaron brought
his car very nearly off the road and to the curbing in
front of Mrs. Askew's house but not quite and he laid
himself full out the sidewindow from the chest up.

Mr. Bridger's labor took the form of some serious

peering, but serious peering, especially from a rooftop, can stir people appreciably and soon enough Mrs. Askew found herself in the company of the widow Mrs. Jennings W. Hayes and the bald Jeeter Throckmorton and Miss Bernice Fay Frazier and her sister, Mrs. Estelle Frazier Singletary, who lived across town on the ninth fairway with Mr. Estelle Singletary but had happily timed her visit. Mrs. Askew introduced the ladies to Mr. Bridger and introduced Mr. Bridger to the ladies, and then attempted to explain the nature of her gutter dilemma breaking off from time to time to field inquiries from Mr. Aaron down on the street. Of course at length the topic of gutters lost the majority of its appeal, and because the issue was still much on her mind Mrs. Askew touched briefly upon the delicate subject of piles and made mention of Mrs. Bridger's suffering aunt which generated noticeable feeling among the ladies who all laid their heads back and openly expressed their deep regret and sympathy for which Mr. Bridger said, "Thank you," from the roof.

On several occasions Mr. Askew reminded Mr. Bridger to fetch down the Thursday *Chronicle* from beside the toilet vent and invariably Mr. Bridger would stand up from his squat long enough to rehike his pants and tall her, "Yes ma'm," but chiefly Mrs. Askew found herself engaged in a lively exchange of pleasantries with her neighbors and Mrs. Estelle Singletary which were punctuated every now and again by questions from Mr. Tiny Aaron down on the road in his Impala who had dropped off the pace some and was just getting up to the piles. Mrs. Askew and her neighbors had plenty to talk about since even though they all lived within plain sight of each other not one of them ever went much of anywhere outside except to church on Sundays and while Mrs. Askew attended the Methodist church on Harker Avenue, the widow Mrs. Jennings W. Hayes gathered with the dissenting Pres-

byterians on the by-pass, and the bald Jeeter Throckmorton and Miss Bernice Fay Frazier both took themselves off to separate Baptist services, the bald Jeeter
being a First Baptist Church of Neely Baptist and Miss
Frazier, along with her sister, Mrs. Estelle Singletary, a
Calgary Free Will Baptist, the two of which were possibly the same species but were not hardly the same
animal. From all reports Mr. Tiny Aaron was generally
taken to be a regular heathen. So the ladies did not
run together much of a Sunday and did not run together much any other time either mostly because the
weather did not ever seem to suit them. In summer-
time the air was far too still and hot to be ventured
into while in wintertime the days were entirely too
short and cold. Autumn provided occasional pleasant
afternoons, but the ladies did not care for the north-
erly breezes, and though springtime held considerable
appeal the days were altogether far too changeable to
be relied upon. Consequently, Mrs. Askew and the
widow Mrs. Jennings W. Hayes and the bald Jeeter
Throckmorton and Miss Bernice Fay Frazier all
watched their stories on television most all afternoon
and most every afternoon except for Miss Bernice Fay
Frazier who was visited by her sister each Friday at
2:00 p.m. and so got the opportunity to haggle with
and snap at somebody on a regular basis.

The ladies were understandably all astir with news
once the guttering and the piles gave way to let them
air it, and the widow Mrs. Jennings W. Hayes commenced the proceedings by announcing that her
daughter, not the oldest daughter Jonellen Marie
Hayes but her next oldest daughter Rachel Suzanne
Hayes, had formed an attachment with a gentleman of
the law in Raleigh who was, the widow Mrs. Jennings
W. Hayes said, going places. Mrs. Estelle Singletary
told Mrs. Hayes she had a nephew that was a lawyer in
Americus, Georgia, and her and her sister, Miss Bernice Fay Frazier, both expressed their belief that he

was going places also. Then Mrs. Askew wondered did anybody know just what Tuttle it was that had died in Yanceyville, and the bald Jeeter said she'd heard it wasn't a native Yanceyville Tuttle but some sort of imported and naturalized Tuttle instead, and the widow Mrs. Jennings W. Hayes, who had gotten the same story from a cousin of hers in Wentworth, threw in with the bald Jeeter on the Tuttle matter while Mrs. Estelle Singletary made a point to say that she herself did not associate with Tuttles as a rule. Subsequently, Miss Bernice Fay Frazier recollected that on the previous Tuesday whole fryers had been on sale at the Big Apple for 47¢ a pound and she said she'd bought one but wished she'd bought two, and Mrs. Askew asked were they meaty to which Miss Bernice Fay Frazier replied yes they were and Mrs. Estelle Singletary said she'd bought three herself which prompted Miss Bernice Fay Frazier to reconsider and announce that she wished she'd bought three also. Mrs. Askew had not bought any chickens and though she wished she had also she did not set her desires at any particular number of whole fryers but instead persevered with the topic of edibles and was fixing to relate the main details of a magazine article she'd read on the uses of ornamental kale when Mr. Tiny Aaron from out the sidewindow of his stark white Impala down on the road set in to telling how he'd had a pilectomy himself in 1962, news of which somehow jarred Mrs. Askew back to business at hand and she made a point of reminding Mr. Bridger to fetch down the *Chronicle* from beside the toilet vent, so naturally Mr. Bridger stood up from his squat, rehiked his pants, and told her, "Yes ma'm."

While the ladies discussed garden vegetables which led to produce in general and culminated in a lively debate on the value of roughage so as to tie back in with the pilectomy that Mr. Tiny Aaron was describing from down on the road with both hands and his mouth

too, Mr. Bridger squatted across the front pitch of
Mrs. Askew's roof and tested Mr. Mountcastle's
plumber's dope patching with his finger. Once he'd satisfied himself that all the gutter holes were properly
filled or once he'd grown suitably weary of squatting,
whichever came first, Mr. Bridger climbed to the peak
of the house and stretched and straightened and
worked his back, taking particular care to massage the
pelvic bone he had fractured in the spring of 1977
when he fell off his ladder with his scraper and his
putty knife and his softball-sized lump of window glazing direct into Mrs. Zeno Stiers's forsythia bush. But
he did not linger unduly on the point of the roof and
was just proceeding to vanish by degrees down the far
slope when Mrs. Askew hollered up to him that everything was fine back there, that there was no trouble at
all, that there wasn't a leak or a drip or a puddle anywhere ever, to all of which Mr. Bridger waved his hand
back over his head before disappearing down to the far
gutter where, presumably, he squatted and tested and
grew weary all over again.

Mrs. Askew and the bald Jeeter Throckmorton and
Miss Bernice Fay Frazier and her sister, Mrs. Estelle
Frazier Singletary, were all analyzing the contents of
the widow Mrs. Jennings W. Hayes's special garden
salad dressing recipe and Mr. Tiny Aaron was just getting around to the virtues of proctology when Mr.
Bridger climbed down off the roof and approached
Mrs. Askew with his findings. He said he did believe
he could clear up Mrs. Askew's troubles with a solitary
coat of sealer and Mrs. Askew replied that she was
pleased to hear it and Mrs. Estelle Singletary told the
widow Mrs. Hayes she did not see any call for sesame
since it didn't seem much of a compliment to the remaining spices and the widow Mrs. Hayes objected
and became peevish. Mr. Bridger estimated he could
finish the job in no more than a couple of hours which
Mrs. Askew replied was agreeable to her and the bald

Jeeter ventured to say the sesame struck her as particularly appealing which stirred the widow Mrs. Hayes to theorize it was the sesame that enhanced the parsley flakes so enormously and down on the road Mr. Tiny Aaron set in to describing something with his hands which did not appear quite so large as a breadbox but very nearly. Then Mr. Bridger removed a small pad of white paper and a stubby pencil from his shirt pocket, scribbled a figure on the top sheet, and tore it loose and handed it to Mrs. Askew who immediately and utterly usurped the prominence the widow Mrs. Jennings W. Hayes's garden salad dressing had enjoyed for such a considerable spell. And although Mrs. Askew dodged and twisted and maneuvered extensively, they all saw it anyway except for the bald Jeeter who got told what it was by Mrs. Estelle Singletary who decided straight off she would not pay it if it was her. Miss Bernice Fay Frazier, in an exceptional lapse in haggling and snapping, threw in with her sister and condemned the figure as unreasonable, but the widow Mrs. Jennings W. Hayes who had had a plumber in to replace her kitchen taps in 1975 took a more moderate view, and the bald Jeeter Throckmorton said it did not seem to her such an awful lot of money either. So Mrs. Askew weighed off the various opinions and just prior to settling her own mind asked Mr. Bridger when he could possibly do the work, and Mr. Bridger told her first thing Monday morning which very likely meant Monday afternoon and could even be construed as Tuesday, but since Mrs. Askew did not believe she could get anybody else before then and since Mrs. Askew held the recommendation of an Eden Mountcastle in extraordinarily high regard she told Mr. Bridger to come ahead Monday morning which would certainly not be Monday morning at all but maybe Monday afternoon and probably Tuesday with Wednesday not entirely out of the realm of possibility. And then Mrs. Askew laid her head beck momentarily and said she did wish Mr. Bridger had recollected to fetch down the Thursday *Chronicle* from beside the toilet vent to which Mr. Bridger responded by sucking a dab of saliva between his front teeth.

He did in fact come back on the actual Monday after the Friday of his estimate when he said he would in fact come back and which happened to be the particular bald Jeeter Throckmorton Monday in August though nobody knew it was or even would be when Mr. Bridger brought his Country Squire wagon up the concrete runners Mrs. Askew called her driveway. He arrived in the middle of the afternoon and had full well intended to arrive in the middle of the morning but along about lunchtime Mr. Bridger discovered the middle of the morning was not around to arrive in anymore and so settled for the middle of the afternoon. Mrs. Askew had not expected him until along about Tuesday evening and consequently was not looking for Mr. Bridger and did not know he had returned until she heard something on the roof that she hoped was not a squirrel and in her great hurry to get out the front door, off the stoop, and into the yard, Mrs. Askew very nearly ran down Miss Bernice Fay Frazier who was standing on the walk with the widow Mrs. Jennings W. Hayes and the widow Mrs. Jennings W. Hayes's cleaning woman Shareena Moncrief of the Macedonia Avenue Moncriefs. They were all three looking at the front gutter or at the shingles or at the chimney stack, Mrs. Askew could not determine which though she was certain they were not looking at Mr. Bridger who had crossed over the peak of the house so as to commence his work on the backside. Mrs. Askew said she had not expected him to arrive so soon, and Miss Bernice Fay Frazier admitted she had not expected him to arrive so soon either which prompted the widow Mrs. Jennings W. Hayes to observe that she had not expected him to arrive so soon herself while Shareena Moncrief, who had not had any expectation to speak of, said nothing whatsoever.

As Mrs. Askew figured, they could all walk around to the backyard and watch Mr. Bridger from there or they could not walk around to the backyard and wait for him where they were, and Shareena Moncrief wanted to know just what she'd see if she took the trouble to walk around to the backyard, so Mrs. Askew, who did not understand much of what Mr. Bridger was up to, explained the entire process to Shareena Moncrief with the aid and assistance of Miss Bernice Fay Frazier and the widow Mrs. Jennings W. Hayes, who did not understand any of what Mr. Bridger was up to. As a result Shareena Moncrief decided not to circle around to Mrs. Askew's backyard and chose not to linger in Mrs. Askew's frontyard either but returned to the widow Mrs. Jennings W. Hayes's house so as to sanitize the upstairs toilet bowl which seemed to her altogether more promising than the prospect of watching Mr. Bridger do to a gutter what Mrs. Askew and Miss Bernice Fay Frazier and the widow Mrs. Jennings W. Hayes insisted he was going to do to a gutter. And when there were three of them not counting Mrs. Bridger instead of four of them not counting Mrs. Bridger, Miss Bernice Fay Frazier said out loud but to the widow Mrs. Jennings W. Hayes mostly, "I do believe the colored are entirely beyond me. Entirely," and near about the middle of the widow Mrs. Jennings W. Hayes's admitting that the colored were entirely beyond her also, except for Shareena Moncrief who was only partially beyond her, Mrs. Askew stepped backwards so as to glance full onto the bald Jeeter Throckmorton's frontporch and said, "Where is she, I wonder?"

Miss Bernice Fay Frazier wanted to know just who George Washington Carver was anyway, and so the widow Mrs. Jennings W. Hayes, whose partial comprehension of negrodom seemed to encompass the George Washington Carver question also, at least partially, set about with a few prefatory remarks on the significance of the peanut before addressing herself full onto the matter of Mr. Carver proper who proved to be considerably more elusive and mysterious than the peanut and who the widow Mrs. Jennings W. Hayes at last identified, following an extended bout of pondering and finger biting, as a small, curly-headed man.

"Do you think she's sick?" Mrs. Askew said.

"Who?" Miss Frazier asked her.

And Mrs. Askew stepped backwards again so as to look full onto the bald Jeeter Throckmorton's front porch.

"She's likely out to town," Miss Frazier said. "Don't you suspect?"

"I suppose," Mrs. Askew told her and lay back on her heels so as to peer around the porch stanchions.

The widow Mrs. Jennings W. Hayes decided Mr. Carver had most resembled snuff in color. "Like Tube Rose," she said. "Like Tube Rose in a can."

But Miss Bernice Fay Frazier grew testy and told the widow Mrs. Hayes the comparison was utterly lost on her since she did not and had never dipped herself and could not tolerate anyone who did dip. It seems snuff users were near about as far beyond Miss Frazier as negroes were. She said she could not ever hope to comprehend how people could befoul their mouths so with snuff or plug chew or even the buttends of cigarettes and cigars. Miss Frazier said she'd just as soon eat dirt as use tobacco which reminded the widow Mrs. Jennings W. Hayes that she'd seen pickaninnies eat dirt out of a clay bank across the road from her brother's house and Miss Frazier recollected she'd heard tell of such a thing before. "I wonder why it is?" Miss Frazier said, and since the widow Mrs. Jennings W. Hayes could not get a handle on it herself, they put it down as just one more item that was entirely beyond them.

Mrs. Askew had slipped off in the midst of Miss Bernice Fay Frazier's snuff tirade, or anyway it ap-

peared to Miss Frazier and it appeared to the widow
Mrs. Hayes that Mrs. Askew had slipped off though
actually she had walked direct across her sideyard to
the Throckmorton flagstones and up the steps onto the
front porch but had gone unnoticed by Miss Frazier
and the widow Mrs. Hayes who had been blinded by
quandaries at the time. Because the front screen was
latched shut, Mrs. Askew could not get at the Throckmorton brass doorknocker and instead beat on the
doorframe with her knuckles and called out to the bald
Jeeter in an extraordinarily shrill and altogether ar-
resting voice that surely penetrated the frame walls of
the Throckmorton house and very probably got into
the block cellar also. But nonetheless Mrs. Askew
could not seem to raise the bald Jeeter no matter how
she screeched and no matter how she banged and she
could not seem to see the bald Jeeter either once she
had left off screeching and had left off banging and had
instead laid her face first against the windowglass to
the left of the door and then against the windowglass
to the right of the door. In fact, the sum total and
accumulation of Mrs. Askew's various activities, that
would be the screeching and the banging and the glaring, did not gain her an iota of satisfaction until she
augmented them with some momentary peeping,
mostly into the bald Jeeter's black metal postbox
where Mrs. Askew discovered a water bill and a Value
Days leaflet from the downtown Rose's which she
dropped her chin and looked at like they were a pair of
garden slugs. Then she hooted and waved the bald
Jeeter's mail at Miss Bernice Fay Frazier and the
widow Mrs. Jennings W. Hayes who watched the display briefly before exchanging observations and concluding that Mrs. Askew's intentions, though not
entirely beyond them, were very nearly entirely
beyond them.

With the water bill and the leaflet too still in hand,
Mrs. Askew scooted off the porch and around the far

side of the house to the back door, or anyway she produced the illusion of scooting without bothering to produce the velocity scooting generally calls for. She worked her arms and her legs and wagged her head and puffed and blew most furiously and thereby exhibited all of the trappings of highspeed locomotion while remaining almost utterly speedless and quite thoroughly unlocomoted. So Mrs. Askew cleared the porch and rounded the far corner of the house with considerable vigor but hardly any momentum to speak of. She tried to search out a trace of the bald Jeeter in the side windows as she passed them by but scooting and glaring, even the illusion of scooting in combination with actual glaring, did not much compliment each other, so after she flashed on by the dining room Mrs. Askew completely devoted her energies and attention to working her arms and her legs and wagging her head and puffing and blowing until at last she arrived at the backporch, yanked on the screendoor, and found it also to be latched from the inside. Naturally she lit out around the near corner towards the door off the mudroom and tried it as a last resort but the bolt held fast and Mrs. Askew could only peer in through the doorlight at the washer and the dryer and the bald Jeeter's straw sunhat hanging on a peg.

Miss Bernice Fay Frazier and the widow Mrs. Jennings W. Hayes still could not between them comprehend the significance of a water bill and a Rose's Value Days leaflet even once Miss Frazier had held the leaflet and eyed it while the widow Mrs. Hayes held and eyed the water bill after which they exchanged correspondences and held and eyed the item they had not held and eyed previously. For her part Mrs. Askew grabbed onto her knees and attempted to draw a full and regular breath and consequently was of little aid to Miss Frazier and the widow Mrs. Hayes who had discarded the water bill completely and were together perusing the Value Days leaflet and discussing the

merits of panty hose when Mrs. Askew finally mus-
tered enough wind to suggest that one or the other or
both of them call Mr. Bridger down off the roof which
Miss Frazier obliged her in primarily though the widow
Mrs. Hayes attempted to oblige her in it also but could
not manage much more than a squeak and it was not
the squeak from the widow Mrs. Hayes but was instead the full-fledged invitation from Miss Bernice Fay
Frazier that fetched Mr. Bridger up to the peak of the
house and away from whatever it was he had been
doing to the back gutter which not Miss Frazier or the
widow Mrs. Hayes or Mrs. Askew either had much of
a grip on or could even convince Miss Shareena Moncrief to look at and once Mr. Bridger arrived at the
peak of the roof he figured immediately that Miss Bernice Fay Frazier and the widow Mrs. Jennings W.
Hayes required his prompt assistance in treating what
appeared to be Mrs. Askew's coronary, so Mr. Bridger
scampered on down the rise to his ladder in as much as
Mr. Bridger could scamper anywhere and he actually
gave the impression of haste as he proceeded to the
ground where he suggested to Mrs. Askew that she
stretch out on the grass which Mrs. Askew did not
much appreciate coming from her gutterpainter.

She got her breath back presently, or anyway got
part of her breath back, enough of her breath back
that is to tell Miss Bernice Fay Frazier and the widow
Mrs. Hayes and Mr. Derwood Bridger what she suspected had went with the bald Jeeter Throckmorton,
but even with the latched doors and the water bill and
the Rose's Value Days leaflet Miss Bernice Fay Frazier
and the widow Mrs. Jennings W. Hayes continued to
imagine that the bald Jeeter was only out to town for
the afternoon and Mr. Derwood Bridger, when called
upon for his opinion, wanted to know was the bald
Jeeter Throckmorton the one with the hooked nose or
the other one, and Miss Bernice Fay Frazier told him
the one with the hooked nose had been Mrs. Estelle

Singletary and it wasn't a hooked nose anyway, it was an aquiline nose, her daddy's aquiline nose. She said the bald Jeeter had been the bald one.

"Bald where?" Mr. Bridger asked her.

"All up underneath her wig," Miss Frazier said.

"Was that a wig?" Mr. Bridger asked her.

"Pure horsehair," Miss Frazier said.

"Well I'll be," Mr. Bridger exclaimed. "I'd never have known it."

"Her grandmother stitched it off a chestnut mare," the widow Mrs. Jennings W. Hayes said. "The thing must be fifty years old and when it gets wet you can still get a whiff of the stable every now and again."

"Well I'll be," Mr. Bridger exclaimed. "Isn't that the most peculiar thing?" and he looked direct at Mrs. Askew so as to allow her the chance to agree that the bald Jeeter Throckmorton's chestnut wig was in fact a most peculiar thing but Mrs. Askew did not seem to have any opinion on the matter and instead told Mr. Bridger and told Miss Bernice Fay Frazier and told the widow Mrs. Jennings W. Hayes, "The woman could be expiring this very minute."

"Oh, come now!" Miss Frazier said.

"Yes, really!" the widow Mrs. Hayes added.

"Expiring?" Mr. Bridger wanted to know, and Mrs. Askew told him about the latched doors and the screeching and the banging and the water bill and the Rose's Value Days leaflet and just talking about all the scooting she did took Mrs. Askew's breath all over again and even stirred Mr. Bridger up some which in turn affected Miss Frazier and the widow Mrs. Hayes who had not previously thought Mr. Bridger capable of being stirred up so they became a little agitated themselves and soon enough the four of them together were scooting across Mrs. Askew's sideyard toward the bald Jeeter Throckmorton's house, the ladies toting with them their heightened anxiety and Mr. Bridger toting with him his thirty-foot aluminum extension ladder.

Mrs. Askew screeched and banged at the front door and Miss Bernice Fay Frazier and the widow Mrs. Jennings W. Hayes each took a front window to screech and bang at while Mr. Bridger stood on the lawn with his ladder and bellowed towards the upstairs, but the bald Jeeter did not answer to the screeching and the banging and did not answer to the bellowing either so Mrs. Askew and Miss Bernice Fay Frazier and the widow Mrs. Hayes along with Mr. Bridger and his aluminum extension ladder all circled round to the back of the house and set up a clamor there which proved equally fruitless and left them only the mudroom door to cause an uproar at and after an especially violent outburst did not draw the bald Jeeter, Miss Bernice Fay Frazier and the widow Mrs. Hayes and Mr. Bridger all put their faces to the doorlight and Mrs. Askew directed them towards the bald Jeeter's sunhat hanging on a peg which seemed a particularly forlorn sight under the circumstances.

The ladies decided Mr. Bridger should climb up to the bedroom window and look in but they could not decide between them which window exactly was the bedroom window since the windows did not look the same on the outside as they did on the inside but they did all agree that the little window was the bathroom window and they did all agree it would not be seemly for Mr. Bridger to look in it. So they debated as to a proper choice for a bedroom window and all landed upon the same one eventually and Mr. Bridger extended his ladder, laid the ends of it against the clapboard, and climbed on up to the sill of what turned out to be the sewing room window and he verified to the ladies that the bald Jeeter was not sewing presently and apparently had not expired sewing, so Mrs. Askew and Miss Frazier and the widow Mrs. Hayes agreed straightaway that the remaining upper window was in fact the bedroom window and they each in turn suggested they had felt it was the bedroom window all along. Miss Frazier went so far as to wonder out loud what business Mr. Bridger had looking into the bald Jeeter's sewing room anyway and her and Mrs. Askew and the widow Mrs. Hayes all encouraged Mr. Bridger to slide his ladder on down to where he should have put it in the first place which Mr. Bridger promptly obliged them in doing and up he went again, this time past the genuine bedroom windowsill and to the genuine bedroom window. The bottom sash was partway up and Mr. Bridger put his nose against the screen, laid his hand across his forehead, and called out, "Mrs. Jeeter, Mrs. Jeeter," which Miss Frazier and the widow Mrs. Hayes neither one could stand for and together they shrieked, "Throckmorton!" just in time for Mr. Bridger to leave off clean after the initial pair of Jeeters and pick up with Throckmorton directly. And he called out again and yelled and hollered and shrieked some himself but didn't seem to get any return from it and at last he did not say anything more but simply peered in through the screen for a spell and then he left off peering also so as to look down at Mrs. Askew and Miss Bernice Fay Frazier and the widow Mrs. Jennings W. Hayes and tell them, "She's gone."

"You see," Miss Frazier said, "probably to town."

"No ma'm," Mr. Brider told her. "I mean she's gone and I don't mean to town. She's Gone."

And Mrs. Askew looked up at Mr. Bridger in sheer undisguised puzzlement and dismay. "Do you mean?" Mrs. Askew said and left off talking but persisted in moving her mouth.

"Yes ma'm,' Mr. Bridger told her. "Gone."

"This breaks my heart," Mrs. Askew said to Mr. Bridger. "This just breaks my heart," Mrs. Askew said to Miss Frazier and the widow Mrs. Hayes who concluded it just broke their hearts also and told Mrs. Askew as much while Mr. Bridger looked through the screen again to confirm his diagnosis and saw precisely what he had seen before which was the bald Jeeter

Throckmorton lying on her side partway under the bedclothes and seeming for all the world very much asleep.

"Why I just saw her on Friday," Mrs. Askew said. "Don't you recall we were all out on the walk and I showed her the gutter estimate and she said to me, 'It's not such an awful lot of money.' Those were her very words. 'It's not such an awful lot of money,' she said."

"She did, she surely did," the widow Mrs. Hayes added. "I heard her myself."

"She had a way with figures," Mrs. Askew said, "always did have a way with figures."

"She did, she surely did," the widow Mrs. Hayes added.

"Saturday, Saturday I saw her," Miss Frazier started in. "I saw her in the sideyard with the water sprinkler. She set it in her azalea bed." And Miss Frazier paused to draw up her lips into an ever so slight and bittersweet smile. "Do you recollect the way she had of stooping over so as not to dump her wig off?"

"I do," the widow Mrs. Hayes said, "I surely do."

"She was a fine woman," Mrs. Askew added.

"She was," the widow Mrs. Hayes said. "She surely was."

"A fine woman indeed," Miss Frazier said. "We were like this."

"So were we," Mrs. Askew announced.

"We were too," the widow Mrs. Hayes added. "We surely were." And the ladies all held up their fingers towards Mr. Bridger who had backed down the ladder three rungs before advancing two rungs up it again to peek through the window screen and satisfy himself altogether. "Like sisters," the widow Mrs. Hayes said.

"The same as," Mrs. Askew added.

"Precisely like sisters," Miss Frazier agreed.

And Mr. Bridger wrapped his hands around the nearest rung, laid his nose atop his knuckles, and said to himself, "Lord, the woman's bald as an egg."

Mrs. Askew called the sheriff because she had experience in calling the sheriff since she had done it before in 1967 when Mr. Askew had his stroke though that was Sheriff Carl Benjamin Browner who drowned himself in the bathtub in 1974 and so had surrendered the office, in a manner of speaking, to deputy Burton who took over the desk and the paraphernalia and the title and instituted his own manner of bluster and blow but still could not get anybody much to call him sheriff and say it the way that everybody everywhere had said it to Mr. Browner. Sheriff Burton came himself because he was not doing anything otherwise and out of reflex he backed up the ladies and backed up Mr. Bridger off and away from the scene of the investigation and straightaway proceeded up the ladder without any forethought to speak of so it was not until he reached the windowsill and prepared himself to look through it that he realized how uncommonly high off the ground he had come to be, and almost simultaneously he realized how thoroughly frightful it was to him to find himself so uncommonly high off the ground so he snatched at the ladder with every attachment he had to snatch with and him and the ladder together lurched and rattled and hooted and generally made as much fuss as a cat in a treetop.

Mr. Bridger, who was professionally acquainted with the sheriff, threw his arms across his chest and called out in an especially sweet voice, "You all right up there?" to which Sheriff Burton attempted to make prompt reply but could not seem to bring his head around to the left and he could not seem to bring his head around to the right though he appeared inclined to do one or the other or both but was prevented from any of it by the realization of his uncommon height which appeared to be running through his body like an electric charge. Consequently, Sheriff Burton addressed the windowsill directly beneath his nose and told it of the serious misgivings his present predicament had inspired in him. He said, mostly to the windowsill but somewhat to the window casing also, he would be pleased to be fetched straightaway into the bedroom. He said he would be highly gratified to whoever might fetch him. He said he would be most highly gratified. So Mr. Bridger commenced to cast around for a way into the house, not that he desired any special gratification but more because he preferred his ladder without any sort of terrified public official clinging to the top of it. He was able to get himself in through an unlatched back window and proceeded on upstairs to the bald Jeeter Throckmorton's bedroom where he removed the screen and brought the sheriff on into the house mostly by way of the back of his pants. But even once Sheriff Burton found himself safe on the hardwood he did not seem especially highly gratified unless a quick nod of the head can be construed as a gesture of heartfelt thanksgiving. Chiefly the sheriff had his hat to worry with. It had gone awry in all of the excitement so he crossed over to the bald Jeeter's vanity and put it to rights. Then of course there was the bald Jeeter to see to and the sheriff checked her pulse at her neck and checked her pulse at her wrist and laid his hand on her forehead prior to checking her pulse at her neck again. Then he stood up from the bed, took his hat entirely off his head, and fingered the brim of it as he announced to Mr. Bridger, "This woman's deceased."

"Well I'll be goddamned," Mr. Bridger shot back at him, "and I thought she was only bald."

Sheriff Burton's patrol car out by the curb in front of the bald Jeeter Throckmorton's house had attracted an appreciable crowd in the way of most official vehicles and Mrs. Askew and Miss Bernice Fay Frazier and the widow Mrs. Hayes, who were all three together narrating and enacting the bald Jeeter Throckmorton story, had just raised their fingers prefatory to waving them at the crowd when the number one hearse from

Commander Avery Tuttle's Heavenly Rest turned off the boulevard and glided on up the street in that way hearses have of gliding. Mr. Dunn slipped it in behind the sheriff's car without ever accelerating without ever seeming to brake either and him and Mr. Hazlip did not exactly climb out the side doors like you would from a Rambler but fairly much emerged fullblown into the sunlight looking suitably somber and grim. They removed a collapsible chrome gurney from the back compartment and toted it on into the house, and all of the residents roundabout who had not seen fit to venture out on account of a patrol car alone could not stay away from a patrol car in combination with Commander Avery's number one hearse so the crowd expanded and swelled and Mrs. Askew and Miss Frazier and the widow Mrs. Hayes felt obliged to backtrack some for the benefit of the latecomers which left the earlycomers to dawdle and chat and peer in through the tinted glass at the insides of the hearse. Mrs. Askew had just arrived at not such an awful lot of money when Mr. Hazlip passed through the Throckmorton front doorway hindquarters foremost with the collapsible chrome gurney entirely uncollapsed and in tow, and since circumstances seemed to call for an intermission Mrs. Askew left off talking and not Miss Frazier or the widow Mrs. Hayes either one set in and together the three of them joined with the rest of the crowd in watching the progress of the corpse.

Now there had been comparable excitement only two weeks previous when Mr. Peterson from up the street got taken off in an ambulance to the Annie Gattis Memorial Hospital, but it had not been the same sort of excitement exactly on account of how Mr. Peterson had been down with the yellow jaundice for several weeks and had openly contemplated going to the hospital and had discussed the possibility with Mrs. Peterson who had in turn discussed it with several of her close acquaintants and even a neighbor or two.

So when the ambulance finally did come for Mr. Peterson and the attendants carted him out into the afternoon looking for all the world like a summer squash in pajamas nobody much among the onlookers was especially agitated by the proceedings since most everybody had expected Mr. Peterson to look how he looked and had figured he would eventually go where he went. But not anybody really had anticipated that when next the bald Jeeter Throckmorton ventured out into her frontyard she would venture out into it dead, so this was probably one of what the Presbyterian Reverend Mr. Holroyd calls those sheer unforeseen vicissitudes of this our life on His planet and as such took a thoroughgoing hold of the neighbors roundabout or more likely it was just the sheer unforseenness of this particular vicissitude that got a grip on people since most everybody was usually on the lookout for a vicissitude where they could find one, but there were vicissitudes and then there were vicissitudes and the bald Jeeter Throckmorton vicissitude seemed especially sheer and excessively unforeseen mostly because the bald Jeeter had not been sick or ailing or in the least way afflicted, only bald.

Mr. Hazlip and Mr. Dunn carried the gurney down the front steps and commenced to rolling it again once they got onto the sidewalk but the collapsible chrome gurney did not glide quite like the hearse did and every three or four paces Mr. Hazlip had to stoop and attend to the front left wheel which insisted on whirling around and rattling and skidding and generally doing most every ungrim and unsomber thing it could manage. Consequently the onlookers got an extended opportunity to view the corpse or anyway to view the bulk of the corpse since the bulk of the corpse was all they could view on account of how the actual corpse itself had been covered over with a thin green blanket, but in the course of his nearly incessant stooping and rising Mr. Hazlip accidentally uncovered a piece of the

bald Jeeter so partway down the sidewalk the plain
bulk got complimented with an actual naked elbow
which proved immeasurably satisfying to the crowd
collected roundabout who had expected bulk alone
and so took the naked elbow as good fortune.

Sheriff Burton, who along with Mr. Bridger had departed from the house near about when the corpse did,
opened the back hearse door for Mr. Hazlip and Mr.
Dunn who slid the collapsible chrome gurney on inside
where it did in fact collapse, and Mr. Hazlip and Mr.
Dunn, without the front left wheel to hinder them any,
became suitably grim and somber all over again while
Sheriff Burton commenced to forage among the onlookers for details and came across Mrs. Askew who
had left off at not such an awful lot of money and so
picked up from that very spot. Mr. Dunn started the
hearse and brought it away from the curbing slow and
stately so as to allow the onlookers to gape in through
the tinted glass and pay their respects to the bulk and
naked elbow of the bald Jeeter Throckmorton, and
folks generally told each other what a shame it was
and told each other what a surprise it was and told
each other what a downright shock it was except for
Miss Bernice Fay Frazier who waved her fingers at the
gentleman next to her and told him, "We were like
this."

"Yes ma'm," Mr. Bridger said, "I've heard."

AND THEN it was the summer we lost the bald Jeeter
which we figured to be enough for any one season out
of any one year and so we did not imagine it would
become the summer of anything else, did not suspect it
would become worse or not worse really but more so
that it was not just the summer we lost the bald Jeeter
but was that too, was that on top of and along with
everything else. Once Mr. Hazlip and Mr. Dunn carted
the bald Jeeter out the front door and down the steps
there was not anybody of the home remaining, so at

the suggestion of Sheriff Burton, who did not ever only suggest anything but instead usually ordered and proclaimed what he had started out suggesting, Mrs. Askew and Miss Bernice Fay Frazier and the widow Mrs. Jennings W. Hayes retired to Mrs. Askew's kitchen where Mrs. Askew's black telephone hung on the wall and they took turns calling the near relations. Since it was after all Mrs. Askew's kitchen and Mrs. Askew's telephone Mrs. Askew got to call the bald Jeeter's only daughter little Ivy Jeeter Throckmorton Lanier who had married an insurance agent from Greensboro and together they lived there behind the Friendly Shopping Center along with three children, a cat, two painted turtles, a halfdozen tropical fish—give or take your occasional floater—and one Lhasa Apso complete with an assortment of forelock ribbons. According to Miss Frazier and the widow Mrs. Hayes, Mrs. Askew proved delicate and tactful in her grievious capacity, especially in such a "time of crisis," Miss Frazier added, but Mrs. Askew and the widow Mrs. Hayes took issue with Miss Frazier's assessment of the predicament and persuaded her towards the viewpoint that the crisis part of the thing had ended along about when the bald Jeeter did. Now they were full well into the tragic end of it, as far as Mrs. Askew and the widow Mrs. Hayes could tell, which they figured was the place all crises got to if they didn't somehow resolve themselves otherwise. So Miss Frazier stood corrected, which was near about her least favorite way to stand, and to relieve the agony of it some she took it upon herself to call the bald Jeeter's only sister the fat Jeeter in Oregon Hill even though the widow Mrs. Hayes had previously expressed her desire to call the fat Jeeter, but Miss Frazier was considerably taller and stouter and altogether bigger than the widow Mrs. Hayes which counted for something even among old ladies, so when Miss Frazier took ahold of the receiver the widow Mrs. Hayes let her.

Once the bald Jeeter's crisis resolved itself direct
into a tragedy there were not any genuine Jeeters left
but for the fat Jeeter who counted as one Jeeter only
but possessed the volume for several. The momma
Jeeter and the daddy Jeeter had both passed on in
1963, one at the first of the year and the other at the
end of it, which left only three actual Jeeters including
the bald Jeeter and the fat Jeeter and their grandmomma Jeeter who was actually not a Jeeter but had
married into Jeeterdom and through the years had assumed, assimilated and otherwise sopped up everything it was to be a Jeeter and so had become one as
far as anybody that mattered was concerned. Grandmomma Jeeter lived very nearly forever or anyway to
the closest approximation of forever that anyone anywhere around could come up with, even the clergy
who generally paid some attention to the subject by
occupation. She celebrated her one hundredth birthday three years running just so as to hit it once since
she did not own the proper documents or suitable
memory to verify the where and the when of her coming about. So one year in Oregon Hill and the next
year in Neely and the next year in Leaksville Grandmomma Jeeter got a party first in a Baptist and then a
Presbyterian and then a Methodist fellowship hall, and
hordes of people she was not well acquainted with
made her speeches and gave her presents and cooked
her dinner and for her part Grandmomma Jeeter told
them all to go straight to perdition which not any of
them were offended by, not even those people who
were usually offended by everything, since Grandmomma Jeeter had survived to ninety-nine or one
hundred or one hundred and one and so could not
manage an utterance that wasn't sagacious or amusing
or at least excusable. Nobody much ever seemed to
want to know anything from her except how she'd gotten to be as old as she'd gotten to be and when she told
them they didn't want to know that either because

Grandmomma Jeeter smoked Pall Mall cigarettes out of the maroon pack and daily drank the whiskey her grandnephew made in a ravine behind the chicken-house which anyway he called whiskey and she called whiskey but was more in the line of a petroleum product and she chewed plug tobacco and swore in a most profane and accomplished manner and on Labor Day of her eighty-second year she had had relations with a man from Danville and at Christmastime had announced her pregnancy which turned out to be gas, and while all of this was very fine news for the ilk that smoked and drank and chewed and swore and fornicated it did not much comfort the sorts of people who collected at Baptist and Presbyterian and Methodist fellowship halls and who generally liked to figure the Lord did not reward the brand of living that Grandmomma Jeeter had been rewarded for.

She did die at last, however, but not until the June of the summer before the summer we lost the bald Jeeter when she was nearly done her one hundred and tenth or one hundred and ninth or one hundred and eleventh year. A cold which settled in her chest had turned into pneumonia and strangled her and we were all very sorry to see her go. The people that smoked and drank and chewed and swore and fornicated said she'd had a full and useful life and the people that didn't said she'd probably still be with us if not for the smoking and the drinking and the chewing and the swearing and the fornicating while the remaining Jeeters themselves did not say much of anything partly because Jeeters by nature did not ever have much of anything to say and partly because there weren't but two Jeeters remaining, them of course being the bald and the fat.

So the death of the bald Jeeter just over a year after the death of Grandmomma Jeeter left the fat Jeeter all by herself as far as Jeeters went but not entirely all by herself otherwise since the fat Jeeter had managed to hook a Lynch early on and had gotten a pair of Jeeter Lynches by him in the course of the years. The fat Jeeter's Lynch, who was Raeford Lynch, did not come direct from Oregon Hill Lynches but derived mostly from Stacy Lynches or anyway from a combination of Stacy Lynches and Oregon Hill Lynches who themselves were part diluted with Ruffin Lynches which was not a pure sort of Lynch but was a Lynch descended from a pair of Mebane Lynches who had in fact been Stacy Lynches until they moved to Mebane. Raeford Lynch had three verifiable brothers in Benton, Jip, and Harland Lynch and one verifiable sister in Vergie Lynch and then there was William Petworth Lynch the lastborn who Raeford's momma named out of a magazine and raised close in to home which left William Petworth unverifiable as a brother and unverifiable as a sister but more along the lines of a form of brother who should have been a sister. Benton, Jip, and Harland Lynch all married prior to Raeford and produced between them seventeen children which was not in any way excessive or out of the ordinary since their gender of Stacy Lynch generally took wives about as fertile as compost, but Raeford could never seem to manage more than his meager pair mostly on account of the fat Jeeter who was plenty fat enough to say no and mean it. As for Vergie Lynch, she had triplets by a jackleg pentecostal preacher and then took William Petworth in once her mother died since William Petworth did not seem to have use enough for women to marry one and since William Petworth's daddy did not seem to have use enough for William Petworth to abide the sight of him.

The Lynch boys all brought their wives to Oregon Hill and farmed for a living on the land their daddy had parceled out to them, that is all the Lynch boys except for Raeford who cultivated chickens and cultivated speckled eggs instead in the dilapidated henhouse with the localized ammonia cloud that he got when

he got the fat Jeeter. The momma Jeeter and the
daddy Jeeter, who could never seem to make a go of it
with the chickens or the speckled eggs either, figured a
Lynch might possibly possess the wherewithal to reju-
venate what they themselves had not ever threatened
to juvenate in the first place. So there was a general
optimism and rosiness in Jeeterdom once the fat Jeeter
hooked a Lynch since the bald Jeeter before her had
only managed to land a Throckmorton who was from
notoriously worthless stock and consequently did not
give much rise to cheeriness or rosiness or general optimism. And in a surge of high spirits and good will the
momma Jeeter and the daddy Jeeter bought for Raeford Lynch and for the fat Jeeter Lynch a brand new
never before lived in mobile home which arrived behind the truck cab complete with curtains and carpet
and doormats and coathangers and appliances and
Mediterranean furniture and plates and glasses and
ashtrays and coasters and silverware and two oven
mitts and a halfdozen floorlamps and bedlinen and a
toilet bowl brush and a New Testament in each nightstand and a complimentary bathmat and shower cap
along with a bound up roll of shiny silver aluminum
skirting that would run around the outside to hide the
block pylons. The daddy Jeeter had the thing parked
next to the henhouse but upwind from it which was a
fine enough gesture but a fairly empty one on account
of how the chicken smell did not blow so much as radi-
ate, and accordingly a housetrailer next to the henhouse, even next to the upwind side of the henhouse,
was still atop the meaty part of ground zero.

Raeford Lynch set in straightaway to put the
chicken and speckled egg business to rights while the
fat Jeeter set in just as straightaway to whatever it was
she did which did not seem at all connected with
chickens or speckled eggs but had instead some attachment to red nail lacquer and honey grahams by the
box. But if the fat Jeeter attempted less she accom-

plished more mostly because her husband had waded into the middle of some serious and headlong dilapidation and dilapidation is simply one of those things that cannot be properly halted or excised once it has become serious and once it has become headlong. So the fat Jeeter Lynch passed her days painting all eight of her nails—she did not have enough of a sliver on each little toe to lay a brush to—and devouring graham crackers direct from the wax paper wrappers along with the odd boxful of vanilla wafers while her husband went over to the henhouse every morning and endeavored to flag down the ongoing destruction. He hammered and sawed and drilled and stapled and tacked and taped and tied and beat and banged and did in fact manage a partial and temporary rejuvenation but the chickens pecked away indiscriminately at the rejuvenated items as well as the dilapidated ones and so persisted in unrejuvenating and redilapidating every little repair and improvement Raeford Lynch bothered to make, so he rehammered and resawed and redrilled and restapled and tacked and taped and tied and beat and banged all over again while his energy and drive lasted, but of course the chickens won outright in the end, or the dilapidation won, or maybe it was the combination of chickens and dilapidation along with a touch of flatout Jeeter destiny that vanquished Raeford Lynch in the end because in the end vanquished is certainly exactly what he got. He still passed his days in the chickenhouse and left the fat Jeeter to do what she did in the trailer, but anymore Mr. Lynch did not hammer or saw or drill or staple or tack or tape or tie or beat or bang but mostly sat in a metal chair canted up against a roof stanchion and watched the speckled eggs roll out of the roosting boxes and down the wooden troughs as any number of unoccupied hens untied his shoes for him and frayed the laces until they decided all at once and together to flap and squawk and pick themselves up off the dirt floor so as to land somewhere else.

Each evening in the Jeeter Lynch trailer was generally very nearly identical to all the other evenings in the Jeeter Lynch trailer. Raeford Lynch would sit on the sofa with his second third fourth or fifth beer in hand and tell the fat Jeeter what the chickens had done in the course of the day which usually ranged from eggs to shoelaces to the manufacture of chickenshit since chickens do not lead lives of extraordinary diversity, and the fat Jeeter would blow on her fingers and ponder over what she might thaw or open or send Raeford down the road to fetch for supper. And once the fat Jeeter had fried or unwrapped or heated in a pot whatever it was she had decided on and once she had piled the supper dishes in the sink on top of the lunch dishes and the breakfast dishes so they could all ferment together, there was the radio to listen to for entertainment and the chickens to smell and the scintillating banter to partake of and for Mr. Raeford Lynch some earnest urinating to engage in and for the fat Jeeter Lynch some extensive foraging to see after straight up until bedtime when the fat Jeeter would retire and Mr. Raeford Lynch would retire just behind her and plead and beg and moan and set up the most terrible lament imaginable. But there was quite sufficiently enough of the fat Jeeter hanging out of her nightgown to make up two Raeford Lynches, so when the pleading and the begging and the moaning and the terrible lamenting proved ineffective and prompted Mr. Lynch to a hands-on assault the fat Jeeter would fling him against the far wall where Mr. Raeford Lynch and his bladder and his libido would all slide down the paneling and pile up on the carpet. From there on the floor Mr. Lynch would make himself pathetic and plead and beg and moan and commence to lament all over again, but he could never seem to get pathetic enough to persuade the fat Jeeter to say yes since she invariably said "No," or almost invariably anyway except maybe for twice when she did in fact say yes or possibly did not say no with the proper authority or perhaps was even asleep.

Most of the Jeeters and a majority of Lynches did not expect a baby to arrive when it did arrive primarily because the fat Jeeter did not appear to be expecting one herself. She failed to do any additional swelling so as to be noticeable and initially she figured the twitching and the stomping and the rolling around in her belly for a honey graham affliction, but the pharmacist at the Rexall set her straight directly and she brought the happy news on home to Mr. Raeford who got thrashed all throughout the trailer and managed to pile up in a great variety of locations. The baby itself arrived along about the fat Jeeter and Mr. Raeford Lynch's first wedding anniversary and at the time Mr. Raeford Lynch was feeling especially warm towards his brother Benton who had made the Jeeter Lynches a gift of four bias belted truck tires to lay on the trailer roof against strong winds, so he named his boy Raeford Benton Lynch partly on account of his brother's generosity and partly on account of his own derring-do and perilous exploits. They called the boy Benton so as to keep things uncomplicated around the trailer, and he stayed inside with his momma and wailed at her while she painted her nails until he was big enough to accompany his daddy down to the chickenhouse and screech at the chickens. He did not much resemble a Jeeter and did not much resemble a Lynch and did not much resemble any logical combination of Jeeters and Lynches either but showed a most remarkable likeness to Mrs. Phillip J. King's sister-in-law's mother who lived in Pittsboro but came through Neely every now and again on her way to somewhere else. She was a gangly woman with pointy elbows and an equally pointy Adam's apple and a face all hollowed and carved out and a prominent chin and a prominent nose and a mouth full of big square teeth and just the kind of aspect in general that made you want to saddle her up and ride her around the block, and even when he was only two feet tall Benton Lynch was just as gangly and pointy and carved out and prominent and toothsome himself which was not the way of Lynches and was not in the way of Jeeters either and was truly not much in the way of Mrs. Phillip J. King's sister-in-law's mother who started out as a regular girlchild and got homely later when she blossomed.

So the fat Jeeter told everybody he had mostly Lynch to him and Raeford Lynch told everybody he was primarily Jeeter and all the non-Lynches and non-Jeeters roundabout debated as to whether it was a mule or a jackass in the woodpile while Benton Lynch himself grew increasingly ganglier and pointier and more carved out and prominent and toothsome. He was not an extraordinarily bright child, was not even intelligent in any sort of ordinary way—which could have been Jeeter, Lynch, mule, or jackass—and when at last he turned seven and went into the first grade at the primary school in Ruffin he did not graduate up a level until six months after his ninth birthday on account of some general difficulties with shoe-tying and the alphabet and numbers and everything else otherwise except for lunch. By the time he did reach the second grade, the fat Jeeter had said yes on the only other occasion she would say yes or had not said no anyway or maybe even had slept through it and Benton Lynch found himself with a little brother that he did not get the opportunity to expect or anticipate since his momma did not ever swell or bloat up sufficiently to stir his interest, did not really do anything unusual in the course of her nine months except throw his daddy against the paneling most evenings. The fat Jeeter named this one herself without any assistance whatsoever from Raeford Lynch or his brothers or their truck tires as she called him Otway Burns Lynch which was not from any Jeeters and was not from any Lynches and was not from any combination thereof but came direct off the "points of interest" portion of a state road map. Otway Burns Lynch did not start out gangly or pointy or carved out or prominent or toothsome but was a fairly regular baby and looked a little bit like his momma and a little bit like his daddy and a little bit like a week-old shoat. He did not wail like Benton Lynch had wailed and he did not screech like Benton Lynch had screeched and when he was old enough to walk with Benton and his daddy out to Mr. Newsome's store on the highway he did not get fed sugarcubes out of Mr. Newsome's coatpocket like Benton Lynch had been fed sugarcubes.

Otway Burns Lynch did not turn out to be such an extraordinarily bright child himself but appeared very nearly incandescent next to his brother who in five years of schooling had advanced to the third grade and who worked at his lessons and paid some considerable attention to his teachers but could not seem to keep whatever went in through his ears from running out the bottoms of his feet. Otway Burns Lynch caught Benton in the fifth grade and left him there, and once his own brother passed him up Benton seemed to lose his enthusiasm for schoolwork which did not matter much since he'd lacked the aptitude for it all along and so two weeks into the sixth grade he quit on account of what most folks said was the Lynch in him and what other folks said was the Jeeter in him and what some folks said was the combination of mule and jackass. Of course he set out on a career in chickens directly or anyway set down on one with his daddy who gave Benton his own folding metal chair and his own roof stanchion to lay it up against, while for his part Otway Burns Lynch persisted in his schoolwork and continued at the end of every quarter to bring home average marks which Jeeters and Lynches and Jeeter-Lynches and neighbors of Jeeters and Lynches and Jeeter-Lynches and even people who'd only heard tell of Jeeters and Lynches and Jeeter-Lynches all took to be a phenomenal accomplishment coming as it did from Otway Burns who had no call to be phenomenal or accomplished either since he was not purely Jeeter and was not purely Lynch but had distillated and precipitated from a mixture of Jeeters and Lynches who were not hardly anything pure and should have been less than anything diluted. But Otway Burns Lynch became something nonetheless and the theory roundabout had it that Otway Burns had gotten what he was supposed to get at birth and had somehow also managed to collect what Benton Lynch had neglected to pick up for himself, and so with perseverance and the sweat of his brow Otway Burns Lynch became quite capable and mediocre and Benton Lynch, who persevered and sweated some himself, could not ever rise much above cipherdom.

He was not blatantly stupid or outright idiotic. There was not anything blatant or outright about him, not anything at all. He mostly simply was not. Of course there was the pointiness and the gangliness and the square teeth but there did not seem to be any of him otherwise, certainly not anything blatant or outright and really not anything measurably stupid or idiotic, simply not anything. He wasn't. He had no personality to speak of, no distinguishing mannerisms, no funny little nervous cough, no particular way of standing or of leaning or of sitting, no special laugh, no favorite turn of phrase, no pants or shoes or shirt or hat he was partial to, and no Jeeter accent or Lynch accent or Jeeter-Lynch accent that was detectable since he did not ever ask any whys or wherefores, did not wonder or speculate or declare or reckon or wish or hope or imagine, did not ever say anything much except for yes and except for no. He had only his prominent features and his general angularity, which birth itself had put him in possession of, and had bothered to accumulate nothing otherwise. He was not his daddy's son, was not his momma's boy, and did not favor his brother or his grandparents or his aunts or his uncles or any strain of family on one side or the other that did not reside in the barnyard. He had not grown to be a Lynch and had not grown to be a Jeeter and had not grown to be a Jeeter-Lynch, had become nothing really from the moment he was named and designated except taller and pointier and more extraordinarily hollowed out on the outside and maybe extraordinarily hollowed out on the inside too or primarily vacant anyway which could have been how he started but certainly was how he ended up because even by the time he quit school for the chickenhouse he already mostly wasn't. Mostly he simply was not. His daddy laid back against his stanchion in his chair and made exaggerated claims about this and exaggerated claims about that and Benton Lynch sat and the chickens laid and squawked and pecked at his shoelaces and Benton Lynch sat and the chickenhouse dilapidated and fell away all around him amid the feathers and the ammonia and the uproar and Benton Lynch sat and when his daddy spied a particularly comely bird and left off soliloquizing long enough to say to his boy, "You think I can spit on that hen yonder?" Benton Lynch sat and eyed his daddy and eyed the chicken in question and sometimes he said, "Yes," and sometimes he said, "No."

Otway Burns graduated high school, which no Lynch or Jeeter before him had ever succeeded at, and his average marks and ordinary capabilities got him a diploma which indicated and duly certified the exact level of mediocrity he had risen to, a level of course unparalleled among Jeeters and unparalleled among Lynches, and the diploma in turn got him a position at the American Tobacco plant between Oregon Hill and Neely where Otway Burns pushed cigarettes around all day on a cart and received along with his weekly paycheck a promise of advancement if not the actual advancement itself. And even if it was only cigarettes and even if it was only a cart to push them around on, Otway Burns Lynch had in fact succeeded and had in fact advanced because it was not sweetpotatoes or alfalfa or corn or short grain or beef cows or manure or chickens or eggs or feathers or ammonia or any other item that Jeeters and Lynches tended to grow or rear or market or just be blessed with. Once he'd accumulated three months' worth of pay, Otway Burns Lynch moved out of the trailer and took a room on the north end of Neely with the second Mrs. Cummings who had been the first Mrs. Tadlock before she became the second Mrs. Cummings and who had commenced to rent out the various parts of the late Mr. Cummings's house almost before they could put the dirt on top of him. So the remaining Jeeter-Lynches expanded some in the trailer once Otway Burns Lynch vacated his part of it, or anyway two of the three remaining Jeeter-Lynches expanded some since the fat Jeeter was always about as expanded as she could get, and then Benton Lynch did a little vacating on his own and left more room than Mr. Raeford by himself could expand into. He did not announce his departure and did not seem to prepare or plan for it but just stuffed two shirts into a paper sack and went, and for a month and a half, nearly two months, he stayed gone and Mr. Raeford Lynch wondered where he was from the chickenhouse while the fat Jeeter wondered where he was from the dinette in the trailer and then in the evenings they would get together over something thawed or fried or sent out for and wonder out loud at each other until at last after his nearly two months Benton Lynch just showed up one night, came direct into the trailer, and sat down on the Mediterranean sofa beside Mr. Raeford Lynch who dropped his mouth open and said, "You're back."

And Benton Lynch looked at him with that pointy, prominent, carved and hollowed out face and told him, "Yes," by way of explanation.

He stayed on after that, stayed on right up to the summer we lost the bald Jeeter or anyway right up to the May just prior to the summer we lost the Bald Jeeter, and then he up and went again not even with shirts this time or a sack to put them in but just up and went and stayed gone through Independence Day and almost until August before he came home in the very middle of the afternoon and proceeded direct to the chickenhouse where his daddy brushed the chickens and the feathers and the hardened chickenshit off Benton's chairseat and told him he was back again, told him he certainly was back indeed, which Benton Lynch agreed with twice prior to canting himself against his stanchion so as to watch the speckled eggs roll out of the roosting boxes and down the wooden troughs while the chickens pecked at his shoestrings and squawked and flapped and rose off of and settled onto the dirt floor. And then we lost the bald Jeeter which transformed a regular June and a regular July and the better part of a regular August into the summer we lost the bald Jeeter and that was sufficiently lamentable for one season out of one year as far as most of us were concerned and so we did not imagine it would become the summer of anything else, did not suspect it would become worse or more or be compounded by anybody anyhow especially by Benton Lynch who nobody much had ever seen or even heard of or could have recollected anyway. But it did get worse and more and compounded and Benton Lynch got himself thoroughly recollected, all of it commencing together on the afternoon of Monday August the twenty-ninth when the fat Jeeter picked up her phone receiver and said, "Whut?" into it.

She did not know Miss Bernice Fay Frazier from Harry's fuzzy cat and could not at all make out Miss Frazier's business on account of the excessive tact and delicacy Miss Frazier's grievous capacity had inspired in her. But at length once she'd made two or three dozen laps all roundabout the dilemma, Miss Frazier set onto the crisis and tragedy part of the matter and managed to refer specifically to the individual in question any number of times until she got a legitimate shriek out of the fat Jeeter and gauged her success accordingly. Miss Frazier set about explaining the details and circumstances of the afternoon but the fat Jeeter had thrown down the phone receiver on the dinette table after her initial shriek and so Miss Fazier squandered the best part of her tact and delicacy primarily on a half-eaten Little Debbie fudge twirl. The fat Jeeter shrieked again once she got outside on the trailer steps and when she hit the ground she attempted to shriek all the way down to the chickenhouse but did not have the wind for more than an extended whimper and consequently not the hens or Mr. Raeford Lynch or Benton Lynch either heard her coming and so levitated together when the fat Jeeter burst in through the chickenhouse door and cut loose with some genuine anguish.

She could not be consoled, could not at first be comprehended. "Deaddeaddead," the fat Jeeter wailed.

"Who?" Mr. Lynch asked her. "Dead where from what?"

"Gonegonegone," the fat Jeeter wailed. "Deaddeaddead."

"Where? Who?" Mr. Lynch asked her. "Dead how?"

"Gone and dead," the fat Jeeter cried. "Deaddeaddead and gonegonegone." And the fat Jeeter raised her hands and covered her face with her ten fleshy fingers and she said, "Oooo," and shook and sobbed and dropped to the floor full on top of one hen and partway on top of another and together the three of them moaned and shrieked and squawked and lamented until Mr. Raeford Lynch and Mr. Benton Lynch each took the fat Jeeter under an arm and managed to hoist her.

"Who is it, momma?" Mr. Raeford demanded.

And the fat Jeeter turned her head sideways and looked at Mr. Raeford like he'd just crawled up out of a hole in the ground.

"Momma, who is it that's dead and gone?" Mr. Raeford wanted to know.

And the fat Jeeter cried, "Oooohhh," and stretched and worked her face until her eyes just up and disappeared in the folds of it. "Deaddeaddead," she said. "Gonegonegone," and then she spun around and scampered on out the chickenhouse door in as much as the fat Jeeter could spin and in as much as she could scamper.

Mr. Raeford caught up with her midway between the chickenhouse and the trailer and got from her what he'd been after all along, but she still could not be consoled even once she got comprehended and the fat Jeeter worked her way loose from Mr. Raeford and proceeded on back to the trailer all wild and incoherent with grief while Mr. Raeford returned to the chickenhouse and vented himself. "Goddamn it all," he said and beat the doorjamb as he passed by it. "She was a fine woman, a fine woman. Goddamn it all." And Mr. Raeford stomped around the perimeters of the chickenhouse kicking at the hens and swearing and flailing his arms in the air and generally putting on a regular pageant for Benton Lynch who watched overtop his pointy nose from his chair against his roof stanchion. "It ain't fair," Mr. Raeford said, "it ain't never fair but this time it ain't fair especial. Shit." And he kicked at a convenient collection of chickens which mostly got clear of his foot except for one particularly sluggish animal that had been sat on previously and now got booted too. "A fine woman," Mr. Raeford said, "such a fine woman," and he threw himself into his chair and launched his chair back against his stanchion in one reckless burst of blasphemous energy which he terminated and punctuated with a "Shitfuckitshitshit." And

Mr. Raeford did commence to settle down once he got seated but he spat out his vexation at intervals for an extended spell and went through a dozen shits, five or six goddamn it alls, and a couple of fuck its until he slipped finally into a kind of even tempered silence that did not get interrupted by anything more savage and offensive than a grunt every now and again. Then he made several demonstrative exhalations so as to illustrate precisely how put out he was and after that commenced to chew his fingernails and ponder a batch of chickens off to his left which he paid impressive and grave attention to right up to the moment he opened his mouth and said. "You think I can spit on that hen yonder?"

And Benton Lynch looked from his daddy to the chicken in question and then back to his daddy again and told him, "No."

Mrs. ASKEW and the widow Mrs. Hayes and Miss Bernice Fay Frazier along with her sister, Mrs. Estelle Frazier Singletary, set up vigil in the bald Jeeter Throckmorton house along about suppertime black Monday, they called it, and right off went all throughout the premises making ready for the family and the anticipated horde of unattached but equally bereaved acquaintances. Mrs. Askew and Miss Bernice Fay Frazier changed the linen on the deathbed and made it up and Miss Frazier said just the sight of the old fitted sheet and topsheet and pillowcase balled up in the corner by the dresser sent shivers up and down her backbone and Mrs. Askew said it gave her the chills too and she said, as far as she could figure, it must be awful to die and Miss Frazier said she believed it probably was. Mrs. Estelle Singletary vacuumed and dusted in the downstairs and every ten or twelve minutes interrupted herself and hunted up the widow Mrs. Hayes so as to openly express her surprise that the bald

Jeeter had not been a tidier woman which was, the widow Mrs. Hayes agreed, a sad truth and together they would commiserate over several of the bald Jeeter's more noticeable failings until Mrs. Singletary decided to go back to the Electrolux and seek out some new and disturbing untidiness.

Little Ivy Jeeter Throckmorton Lanier and her husband and her two boys and one girl and her Lhasa Apso with its black forelock ribbon all arrived at the bald Jeeter Throckmorton house just as Mrs. Askew and Miss Bernice Fay Frazier and Mrs. Estelle Frazier Singletary and the widow Mrs. Hayes were fishing through some personal items in a highboy that they had not really intended to fish through but did anyway once the straightening and dusting and vacuuming gave out. In the course of the trip from Greensboro to Neely little Ivy had managed to work herself full into the throes of hysteria and so did not notice straight off that she had caught Mrs. Askew and Miss Frazier and Mrs. Frazier Singletary and the widow Mrs. Hayes in the middle of anything which gave them the opportunity to stick the report cards and the photographs and the old yellowed letters down between the sofa cushions while little Ivy paced and fretted and her husband took the Lhasa Apso into the shrubbery to evacuate itself. She could not believe her mother was gone even once she had visited the deathbed and had sat through a complete performance of the bald Jeeter Throckmorton story, she simply could not believe it even once Mrs. Askew and Miss Frazier and the widow Mrs. Hayes all assured her that the bald Jeeter was indeed gone, that they had seen her go themselves or the bulk and the naked elbow of her anyway. But still she could not believe it, or would not believe it, and threw herself onto the sofa and commenced to blubber into her hands and her husband returned from the shrubbery with the dog and then she blubbered on him instead.

The fat Jeeter and Mr. Raeford Lynch and their boy

Benton arrived considerably later than little Ivy and her family mostly on account of the fat Jeeter herself who could not leave off shrieking long enough to put a dress on, and little Ivy and the fat Jeeter fell into each other's arms right off and the one of them blubbered while the other wheezed and moaned until they dropped onto the sofa together and became uniformly hysterical. Mr. Raeford got treated to his own personal three-part reenactment of the bald Jeeter Throckmorton story which vexed him afresh and he spiced the narrative with several goddamn it alls for each of which he begged pardon and received it while Benton Lynch stood with his back to the front doorframe and got talked at by little Ivy Jeeter Throckmorton Lanier's husband which was not a pretty sight seeing as how a man with only a "yes" and a "no" in his entire arsenal is hardly a match for a bona fide insurance agent. So Benton Lynch sometimes said, "Yes," and sometimes said, "No," as Mr. Lanier told him every tellable item concerning the bald Jeeter's coverage and Mr. Raeford occasionally let out a goddamn it all and the accompanying excuse me as the ladies told him all about the bulk and naked elbow and little Ivy blubbered and wheezed and the fat Jeeter wheezed and blubbered as they sat on the sofa holding each other in their arms.

Otway Burns Lynch got to the house shortly after his momma and daddy and brother did and wearing a new blue suit he'd paid on and a necktie he'd bought outright which in combination with his black oxfords and his dire expression made him the picture of proper and comely grieviousness unlike his daddy and unlike his brother who did not own blue suits but wore instead identical dishwater brown suits and starched white shirts buttoned up to the chin and no neckties whatsoever and not oxfords either but brogans brushed up and done over a little all of which failed to suggest anything proper and comely, especially grieviousness. Otway Burns took Mr. Lanier's hand, shook it, and bowed like a Chinaman and told him how distressed and saddened he was over the news of Mrs. Bald Jeeter Throckmorton's untimely death and then he advanced on to the sofa and dipped towards little Ivy Jeeter and told her and his momma much the same thing after which he greeted Mrs. Askew and Miss Frazier and Mrs. Frazier Singletary and the widow Mrs. Hayes each in turn and took them all fairly much by surprise since they had not expected any natural manners in a Jeeter-Lynch and had not anticipated that Otway Burns could develop any pushing cigarettes around on a cart, so they watched him and waited for him to show the Jeeter in him or at least a touch of the Lynch but instead he struck up a policy discussion with Mr. Lanier and appeared actively interested in the progress of it.

Along about seven o'clock the first casserole showed up in the company of a dozen deviled eggs and shortly afterwards the initial chicken pieces arrived followed close behind by a yokeless layer cake and some manner of waldorf salad in a punchbowl. Mrs. Lassister of Draper carried over a platterful of Mrs. Lassister's hot dry-cured sausage sliced up and skewered on toothpicks and the firechief Mr. Pipkin's wife, Louise, brought by a tin box full of after dinner mints, mostly pink ones. Fresh potato salad came up the walk every quarter hour or so and consequently outdid every form of chicken—baked, fried, barbecued, and stewed—which arrived about as frequently but not quite. Mrs. Phillip J. King stopped in with a devil's food cake that she'd bought at the Big Apple and put on a legitimate cake plate but could not disguise anyway and a Mrs. Hastings of the Leaksville Vernell Hastinges brought by the only pigs-in-a-blanket of the evening. Inez Benfield carried over several biscuits and her own variety of waldorf salad which far more resembled the genuine article than what had pre-

viously arrived in the punchbowl, and the Drumm
twins, May and Halley Verna, both came in with cus-
tard pies although and maybe because they had not
consulted on the matter. Mr. Emmet Dabb brought
the beverage in a five gallon bucket and it was lemonade with gingerale in it or gingerale with lemonade in
it or maybe limeade with Seven-Up in it, nobody could
determine which and Mr. Dabb wasn't talking, and
once the kitchen counter and the hutchtop and the
dining room table were all covered over with trays and
saucers and platters and serving bowls the Reverend
Mr. Lynwood Wilkerson showed up with his appetite
and paid his condolences to the daughter and paid his
condolences to the sister and then blessed the food and
went ahead and had some straightaway since he was so
close to it anyhow.

Everybody told little Ivy and the fat Jeeter what a
shame it was and what a surprise it was and what a
downright shock it was and then told each other much
the same thing, and for the benefit of those people
who did not witness the initial performance or any
subsequent performance thereof, Mrs. Askew and
Miss Frazier and the widow Mrs. Hayes staged a fairly
elaborate and painfully detailed production of the bald
Jeeter Throckmorton story which concluded with the
traditional waving of fingers. There was not much talk
of the bald Jeeter after that and folks generally ate
some of everything and a lot of some things and attempted to break Mr. Dabb's punch down into its various components. Little Ivy and the fat Jeeter
circulated and endeavored to be pleasant but were not
entirely successful mostly on account of their bereave-
ment though the fat Jeeter had never been blessed
with a native pleasantness anyway. Otway Burns traveled roundabout the living room and the dining room
and the kitchen bobbing like a coolie and his daddy
exhibited his vexation to whoever appeared able to
stand still for it. As for Benton Lynch, he got put on

the sofa by Mr. Tiny Aaron who sat down with him and talked at him in a most steadfast and earnest sort of way, and Mr. Aaron seemed particularly animated and worked his arms and laughed and slapped himself on the leg and slapped Benton Lynch on the leg and howled a time or two, but even when he got slapped and pounded and had his face laughed into and his whole self howled at Benton Lynch did not seem anything in return but pointy and prominent and hollowed out and very much absent otherwise, and only once when Tiny Aaron set in with his hands describing an item that was near about exactly the size of a bread box did Benton Lynch say something back that was not just yes and not just no but very much resembled half of a conversation and rendered Benton Lynch something other than just pointy and prominent and hollowed out if only for the time being. And then Tiny Aaron laughed again and slapped himself again and slapped Benton Lynch again and howled once more before he slipped his fingers down between two of the sofa cushions where he discovered little Ivy Jeeter Throckmorton Lanier's third-grade report card and brought it out into the lamplight to peruse it.

Commander Avery Tuttle had laid out the bald Jeeter in a lustrous mahogany casket with antique brass attachments and little Ivy and the fat Jeeter had personally seen to her apparel. Now on several occasions the bald Jeeter had requested to be buried in her blue cotton suit and her matching white blouse with the geraniums on it and her navy pumps and the brunette horsehair wig, but when the time came to actually do the burying little Ivy and the fat Jeeter found they objected to the suit and the blouse and the pumps and the brunette wig and they figured the bald Jeeter would have objected to them also if she could have ever seen for herself exactly how little they did for her. So they substituted the chestnut wig for the brunette wig on account of how it brought out the color in the bald Jeeter's eyes, which did not seem much of a consideration in this particular case but got by anyhow, and they replaced the blue suit and the geraniumed blouse and the navy pumps with a gauzy brown dress and a pair of oxblood heels, and then they stood off across the parlor and assessed the improvement which little Ivy and the fat Jeeter both considered to be appreciable. Of course they called in Commander Avery to verify their opinion in the matter with his own official opinion in the matter and the commander stuck the first two fingers of his right hand into his fob pocket and circled the casket at close range prior to pacing all throughout the room so as to get the fullest picture of the situation, and when he had formulated his official opinion he addressed himself to little Ivy and to the fat Jeeter and told them exactly what it was they had wanted him to tell them which was about all the commander was good for since he did not ever have an official opinion but the right one.

The bald Jeeter got viewed from seven o'clock to nine o'clock on the Tuesday evening following black Monday and the people who viewed her were most generally the people who had gorged themselves in her honor the night previous except for the addition of little Buford Needham and his son Paul and Paul's wife Mary Margaret Vance Needham and of course the bald Jeeter herself who added a kind of gravity to the proceedings that had been absent from the potato salad and the chicken pieces and the rest of the buffet. Little Ivy and the fat Jeeter had perched themselves together on a Duncan Phyfe settee by the main parlor door so as to receive the mourners and Otway Burns Lynch and Mr. Raeford Lynch circulated as a team with one bowing and the other swearing. Mrs. Askew and Miss Frazier and the widow Mrs. Hayes lingered by the casket and intermittently gave command performances of the bald Jeeter Throckmorton story which did not differ substantially from any of their earlier perform-

ances except for the not such an awful lot of money
passage immediately after which Mrs. Askew and Miss
Frazier and the widow Mrs. Hayes would all three gaze
rather longingly at the bald Jeeter's earthly remains
and so inflate the drama some. Benton Lynch did not
ever enter into the parlor proper but slipped off to one
side of the porch in the shadows and did not have anything to do with anybody—not even so much as a solitary yes or a solitary no—until Mr. Tiny Aaron
brought his stark white Impala up to the curbing and
Benton went down to the street to meet him. They
talked at the back bumper for a spell, or anyway Tiny
Aaron talked and indicated and laughed and hooted
and slapped himself and eventually turned the key in
the trunklid so as to open it and he fetched from the
trunk a particular item which he examined briefly prior
to handing it over to Benton Lynch who examined it a
little less briefly for himself. Mrs. Harold McKinney of
the block and mortar McKinney's said later she had
been suspicious, said later she had been highly suspicious when she passed the stark white Impala with the
open trunklid on her way into the Heavenly Rest. She
told everybody she had figured they were transacting.
She told everybody she had suspected they were up to
exactly what it turned out they were up to. But that
was after he had done what he did, and that was after
we'd all found out for ourselves precisely what Mrs.
McKinney insisted she'd figured and suspected and
been mostly highly suspicious of all along.

Benton Lynch did not make for one of your more
eminent pall bearers. His daddy and his brother and
little Ivy's husband and Mr. Pittman from the icehouse
all served well enough and carried out their business in
a stately and altogether acceptable manner but Benton
was just bones and joints and pointy outcroppings and
appeared to have attached himself to the coffin like a
spiny burr to a pantleg. He did not mar the proceedings much however since once the time came for the

coffin to leave the premises the congregation had already been near about eulogized and brethrened to death by the Reverend Mr. Lynwood Wilkerson who had a way with words if sheer bulk and volume counted for anything. Mrs. Edith Sudwick Hargrave capped off the eulogy with a recitation of her poetical tribute to the bald Jeeter that did not have much of a nugget but would have been fine to waltz to, and eventually when she did surrender the floor she surrendered it to Mr. Tupperman who claimed to be a tenor and who collaborated with Miss Frankie Dull, who claimed to be an organist, on a version of "Up a Lazy River" that they both alleged to be music. To close out the whole business the Reverend Mr. Wilkerson benedicted at the foot of the altar for a full quarter hour and thereby thoroughly numbed anybody who might have avoided stupefication earlier, so consequently Benton Lynch went fairly unnoticed as he clung to the side of the casket all thorny and inappropriate down the aisle and out the chapel doors.

Commander Avery had scheduled the funeral service for two o'clock the Wednesday after black Monday which seemed to the family and the mourning party too an altogether convenient and agreeable time for the proceedings for as long as the proceedings confined themselves to the commander's air-cooled chapel, but once the bald Jeeter had been thoroughly eulogized and tributized and passably serenaded under the air-cooled chapel roof she got hauled on out to the hearse and carted off to the cemetery which was not air-cooled exactly and was hardly a desirable place to spend the shank of the afternoon on the thirty-first of August. There was not much relief from the sun within the cemetery except for a row of cedars of Lebanon just above the Pettigrews but the underside of a cedar of Lebanon is generally about as cool and shady as the hilt of a cornstalk, so there was really not any relief within the cemetery aside, of course, from Com-

mander Avery's green canvas awning over the grave-
site which looked cool and inviting enough but was in
actuality a kind of open-air oven.

The family got seated in metal chairs next to the
dirtpile next to the open grave where they all boasted
together and the unrelated mourners collected along
the perimeters of the awning where they dabbed at
themselves with Kleenexes and handkerchiefs and
bandannas and waved off the sweatbees and gnats and
the greenheaded flies. The Reverend Mr. Wilkerson
had unaccountably retained a good degree of his vigor
and proved to be the windiest item roundabout. He
prayed and re-eulogized and generally carried on for
the most unbearable span of time interrupting himself
only on one occasion when the widow Mrs. Jennings
W. Hayes fell out in a faint on account of what she
claimed later was excessive grief but got caught by Mr.
Pittman who laid her down against a headstone so she
could be attended to by Mrs. Askew and Miss Bernice
Fay Frazier who said they felt a little weak in the knees
themselves but held up nonetheless. Eventually the
ceremony did in fact conclude when the Reverend Mr.
Wilkerson lowered the bald Jeeter on into the ground
next to her husband, Mr. Braxton Porter Throckmorton the third, and then tossed a little dirt in after her
and benedicted briefly, or anyway the official religious
part of the ceremony ended with the lowering and the
praying and the benedicting but nobody moved to go
anywhere until Mrs. Jack Vestal, a self-avowed funeral
enthusiast who had very nearly been acquainted with
the bald Jeeter, stepped forward from out of the
crowd, wailed, "Farewell, brave soul!" and flung her
good linen handkerchief on in after the coffin thereby
punctuating and finalizing what the reverend had previously sanctified. And then and only then did the
mourners and the family and the clergy and the funeral
home personnel commence to agitate and disperse
since anymore Mrs. Jack Vestal's good linen handker-

chief was about as significant to a Neely funeral as the corpse itself.

Seeing as how little Ivy's husband had elected to tend to the children, Otway Burns Lynch put one arm around little Ivy and laid as much of the other as he could manage around his mother and ushered the ladies off to the family limousine. Mr. Raeford Lynch followed close behind them all vexed afresh and kicking at the ground to show it, and Benton Lynch came along somewhere afterwards putting on his usual display which was not a display really but more along the lines of a vanishing act, so likely as not nobody much noticed Benton as he progressed from the canopy across the slope to the limousine but most everybody recollected having noticed him once he did what he would do, most everybody recollected every little thing about him once he had rendered himself so entirely and utterly recollectable, but nobody much noticed him climb into the back of the car beside his daddy and nobody much said poor Benton Lynch like they said poor little Ivy and poor fat Jeeter and poor Raeford and poor Otway Burns, but Benton Lynch was still not anything when we laid the bald Jeeter under the headstone and the red clay and left her behind the iron cemetery fence, was not anything at all really and would not become a man of consequence for a spell yet.

*T*WELVE DAYS later, twelve days to the hour exactly later outside of Draper on the Wentworth road it all commenced, all got thoroughly under way at Mr. J. Earl Busick's place of business which was part service station part store part social hall and part living tribute and monument to grime and neglect. Mr. Busick sold Sunoco gasoline and diesel fuel and kerosene and potted meat and fishing floats and hinged Barlows and loafbread and combs and two dollar pocket watches

and camphorated liniment and Pepsi-Cola and cigarettes mostly. His opinions he gave away, and in the
middle of the afternoon of Friday September twelfth
he was treating Mr. Tommy Winn and Mr. C. W. Bobbit to his viewpoint on the federal tobacco subsidy pro-
gram which was quite possibly the freest and most
strident opinion in Mr. Busick's entire repertoire. Mr.
Tommy Winn, who was of a mind with Mr. Busick on
the topic, spat periodically into a soup can and volunteered a yes sir and sometimes a yes sir indeed whenever Mr. Busick paused to draw breath, while Mr. C.
W. Bobbit, who did not have any of one arm and only
part of the other ever since he plowed up a nest of
yellowjackets and bailed under the tractor to get clear
of them, held a cigarette between his lips and squinted
through the rising smoke.

They all three heard the spring on the door draw
out and heard it draw in again and they all three
looked around to see the who of it, so they all three
saw him, or anyway saw the side of his head and the
sharp tip of his nose as he bent over the drinkbox but
they did not to a man find him extraordinarily riveting
and so returned their attention to the tobacco subsidy
matter and Mr. Busick skewered his congressmen and
basted his senators and got yes sired and yes sir in-
deeded by Mr. Winn and squinted at by Mr. Bobbit.
And then he came away from the drinkbox and set his
Pepsi-Cola and his sack of salted nuts down on the
counter by the cash register and leaned there on the
heels of his hands so as to display the other side of his
head and give a fresh perspective on the sharp tip of
his nose, and only Mr. Busick, who was very nearly
looking at him anyway, looked at him this time and he
told him, "Be right there, buddy," but did not stir himself noticeably and persisted in his accusations and his
complaints and his general indignation until it suited
him to break off and cross around behind the counter
where he rang up the Pepsi-Cola and rang up the sack

of nuts and stopped the cash drawer with his stomach. "Sixty-three cents," he said and looked full and front on at both sides of the head and all of the nose and the rest of the face in general no single part of which twitched or moved or seemed at all lively, and when neither hand went up to a pocket, when neither hand went anywhere at all, Mr. Busick said, "Sixty-three cents," one more time and waited with the cash drawer against his stomach.

And though the hands still did not go anywhere in particular, the mouth gathered itself up and said, "You know who I am?"

And Mr. Busick turned his bottom lip partway inside out and pondered the face briefly. "Tommy, C. W., you know this boy here?" he said, still pondering but not so earnestly as before.

"No sir," Mr. Winn told him and Mr. Bobbit shook his head no.

"Might pass for a Littlejohn," Mr. Busick said, "might pass for a Ralph Littlejohn Littlejohn."

"No sir," Mr. Winn told him, "Littlejohns ain't got them teeth," and Mr. Bobbit shook his head no.

"You ain't a Holloway are you?" Mr. Busick wondered. "Holloways got them teeth." But the pointy nose wagged ever so slightly from side to side and Mr. Busick blew out a breath and said, "Well I don't know what you are. I don't believe I've ever laid eyes on you."

"You don't know who I am?"

"Shit, buddy," Mr. Busick said, "I ain't got no idea."

"I'll tell you then." And the right hand left the counter slow and deliberate and proceeded upwards to the button of a jacket which Mr. Busick had not paid much mind to previously but which he recollected struck him at that moment as the nearest thing to turd colored he'd ever seen in an article of clothing with turd colored buttons to match it, and the fingers unfastened first one turd colored button and then the other one so as to allow the hand to proceed on inside the jacket folds from which it returned presently in the company of what Mr. Busick identified later as a regular cannon and which in fact turned out to be a Harrington and Richardson Buntline revolver of extraordinarily high caliber, sufficiently high anyway to have made a sizable hole in Mr. Busick, probably near about the girth of a bathtub drain.

They all heard him draw the hammer back, even Mr. Winn and Mr. Bobbit who had not seen the artillery previously heard the first click and the second right behind it and the third right behind that and Mr. Winn said, "Oh Jesus," and stood up out of his chair and Mr. Bobbit who did not ever say much of anything stood up out of his chair without saying much of anything and they watched him draw a bead along about Mr. Busick's midsection and they heard him tell Mr. Busick, "If you don't give me what's in that drawer there, I'm the man's gonna blow your balls clean to Fuquay-Varina."

And Mr. Busick, who had raised his hands high over his head and backed up against the cigarette rack, labored to get up some spit and said, "Where's that?"

Two

HE WAS an Overhill, not one of the banking Overhills or one of the milling Overhills, not even one of the feed and grain Overhill-Dexters, but an Overhill nonetheless, a foreign and maybe even exotic strain of Overhill who had no connections in Neely or Leaksville or Spray or Draper or Yanceyville or even Greensboro or Winston-Salem or Raleigh or Charlotte but who instead hailed absolutely and completely from a place called Altoona which did not seem to be anywhere anybody knew about. He was standing by the counter in Mr. Newsome's store on the highway eating candied corn out of his fist and talking to Mr. Newsome with his foot resting atop the handwoven seat of one of Mr. Newsome's ladderback chairs which was not a place Mr. Newsome generally allowed a foot to rest but he was a large Overhill, a very broad and sturdy Overhill, and Mr. Newsome did not come from valiant or otherwise distinguished stock himself. So Mr. Overhill talked at Mr. Newsome with his mouth always at least partly full of candied corn and his foot a little burdensome on the webbing and Mr. Newsome listened to Mr. Overhill and made himself most thoroughly agreeable and very nearly pleasant.

The fat Jeeter had run out of graham crackers, had even turned up the wax paper and run out of crumbs and broken corners and was commencing to make trouble with the vanilla wafers when she gave Benton Lynch a dollar and sent him up the road with it. Mr.

Overhill had some firm ideas on the subject of nuclear
energy and he was just setting out to expand upon
them as Benton Lynch stepped through Mr. Newsome's doorway and proceeded on to the back of the
store where Mr. Newsome kept his dried beans and his
cookies and his unplugged pinball machine. Mr. Overhill said he had seen some plutonium once, said he had
held a lump of it in the very palm of his hand and Mr.
Newsome made an altogether pleasant and agreeable
exclamation of wonderment and awe that Mr. Overhill
paused to allow for prior to expanding still further
which he managed with considerable ease and grace
since he was a highly expansive individual by nature.
Benton Lynch stood and waited behind Mr. Overhill
and off to one side of him a little with his momma's
dollar and his momma's box of graham crackers while
Mr. Overhill explained to Mr. Newsome the principles
of megatonnage and kilowattage and Mr. Newsome
whistled between his teeth when there seemed a call
for it and Benton Lynch just stood and just waited and
did not look anywhere and did not say anything until
Mr. Overhill tossed his head back and laid in a new
supply of candied corn when Mr. Newsome waved
Benton Lynch and his dollar and his crackerbox flush
up to the counter.

"Hello boy," Mr. Overhill said and eyed Benton
Lynch sideways and at a slant, and he chewed and
swallowed and cleaned out a hollow with the tip of his
tongue. "Tell me something," and he knocked down a
few more kernels prefatory to expanding clear off the
nuclear energy issue and onto another item entirely,
which was a particular talent with him, "you like
money, son?" he said.

Mr. Newsome took the fat Jeeter's dollar out of
Benton's hand and put the fat Jeeter's nickel and two
pennies back into it and Benton Lynch closed his
fingers around the coins and looked full at Mr. Overhill who had run the most of his right hand into his

mouth clear up to the knuckles, or along about his adenoids anyway, and was doing some serious excavation which he interrupted and departed from long enough to say, "Huh?" when it did not appear that Benton Lynch had an opinion on money one way or the other. "I mean can you use some cash?" Mr. Overhill asked once he'd unstuck whatever he unstuck and swallowed it.

"Yes," Benton Lynch said.

"You know how to dig a hole, boy?" Mr. Overhill asked.

"Yes," Benton Lynch said.

"Ain't much to you. Bones mostly," Mr. Overhill said, and Mr. Newsome blew through his nose and told him, "Lynches."

"But you ain't scared of work are you boy? You ain't scared of a shovel and a pick are you?"

"No," Benton Lynch said.

"Then why don't you come along and dig some holes with us," Mr. Overhill suggested.

"Where?" Benton Lynch said.

"In the ground, boy," Mr. Overhill told him and Mr. Overhill and Mr. Newsome showed each other their teeth. "Seventeen dollars a hole," Mr. Overhill added, "cash money on the spot. Truck's around back, be here till nightfall. You just give it a little attention."

And Benton Lynch did not say he would and did not say he wouldn't but left with his momma's crackers and his momma's seven cents.

"Fine sort," Mr. Overhill observed, and Mr. Newsome said, "Shit," in a manner that was not especially pleasant or particularly agreeable.

It was a Dodge truck, a faded red Dodge halfton pickup with an aluminum cap on the bed and near about a full load what with the two negroes, a fat one and a paltry one, and a wiry tattooed white boy and some other additional manner of being squatted against the fender well who was too black to be white and too white to be black. Mr. Overhill stirred up a place for Benton Lynch who climbed in over the tailgate with his paper sack and lowered himself between the tattooed white boy and the thickest part of a pick handle and then the truck lurched and sputtered and gradually wound out through the gears as Mr. Overhill headed south down the 29 highway towards Greensboro. The air in the bed was hot and close and foul-smelling even though the louvered side windows were standing straight out and the back glass had been tied open against the ceiling. They were all stretched across the same blanket, or anyway three of them were—the fat negro and the paltry negro and the wiry tattooed white boy—laying uniformly on their sides with their heads in the crooks of their arms. Benton Lynch sat with his back against the left fender well and opposite him whatever it was crouched like a toad against the right fender well and picked at his cheek and jittered and jerked in a quick, nervy, almost reptilian fashion.

At Greensboro Mr. Overhill got on the interstate and the wiry tattooed white boy woke up and crawled across the fat negro and the paltry negro who cursed him and swore him and threatened him prior to joining him at the tailgate where they all three pissed onto the highway and spat and coughed and then crawled back to where they'd come from and laid down on their sides with their heads in the crooks of their arms. Benton Lynch dozed off along about Colfax and slept entirely through Winston-Salem and near about to Clemmons when he woke up of a sudden and shook his head and blinked and squinted until he could make out the tattooed white boy and the two negroes and the vacant fender well across the way, and he squinted again and blinked again and shook his head again and still could only see the tattooed white boy and the two negroes and the vacant fender well until a voice said, "Hey," so close into his ear that he could feel the breath and then "Hey" again, and like as not Benton

Lynch would have leapt over the tailgate and out into the road but for the hand on his arm that held him, squeezed him, pulled at him in nervous fits and snatches.

It was squatting there at his shoulder with its face in his face and it said, "Hey, listen listen," in a sharp airy whisper. "We stepped in some shit, stepped in some big, big shit. There wasn't nothing we could do, wasn't no place we could go. We was pinned in a stinking mudhole and him in the trees and the bushes all round-about just shooting and shooting and shooting and shooting. Greased two of us straight off, just blown right the fuck up. Got that cocksucker Drexler in the throat, blood running down his arms and dripping off his fingers, and wasn't nothing we could do, wasn't no place we could go, just squirm around in the mud and try to sink clean outta sight. Then we heard them coming, heard them way off even with the guns and the bullets and the screaming we heard them coming, and the mud commenced to shake and the water commenced to pitch and every loose piece of shit just picked up and left. They was two of them and they was bringing it, bringing it, raining it all over him. Rockets, flex guns, fifties in the door pissing full into the trees and into the bushes bringing it, bringing it, raining it all over him. Then the one came down and picked up some of us and the other came down and picked up the rest of us and we was at sixty, seventy-five, maybe eighty feet when he got the door gunner, got him clean and rolled him on out the door but he hung up on a sled—an arm, a leg, the rest of him just dangling—and he shot him to pieces, shot him the fuck up, killed him and killed him and killed him, and I grabbed onto the fifties and pissed it all over him, rained it, brought it, shot up the whole goddamn jungle, just cut it to little fucking bits, and when we got clear, when we got out, when we got clean gone the captain up on the stick said to me, 'Outstanding, son. Outstanding,' he

said, and me and this guy we untangled the door gunner and dropped him into the treetops."

Benton Lynch had backed up the fender well and
was sitting on top of it. "Big shit," it said. "Bit, big
shit," it said, and it twitched in a half dozen different
places all at once, or at least almost all at once, and it
laughed not like Mr. Newsome's petty nosetooting or
Mr. Overhill's deep, jolly HawHaw and not as flat and
unfunny as what passed for laughter in Mr. Raeford
Lynch and very nearly only louder and wilder and
more mean-spirited. And it shook and flinched and
jerked and bobbed until the fat negro lifted his head
off the crook of his arm and swung his foot a hard,
vicious kick that hit it across the shoulder and partway
onto the chest. "Get away from him," he said. "Get on
away." And it laughed again, louder and wilder and
even more mean-spirited and got kicked twice more by
the fat negro and threatened and cursed at by the
paltry negro and the wiry tattooed white boy and then
it slipped away, slipped on back to where it came from,
and the fat negro told Benton Lynch, "Don't listen to
him. He ain't never killed nobody. He ain't never been
nowhere."

By morning they were beyond Asheville, beyond
Gatlinburg even and had come into a place that was
not a place really, not a civilized place anyway or not a
civilized place any longer but merely an interruption in
the vines and the brambles and the laurel thickets and
not truly a full-fledged interruption either but just a
distraction from the undergrowth in the form of a
block grocery, two green metal trash bins, and several
dozen unpainted, untended to, entirely unlivable, and
fully inhabited houses all of which taken together con-
stituted the township of Lemly as had once been designated and certified by a rectangular white sign with
black lettering beside the grocery but the honeysuckle
had long since come up out of the ditch to strangle it
off. Lemly was situated in what some residents called a

creek bottom and other residents called a ravine and
what the majority of the seasonal Floridians roundabout referred to as a valley but which was actually a
deep and sunless hole in the ground flanked to the
north and the east by one ridge and flanked to the
south and the west by another. Lemly had no industry
whatsoever and little agriculture to speak of unless
mildew counted for something, did not have anything
really, not even any Lemlys any longer in the very
place founded and originated by a pair of Lemly
brothers and their wives who had settled on the creekbank and thrived there but whose sons and daughters
and grandchildren and greatgrandchildren had attempted to move up the slope onto the land they beat
back the forest to possess and inhabit and live from but
never could really possess, never could actually live
from, and could only fully inhabit for that briefest of
moments between the beating back and the first new
sprouts and shoots and vines which spread down the
mountainside across the pastures and beanfields and
up to the very houses and outbuildings which had
commenced to sag and rot and fall away almost before
the sound of the hammers and the saws had died off
entirely. So Lemly had been abandoned by virtually all
of its willful natives which meant actual and full-
blooded Lemlys mostly since actual and full-blooded
Lemlys were generally driven to seek the sort of success and satisfaction their creek bottom refused them,
and the block store and the trash bins and the ruinous
houses and the overgrown pastures and garden plots
had been left to Dinkinses and Greers and McDonalds
and Earps and Donahoos and Rawlses and McCoys
who apparently had not inherited any appreciable
gumption and determination and had failed to culti-
vate any on their own and so were content with the
underbrush and the mildew and the general dilapidation roundabout. Only Mr. Raymond Dance Greer
who owned the block store made anything in the way

of a living while two McDonalds and an Earp collected and sold mayapple and ginseng root as a diversion of sorts. Otherwise Lemlyites by and large got their livelihood signing checks at the first of each month and applying for supplements in the middle of each month and they occupied themselves watching what traffic passed through Lemly from day to day which didn't ever amount to much since Lemly was not on the way to anywhere in particular.

Consequently Mr. Overhill's red Dodge pickup truck got noticed and observed straight off even though it arrived early on in the day before Lemly was fully astir which it would not be until at least midmorning since there was not much in Lemly to get astir over. And Mr. Overhill compounded his impact some by delivering four short blasts on his truckhorn as he rolled to a stop in front of the block grocery just like he always did when he got to where he was going since with the absence of trumpets it was the closest thing to a fanfare he could muster. He stepped out of the cab and stretched himself and then went on into the store where he purchased a half dozen cellophane packets of candied corn and engaged Mr. Raymond Dance Greer in a varied and far-reaching conversation which commenced with a dual analysis of the localized cloud formations, fell off some midway as Mr. Greer drew Mr. Overhill a roadmap on the detached end panel of a cigarette carton, and then picked up again and carried on in a most lively and energetic fashion to an ever so boisterous climax which saw Mr. Overhill recite to Mr. Greer a snatch of poetry he had read over a urinal in Charlotte.

Occasionally consulting the end panel of the cigarette carton, Mr. Overhill drove back out of Lemly the way he had come in and turned off the main road onto a secondary one that proceeded paved for a half mile or so and then went to gravel and curled down the mountainside towards the creek bottom where it

straightened out and followed the bank of what was
known locally as Little Roaring Fork which came off of
Big Roaring Fork to the north which itself originated
just above the confluence of the French Broad River
and Flatwoods Creek. Mr. Overhill kept to the creekbank for a considerable ways, several miles anyhow,
and when he did eventually pull the truck off the side
of the road and beat out a salute on the horn it did not
appear he had come to a place worth stopping and
beeping over but he left the cab with his usual resolve
and after casting around for a break in the underbrush
struck out between a pair of locust trees up a fairly
well-trod footpath. The paltry negro lowered the tailgate and rolled out into the road followed by the fat
negro and the wiry tattooed white boy who was ever
excruciatingly attentive to his bladder and straightaway
waded on into the weeds to relieve himself where he
was joined by the fat negro who near about filled up
the wiry tattooed white boy's left shoe and so got
chased up the slope and into the woods and back out
again to the great amusement of the paltry negro who
had taken up a position directly in the middle of the
gravel road where he figured no snakes could slip up
on him. Benton Lynch brought himself and his paper
sack out of the truckbed and stood by the left rear tire
doing nothing in particular and lastly it came away
from the fender well and onto the tailgate where it
squatted and picked at itself. They called it the critter,
the fat negro and the paltry negro and the wiry tattooed white boy did anyhow, while Mr. Overhill insisted on referring to it as Dwight, and it was not a
negro as Benton Lynch had suspected right off, not by
race anyway, but it was black enough what with the
grit and the grime and the dust and the general filth
that had collected and caked up on its face and on its
neck and on its forearms and on the backs and fronts
of its hands and on its ankles and all throughout its
trousers and its button-up shirt and on into the hair on

its head which did not lay down anywhere but stood up
in the knots and mats and greasy swirls all over, and it
raked out its ears with a fingernail and then without
even bothering to stand up urinated off the end of the
tailgate and into the road or primarily into the road
but partly onto the tailgate itself so that a slight but
measurable puddle formed under its haunches and
around its feet and the paltry negro said, "You nasty
motherfucker, you," and tried to appear thoroughly
disgusted but could not.

Mr. Overhill hooted from up the slope and the fat
negro and the wiry tattooed white boy and the paltry
negro scanned the hillside but couldn't find him out
amid the trees and the brambles and the leafy bushes
so he hooted again and waved his arms over his head
and the wiry tattooed white boy spotted him under a
cucumber tree and hooted back.

"Come ahead," Mr. Overhill hollered.

And the wiry tattooed white boy yelled, "Awright,"
and the fat negro yelled, "Awright," just behind him
and the paltry negro said, "Sho nuff, asshole," with no
considerable volume to speak of and the fat negro
fetched the picks and shovels and distributed them all
around so everybody got one of each except for the
critter who brought a garden trowel out from a corner
of the truckbed and stuck the handle of it in his back
pocket and then lit out between the locust trees and up
the footpath. The paltry negro did not wish to walk in
front of the fat negro and the wiry tattooed white boy
and Benton Lynch and did not wish to come along
behind them but desired to climb the trail somewhere
in the midst of the three of them so as to be suitably
insulated from the wildlife roundabout. However, he
could not decide if he wanted to go second behind the
fat negro or third behind the wiry tattooed white boy
and when he was at last pressed to choose he settled
on third but reconsidered partway through the weeds
and fairly much scaled the wiry tattooed white boy's

backside in an effort to jump ahead a spot but the wiry tattooed white boy resisted and the two of them got all tangled up together on the trail and pushed each other and swore each other and yanked each other around and when the paltry negro had gotten where he wanted to get he swung his pick and his shovel up onto his shoulder and called the wiry tattooed white boy a sorry motherfucker and called the fat negro a stupid motherfucker and turned all the way around to Benton Lynch to tell him what a homely motherfucker he was which was only the second thing he'd had yet to say to Benton Lynch the first having come somewhere along about Statesville sometime along about the middle of the night when Mr. Overhill had stopped for gas and the paltry negro had noticed Benton Lynch against the fender well and had raised his head up off the crook of his arm and said, "Damn boy, ain't you ugly."

The trail cut back and forth across the hillside and eventually gave out on a grassy plateau where Mr. Overhill waited to direct the four of them around the rotted and tumbled down remains of a Baptist sanctuary on the far side of which lay a modest graveyard bordered round by an iron fence, and though it was small and sparsely populated as graveyards go it was nonetheless an extraordinary sight there in the middle of the woods beside an abandoned and collapsed church because it was so utterly and absolutely well tended to in a run of country where everything else was going to ruin unchecked. The grass around the headstones and on the mounded graves themselves had been clipped and weeded and throughout the plots were decorated with flowers in foil-wrapped vases and ribbons and flags and a varied assortment of personal effects and mementos, or the majority of them were decorated anyway except for that of Mr. Robert Earl Earp 1897–1956 Asleep in the Redeemer's Arms whose plot was as neat and scrupulously tended to as any of the others but was entirely unadorned and col-

orless and so somehow suggested that Mr. Robert Earl
Earp was more frankly dead and perished than his
neighbors, especially his neighbor to his immediate
left, Mrs. Ida Dinkins McCoy 1904–1967 Gone to
God who had plastic jonquils and bows at her feet and
a gilt-framed picture of herself embedded in her headstone. Apparently Mrs. Ida Dinkins McCoy had not
made her way in the world on account of her good
looks.

Mr. Overhill stepped aside at the gate and the fat
negro and the paltry negro and the wiry tattooed white
boy and Benton Lynch filed past him into the cemetery. The critter was on his knees astride Mrs. Emma
Vance Lemly 1821–1889 Loving Wife and Mother. He
had already taken the sod off and was commencing to
break up the underlying earth with the point of his
trowel. The wiry tattooed white boy dropped his pick
and shovel down across her husband, Colonel George
Fentress Lemly 1819–1863 Brave and Just—Peace Be
His Reward, and removed the flags and the vase of
zinnias and tossed aside the shovel and raised the pick
and said, "Probe that thing, you greasy bastard," to
which the critter bared his teeth and wiped his forehead on his shirtsleeve. Benton Lynch did not go anywhere much once he got inside the cemetery gate but
just stood for a spell in between a row of graves with
his shovel handle against his chest and his pick handle
against his beltbuckle. The paltry negro had settled on
a Greer, a fairly recent Greer, and the fat negro had
laid claim to yet another Lemly, William George
Lemly 1859–1928 From His Labors Delivered, and the
fat negro was removing some of the greenery from
roundabout Mr. Lemly's midsection when he noticed
Benton Lynch standing there between a Dinkins and a
Donahoo not seeming inclined to go anywhere much
and not seeming inclined to commence anything
hardly, and maybe it was the hollowed out and prominent features and maybe it was the general pointiness

and maybe it was the usual vacant expression in combination with the hollowed out and prominent features and the general pointiness all of which together suggested perplexity to the fat negro who figured perplexity was what it had to be and so left off with Mr. William George Lemly momentarily and explained to Benton Lynch, "They's a dam going up somewhere, somewhere up on the creek, up on the river, somewhere," and he jerked his head in what he figured for a likely direction. "Put all this under water, all these trees and this mess here, these dead folks and some of these live ones too, and it ain't no matter much to cover up all these trees and all these live folks round here and all their mess, but cain't cover up these dead folks, cain't cover up the first one of them. Just cain't. So ain't nothing to do but take them up from this place and put them some place else, ain't nothing to do otherwise. Dam folks paying him, he paying us, ain't nothing to do otherwise," and the fat negro tossed his pick aside and set about scraping the sod off Mr. Lemly while Benton Lynch stood as he had stood previously in all of his angularity and his pointiness which somehow suggested to the fat negro a greatly diminished perplexity and he pointed to the nearest Dinkins with the end of his shovel handle, a Mr. Robert Lloyd Dinkins 1917–1972 Sleep Everlasting, and said, "Start on that one there. He ain't been dead long, probably still in the box."

Benton Lynch was up to his shins when the first pair of Lemlys climbed the trail from the creekbottom and joined Mr. Overhill at the cemetery gate. They had received their due notification, Mr. Overhill called it, back in March and so had set aside the entire morning and part of the afternoon to cross the border from Ashe county and fetch their daddy and their granddaddy and their grandmomma and their grandmomma's sister Heloise Simpkins Vance McCoy. They were clean and neat and somber and favored remarkably, appeared in fact to be two different stages of the same existence. They shared the Lemly nose and the broad Lemly brow and the red Lemly ears with the dainty Lemly earlobes and when they leaned against the fence with Mr. Overhill they both crossed their arms over their chests and inclined their heads in precisely the same fashion. Of course Mr. Overhill engaged them in conversation straightaway and whenever it seemed that one Lemly or the other or both were paying inordinate attention to the activity around them he started in afresh on an untried topic so as to divert the pair of them some mostly on account of the critter who was not especially clean or neat or somber and who was just before bringing Grandmother Lemly up out of the ground. He had put the trowel aside and was digging with his bare hands, throwing the dirt up between his legs like a dog and grunting and dripping sweat and making for his usual unseemly spectacle which Mr. Overhill did not believe was the kind of thing a person should see in conjunction with his dead relations so he developed a sudden and burning curiosity as to the indigenous foliage, especially as to the indigenous foliage down around the collapsed sanctuary and he led both Lemlys out of the cemetery and down the hill, told them they needed to identify an item or two for him, told them they simply had to put his mind at ease.

The critter struck pure grandmother soon after Mr. Overhill and the Lemlys had dropped over the rise and out of sight or anyway the general consensus was that the critter had struck relatively pure grandmother since once he held up a trowelful of the substance in question for a ruling he got an "Uh huh" from the fat negro and an "Uh huh" from the wiry tattooed white boy and a "That's the bitch" from the paltry negro who was the one this time to notice the hollowed out and prominent features and the general pointiness and the usual vacant expression which he did not take for perplexity exactly but which instead suggested to him a kind of thoroughgoing idiocy and he rested the point of his shovel on his shoetop and turned his head sideways and very nearly addressed Benton Lynch with "Black dirt's dirt. Yellow dirt's clay. Gray dirt's folks. Ain't a goddamn thing to it."

The critter put Mrs. Emma Vance Lemly 1821–1889 Loving Wife and Mother into one of the Ziploc plastic bags Mr. Overhill had piled up at the cemetery gate. She was damp and coarse and a little lumpy and bony and splintery every now and again, and he burped the air off of her and sealed her up and dropped her behind her headstone prior to taking himself and his trowel off a plot to the left so as to commence work on Mrs. Heloise Simpkins Vance McCoy 1825–1887 Beloved and Cherished Wife of Jackson Caswell McCoy with whom she shared her granite marker. The wiry tattooed white boy hit a vein of fairly dense and incontestable Colonel Lemly just after the critter had bagged up the Mrs. and just prior to the return of Mr. Overhill and the only live Lemlys roundabout who had fairly much exhausted themselves with identifying half of the forest and speculating over the rest of it. Like his wife the colonel was gray and damp and coarse and lumpy with bone and with splinters but lumpy as well with a good half dozen extremely well-preserved brass coatbuttons and one gold matchsafe which the Lemlys arrived in time to retrieve before it got burped and Ziplocked. The paltry negro interrupted the surfacing of Lemlys with his recent Greer whose hardwood casket he inadvertently punctured with his pick but who otherwise did not appear excessively damaged or decayed or deteriorated and who in fact had retained sufficient bulk to call for the paltry negro and the fat negro and the wiry tattooed white boy along with Mr. Overhill himself to fetch him up out of his hole in the ground, and as a favor to the living Lemlys Mr. Overhill lifted the casket lid to expose the paltry negro's

recent Greer who one of the Lemlys believed he had
fished with on three different occasions and him and
his brother peered in at the Greer in question, who
was not in any way hideous or frightening but whose
mouth had opened up some and whose skin had tight-
ened up some and who did appear in general most con-
vincingly deceased, and after the pair of Lemlys had
consulted on the matter the Lemly that had been fishing with a Greer decided it had not been this particular
Greer.

A Dinkins, two Earps, and a vagrant strain of
Jemison who had some Earp to him but not a good
deal of Earp showed up at the cemetery just as Mr.
Overhill was letting the lid back down on the paltry
negro's Greer. They had not come up the trail from the
creekbottom but had stepped out from the undergrowth above the ruined church and the cemetery
where no trail or footpaths or even deer run appeared
to be. The four of them jerked their heads at the
Lemlys and the Lemlys jerked their heads in return as
the Dinkins and the two Earps along with the diluted
Jemison took up positions against the high side of the
fence opposite the gate and proceeded to ponder over
the ongoing excavation, proceeded to ponder without
any talk and without much interruption except for
some spitting on the part of the Earps who chewed and
some drooling on the part of the Dinkins who dipped
and some general fidgeting on the part of the Jemison
who fidgeted. As a group they were not nearly so pink
and robust as the Lemlys, did not possess the broad
Lemly brow or the fleshy Lemly ears or the straight
and proper Lemly nose but were instead slight and
drawn and waxen and predominantly eye sockets,
deep and near about purple eye sockets which the
Earps had the deepest and purplest of followed by the
Dinkins and concluding with the Jemison who appeared as if he had slept once maybe.

Mr. Overhill crossed the cemetery and met them all

hail and forthrightly but did not generate any considerable enthusiasm and so carried the bulk of the conversation himself which was not in fact a conversation really but more truly took the form of an extemporaneous panegyric on the local countryside delivered by Mr. Overhill with much energy and some highly dramatic gesticulation but received with only the usual spitting and the usual drooling and an altogether unextraordinary display of fidgeting. The Dinkins and the shorter of the two Earps did not seem inclined or able to speak and the remaining Earp would not speak until Mr. Overhill insisted on knowing who they had come to fetch away, if that was their purpose, to which the remaining Earp wiped his mouth with the back of his hand and said, "Daddy."

"Daddy who?" Mr. Overhill asked him.

"Earp," the remaining Earp said, and though he got probed and examined and prodded he could not be made to elaborate on or embellish his answer any further, could not be made to do anything really but spit on the iron cemetery fence and could not be kept from that. The Jemison did volunteer that he had a cousin across the way in the far corner and he pointed out the headstone to Mr. Overhill, the headstone of his cousin, his second cousin on his mother's side which would be his mother's sister's daughter's child, but he had not come to fetch away his cousin, had not been well acquainted with him actually on account of a rift between his mother and his mother's sister which had developed during a land dispute upon the death of his granddaddy who fell off the listening rock in March of 1935 and got broke all to pieces. The Jemison decided his was strictly a social call and told Mr. Overhill as much and fidgeted and finally shut up.

Mr. Overhill left the fence and wandered throughout the cemetery in search of all the resident Earps and pointed to each one he came across and judged the reaction on the taller Earp and the shorter Earp

also who between them did not show much sign of life
until Mr. Overhill arrived at and indicated Mr. Phillip
Reid Earp 1902–1965 Jesus Called upon which the
shorter Earp glanced at the taller Earp who managed
an ever so slight nod of the head in between two exceedingly demonstrative expectorations. So Mr. Overhill put the wiry tattooed white boy on the appropriate
Earp straightaway or almost straightaway anyhow once
he had handed the deceased and bagged up Lemlys
over the fence to the pair of live Lemlys who had decided to unseal their granddaddy and separate him
from his brass coatbuttons which they set about directly. The fat negro had partly uncovered William
George Lemly when Benton Lynch finally struck his
Dinkins or struck the laminated coffinlid of his Dinkins which was still firm and solid and so did not give
way to the tip end of the shovel. The fat negro's
Lemly, however, did not have much box left and had
predominantly come to pieces himself except from the
knees down where he had retained the cuffs of his
pants and the entire of his shoes, and there was so
much corpse and so little coffin that after the digging
and the sorting and the burping and the Ziplocking the
fat negro ended up with a three bag Lemly. Benton
Lynch scraped the dirt off his Dinkins's coffinlid and
attempted to prize the box up some with his shovel but
could not and so was assisted by the fat negro and the
paltry negro along with Mr. Overhill and four equal
lengths of rope which the paltry negro tied to the casket handles once he took them from Benton Lynch
who had been handed them by Mr. Overhill but had
only eyed them there across his palm with his usual
angularity and pointiness and general vacancy, and the
four of them together along with their rope and aided
by a touch of scorching profanity from the paltry negro
brought Mr. Robert Lloyd Dinkins up into the sunlight
which made for five empty holes in the cemetery and
in keeping with his usual practice Mr. Overhill went

round to each fresh mound of dirt and dropped upon it
a ten, a five, and two one dollar bills.

By the top of the noon hour the critter had already
bagged up the live Lemlys' grandmomma's sister who
proved to be extraordinarily powdery considering her
depth and the wiry tattooed white boy had sunk himself about halfway to his Earp when Mr. Overhill
called for lunch. He apologized to the Dinkins and the
Earps and the Jemison for the delay and they drooled
and spat and fidgeted respectively, and him and the fat
negro and the paltry negro tried to hand the three bag
Lemly over the cemetery fence to the live Lemlys
thinking it was their daddy and would thereby fill the
Lemly order, but it was not their daddy after all and
turned out to be their daddy's oldest brother who the
live Lemlys had known as children but had not ever
cherished much and did not want to carry home with
them, so Mr. Overhill apologized to the Lemlys for the
delay just as he had apologized to the Dinkins and the
Earps and the Jemison and they told him not to fret
over it and went back to stirring their grandmomma's
sister with a stick.

They had lunch at the block grocery, rode there on
the open tailgate except for Mr. Overhill who drove
and except for the critter who squatted beside the
fender well. Mr. Overhill bought Pepsi-Colas and saltines and potted meat and fig newtons and he distributed the drinks himself but gave over the food sack to
the fat negro who set aside an entire sleeve of crackers
and two cans of potted meat and a dozen fig newtons
before throwing the bag at the paltry negro and hitting
him square in the head with it which touched off a
full-fledged invective festival with the paltry negro and
the fat negro as the prime participants but with meaningful contributions from the wiry tattooed white boy
who got the bag himself eventually, mostly in the neck
and shoulders, and then got relieved of it from behind
by the critter who pilfered through it prior to dropping

it in Benton Lynch's lap. Mr. Overhill ate in the store,
candied corn primarily, and told Mr. Greer about a
woman he'd known in Clarksburg, West Virginia, and
the fat negro got choked on a saltine and coughed
some Pepsi up through his nose which the paltry negro
found exceedingly satisfying and to celebrate raised his
left haunch up off the tailgate and farted in one brief
resounding pop which prompted several strident and
near about violent objections from the wiry tattooed
white boy who held bodily functions in the highest regard and took an especially dim view on all recreational farting and burping and told the paltry negro as
much in the strongest and gravest language he could
manage and then got burped at by both the negroes
together and farted on by the critter and so stormed
off around the block store in a fit of pique and urinated into Mr. Greer's trashcan to relieve his agitation
some.

By the time Mr. Overhill returned to the cemetery
with his charges, the Lemlys and the Dinkins and the
Earps and the Jemison had been joined by a McCoy,
two Donahoos and a Kemp. The Kemp's dead relations were all in South Carolina and he had come primarily to see the Donahoos' uncle but perused the
bagged-up Lemlys with considerable interest and
helped himself to a peek at the paltry negro's Greer.
The Donahoos had come primarily to see their uncle
also but did not have any plans for him past the seeing
of him and so volunteered their assistance and volunteered the assistance of the Kemp, who was not ever
very quick to volunteer it on his own, in the eventual
hauling off of the McCoy's sister-in-law, Ida Dinkins
McCoy of the embedded portrait. The actual upright
McCoy was Miss Vera Jane McCoy from Flatwoods
who did not have an actual upright sister and had
always considered Mrs. Ida Dinkins McCoy the closest
thing to one when she was actual and upright herself,
and Miss Vera Jane McCoy from Flatwoods took ahold

of Mr. Overhill's elbow from the underside once Mr. Overhill reached the cemetery and she led him round to her sister-in-law's plot as she told him all about the funeral and all about the mourners and all about the eulogy and all about the preacher who delivered it and all about the preacher's youngest daughter that had gotten herself pregnant by a Lutheran. Then she gazed upon the plastic jonquils and the bows and the gilt-framed photograph and said, "Lord, she was a handsome woman."

And Mr. Overhill told her, "Yes," told her, "Lord," told her, "Well now."

Benton Lynch got put on the actual upright McCoy's sister-in-law and the fat negro set in on the Donahoos' uncle while the paltry negro commenced with the true and verifiable Lemly daddy and the wiry tattooed white boy persisted with his Earp. Mr. Overhill put the critter to work on a Rawls once he determined there were not any Rawlses present and then he visited with the Lemlys who had successfully fished a gold pendant out from their grandmomma's sister. Mrs. Ida Dinkins McCoy did not appear very pleased with Benton Lynch from her gilt frame and he took off his shirt and covered her up with it but could not forget she was behind his shirttail looking at him and so remained uneasy. He was blistered already underneath his fingers or underneath six of his fingers anyway and consequently he could not effectively shovel with the shovel and could not effectively pick with the pick and thereby fell off the pace of the others which he had never really been up to in the first place. If anything the critter troweled up his Rawls with a kind of velocity he had not even approached on either one of his Lemlys and the wiry tattooed white boy and the paltry negro dug with appreciable energy and rhythm themselves while the fat negro, who was a little too fat and just a touch too sorry to put in an entire day's worth of hard and honest labor, dwindled some but hardly like

Benton Lynch had dwindled and was continuing to dwindle on account of his general weariness and on account of his six blisters two of which had popped open and four more of which were about to.

The critter had his Rawls sifted out, bagged, and Ziplocked before Benton Lynch was even halfway down to Mrs. Ida Dinkins McCoy who continued to glare at him from underneath his shirttail, and as much as Mr. Overhill had resisted it, as much as he had wished to avoid it altogether, he directed the critter to assist Benton Lynch so as to expedite matters and Mr. Overhill himself took charge of Miss Vera Jane McCoy by offering her his elbow and strolling with her down to the collapsed sanctuary where he initiated a discussion of Lutherans about whom Miss McCoy held some exceptionally emphatic opinions. The critter was not extraordinarily fond of sharing his hole even if it wasn't his hole in the first place and he fairly much moved Benton Lynch clean up out of it and troweled and grunted and sweated and wheezed and sprayed dirt like a hound down to the casketlid while Benton Lynch squatted on the lip of the grave and licked his blisters. Mr. Overhill squired Miss Vera Jane McCoy back up the hillside just as her sister-in-law was getting hefted up into the sunlight by the critter and the paltry negro and the fat negro along with Benton Lynch and four strands of rope, and the upright and actual McCoy, who seemed to have a certain flair for the preposterous, rushed in through the cemetery gate to her sister-in-law's casket and brushed the remaining dirt off the top of it and said, "Oh hello Ida dear," and then she knocked with her knuckles on the coffinlid and the fat negro and the paltry negro each drew a breath and listened.

The actual and upright McCoy had begun to marshal the pair of Donahoos and the solitary Kemp into a squad of bearers just as the paltry negro and the fat negro and Benton Lynch were helping to snatch the wiry tattooed white boy's Earp up out of the ground, and the Dinkins and the two Earps and the vagrant strain of Jemison did not greet the boxed-up deceased Earp in any particular way, did not even wipe the dirt clean from the coffinlid but just drooled and spat and fidgeted respectively prior to taking up a coffinhandle apiece and carrying the Earps' daddy out the cemetery gate and up the hillside into the woods. They were followed directly by the actual and upright McCoy and the pair of Donahoos along with the solitary Kemp who had commenced to complain of a crooked spine when time came to lift the coffin, had commenced to complain most fornlornly and resolutely, and so had been given to carry instead the gilt-framed portrait of the actual and upright McCoy's sister-in-law which Mr. Overhill had prized out of the headstone. So the actual and upright McCoy herself grabbed onto the backend of the casket and the Donahoos took ahold of opposite sides of the middle of it and the solitary and afflicted Kemp led them into the woods out from which there came presently a ponderous thud which was certainly the sound of the dropping of the sister-in-law and which was followed by the clamor of several harsh, strident, and near about outraged voices raised all at once and together which was certainly the sound of the berating of the Kemp.

The Lemlys got some help with their daddy from the fat negro, and the paltry negro and the wiry tattooed white boy carried grandmomma Lemly and granddaddy Lemly while Benton Lynch toted grandmomma Lemly's powdery sister on down the slope to the creek bottom. So as not to go entirely unproductive Mr. Overhill carried as much of the unwanted three bag Lemly as he could manage, which turned out to be two bags' worth, and the critter brought down the paltry negro's Greer by himself on his back. The four dead Lemlys that were departing with the two live Lemlys got loaded into the bed of the Lemly truck, and the two thirds of the three bag Lemly along with the entire of the boxed up Greer got set down on the roadside and left there temporarily. The fat negro had near about completely uncovered the Donahoos' uncle prior to the departure of the Lemlys and so returned to the cemetery and with the assistance of the wiry tattooed white boy and the paltry negro and Benton Lynch hoisted out of the ground this particular deceased Donahoo who the live Donahoos had said they had come to see but had neglected to even visit with, and the fat negro and the paltry negro took up either end of the Donahoos' uncle and carried him down to the roadside followed by Benton Lynch with an armful of the critter's Rawls in a bag followed by the wiry tattooed white boy and the critter himself with Benton Lynch's Dinkins between them and punctuated by Mr. Overhill with the third bag of the three bag Lemly. The fat negro and the paltry negro set their Donahoo next to the Greer and the critter and the wiry tattooed white boy laid down the Dinkins alongside him while Benton Lynch, without considering why he shouldn't put his Rawls in a bag down with two thirds of the Lemly so when Mr. Overhill arrived with the remaining third and commenced to label the various corpses in their various forms, he could not decipher which three of the four bags was Lemly and which one of the four bags was Rawls. He examined the dirt, questioned Benton Lynch, and solicited opinions from both the negroes and the wiry tattooed white boy too, but still was not satisfied that the Rawls was a Rawls and the Lemly all Lemly even once he had labeled them Rawls and Lemly. It seemed far more likely to Mr. Overhill that the Lemly was only mostly Lemly and the Rawls very possibly entirely part Lemly, but he went ahead and tagged and designated them anyway since it did not matter much who was what now that the both of them were compost.

Mr. Overhill drove the red Dodge pickup out of the

creekbottom to the block grocery after a carton of cold Pepsi-Colas, and the fat negro and the paltry negro and the wiry tattooed white boy along with Benton Lynch and the critter returned to the cemetery where they selected new and unearthed Donahoos and Dinkinses and McCoys and Rawlses and Lemlys for themselves. Work ceased temporarily when Mr. Overhill came back and passed out the bottles and divvied up a packet of candied corn but it resumed presently to the accompaniment of an irregular but lively melody that Mr. Overhill whistled through his teeth as he wandered about the cemetery dropping the seventeen dollars onto the dirt mounds he had not dropped the seventeen dollars onto previously and pausing to gaze into the five halfdug, halfpicked, halftroweled holes. Towards the end of the afternoon a storm rolled in over the mountaintop preceded by great bursts of thunder and wind that turned the treeleaves backside up and then the rain itself advanced down the mountainside rattling in the treetops and beating the brush and finally arriving at the cemetery clearing in plump, soaking drops, first one and then another and then a half dozen and a dozen and then all of the rest at once staining the granite markers and dripping from the iron fence and running off the necks and faces of the fat negro who dug and the paltry negro who dug and the wiry tattooed white boy who dug and the critter who troweled and Mr. Overhill who grinned and whistled and off of the pointy nose and down into the carved out hollows of Benton Lynch who laid his shovel handle against his chest and looked all around himself.

At 5:30 promptly the paltry negro gathered all of the shovels and the picks and deposited them beneath the least collapsed part of the collapsed Baptist sanctuary. The critter who had succeeded in reaching what was in this case his Dinkins attempted to trowel him up into a sack and thereby close out the day but his Din-

kins had become muddy in the rain and would not well
lend himself to troweling or bagging or burping, so the
critter dumped what little Dinkins he'd collected back
into the hole with the rest of the Dinkins he'd yet to
collect and pocketed his trowel for the night. Mr.
Overhill brought the fixings out of the cab and set
about preparing supper. The wiry tattooed white boy
and the fat negro stripped naked and carried their
towels and a half-empty jug of pink dish detergent
down to the creek where they were determined to
bathe even after they stuck their toes into the water
and drew them out again. The paltry negro was determined to bathe also but was determined as well not to
stray from the middle of the gravel road which put him
in a considerable dilemma and he had not even begun
to puzzle it out when Benton Lynch, who had not previously given much thought to bathing, determined
that he would wash after all and started down the slope
to the creekbank in the immediate company of the
paltry negro who did not much mind underbrush when
someone else beat it back. The critter squatted on the
tailgate and scratched himself, apparently indifferent
to and entirely immune from the attempted hygiene all
around him.

   The wiry tattooed white boy sat down in a knee-
deep eddy after the fat negro dared him to and all of
his skin went to gooseflesh even the dragon on his left
bicep and the serpent on his right bicep and the Marlene in a red heart on his right forearm. He poured
pink dish detergent all over himself and lathered up
and then lay back in the water ever so briefly prior to
leaping bolt upright and standing all sudsy and thoroughly goosebumped on the creekbed with a tortured
little knot of skin where his testicles had been before
they crawled up inside his stomach. The mere sight of
him convinced the fat negro and the paltry negro too
that they did not wish to get as entirely clean as they
had thought previously and the both of them ended up

washing their hands mostly while Benton Lynch removed his clothes, soaped himself all over, and waded
on out into the center of the creek where he vanished
with hardly a ripple and stayed vanished for what
seemed a lengthy spell to the fat negro and the paltry
negro and for what seemed an incredibly lengthy spell
to the wiry tattooed white boy who had been vanished
briefly himself. And when he at last did resurface he
came up soapless but apparently unaffected otherwise
and waded out of the creek past the wiry tattooed
white boy and the fat negro and the paltry negro who
asked him was he a crazy motherfucker or what.

Mr. Overhill had attempted to build a fire, had
heaped up some wet sticks anyway, but did not ever
strike a match to them and instead started the truck
engine and placed the three cans of corned beef hash
and the jar of creamed onions on the manifold to heat
them up some. He tended to himself with undiluted
drafts of Ancient Age which he took direct from a pint
bottle which he kept discreetly in a paper sack even in
a densely wooded creekbottom in the middle of nowhere with no natives roundabout but for bagged up
and boxed up dead ones. However, the manifold did
not seem to have much effect on the three cans of
corned beef hash and the jar of creamed onions mostly
because they fell off it once Mr. Overhill himself got
sufficiently heated up and hit the gearshift with his
knee, and even though he discovered them on the
ground soon thereafter and returned them to the engine he set the onions atop the battery and balanced
the cans of corned beef on the tire jack bolted to the
wheel well neither of which tended to heat up quite as
dramatically as the manifold did. Consequently, aside
from Mr. Overhill himself, nothing really got warmed
up for supper and Mr. Overhill portioned out the tepid
hash and the onions into coffee cups and divided the
remaining saltines equally and then joined the fat
negro and the paltry negro and the wiry tattooed white

boy and Benton Lynch and the critter at the tailgate of
the truck where they ate in the company of a Greer
and a Dinkins and a Donahoo and a Rawls and a
Lemly who lay in a bunch on the roadside. And after
they had eaten, and after the fat negro and the paltry
negro and the critter had burped and farted the wiry
tattooed white boy into a vicious fit, and after Mr.
Overhill had told three times a joke about a shoesalesman he had told two times earlier in the day, they all
settled in for the night, Mr. Overhill in the cab of the
truck with his sack of Ancient Age and the fat negro
and the paltry negro and the wiry tattooed white boy
and the critter and Benton Lynch in the bed of the
truck with the paltry negro's dope which went round
between the paltry negro and the fat negro and the
wiry tattooed white boy as they lay with their heads on
their arms and watched the darkness come into the
creekbottom, lay in silence mostly and watched in silence primarily except for the paltry negro who said,
"Whus at?" with most every breath he could draw.

In another half a day they had the cemetery by the
dilapidated church emptied of its Lemlys and its
Greers and its Rawlses and its Dinkinses and its
McCoys and its Donahoos and its Earps who lay together in their bags and boxes on the roadside until
Mr. Overhill and the fat negro could load them into
the truckbed and drive them up the gravel road and
out through Lemly past the block store and the trash
bins and the shabby ruinous house and up onto a
square of sufficiently high and newly sanctified ground
where they set them out again in their various bags and
their various boxes. And when there were no more
Lemlys and no more Greers and no more Rawlses and
Dinkinses and McCoys and Donahoos and Earps by
the roadside in the creekbottom, Mr. Overhill and the
fat negro carried away all the picks and the shovels and
even the trowel too along with the paltry negro and
Benton Lynch and the wiry tattooed white boy and the

critter who had come out the iron gate and away from
the markers and the vases and the flags and the mementos, away from the collapsed sanctuary and down
the trail between the locust trees. They dug new holes
on the high ground, holes not as deep as the original
holes but suitable nonetheless for the plastic bags and
the wooden and the metal and the laminated caskets,
and Mr. Overhill counted out the appropriate number
of new tin markers from a five gallon bucket and wrote
the names across them with a wax pencil and he stuck
one in the ground at the head of each finished grave
and dropped onto the red dirt still the ten and the five
and the two ones though the holes were not so deep as
before and not so broad and not so long. They were
finished before 5:30 even and the paltry negro collected the picks and the shovels and packed them away
in the truckbed while Mr. Overhill built a fire and successfully heated four cans of Dinty Moore stew. There
was no creek to bathe in so there was not any lathering
up or rinsing off or even any handwashing to speak of,
just another joke from Mr. Overhill about another
shoesalesman and more saltines and more Ancient
Age and more dope and then treefrogs and darkness
and sleep. They left in the night and so were already
somewhere else by daylight, beyond Chattanooga this
time, just beyond it on a hillside studded with tombstones and carved markers and one ghastly marble
mausoleum, and the fat negro rolled out of the
truckbed and pointed across the cemetery to first one
rise and then another and then another. "Yonder," he
said, "and yonder, and yonder too. Condominyums."

Mr. Busick did not consider himself done with his
testicles though he had been accused of as much by
Mrs. Busick ever since about 1972 or anyway that's
what Mr. Tommy Winn said and that's what Mr. C. W.
Bobbit nodded over and that's what Mr. Busick him-

self smirked at while Deputy Mercer apparently made
a note about it on his little pad of paper that swung
open from the top. Mr. Busick said it did not seem
fitting to him his testicles should go to a place he'd
never been to himself, did not seem fitting in the least
especially since he always took them wherever he went
and what he most desired to know from Deputy
Mercer or Mr. Tommy Winn or Mr. C. W. Bobbit either one was what in the hell was a Fuquay-Varina
anyhow and where in the hell was it in the first place,
and Mr. Tommy Winn spoke up straight off and told
him it was where all the best testicles go this time of
year and Mr. C. W. Bobbit, who hardly ever added or
contributed much of anything, this time did in fact add
and contribute, "A regular rash of them," which Mr.
Busick and Mr. Winn together yipped and howled over
and Deputy Mercer made a note about, and Mr. Bobbit recrossed his legs and rolled his cigarette the width
of his mouth and said he believed he was itching to go
there himself, and Mr. Busick and Mr. Winn near
about expired from breathlessness.

Deputy Mercer wanted to know did the alleged
gunman, he called him, have any distinguishing features and Mr. Busick told him he had nothing but from
the nose out in all directions, so they commenced to
work their way down from the top of his head which
Mr. Busick and Mr. Winn and Mr. Bobbit all agreed
had been fairly distinguishing itself what with its fullblown and glorious pointiness. Mr. Busick estimated a
half a foot between the eyebrows and the hairline but
Mr. Winn begged to differ and could not see fit to
allow for more than four inches while Mr. Bobbit did
not recollect any eyebrows straightoff but was presently reminded of them by Mr. Busick. They all agreed
his eyes had been of the sunken variety, probably of
the extraordinarily sunken variety, and Mr. Busick was
convinced they had been black but Mr. Winn was
equally convinced they had been brown and Mr. Bob-

bit was convinced they had been either brown or black, so Deputy Mercer offered up dark as an alternative and it was agreeable to Mr. Winn and agreeable to Mr. Bobbit but was not in the least agreeable to Mr. Busick who insisted on black since it was after all his testicles that had been threatened.

They did not differ much on the nose except in the magnitude of it and Mr. Busick eventually retreated from his initial estimation and threw in with Mr. Winn and Mr. Bobbitt who had themselves described to the deputy a nearly implausible organ and so welcomed the assistance of Mr. Busick whose threatened testicles seemed to lend him more credence than they possessed. The mouth was not a matter of much dissension either since they all agreed on the thinness of the lips and fairly completely agreed on the sheer bulk and squareness of the teeth, but they had some difficulty in conveying their impressions to Deputy Mercer who did not know any Holloways personally and had not been raised around horses except for Mr. Ed. So after casting around for a comparable item that was not a Holloway and not a horse either Mr. Winn at last struck upon Chiclets, which the deputy had never even heard of, and Mr. Busick plucked a box of the big ones off the candy rack and laid out a half dozen of them across the top of the drinkbox and Deputy Mercer studied and puzzled over them momentarily prior to announcing that he believed he got the gist of the thing. Talk of the Adam's apple called for several nectarines and a tangelo out from Mr. Busick's meager produce bin and the tangelo eventually took the majority on account of it was the size of a true and healthy nectarine while Mr. Busick's nectarines had gone unbought and were rather slight and withered, and once Mr. Busick and Mr. Winn and Mr. Bobbit had in fact settled on the nectarine-sized tangelo for their model, Mr. Winn rolled up his left pantleg and Mr. Busick held the fruit in question against Mr. Winn's naked shinbone so as to illustrate the relàtionship between the Adam's apple and the neck since none of the actual necks present could even approach the alleged gunman's neck, at least not in the area of tubularity, Mr. Busick called it, much to the delight of Deputy Mercer who threw open his pad and set his pencil to scratching.

There was not much fuss or disagreement about those parts of the alleged gunman underneath the head and neck of him. Mr. Busick and Mr. Winn and Mr. Bobbit were all convinced he had stood well over six feet tall and they all recollected he had worn brown shoes and blue trousers and some sort of dress jacket, some sort of turd-colored dress jacket, Mr. Busick said, with turd-colored buttons, and now that Mr. Busick mentioned it Mr. Winn and Mr. Bobbit believed turd-colored was just the thing it was, just precisely the thing it was, and they rendered themselves emphatic with the deputy who licked the tipend of his pencil and made out to write turd-colored on his pad but did not. The gun was the final item to be analyzed and described, and though Mr. Busick and Mr. Winn and Mr. Bobbit all agreed it had been a pistol or a revolver or not a rifle anyway, they could not settle on a caliber between them and Mr. Winn proposed .38 while Mr. Bobbit insisted on .45 and Mr. Busick wandered around in the fifties tossing out whatever seemed likely at the moment, so the deputy suggested high caliber and Mr. Busick, with the thumb and forefinger of his right hand, described the diameter of the bore and the deputy suggested very high caliber to which Mr. Busick added a very on his own.

And that was near about the conclusion of the fact gathering and the statement taking and the general describing of the culprit except for a final question on the part of Deputy Mercer who asked Mr. Busick, "You have any idea at all who he was? Any idea?"

And Mr. Busick told him, "My travel agent, I guess," which Mr. Winn and Mr. Bobbit went into fits over.

They ran the whole story, not just in Draper and Wentworth but in Neely too on the bottom half of the front page of the *Chronicle* under some exceptionally inky headlines, and from his office in the town hall on the square Sheriff Burton creased the paper midway and set it aside on his desk and then took it up again and then set it aside again and then picked at his badge and fidgeted with his whistle prior to laying back against the wall on two legs of his chair prior to setting full onto the floor again and crossing his arms over his chest. Lawlessness generally got quite completely away from him, made him uneasy and agitated, especially serious lawlessness, malicious and dangerous lawlessness of which armed robbery was at the pure pinnacle next to homicide, which the sheriff did not hardly ever get any of, and just after suicide, which the sheriff most usually annually got some of but which was not an appreciable challenge to him since ordinarily the victim was the sole culprit also, and somewhere in the vicinity of mass murder with a garden implement or such, which the sheriff could only hope for and salivate over. So he was understandably edgy what with an actual offense with a very high caliber revolver, and the sheriff laid his palms flat out on his desktop and said to himself, "*Very* high caliber," in a deep and ominous sort of way.

It was going on a month since the sheriff had investigated any sort of violence whatsoever and the last episode had been a passionate but not a lethal outburst north on the 29 highway at the home of Mr. Jules Henry Graham, the least son of Mr. Lamont Graham of Ruffin. Mr. Jules Henry had built himself a house back a ways off the road and had taken a wife and raised a family in it all the while making improvements and embellishments in the form of shrubs and saplings and trumpet flowers and pine bark mulch and a two acre kidney-shaped pond out front between the house and the roadside. Mr. Jules Henry had taken care to place a few drooping willow trees here and there around the water and had set out a number of pink and white azaleas and sown some grass and some ivy and had situated two concrete benches in two picturesque and enticing locations and so had generally made for himself a lush and comely garden spot that he could sit on his front porch and admire, and it was equally admirable from the highway, maybe even especially admirable from the highway on account of how little else there was roundabout worth looking at hard except maybe for the Knights of Columbus clubhouse which was situated off the lefthand side of the road in a cedar grove and which the knights themselves had painted pink and green thereby transforming a fairly harmless and unobtrusive frame structure into the sort of thing your eyes went to even if your stomach resisted. But people generally sped up as they looked at the Knights of Columbus clubhouse and they generally slowed down as they looked at Mr. Jules Henry's lush and comely frontyard pond.

Now Mr. Jules Henry Graham's house and grounds lay almost precisely midway between the Texaco station at the outskirts of Neely and the American Tobacco Company's cigarette plant north towards Danville, so three times a day when the shifts changed a great assortment of people set out from Neely going north and an equally great assortment of people set out from the cigarette plant coming south and they all sped up at the Knights of Columbus clubhouse and they all slowed down at Mr. Jules Henry's garden spot but probably nobody slowed down so much as Mr. Sleepy Pitts slowed down since in his years of driving from Neely to the plant and back again he had watched the property before Mr. Graham's house go from a brambly field to a bulldozed out hole in the ground to a seepy puddle to a fullblown pond to a fullblown and comely and lush and verdant pond with grassy banks and decorative azaleas roundabout and

thick viny willows on the water's edge and just generally the fishiest aspect of any body of water in any part
of the surrounding countryside, and Mr. Sleepy Pitts,
who always traveled with his rod and his reel disassembled and hanging behind him in the truck cab, was
one to take notice of fishy places, especially exceptionally fishy places, so while everybody else slowed down
in the road Sleepy Pitts near about stopped in it and
envisioned the bass and the bream and maybe even the
crappie too all across the pond bottom and suspended
thick and bounteous throughout the depths of the
water.

He was not personally acquainted with Mr. Jules
Henry Graham but had grown up with one of Mr.
Jules Henry's nephews, Mr. Robert Porter Graham,
and consequently figured he could introduce himself as
a friend of the family and so stopped in early one evening on his way back to Neely and found Mr. Jules
Henry on his frontporch swing with the *Chronicle* in
his lap and his Dr. Grabow out of the corner of his
mouth smoking and spewing and sparking up most
successfully. Mr. Jules Henry had never been much of
a talker and Sleepy Pitts was not one to flap and carry
on himself, so after the initial hellos and an odd word
or two from each party on the health and well-being of
Mr. Robert Porter Graham, not much got said straight
off and Mr. Jules Henry smoked and gazed out over
his lush and comely garden spot for himself and made
several appreciative noises in his neck prior to telling
Mr. Jules Henry outright that he had himself a lovely
pond to sit and look at and Mr. Jules Henry said yes he
did and nodded in agreement. And that was the end of
the lively banter for another spell until Mrs. Jules
Henry finished the dishes and came out onto the porch
where she got introduced to Sleepy Pitts partly by Mr.
Jules Henry who pointed and partly by Sleepy Pitts
who spoke. Mrs. Jules Henry set herself down on the
porch swing beside her husband and undertook to

strike up a conversation which Sleepy Pitts at first had
a very small role in, which Mr. Jules Henry never contributed to, and which Mrs. Jules Henry ultimately
transformed into an exceedingly aimless recitation
commencing with the general humidity and winding
round to a local history of the kidney stone including
who had got them, who had passed them, and who had
had them surgically excised. Mrs. Jules Henry said
kidney stones were much on her mind of late; she
could not explain why exactly.

It was an exceedingly long way from kidney stones
to bass and bream and maybe crappie too. Actually it
is an exceedingly long way from kidney stones to most
everything else, and it was precisely the sort of exceedingly long way that Sleepy Pitts did not travel well
at all, especially since he had to go unassisted by Mr.
Jules Henry, who complacently smoked his Dr. Grabow from the porch swing, and unassisted as well by
Mrs. Jules Henry, who could be led off the subject of
kidney stones specifically but could not seem to be diverted from human suffering in general. So Sleepy
Pitts got to where he wanted to go a piece at a time
and went by way of drownings and shark attacks and
boating accidents and mercury poisoning which all
served to introduce water and served to introduce fish
and consequently cushioned the blow some when
Sleepy Pitts opened his mouth and told Mrs. Jules
Henry she had herself a lovely pond to sit and look at
to which Mrs. Jules Henry said yes she did and nodded
in agreement. "Truly lovely," Sleepy Pitts added and
made a general racket in his neck which somehow reminded Mrs. Jules Henry of a gentleman she knew in
Burlington who had a hole in his throat and talked
through what appeared to be a flashlight and she was
setting herself to elaborate some on his affliction when
Sleepy Pitts came straight out and asked Mr. Jules
Henry or Mrs. Jules Henry either one if a man might
fish in their pond sometime or another, and Mrs. Jules

Henry looked at Mr. Jules Henry who removed his pipe from his mouth, tamped the ash and tobacco with the end of his finger, and said, "A man might."

And Mrs. Jules Henry told him, "Jules Henry!" in a stern and altogether displeased sort of way and Mr. Jules Henry waved his open hand at her and returned his pipe to his mouth.

"I'd be willing to pay," Sleepy Pitts said. "I'd insist on it."

And Mr. Jules Henry replied, "Two dollars," which got him another Jules Henry! from Mrs. Jules Henry who herself got waved off and hushed up all over again.

And Mr. Sleepy Pitts said that was a fair and just price for the privilege of sitting and looking at and fishing from such a lovely pond and he paid the money and made plans to return a week to the day later so as to anticipate the privilege more thoroughly and then he thanked Mr. Jules Henry, who folded the bills and slipped them into his shirtpocket, and thanked Mrs. Jules Henry, who laid the fingers on her right hand against the bottom of her stomach and said she had a pain, said she had a hot shooting pain, said she believed it was appendicitis, said she had known a woman whose appendix had burst wide open on her.

Mrs. Sleepy Pitts was not disposed to fish herself and was not disposed to tolerate fishing in other people, especially not in Mr. Sleepy Pitts, so somehow or another on the day he had set aside to collect his two dollars' worth of fishing Mr. Sleepy Pitts neglected to tell Mrs. Sleepy Pitts that he was not going to the cigarette factory, or was only going partway to the cigarette factory anyhow, and since he got up when he usually got up and did all of what he usually did and departed when he usually departed Mrs. Sleepy Pitts had no call to suspect he was not going where he usually went, but he was not and this time pulled off the road instead of stopping in it and got his tackle out from the glove compartment and his disassembled fishing rod off the window rack and proceeded down the roadbank to Mr. Jules Henry Graham's lush and comely garden spot. Sleepy Pitts had pondered and considered and scrutinized and hypothesized for a week now and had at last concluded he would commence with his purple worm followed by the black one and then the red one and would cap off the morning with his green speckled Jitterbug just prior to lunch which Sleepy Pitts had brought in his usual box and had decided he would enjoy from Mr. Jules Henry's furthest concrete bench. He planned to concentrate chiefly on bream throughout the early afternoon and so intended to change over to a cork float and a sinker and a number six hook baited with lightly salted fried dough from a batch he had mixed up at great peril, a batch Mrs. Sleepy Pitts had smelled cooking and had got told was an omelette. He figured he would dispense with the float in the shank of the afternoon and fish for whatever might be on the bottom until the shift changed and then maybe he would keep a bass or a bream or two or possibly a crappie and carry them home to Mrs. Sleepy Pitts who would get told something or another.

But after the purple worm and well into the black one Sleepy Pitts had not hooked anything but part of a treestump and throughout the red worm and on into the Jitterbug he did not attract even a detectable nip and so sat down to lunch perplexed and somewhat agitated. Mr. Jules Henry came around the house and into the frontyard where he piddled with his nandinas while Sleepy Pitts ate his lunch and Sleepy Pitts hooted and waved at him from the concrete bench and held his empty stringer up over his head and in return Mr. Jules Henry saluted with his pruning shears. Sleepy Pitts attached his float and his sinkers form there on the concrete bench and he pinched off a piece of dough and baited his number six hook with it and then

laid the whole business out in a shady patch of water
underneath the boughs of a willow tree and squatted
on the pondbank from where he studied the bobber
and held the rod with the tipends of his fingers, but
nothing took the bait, nothing took a piece of the bait,
nothing even went by and smelled it as far as Sleepy
Pitts could tell and he flung the line out of the shade
towards the deeper water and adjusted his squat some
and watched the bobber and felt of the rod all over
again but nothing took the bait or a piece of the bait or
sniffed at it there either. So he commenced to circle
the pond, pausing to fling his baited hook in what
looked to be the fishiest places and he went from the
north end to the south end to the north end to the
sound end again with the same pinch of unnibbled-at
and entirely unthreatened dough wrapped roundabout
his hook. Then he raised the float so as to drop the
sinkers and the hook some and he recircled and re-
flung and resquatted at most every place he'd circled
to and flung and squatted at previously but with about
the same results, or actually with precisely the same
results, and so he lowered the hook, lowered it past
where it had been lowered to before, and circled and
flung and squatted all over again but in the opposite
direction this time and so was unsuccessful at last in
the very place he had been unsuccessful at first. Eventually he took the float off the line and put it in his
shirtpocket and he changed the bait first for a piece off
the top of his doughball and then for a piece off the
bottom of his doughball and then for a piece direct
from the center of his doughball, but the floatless re-
doughed hook did not seem to attract any more notice
than the floated doughed hook or the green speckled
Jitterbug or the red worm or the black worm or the
purple worm either, and Sleepy Pitts was near about
used up with circling and flinging and squatting when
the tailend of the second shift going north commenced
to meet the frontend of the first shift coming south up

the roadbank on the highway and Sleepy Pitts un-
baited his hook and cut his tackle loose and took his
rod to pieces.

He felt obliged to thank Mr. Jules Henry for the
opportunity to fish his pond, even though the two dollars had only bought him considerable risk and aggra-
vation and a slight sunburn on his forearms, and he
spied Mr. Jules Henry on his porch swing with his Dr.
Grabow and his *Chronicle* and proceeded on up to talk
to him. Sleepy Pitts was most grateful, or anyway later
he recollected and insisted that he had been most
grateful at the outset, and again he held up the stringer
for examination, it being as empty and as dry as it had
been previously, and he told Mr. Jules Henry, "I tried
everywhere, tried every manner of lure and bait I had,
but didn't catch a one of them rascals, didn't even get
a nibble. I went all roundabout that thing and couldn't
even get a bite."

And Mr. Jules Henry, all serene and placid like
usual, creased his paper and extracted his Dr. Grabow
from his mouth and said, "I didn't think you would.
Ain't no fish in it."

They called it a lashing but it wasn't an actual and
legitimate lashing, or anyway Sheriff Burton called it a
lashing though he himself admitted to being torn between a lashing and a flogging and had even flirted
with a flaying before he knew exactly what a flaying
was, but it was probably more like a whipping than
a lashing or a flogging and was certainly more like a
whipping than a flaying, though it would have been a
lashing if Sleepy Pitts had selected the little end of the
rod which had considerable spring to it and so would
have been the ideal device to lash with, and it would
have been a flogging if Sleepy Pitts had selected the
big end of the rod which was fairly thoroughly stiff and
unspringy and so would have been the ideal device to
flog with, but Sleepy Pitts selected the middle part of
the rod which was not especially springy or especially

stiff either and so was the ideal device to do to Mr.
Jules Henry what it did to him. Mrs. Jules Henry
heard the fuss from the kitchen and came bolting out
onto the porch where she attempted to interfere in the
proceedings but was delivered a vicious backhanded
blow, she called it, and thereby got prevented from
succeeding at any serious or useful interfering and so
laid idly by as that man, that cruel and mean-hearted
man, she called him, raised whelps all about her husband's person. Understandably Mr. Jules Henry had
dropped his Dr. Grabow and had let go his *Chronicle*
and had drawn himself up into a knot on the porch
swing with his arms over his head and he absorbed the
majority of the punishment from the elbows out, except for the few stray blows which fell elsewhere every
now and again, and probably would have continued to
absorb the punishment from the elbows out and otherwise if Mr. Sleepy Pitts had not come to himself and
regained his native disposition which usually did not
show anything in the way of lashing or flogging or
whipping even since they did not call Sleepy Sleepy on
account of his quick and violent temper.

He gave himself up, drove directly to the town hall,
and took himself and his piece of fishing rod on into
the sheriff's office and surrendered which deflated the
whole enterprise some for the sheriff who generally
liked to go out and fetch his culprits but presently the
business took on a new luster when Mr. and Mrs. Jules
Henry Graham showed up to discover that Sheriff
Burton had gone ahead and caught who they hadn't
even turned in yet which was a matter of some amazement especially to Mrs. Jules Henry who had not been
whelped and beat up about the forearms and so was
not distracted by the discomfort. Of course Mr. Sleepy
Pitts had already confessed to the whipping and had
already detailed the entire affair to Sheriff Burton and
had already apologized for the most of it prior to getting put away in the lockup where Sheriff Burton took

Mrs. Jules Henry for purposes of identification and
where Mr. Sleepy Pitts apologized all over again but
apparently with little effect on Mrs. Jules Henry who
would not speak directly to him and would not look
directly at him but instead expressed her profound displeasure to Sheriff Burton who in turn expressed it to
Sleepy Pitts.

Mr. Jules Henry was probably about as profoundly
displeased as Mrs. Jules Henry was but he could not
keep his mind on his displeasure on account of the
whelps and the bruises and the various abrasions primarily on his forearms but to some degree about his
person in general and he sat alone and untended to in
a hard-back chair against the wall of the sheriff's office
until the mayor's secretary discovered him there and
hunted up some salve which she spread roundabout all
but the most private places where Mr. Jules Henry figured he had a whelp or two as well but had not really
looked to see. The sheriff called Mrs. Sleepy Pitts who
was verily astounded to find out her husband was in
the lockup and was even more verily astounded to find
out why and she came over to the town hall straightaway while her surprise still had most of its edge to it
and she apologized to and commiserated with Mr.
Jules Henry, who was all greased up and somewhat
more comfortable than he had been previously, and
then she followed the sheriff and followed Mrs. Jules
Henry back to the lockup where she vilified Mr. Sleepy
Pitts and allowed Mrs. Jules Henry to vilify him also,
and Mr. Sleepy Pitts himself, who was extraordinarily
sorry and repentant, brought his stooped shoulders
and his bowed head just a tad too close to the cell door
and Mrs. Sleepy Pitts shot her arm through the bars
and grabbed onto a serious handful of Mr. Sleepy
Pitts's hair and did some squeezing and some yanking
and some vigorous jerking around which had the effect
of rendering Mr. Sleepy Pitts even more extraordinarily sorry and repentant than he had been previously

and had the effect of bringing some noticeable delight
and pleasure to Mrs. Jules Henry along with some
measurable satisfaction to Mrs. Sleepy Pitts and even
served to substantially reinvigorate the sheriff who had
figured most all the good passion and violence was
over and done with.

But after the squeezing and the yanking and the
jerking around, most all the good passion and violence
was over and done with, and now only a month
beyond the actual lashing of Mr. Jules Henry Graham
by Mr. Sleepy Pitts, or what was called the actual lashing anyway, the sheriff could not recollect who had got
what in the settlement, simply could not recall if Mr.
Jules Henry had been awarded his damages or if Mr.
Sleepy Pitts had been awarded his two dollar fishing
fee or if Mrs. Sleepy Pitts had been awarded her un-
contested divorce. He could not remember anything
much about the episode except for the brief passion
and violence of it, but then it was a theory with the
sheriff that the passion and violence of a thing, no
matter how brief and fleeting, was about all that mattered anyhow, all that mattered to him anyway since he
was in the passion and violence business, or that's what
he told the ladies of the Flower Society and of the
Sewing Club and of the Daughters of the American
Revolution along with the Rotarians and the Knights
of Columbus and the members of the Bi-Monthly
Book Association, what he told most everybody who
invited him out to tell them something prior to hooking his thumbs on his belt and displaying his paraphernalia. So Sheriff Burton could not recollect the justice
end of the Graham-Pitts dispute mainly because he
was not in the justice business, and he could not recollect much of the violence and passion end of it either
mainly because there had not been enough violence
and passion to it to suit him which was his primary
complaint about law enforcement roundabout. So
Sheriff Burton uncrossed his arms and fetched his

Chronicle up off the desktop and read about the robbery all over again and about the threat to Mr. Busick's private parts and about the very high caliber
revolver, and then he packed the paper away by itself
in his leather satchel and locked his top drawer and
straightened his blotter and excused himself for the afternoon.

Sheriff Burton rented out the upstairs of Mrs. Carrie Alice Dunlop Messick's frame house on Ennis
Street behind the Big Apple. Mrs. Carrie Alice Dunlop Messick had lived well for a time and had never
figured she would be reduced to renting out her upstairs, but once Mr. Messick passed away and once
Mrs. Messick's colored housekeeper took up with a
Greyhound driver from Greensboro Mrs. Messick discovered she did not have anybody to hook her screens
and turn her latches at night and since she did not
much care for the independence and the solitude she
decided to rent out her upstairs even though her upstairs had not been built to be rented out, did not have
its own entrance, did not have its own kitchen, did not
have anything really but three bedrooms, one
bathroom, a little slip of a hallway, and prodigious
closet space, but once Sheriff Browner hired on Sheriff
Burton as his deputy and once Deputy Burton commenced to cast around for living quarters, Mrs. Messick concluded and determined she would in fact rent
out her upstairs since having a lawman under her very
own roof seemed near about as good as getting Mr.
Messick back and far surpassed the colored housekeeper who turned latches well enough but would not
venture into the cellar after sunset and hid under the
bedclothes during hard weather.

Sheriff Burton paid Mrs. Messick a nominal
monthly fee and kept the yard and carried out the garbage for his board which he took in what had once
been a glorious dining room at the center of the house
but the plaster had long since cracked open and the

paint had mildewed around the windowlights and the carpet had worn down to the matting most everywhere and Mrs. Messick had established her television in one corner and had stacked her magazines in another and had covered the walls with her daughter-in-law's needlepoint samplers and photographs of her grandchildren and one large and colorful and altogether grisly picture of Christ on the cross which hung beside a smaller less colorful and far less grisly picture of him off it, so the dining room was not so glorious any longer but suited the food well enough since it was not so glorious either.

Mrs. Messick could not eat salt on account of her blood pressure and could not eat shortening or any manner of animal fat and was instructed to stay away from butter and eggs and cream sauces and refined sugar and could not effectively digest beef and did not have much fondness for pork which left chicken primarily, lean chicken baked without the assistance of a sauce or seasonings and served with a piece of whitebread alongside a garden salad and a dietetic peach half on a lettuce leaf all of which usually satisfied Mrs. Messick, who was spindly and wiry and altogether insubstantial, and all of which never satisfied Sheriff Burton who generally retired to the upstairs after supper and ate Cheez Doodles in one of his bedrooms, most often in the bedroom with the bed and the television set which he called his den as opposed to the bedroom with the bed and the table and the straight chair which he called his study and the bedroom with the bed and the dresser and the oval mirror which he called his bedroom.

On the evening of the armed robbery article in the *Chronicle* Sheriff Burton carried the newspaper with him to supper which he did not usually make a habit of on account of Mrs. Messick's low opinion of newspapers, elbows, and such on the tabletop at mealtime, but he begged pardon and as Mrs. Messick brought the icewater in from the kitchen the sheriff began reading aloud those parts of the story that did not deal directly with Mr. Busick's privates which somehow seemed less allowable at the supper table than newspapers or elbows either. Occasionally the sheriff interrupted himself to interpolate or surmise or theorize or hypothesize or expand upon and wander from the actual story itself and thereby bring his vast experience to bear on the circumstances, and Mrs. Messick picked at her shortleg and said, Um Hmm, and said, I see, and said, Oh really, and watched the sheriff throw himself carelessly back in his chair and bring himself earnestly forward out of it and wave his arms and point his finger and take up his bottom lip between his teeth.

The sheriff figured the assailant for a product of socio-economic depravity, a father maybe, a husband surely, and likely laid off from the cigarette plant or the brewery outside Eden or the cotton mill or the quarry at Stokesdale. It was the sheriff's opinion that Mr. Busick had not been in much danger of getting shot, he did not mention precisely where Mr. Busick had not been in much danger of getting shot, and the sheriff imagined the money would go for necessities, food, clothing, and such. But, the sheriff said, and this was the part where he shook his finger, a man's got no right to rob and plunder even to clothe and feed his wife and his little ones. A man's got no right to lawlessness, the sheriff said, and this was the part where he took up his lip between his teeth, and Mrs. Messick, who had not Um Hmmed or I seed or Oh reallyed for a prominent while, left off with her peach half, waved the pointy end of her fork at the sheriff, and told him she had a niece in Stokesdale who made the most exquisite baby blankets and booties and little knit hats, and the sheriff said, "Socio-economic depravity, pure and simple," and Mrs. Messick told him, "And scarves too, fuzzy little scarves with tiny tassels."

The sheriff sat in front of his air circulator and ate

his Cheez Doodles and looked at his television set and every now and again picked up the open *Chronicle* and perused the bottom half of the front of it prior to carrying himself to the big sidewindow in his den and peering out into the evening where there was a felon somewhere, somewhere local and close by. And when the sheriff went to bed at last he went to bed with the open *Chronicle* and read the front of it and the back of it and the middle of it and then folded it over and looked at the inky headlines and at the photograph of Mr. Busick, the victim, and at the photograph of Mr. Winn with his chin dangling alongside Mr. Bobbit with his cigarette and the pieces of his arms, the witnesses, and at the little square of roadmap that was Raleigh mostly and Wendell and Garner and Knightdale and Zebulon and down the 401 highway to the south Fuquay-Varina also with a bold black arrow to indicate and distinguish it.

*T*HEY HAD circled round through Georgia, crossed east through South Carolina, and come north to a place called Bay Leaf which was not much more of a place than Lemly had been but which was preparing and intending to become a place, preparing and intending to become quite a prominent place when the Neuse River backed up and filled the reservoir which it had not done yet on account of the dam which had not been built yet on account of the general discord between the governor and the congress and the various dirt farmers whose property would become lake bottom. For ten years running there had been talk of a dam and talk of a reservoir and there had even been a settlement once and the shoreline had got surveyed and laid out and the trees had got cut down and a portion of the lake bottom had got bought up but something had happened, some vague and political something, and the dam still did not get built though

now everybody expected that it would, even those
people who had previously expected that it wouldn't,
mostly on account of the laid out shoreline and the cut
down trees and the partially bought up lakebottom.
The people of Bay Leaf especially expected and anticipated the dam and expected and anticipated the shoreline mostly because they would be on it or actually
were on it already though it did not appear much of a
shoreline and did not appear much of a lake but must
have been a lake and must have been a shoreline because the price of the land along it and around it and
all roundabout the vicinity of it tripled and then got
bought up in the majority and so what was left qua-
drupled and got bought up too and little clearings got
cut away in the lots and footings got poured and walls
got framed out and houses went up, not your regular
Bay Leaf houses, your lowslung ranch styles with brick
flowerboxes and carports, but wildly geometrical
houses, round houses and octagonal houses and square
and rectangular houses with triangular outcroppings in
the most unexpected places and not a brick to be
found anywhere but rough cypress and rough cedar
and rough fir and plain old chewed up spruce pine
stained and made up to look like cypress and cedar
and fir and no grass around the frontyards but just
pine mulch and exotic shrubbery and dwarf trees and
no grass around the backyards either but just more
pine mulch and more shrubbery and generally a red-
wood deck with some shade to it and a view of the lake
which was not a lake yet, not even a marsh but just an
expanse of scrub and undergrowth and brambles and
treestumps ringed round with houses and ringed round
with concrete boatramps and ringed round with nar-
row wooden floating docks, entirely unbuoyed and
thoroughly unfloating floating docks.

The natives of Bay Leaf, both the lowslung red
brick fulltime natives and the geometrical roughwood
weekend natives were still waiting for the water to rise

when Mr. Overhill drove his red Dodge pickup and his load of equipment and his load of manpower into the limits of the township and brought the whole business to a halt in front of a fairly massive marina that the mayor and the firechief and the town clerk and two insurance agents had all invested in together and had constructed a bit prematurely. Initially they stocked boating and fishing supplies and Styrofoam coolers and sunglasses and waterskis but when the dam didn't get built and the river didn't back up they set in to selling sundry unaquatic items like sportsjackets and neckties and cotton socks and ladies' jewelry and leather tire-tread sandals and handbags and openweave sunhats and loafbread and insecticides and window fans and cold beer, and of course candied corn also which Mr. Overhill bought a half dozen packets of straightaway since he had been without it in the sack or even between his teeth ever since Bennetsville which was a whole state away. The town clerk, who was in charge of the sportsjackets, drew out a map for Mr. Overhill on a piece of box while Mr. Overhill tried on a 42 long in poplin and modeled it for himself in front of the mirror on the men's room door prior to exchanging it for a 44 long in a kind of speckled polyester which he wore to the back of the store and viewed the lakebed which was even less of a lakebed than it had been previously on account of the unmitigated success of the undergrowth, and the sight of the scrub and the brambles and the treestumps stretching far and away into the distance prompted Mr. Overhill to snicker and prompted Mr. Overhill to laugh once outright and prompted Mr. Overhill to holler across the store to the town clerk and ask him when the tide might be coming in which the town clerk did not much appreciate and made a fairly vile reply to which prompted Mr. Overhill to snicker and laugh outright all over again.

They left Bay Leaf the way they'd come in and headed south back down the Falls of the Neuse Road

until they arrived at a territory known as the Harricanes which was not on any map and did not have a
sign to announce it like Lemly or Bay Leaf because it
was not a legitimate and particular place like Lemly
and Bay Leaf were legitimate and particular places
even though just barely. So Mr. Overhill pondered his
piece of box with considerable care but nonetheless
passed his turnoff going to the south and turned
around and drove on by it the other way and then
stopped in the highway on this third run and looked at
the piece of box and peered down an oiled rural road
to his right and then looked at the piece of box again
prior to getting off the highway at last and heading
towards the riverbottom to the strains of a general and
harmonious lament from the paltry negro and the wiry
tattooed white boy who wanted to know where in the
fuck they were going anyway, with the wiry tattooed
white boy supplying the where primarily and the paltry
negro supplying the fuck, and Mr. Overhill told them
he'd be goddamned and bound up in hell if he knew
himself which did not much comfort or satisfy the
paltry negro or the wiry tattooed white boy or the fat
negro either who threw in with a shit yes whenever
there seemed a need for one.

Mr. Overhill proceeded down into the woods at
what he considered a prudent velocity which called for
liberal and fairly indelicate braking on his part and
kicked up some serious nausea in the truckbed thereby
choking off and thoroughly stifling the lamentations
and complaints and sending the fat negro and the
paltry negro and the wiry tattooed white boy to the
tailgate to suck air in the company of an additional and
equally wiry white boy who was not Benton Lynch and
was not the critter either but was Emmet somebody
that Mr. Overhill had picked up on the roadside
beyond Chattanooga. Emmet chewed his tobacco with
Bazooka bubble gum and generally did not clear his
chin when he spat. He had no manners to speak of, did

not wear socks, and had surrendered the majority of his teeth except for one on the top and six on the bottom all of which were turned and twisted roundabout in his mouth so as to face his earlobes. The paltry negro had despised him straight off but could not decide precisely what sort of motherfucker he was and so called him every sort he could think of, and being proficient and meticulous in his profanity the paltry negro could think of a considerable plenty. The fat negro and the wiry tattooed white boy had despised him at length themselves but not until after the first night in the truckbed when the critter abandoned his fender well so as to squat at Emmet's ear and hiss into it, and Emmet sat up on the blanket and eyed the critter and heard him out and at last opened his own mouth and said, "I got this buddy went to Ve it nahm, cut off a pecker and brought it back with him, hung it on the mirror in his Torino. All dried up now, falling to pieces. Never was no big pecker." And the fat negro drew back his foot and delivered Emmet a wallop across the shoulder which sent him into a wild, impotent rage and he wailed, "Hey! Whud I do?" And the fat negro told him, "Shut up," and the wiry tattooed white boy told him, "Shut up," and the paltry negro announced, "Sick motherfucker," which seemed fitting to the moment.

Not any of them became truly ill though Emmet spat out his lump of bubble gum and tobacco prefatory to an upchuck which never arrived and presently Mr. Overhill turned south off the first oiled road onto a second oiled road that ran parallel to the riverbank and so did not call for the prodigious braking and jerking that had been called for previously. The second oiled road off the first oiled road off the highway curled and turned and wound up and wound out through the very heart of the Harricanes though the heart of the Harricanes was the sort of place you could not know you were in until you were out of it, so Mr.

Overhill pondered his piece of box and proceeded
ahead slowing at the sideroads he came up on and
slowing at the houses he passed, extraordinarily
shabby houses with extraordinarily shabby people on
the porches of them come out to see just who it was in
a red Dodge pickup truck passing through the heart of
the Harricanes which Mr. Overhill still did not know
he was in since there was not a sign to tell him, not
even a bullet-riddled vine-obscured sign laid over in a
ditch somewhere, but there was indication enough
otherwise just like in niggertown, niggertown most
everywhere there is one, which has no signs or markers
either but cannot be confused with anywhere else on
account of how what lives there lives. There were
junked cars in the woods and old appliances and regular trash and garbage strewn down the banks of nearly
all the roadside gullies. Chickens ran loose like squir-
rels and off the road beside the houses the hogs and
the pigs were pinned up with planks and wire and most
anything else that would take a nail. Where there was
washing, it hung out on bushes and treelimbs, and
where there were children, they played on the packed
dirt with sticks and rocks or just their own ten fingers
and like everybody else were diverted and enthralled
by the strange and wondrous red Dodge pickup truck
with its exotic load of negroes mostly, or so it appeared, and the Gilchrists and the Currins and the
Sapps and the Parkers and the Firesheetses of the
Harricanes did not see negroes much down in their
riverbottom in their woods and so viewed these with
measurable attention and curiosity. And the fat negro
said to the paltry negro, "These some bad looking
whitefolks."

And the paltry negro said to the fat negro, "Stringy
motherfuckers, ain't they."

And Emmet told the both of them, "Ain't nothing
wrong with these people," and he laid himself partway
out over the tailgate and waved his left arm and

shouted, "Hey there," up the roadbank towards the worst looking, stringiest bunch of whitefolks even he had ever seen and nobody not the adults or the children either bothered to wave back.

"That's right Emmet," the fat negro said, "stir 'em up."

"Stupid motherfucker," the paltry negro told him and pushed him into the fat negro who pushed him back into the paltry negro and the two of them together grabbed onto his arms and threw him up towards the truckcab onto the pick and shovel handles and hard against Benton Lynch and Emmet brought himself upright and wailed, "Hey! Whud I do?"

Mr. Overhill found the cemetery all by himself, or with his piece of box only and without call for instructions and directions from any of the natives who did not seem even to Mr. Overhill much disposed to instruct or direct. Apparently, plenty of people did plenty of dying in the Harricanes because surely there was a mass of them buried there and in a graveyard near about as fine and comely as every other human undertaking roundabout. There had been a fence once, a wooden fence, but apparently the primary parts of it had got hauled off and burnt throughout the winters so there was not much of a fence any longer but just some pieces of a fence remaining along with the entire of a gate which was thoroughly wooden also but had not been knocked down and chopped up likely on account of some sort of localized and collective arrangement which forgave the fence for as long as the gate stood. The consecrated and sanctified inside of the place had grown up near about as high as the unconsecrated and unsanctified outside of the place, and the tombstones and the wooden and granite markers that the freeze had not cracked or pitched about and the rain and the bugs had not eaten away had got covered up anyhow with creeping vine and bramble and milkweed and grass of every variety so that nobody in

particular got found except by accident and good fortune which proved altogether troublesome for Mr.
Overhill who got asked by three strappy and duly notified Gilchrists to find someone in particular, to find
someone in particular quick and straightaway, their
mother as it turned out, or two of thems mother anyway and one of thems aunt, and since these Gilchrists
were as bad looking a bunch of whitefolks as the fat
negro and the paltry negro had ever laid eyes on the
two of them together jumped at the opportunity to
make themselves accommodating and commenced to
beat the bushes for momma Gilchrist which was not
the sort of thing the paltry negro would generally have
any part of on account of the prospect of snakes.

They did not find her as quick and straightaway as
the two sons and the nephew had desired but they did
find her presently off and away under a wateroak and
bound up in some prodigious ivy and together they
uncovered her and brought her up out of the ground
and toted her through the bushes across the cemetery
to the two sons and one nephew who as it turned out
were not inclined or disposed to haul her off but instead prized open the casket lid and helped themselves
to a brooch and a ring and a pendant which had apparently come to momma Gilchrist in a more frivolous
day. Two more duly notified Gilchrists arrived from off
the road and requested of Mr. Overhill three of their
relations, two Gilchrists and a Sapp, which Mr. Overhill dispatched the paltry negro and the fat negro and
the wiry tattooed white boy to see after, and the two
sons and the nephew of momma Gilchrist, sparked by
the literal example of the two new and additional
Gilchrists, put in an order to near about the rest of the
family, and as best as Mr. Overhill could determine
through the weeds and the vines and the variety of
grasses the northeast corner of the cemetery was purely littered with Gilchrists, so he got Benton Lynch and
Emmet and the critter out from the partly dug holes

and sent them off through the brush to join the fat
negro and the paltry negro in turning up Gilchrists primarily which they managed with great swiftness and
considerable ease on account of the soft, loamy, mole-
eaten ground and they kept the three original
Gilchrists and the two additional Gilchrists supplied
with a steady stream of the boxed up and burped and
Ziplocked relations along with a solitary Gilstrap who
got turned up by accident but was plundered through
and picked over nonetheless.

An assortment of Parkers and Currins and several
actual living and breathing Sapps came out from a path
in the woods and joined the three original Gilchrists
and the two additional Gilchrists along with the ever
increasing flow of their dead relations. All four of the
Parkers, who were of a sluggish and sedentary stock,
lowered themselves onto the casketlids of some previously pilfered Gilchrists while both the Currins, who
were not so sluggish and sedentary as Parkers but near
about, squatted on their heels beside the Sapps who as
a rule preferred leaning to sitting or squatting and
would have most likely tilted themselves against the
cemetery fence if the cemetery fence had not been
burnt up beforehand. A Sugg who was cousin to the
Sapps and uncle to one of the Parkers drove up off the
road in a blue Chevrolet Biscayne and wheeled partway on into the cemetery so as to save himself the
trouble of getting out of the car, which was generally
the way with Suggs, and at his request the Sapps
opened up two of the Gilchrists that did not have
Parkers on top of them and the Sugg studied the
corpses prior to delivering a fairly penetrating assessment of the ravages of death followed by several inci-
sive comments on the noses and chins of Gilchrists,
which was a notoriously tender subject with Gilchrists
on account of the size of their noses and the shape of
their chins, and the Sugg was so extraordinarily inci-
sive, not to say frank and blunt and altogether indeli-

cate, that the Gilchrists got hot and agitated straight
off, the three original Gilchrists along with the two additional ones, and the Sugg rolled up his windowglass
in self defense and concluded the matter through his
side vent much to the open and apparent displeasure
of the Gilchrists but much to the delight of the Parkers
and the Currins and the Sapps who ever enjoyed discord and agitation especially if they led to a stomping,
but the Sugg left off provoking the Gilchrists before he
could get himself stomped, which was a particular talent with Suggs, and instead turned his attention to the
critter who had crossed the cemetery toting a two-bag
Gilchrist and set him down with the rest of his relations.

Like usual the critter's hair was knotted and matted
and standing up all over his head and his face and neck
were dirt black mostly except for the tracks where the
sweat had run through and carried the filth away. His
shirt was stiff and gritty and his pants were torn open
at the knees ad smudged and smeared with fingerprints
and crusted food. He was ensconced in his usual bou-
quet which the flies in particular seemed to adore but
which the Gilchrists and the Parkers and the Currins
and the Sapps and the solitary Sugg did not appear to
think much of judging from how they waved their
hands before their faces and wrinkled up the skin
around their noseholes, and the solitary Sugg, who had
again rolled down his window glass once the Gilchrist
threat had passed and dwindled, laid himself partway
out the door and said to the critter, "Great God Almighty, what in the shit are you anyway?" And from
across the cemetery the paltry negro picked up his
head and watched the critter step away from the collection of bagged up and boxed up Gilchrists and step
towards the blue Biscayne with the solitary Sugg partway out the window of it and he said to the fat negro,
"Oh Jesus, we dead."

The critter looked at the Sugg and the Sugg looked

at the critter and when the critter did not make any
sort of audible response to the Sugg's previous question the Sugg asked it again and the critter made a
noise in his throat followed by several additional simi-
lar noises all of which strung together resembled
human speech and the Sugg asked his question a third
time and then studied and scrutinized the critter's lips
so as to possibly decipher and translate the response
which came out about as undecipherable and untrans-
latable as the one before it and just as the Sugg was
fixing his mouth to use it again one of the squatting
Currins, the nearest squatting Currin who had a
proper angle on the whole business, shifted his weight
from one heel to the other and told him, "He's pissing
on your tire, Walter." And the Sugg looked down over
the swell of the door and saw that the critter had
loosed himself from his trousers and was sure enough
bathing the front left blackwall the sight of which sent
the Sugg into an immediate fit of ornate and heathen-
ish swearing and general vilification and the sound of
the wild and unrestrained profanity along with the
sight of the occasional violent gesture prompted the
paltry negro to turn to the fat negro and tell him, "We
all dead men." But then the first Gilchrist snickered
and the second Gilchrist threw in with him, and pretty
soon all of the rest of the Gilchrists were shaking at the
shoulders and the Sapps commenced to wheeze and
the Currins and the Parkers set in to howling outright
and were joined by the critter himself who put his face
up snug to the Sugg's face and laughed his most vicious
and mean-spirited laugh direct into it so that even the
Sapps, who could not generally muster more than a
wheeze, hooted and howled and held themselves about
the waist as the Sugg squirmed and threatened and
swore from the driver's seat of his Biscayne which he
did not ever get out of that being the way with Suggs.

Attracted by the great and open display of mirth
and levity there among the corpses, Mr. Overhill ap-

proached from across the cemetery already laughing
somewhat in anticipation of what he would get told
had kicked up the great and open display of mirth and
the great and open display of levity, and he had not
even circled round to the peed on side of the Biscayne
and had not hardly Haw Hawed two times in succession when a Currin, three Parkers, and both the Sapps
together commenced to run through the episode in all
of its glorious circumstances pointing for effect at the
blotches on the blackwall and pointing for effect at the
departing backside of the critter and pointing for effect
at that portion of the solitary Sugg above the doortop
after which they shook at the shoulders or wheezed or
howled outright or hawhawed depending on their particular disposition. Even the solitary Sugg smirked and
shook some at the shoulders and Mr. Overhill observed out loud but to the Sugg primarily, "That
Dwight, a little wild and high spirited at times but a
fine sort," and he wagged his head and sucked some
air through the gaps in his teeth and said, "A fine
sort," which prompted the solitary Sugg to eye his
blackwall over the doorswell and reply, "Shit," in an
entirely unpersuaded tone of voice.

They were three days turning up Parkers and Currins and Sapps and Suggs and a stray, misplaced
Gilchrist every now and again before anybody showed
up at the cemetery to do something other than pilfer
and plunder and pass the afternoon on a coffinlid them
being Firesheetses, five Firesheetses all together with a
brother and a sister and a momma and a daddy and an
old stooped and brittle granddaddy in black hightop
sneakers. They had come for the granddaddy's late
wife who had been deceased for a dozen years now
and they intended to carry her off with them when the
water rose because, as the granddaddy put it to Mr.
Overhill, she never could swim worth a piddly squat,
and then he laughed like a spook and Mr. Overhill
threw in with him and clapped him hard between his

arthritic shoulder blades and turned to the momma Firesheets and told her, "Your daddy's a regular stitch," and the momma Firesheets lit herself a cigarette and said, "Ain't my daddy."

The daddy Firesheets got him a place atop a Gilchrist and took up with the regular crowd of Parkers and Currins and whatnot and his boy and his girl led Mr. Overhill to their grandmomma's plot and he set the wiry tattooed white boy about the picking and the shoveling of it under the scrutiny of the grand-daddy Firesheets and the momma Firesheets and the brother Firesheets, which did not matter much to the wiry tattooed white boy, but under the scrutiny as well of the sister Firesheets and that was another thing entirely. She appeared to be about sixteen years old, or maybe eighteen years old, or possibly twenty-five years old, the wiry tattooed white boy could not tell exactly from over his shoulder which was the only way he could look at her without seeming to look at her and he did not want to seem to look at her or did not want to get caught at seeming to look at her which might suggest an interest on his part and he did not want to appear interested, so he looked at her over his shoulder whenever he felt she was not looking at him and mostly he did not find her looking at him when he turned to look at her because mostly she was not looking at him anyway. She seemed fairly much a vision from heaven as far as the wiry tattooed white boy was concerned. Her hair was the color of wheatstraw and hung kind of thin and wet looking down the sides of her head with a little break on the left and a little break on the right for the white tops of her ears to stick through and she was slender and supple all over and her arms and her legs and the little fleshy recess at the base of her neck were a pure and milky white except for the mosquito bites and the scabs and one tiny plum-colored birthmark on her thigh. The wiry tattooed white boy surveyed from over his shoulder the parts of her covered up by clothes and decided her breasts were supple and probably milky white also with some plum-colored features of their own and he figured her stomach to be flat and likely milky white itself. Her backside did not appear to him overly round or excessive and he featured it a little more snowy than milky along with her frontside which he was just setting himself to garnish with some wheatstraw of its own when she plucked a cigarette out from her momma's vinyl case, lit it, and drew off the smoke slow and sultry prior to exhaling it through her noseholes and the wiry tattooed white boy got caught up in the grace and beauty of the whole business and commenced to ache all over.

He figured they would marry in the spring of the year when the dogwoods were blooming, marry in a chapel in the woods somewhere on a mild and sunny afternoon with just a touch of a breeze, enough anyway to jiggle the blossoms some, and she would wear a long milky dress and he would wear a black suit with shiny lapels, and all the old women would cry on account of her beauty and all the young women would cry on account of his, and they would have a son and then a daughter and then another son and they would live on an expansive farm with a creek running through it and cows and chickens and rail fences and in a two story hewn timber house that he would build himself, and at night he would sit in his favorite chair with his feet on the stone hearth and drink off some sort of iced and civilized drink as he studied his initials in the mortar. The wiry tattooed white boy, still lost somewhat in his reverie, came out of his button up shirt and came out of his undershirt beneath it and then recollected himself sufficiently to flex his dragon and to flex his serpent and to obscure the most of his Marlene and he jerked his sweatrag out from his back pocket and set about wiping his face and wiping his neck and wiping his arms and he nodded at the momma Firesheets and

at the granddaddy Firesheets and at the brother Firesheets and made a general comment about the humidity of the day for their benefit and then he nodded at
the sister Firesheets and said to her, "Hey babydoll,"
and she threw down the buttend of her cigarette and
told him ever so sweetly, "Go fuck yourself," which set
the wiry tattooed white boy to aching all over afresh.
He always did like a woman with some pluck to her.

Mr. Overhill went out and fetched back the Pepsis
and the potted meat and the saltines before the wiry
tattooed white boy had completely unearthed the
grandmomma Firesheets and so him and the fat negro
and the paltry negro and Benton Lynch and Emmet
and the critter sat in a shady place and watched the
sister Firesheets loiter at the graveside as they ate. The
wiry tattooed white boy said she was a prime item, said
he'd seen her right up tight and figured there weren't
any need to put a bag on it even, but the fat negro said
he'd put a bag on it and the paltry negro said he'd put
a box on it and the wiry tattooed white boy told them
he'd eat it with a spoon to which the paltry negro replied, "Jesus," and puckered up his face. Nobody
asked him but the critter volunteered that he'd strap
her to the bedstead and perform a series of unseemly,
unspeakable, and very nearly unimaginable acts upon
her person all of which the critter described in his
usual excessive detail and the paltry negro said,
"Jesus," and puckered up all over again and the fat
negro puckered up with him and the wiry tattooed
white boy swung both arms at the critter and kicked at
the critter and chased the critter through the high grass
with a stout length of stick. The fat negro and the
paltry negro desired Benton Lynch's opinion about the
matter and they poked at him and jabbed at him and
were generally solicitious of him in a demonstrative
sort of way but Benton Lynch did not even say yes and
did not even say no regardless of the poking and the
jabbing and the general demonstrativity. He simply

looked down the pointy ridge of his nose at the fat
negro and the paltry negro and ate his share of the fig
newtons. The wiry tattooed white boy returned to his
lunch presently without ever having caught the critter
and so without ever having beaten him either and the
critter squatted off out of reach and leered at the wiry
tattooed white boy who still swung the stick when he
figured the critter to be diverted but the critter was
never quite diverted enough to get hit. To cap off the
proceedings the fat negro and the paltry negro and the
critter raised their orifices in the thunderous display of
recreational burping and farting, and Emmet, who had
finished his lunch and so could at last pay attention to
something else, commenced to chant, "Wham, bang,
sweet poontang," in a syncopated rhythm which the
negroes jumped up and danced to.

The wiry tattooed white boy could not find a suitably secluded place for a purgative urination and so
had to return to grandmomma Firesheets all piqued
and agitated and the sight of the sister Firesheets's
milky arms and milky legs and bulbous and flat parts
too compounded the pique and the agitation with a
thoroughgoing erection which rode out from the wiry
tattooed white boy's trousers like a piece of Louisville
Slugger and the wiry tattooed white boy adjusted himself and fidgeted and stepped out of the grave and
stepped back into it again and adjusted himself and
fidgeted some more but did not move any appreciable
amount of dirt, so when Mr. Overhill, who had taken
his lunch with the Gilchrists and the Parkers and the
Currins and whatnot, stopped by to view the wiry tattooed white boy's progress there was not any to view
and he called in both the negroes together to see if
they couldn't help the wiry tattooed white boy make
some, and they did help him make some or rather they
made some themselves while the wiry tattooed white
boy adjusted himself and fidgeted and stepped out of
the grave and stepped back into it again.

The paltry negro told the fat negro he believed now he'd put a crate on it and the fat negro told the paltry negro he believed he'd put a crate on it too and the paltry negro pointed to the front of the wiry tattooed white boy's trousers and figured the wiry tattooed white boy would probably lay that thing to it and the paltry negro stuck his pickhandle into his pants and the fat negro stuck his shovel handle into his pants and the wiry tattooed white boy turned a kind of fruity color and eyed rather slyly the momma Firesheets and the granddaddy Firesheets and the brother Firesheets prior to glancing ever so surreptitiously at the sister Firesheets who fortunately was still not looking at him. And the paltry negro said maybe he'd put a dumpster on it, a big green dumpster, and the fat negro said maybe he would too, and the wiry tattooed white boy lunged at them desperately with the pointy end of his shovel in an attempt to cut off all twenty of their toes.

They had to bring grandmomma Firesheets up with a rope since her box had not given way and the wiry tattooed white boy took off both his shirts all over again and puffed and grunted and flexed his serpent and flexed his dragon and hid his Marlene while Benton Lynch pulled and the fat negro pulled and the paltry negro pulled, and once they'd set her in the high grass the wiry tattooed white boy laid his foot up on the coffinlid, crossed his arms over his knee, and said, "Preeshate it men. Carry on," and the fat negro and the paltry negro and even Benton Lynch too all looked at each other and threw their rope ends down on the ground.

The momma Firesheets and the daddy Firesheets wanted the grandmomma Firesheets in the trunk of their Oldsmobile for the ride back to wherever it was they'd all come from but the granddaddy Firesheets preferred the backseat since the grandmomma Firesheets had always ridden in the backseat previously but the daddy Firesheets explained that with the

grandmomma Firesheets in the backseat the brother
and the sister Firesheets would have to ride in the
trunk which the wiry tattooed white boy objected to
most strenuously and Mr. Overhill opened his mouth
and began to suggest that they tie the grandmomma
Firesheets to the roof of the car but midway through
the wiry tattooed white boy broke in and suggested
that they tie the grandmomma Firesheets to the roof of
the car and he darted off after some rope and darted
back with some in time to puff and grunt and flex onto
the cartop a little portion of the casket which Mr.
Overhill and the daddy Firesheets had already hoisted
the biggest portion of. And the wiry tattooed white
boy tied his rope secure while Mr. Overhill tied his
rope secure and then the wiry tattooed white boy
undid Mr. Overhill's rope and tied it secure all over
again and he told the Firesheetses he believed it would
hold just as Mr. Overhill was telling them he believed
it would hold and then the wiry tattooed white boy
finagled and sidled his way around the car to where the
sister Firesheets was and he gave her his personal as-
surance that her grandmomma would not fall off in the
road and she looked at him full in the face and did not
tell him to go fuck himself which encouraged the wiry
tattooed white boy some so he asked her, "You live
round here?" and though she did not say yes and did
not say no she did not tell him to go fuck himself then
either which emboldened him still further and so he
said to her, "What say me and you go out for a little
walk this evening. I'd be grateful for the company,"
and the sister Firesheets laid her hand direct upon the
most prominent part of the wiry tattooed white boy's
trousers and told him, "Seems you got all the company
you need." The Oldsmobile and the dust from the
Oldsmobile and even the sound of the Oldsmobile
tires on the gravel had all shrunk and dwindled away
before the wiry tattooed white boy could swallow
again and he licked his lips and begged pardon of Mr.

Overhill and escaped into the bushes where he found some purgation and some relief and did in fact just generally fuck himself after a fashion.

At 5:30 promptly the paltry negro gathered all the shovels and the picks and deposited them in the hollow of a thicket while Mr. Overhill directed a tidying up of the cemetery grounds which had become fairly much littered with boxed up and bagged up Gilchrists and Currins and Parkers and Sapps and Suggs boxed up and bagged up in-laws of Gilchrists and Currins and Parkers and Sapps and Suggs who lay loose in the high grass and among the scrub and the bushes in a state of random disgorgement. Mr. Overhill had the fat negro and the wiry tattooed white boy and Benton Lynch and Emmet and the critter put all the Gilchrists with the Gilchrists and all the Currins with the Currins and all the Parkers with the Parkers and the Sapps with the Sapps and the Suggs with the Suggs and all the unattached corpses, of which there were no more than eight or ten, he had piled up together under a pecan tree, and once everybody had been properly segregated and relocated Mr. Overhill retreated to the cemetery gateway and observed the little colonies of related corpses and the one slight collection of unrelated corpses who were all just as dead and decomposed as previously but not nearly so random and disgorged and Mr. Overhill announced he was mightily satisfied with the results and clasped his hands together and shook them over his head and the fat negro replied, "Christ almighty," to the wiry tattooed white boy mostly.

They left the riverbottom for the evening just as they had left the riverbottom for the evening the night before on account of the negroes primarily who refused to sleep in a riverbottom where the sort of white folks lived that lived in this riverbottom, and though Mr. Overhill insisted and explained they were all fine sorts of white folks the negroes remained unpersuaded and continued to refuse to sleep in the riverbottom

until they were not in it any longer. Like on the night
previous Mr. Overhill drove south along the Falls of
the Neuse Road to a little shopping center at the north
extremity of Raleigh where there was a Burger King at
one end and a Bojangles at the other and a drugstore
and a Big Star and a pet grooming salon in between,
and Mr. Overhill had not hardly parked the truck and
climbed out of it when he was greeted by the granddaddy Firesheets who hailed Mr. Overhill from the
canopied sidewalk in front of the drugstore. He was
still wearing his black sneakers from earlier in the day
and was still stooped over and noticeably arthritic but
relatively jolly nonetheless and he hollered to Mr.
Overhill, "How you?" and Mr. Overhill hollered back
at him, "You get the missus home all right?" and the
granddaddy Firesheets told him, "Yes it is," and threw
up his hand at Mr. Overhill prior to venturing on into
the drugstore.

The sound of the granddaddy Firesheets's voice sent
a quiver through the wiry tattooed white boy and he
leapt out of the truckbed and looked all around the
parking lot and along the storefronts for some sign of
the wheatstraw or the milky whiteness but could not
discover any and so he set out in the direction of the
drugstore and the paltry negro yelled after him, "Put a
crate on it," and the fat negro yelled after him, "Or a
dumpster," and the paltry negro added, "Or a quonset
hut," and the fat negro hollered, "Yea," and then
looked at the paltry negro and asked him, "What's a
quonset hut?" and Mr. Overhill turned his broad smiling face on the pair of negroes together and said,
"Quonset huts. I could tell you tales about them
things," and the paltry negro and the fat negro swore
each other through the sides of their mouths.

Emmet and the critter and the negroes and Mr.
Overhill all settled on the Bojangles and struck out
across the parking lot with Emmet in the lead followed
by the critter followed by a gesticulating Mr. Overhill

in the company of the two sullen negroes who walked
with their hands in their pockets and their heads near
about buried between their shoulder blades. The wiry
tattooed white boy had long since disappeared into the
drugstore and Benton Lynch climbed out from the
truckbed and headed off alone towards the Big Star
where he figured he'd get himself a pudding cup and
maybe some pork rinds, but before he'd gotten abreast
of the fertilizer and peat moss on the pallets outside
the wiry tattooed white boy blew by him in a holy rush
and ducked on into the supermarket just the very in-
stant the automatic door had automatically swung
open precisely far enough to suit his wiry self, and
when Benton Lynch came up on him inside the wiry
tattooed white boy was ruminating over a sack of self-
rising flour so as to appear oblivious to the sister Firesheets and the momma Firesheets who were
comparing potato flakes at the far end of the aisle.
Benton Lynch could not find the pudding cups
straightaway on account of how there was no sign suspended from the ceiling that said pudding cups on it,
not even a sign that said anything suggestive of pudding cups on it, so he cast around through the fruits
and the vegetables, searched along the ice cream bin,
and picked through an assortment of Twinkies and
honey buns but could not discover a pudding cup anywhere he had figured a pudding cup might be and consequently he commenced to cast around and search
and pick through a variety of places he figured a pudding cup would not be and eventually he came across
two shelves' worth of the item in question in between
the disinfectant and the catfood and across from the
aluminum foil. He just wanted one vanilla pudding cup
but could not buy one vanilla pudding cup without
buying three additional vanilla pudding cups or five
additional vanilla pudding cups or eleven additional
vanilla pudding cups and he just wanted the one by
itself and could not say if he would ever desire three

more or five more or eleven more and so he had to
decide if he should sacrifice the one pudding cup he
wanted now for some portion of the nineteen pudding
cups he possibly would not want later or accumulate
some portion of the nineteen pudding cups he possibly
would not want later for the sake of one pudding cup
he wanted now. The quandary was considerable and
taxing and Benton Lynch took up in his hands the
twenty-two pudding cups in their three separate bundles and studied his alternatives, and since the quandary was considerable and was taxing and since the
pudding cups in their three separate bundles were
cumbersome and difficult to manage Benton Lynch did
not have the leisure to notice himself getting approached from the catfood end of the aisle and so he
was still thoroughly taxed and emburdened when the
sister Firesheets stepped right up under his nose and
said to him, "I seen you."

And Benton Lynch turned his usual vacant look on
her for a brief moment prior to turning his usual vacant look over his shoulder where he expected to find
the wiry tattooed white boy but did not and so he jos-
tled and repositioned the pudding cups in his grasp and
pondered over what he would say in return which was
a considerable and taxing quandary on its own since
Benton Lynch had not got talked at lately by anybody
but Mr. Overhill and the negroes who generally did
not call for a reply, and he weighed his alternatives and
eventually landed upon and came direct out with
"Where?"

"I seen you in the graveyard with them other boys,"
the sister Firesheets told him. "I seen you help pull up
my grandmomma and I'm grateful."

"You're welcome," Benton Lynch said, and he
looked past the sister Firesheets to the far end of the
aisle where the wiry tattooed white boy had stepped
into view and picked up a can of flea and tic spray and
was perusing the backside of it.

"He's back there ain't he?" she said. "He's back there looking at me, been following me all over this place ever since I come in."

And Benton Lynch looked past her again to the far end of the aisle.

"He ain't nothing to me," she said, "ain't my sort. All his brains in his pants and I don't like them tattoos the least little bit. I mean the human body's a pure and holy thing and there he's painted his all up with pictures of lizards. There's a sickness behind it, I'll tell you that, a genuine sickness." And she whirled around and snapped at the wiry tattooed white boy, "Get on from here. I'm fed up with you, just get on away from me," and the wiry tattooed white boy tried to appear as thoroughly astounded and affronted as he could and he waved the can of flea and tic spray at Benton Lynch and at the sister Firesheets as if that were his genuine article of business and the sister Firesheets told him, "Get on with your mess then. I don't want you trailing me no more," and the wiry tattooed white boy retreated behind a papertowel display and out of sight. "That just sets me off," the sister Firesheets said and laid her milky hands on her hips. "A boy studies your sweet behind so as to get his pecker all stiff and lathered up and then he figures you owe him a place to put it. Well he ain't getting his old lizardy self near me. That just purely sets me off." And Benton Lynch dropped the four pack of vanilla pudding cups and the cans separated from the container and departed in different directions across the linoleum. "What's your name?" the sister Firesheets asked him.

And Benton Lynch told her, "Benton Lynch."

"Mine's Jane Elizabeth Firesheets from my momma and my grandmomma's sister," Jane Elizabeth Firesheets said. "Who you named for?"

"Uncle Benton," Benton Lynch told her.

"On account of what?" Jane Elizabeth Firesheets wanted to know.

"Tires," Benton Lynch told her.

"Well ain't that a thing," Jane Elizabeth Firesheets said. "Where you live?"

"Nowhere much," Benton Lynch told her.

"We got a house out Falls of the Neuse other side of Yates Pond. You know Yates Pond?" Jane Elizabeth Firesheets asked.

And Benton Lynch shook his head yes. He had passed Yates Pond going and coming from the Bojangles the night previous.

"Daddy's going to sell it when the lake comes up," Jane Elizabeth Firesheets said, "and we all moving to Chalybeate Springs. You know Chalybeate Springs?"

And Benton Lynch shook his head no.

"It's down the road some," Jane Elizabeth Firesheets said. "Daddy's got a brother there and they throwing in together on a farm, going to raise tobacco. Daddy ain't never raised no tobacco. Daddy ain't never done much hardly. What's your daddy do?"

"Eggs," Benton Lynch said.

"Momma don't cook eggs on account of granddaddy can't eat eggs and daddy don't like eggs and Raymond—that's my brother, Raymond. He's an asshole—he don't like eggs either. I'll eat them hard boiled and chopped up on a salad like at the salad bar at the Golden Corral but I don't like them much otherwise myself. You ever eaten at the Golden Corral?" Jane Elizabeth Firesheets wanted to know.

And Benton Lynch shook his head no.

Then Jane Elizabeth Firesheets took a halfstep in Benton Lynch's direction and laid the tipends of her fingers on Benton Lynch's bare forearm. "I can judge people straight off," she said, "I got a gift for it, and I can tell you ain't like the rest of them. I mean you ain't colored but you ain't like them white boys either. Especially him," and she jerked her head at the paper-towel display. "I like you," she said and dragged the tipends of her fingers up Benton Lynch's bare forearm almost to the elbow and then back to the wrist. "We live in a little brick house," she said, "a little brick house with green shutters and brown curtains and a yellow buglight on the front porch. Just the other side of Yates Pond," she said. "I'll be home most all night," and she dragged the tipends of her fingers along the back of Benton Lynch's hand and across the tops of the pudding cups prior to turning her back to Benton Lynch and showing him her sweet behind all the way down the aisle.

The wiry tattooed white boy came round the paper-towel display at a dead run and did not stop or even slow down noticeably until he had his wild, antic, and thoroughly flushed face full up in Benton Lynch's face which was not wild or antic or thoroughly flushed either but had maintained its usual pointiness and angularity and general vacancy, and the wiry tattooed white boy shook the can of flea and tic spray at the side of Benton Lynch's head in a most threatening and violent manner and said to him, "I'll fucking kill you. Go ahead, lay one finger on her and I'll fucking kill you. I'll chew you up and spit you out. I mean it," and then the wiry tattooed white boy recommenced his dead run and maintained it to the end of the aisle where he paused briefly to whirl around and fire the can of flea and tic spray at Benton Lynch who in jumping sideways to avoid it dropped the twelve pack of vanilla pudding cups onto the floor which made for sixteen cans of pudding scattered across the linoleum.

The critter had already returned to the truckbed by the time Benton Lynch got back to it on account of the manager of the Bojangles had not allowed him into the restaurant proper but had instead sent him around to the drive-thru where he picked up his supper and carried it with him to the fender well, and he had disposed of most everything but for the greasy box and the unopened towelette and the white meatless chicken bones which lay all around and atop his feet, so Benton Lynch offered him one of the four pudding cups he had at last decided to buy and the critter tore off the top and scooped out the most of the pudding with his fingers and licked out the rest of the pudding with his tongue and then proceeded on to the second pudding cup followed by the third one followed by half of the fourth one and the pudding cup tops and empty pudding cup cans piled up with the white meatless chicken bones at the critter's feet. Emmet returned directly with part of a thigh in one hand and part of a biscuit in the other and soon after the ever gesticulating Mr. Overhill crossed the parking lot in the company of the increasingly sullen negroes and he detained them at the fender of the truck with a lengthy explanation of the convective qualities of corrugated metal but did in fact let them loose at last and the fat negro and the paltry negro threw themselves into the truckbed and the fat negro exhaled most profoundly and the paltry negro said, "Jesus, what a windy motherfucker."

The wiry tattooed white boy did not show up directly and Mr. Overhill raced the engine and blew the horn and circled the parking lot but could not seem to lure him out of wherever he was and so Mr. Overhill dispatched the fat negro after him and while the fat negro was searching through the drugstore the wiry tattooed white boy emerged from the Big Star with his arms full of the momma Firesheets's groceries and with the momma Firesheets herself at this left shoulder and the sister Firesheets somewhere in the vicinity of his right shoulder but not at it precisely. The wiry tattooed white boy chatted with the momma Firesheets and showed his teeth all the way to the Oldsmobile and at intervals he attempted to chat with the sister Firesheets and showed his teeth in her direction too, but the sister Firesheets slowed and hung back some and did not appear enchanted with the general palaver. Mr. Overhill eased up behind the Oldsmobile and sa-

luted the momma Firesheets and saluted the sister
Firesheets and commented on the sheery airy won-
drousness of the evening, he called it, prior to waving
the wiry tattooed white boy on into the truckbed, and
once the wiry tattooed white boy had shook the
momma Firesheets's hand and had nodded at the sister
Firesheets ever so imperially he did in fact climb over
the tailgate into the truckbed and rode around the
parking lot twice before getting dispatched after the fat
negro who he found in the drugstore at the magazine
rack sharing the anniversary issue of *Penthouse* with
the granddaddy Firesheets.

They did not return to the pure heart of the Harricanes but stopped due south at a roadside picnic table
where Mr. Overhill intended to pass the evening so as
to keep the negroes at ease. However, somebody had
deposited the insides of a cantaloupe in the trash barrel chained to a tree next to the picnic table and the
seeds and the pulp and the juices had mixed with the
rest of the garbage and had stewed in the heat thereby
producing a startling and altogether vigorous aroma
which not even Mr. Overhill, who could stand almost
anything, could stand. So they proceeded a little further into the Harricanes than the negroes had desired
they proceed though not nearly so far as the riverbottom and Mr. Overhill pulled off the highway onto a
fireroad and parked temporarily under the spreading
foliage of a pecan tree until the paltry negro objected
on account of how spreading foliage was just the sort
of thing a snake was likely to drop out of in the night,
and consequently Mr. Overhill pulled on down the
road a ways and stopped underneath a white oak
which had some spreading foliage of its own though of
a far more altitudinous variety and Mr. Overhill asked
the paltry negro did the move suit him and the paltry
negro said he guessed it would have to.

The fat negro and the paltry negro and the critter
commenced the evening's activities by expelling their

indigestion all over the wiry tattooed white boy who did not appreciate the gesture much and so grabbed ahold of Emmet and hurled him across the truckbed and Emmet hollered, "Hey! Hey!" and went into his usual impotent rage. Benton Lynch sat on the open tailgate and watched the festivities unoccupied until he picked up his paper sack, which was soft and tissuey at the neck from getting rolled up and rolled back day after day, and he brought out from it not a clean but a rinsed shirt and he returned to it not a clean or a rinsed but a folded shirt and rolled the soft tissuey neck closed again, and not the fat negro or the paltry negro or Emmet or the wiry tattooed white boy either noticed he was gone until he'd already left the fireroad for the highway and only the wiry tattooed white boy got all agitated and irate on account of it and he screamed off into the darkness, "Lynch! Lynch! I'll fucking kill you. One finger on her and you're dead meat. I mean it Lynch. I'll fucking kill you." And the paltry negro said to the fat negro, "That where he off to? Should've took his bag with him, they both gone need one," and the fat negro hooted and the paltry negro hooted himself and Emmet howled once and was setting himself to howl again when he got dragged out of the truckbed by his ears and kicked sharply in the kidneys twice.

Benton Lynch walked a mile and a half along the highway prior to crossing a pasture and circling around Yates Pond to the inhabited side of it and he narrowed down the brick houses with yellow buglights to an even dozen and narrowed down the brick houses with yellow buglights and green shutters to an even half dozen with two additional possibilities that did not have shutters on the actual house but had them instead in the bushes and on the front lawn. However, he could not find but two brick houses with yellow buglights and green shutters and brown window curtains and long sleek Oldsmobiles in the driveway, and when one of the Oldsmobiles turned out to be a Pontiac Benton Lynch stood in the road in front of the Firesheetses' house and wondered to himself what he would do now that he had arrived at where he was going. In fact he dropped off into a kind of funk as he pondered over what he might say to Jane Elizabeth Firesheets and pondered over what she might say to him and as he figured and imagined what him and Jane Elizabeth Firesheets might get worked up enough to do together which was just the sort of thing he had done considerable figuring and imagining about but never truly any of. The whole process remained somewhat vague and mysterious to him though he had seen pictures in magazines and on the backs of his cousin Jerome Lynch's playing cards, pictures of women with tremendous drooping breasts and pictures of gentlemen with tremendous drooping items of their own, but he could not figure precisely how everything got joined up and hooked together and he did not thoroughly understand where the heaping up on the floor came in though he was reasonably certain it came in somewhere. So Benton Lynch stood in the road and puzzled over what went where and puzzled over how it behaved once it got there and consequently did not hear Jane Elizabeth Firesheets call out to him from the screen-in sideporch the first time she did in fact call out and did not hear anything but the noise of it the second time and only realized what the noise was and where it had come from when Jane Elizabeth Firesheets stepped off the porch and into the yard.

She had changed out of her tiny little shorts and her tiny little top and had put on instead a dress with spots on it, and she had pinched her cheeks and colored her lips and her eyelids and had piled her hair up on top of her head where she had twisted it and teased it and just generally annoyed and provoked it into a massy lump. Benton Lynch had never seen such splendor previously, not that he could recollect anyway, and he

stood at the end of the driveway and ventilated his
molars as he puzzled over what went where with some
actual and increasing desperation since he felt himself
developing the what of it which rendered the where of
it ever more crucial, and Jane Elizabeth Firesheets did
not help matters with the tipends of her fingers which
she raked lightly along Benton Lynch's forearm. "I
knew you'd come," she told him. "I've got a gift."

The grandmomma Firesheets had been laid out
along one end of the screened-in porch and the
momma Firesheets had bedecked the top of her with a
schefflera, two peonies in a pot, and a sickly fern so as
to dissipate some of the natural gravity that a casket
generally produces. For her part Jane Elizabeth Firesheets had lit a red Christmas candle along about her
grandmomma's midsection and had arranged beneath
it a plateful of assorted crackers and a plateful of assorted cheese slices and two icy Coca-Colas in the bottle. She set Benton Lynch atop a chaircushion on the
floor and took the one beside it for herself and offered
up the crackers and the cheese and the Coca-Colas
and Benton Lynch ate though he was not particularly hungry and drank though he was not particularly
thirsty and squirmed and fidgeted around on his chaircushion though he was not particularly uncomfortable
while Jane Elizabeth Firesheets herself did not eat and
did not drink and did not squirm or fidget but instead
laid on her elbow and with the tipends of her fingers
on her free hand agonized and perplexed Benton
Lynch still further. She asked him all about himself
and where he'd come from and he tried to describe the
trailer and the henhouse but could not with much effect and he tried to describe his momma and his daddy
but could not with much effect either and he talked
somewhat about his brother, Otway Burns, but only
slightly somewhat since there was not much he knew
about Otway Burns that could be put into words, and
once when he had his mouth open for the cause of

some utterance or another Jane Elizabeth Firesheets reached out and stuck her finger in it. "You've got the biggest teeth I've ever seen," she said, and she wanted to know did they come from his momma's side or his daddy's side and Benton Lynch closed his mouth to ponder over and work up a reply and got squirmy and fidgety all over again on account of the taste of her.

Jane Elizabeth Firesheets said she had previously intended to become a ballerina but had grown and blossomed appreciably of late and so no longer considered herself flatchested enough for serious dancing, and she sat up on her elbows and arched herself so as to enhance her blessings some and she asked Benton Lynch his opinion on the matter but Benton Lynch said he did not know enough about serious dancing to have an opinion on the matter. Jane Elizabeth Firesheets said she figured she'd simply become a radiologist instead because it was in her nature to assist and administer to people, and if not a radiologist she supposed physical therapy might be in her line and she asked Benton Lynch did he know what a physical therapist did and Benton Lynch shook his head no he did not. "A physical therapist does this," Jane Elizabeth Firesheets said and worked her fingers over Benton Lynch's calf muscles, "and this," she said and kneaded Benton Lynch's left thigh, "and this," she said and laid her hand on a place where Benton Lynch, aside from his own, had never had a hand laid and though he remained pointy and angular and hollowed out like usual, his eyes rolled back in his head some so as to render him a little less vacant than ordinary.

"Let's me and you go down to the pondbank," Jane Elizabeth Firesheets said and then garnished and punctuated the suggestion with a vigorous therapeutic flurry, and Benton Lynch worked his throat and moved his mouth and attempted to tell her, "All right," and very nearly did.

The wiry tattooed white boy said he would kill him,

said he would fucking kill him, said he knew where'd
he'd been, said he knew what went on, and said he
would fucking kill him for it first chance he got, and as
they pulled out of the fireroad and onto the highway
the paltry negro said he'd heard her screaming in the
night, said he'd heard her wailing and howling and the
fat negro asked him what it was she'd been wailing and
what it was she'd been howling and the paltry negro
shrieked, "Ben Ton oooohh Ben Ton," and the fat
negro sucked air and the paltry negro giggled and the
critter laughed his low mean laugh and Emmet said,
"Wham, bang," and got kicked in the stomach.

All morning the wiry tattooed white boy said he
would fucking kill him, said it as he shoveled and as he
picked and as he bagged and as he Ziplocked, said it as
he rested and took water, and repeated it every time
he said it just for emphasis, but as the morning wore
on Benton Lynch did not seem any more fucking killed
than he had been previously in the day and with the
standard assortment of Gilchrists and Parkers and
Currins and Sapps and Suggs for an audience he went
about his excavation like usual straight up until lunchtime when Jane Elizabeth Firesheets came out from a
trail in the woods with a bag lunch and hauled Benton
Lynch off into the bushes to eat his share of it. The
wiry tattooed white boy took his potted meat and
crackers on Mr. Overhill's tailgate and announced to
the paltry negro and the fat negro and the critter and
Emmet too that he would fucking kill him that he
would purely assassinate the son-of-a-bitch, and then
he grimly studied the clump of bushes Benton Lynch
and Jane Elizabeth Firesheets had disappeared behind
and the paltry negro said, "Ben Ton oooohh Ben
Ton," in a high excited voice and the fat negro contributed a series of rhythmic vulgar noises which he persisted in until the wiry tattooed white boy whirled
around and hit him full in the face with a handful of
saltines. Of course the fat negro came out of the

truckbed like a shot and him and the wiry tattooed white boy rolled around on the ground together and the fat negro said, "Sho nuff gone be somebody fucking killed here," and the wiry tattooed white boy responded with a colorful ethnic epithet which served to fire the fat negro still further and he wedged the frontal portion of the wiry tattooed white boy's skull in the crook of his arm and attempted to crack it open. Mr. Overhill asked them why didn't they leave off the fighting and leave off the rolling around but he did not get up from the tailgate to do any active separating primarily on account of the attention the scuffle had aroused among the Parkers and the Currins and the Gilchrists and the Sapps and the Suggs who had got up from their coffinlids and come to watch the proceedings. They were uniformly opposed to the fat negro with the exception of a solitary Currin who had a strong personal aversion to tattoos and he urged on the fat negro in a highly animated and excessively vocal sort of way which one of the Parkers found acutely objectionable and he shoved the Currin from behind and advised him not to be so excessively vocal and not to be so highly animated which prompted the Currin to suggest in return that the Parker stick his finger up his ass like usual so as to keep himself out of trouble. But the Parker, not being pliant and suggestible by nature, did not wait for a second highly animated and excessively vocal outburst but straightaway shoved the Currin again and the Currin turned around and broke the Parker's nose which pained the Parker some but did not deter him much and he reached out with his shoving hand and left the Currin bald on the side of his head. Understandably, the Currin yelped and felt himself which presented the Parker with the opportunity to break the Currin's nose which he promptly took advantage of and the Currin pitched over backwards through his neighbors and relations and landed near about on top of the fat negro and the wiry tattooed white boy who were not at this point doing any considerable rolling around on account of general weariness. The Parker followed the Currin through his neighbors and relations and bent down to pick him up off the ground so as to put him back onto it again but the Currin managed to kick the Parker a clean shot in the groin which the Parker did not appreciate much and had not anticipated whatsoever and he groaned and lamented some and stayed bent over sufficiently long enough to get hit upside the head twice prior to stumbling across the cemetery and falling over a marker. Of course the remaining Parkers and Currins and the Gilchrists and the Sapps and the Suggs followed the dispute as it proceeded on around the cemetery grounds which left the fat negro and the wiry tattooed white boy fairly much alone in each other's arms and between the two of them they decided to break off the hostilities for the time being so as to witness the Parker-Currin disagreement which they joined up with and observed under the hickory tree where the Parker was laying it to the Currin with near about the ferocity that the Currin was laying it to the Parker, and the wiry tattooed white boy got so caught up in the vitality of the proceedings that when Benton Lynch arrived and stuck his angular, pointy, and hollowed out face into the crowd to see what was going on the wiry tattooed white boy turned to him and exclaimed, "These men beating the shit out of each other!" but he remembered himself near about immediately and added, "I'm still going to fucking kill you, you know that."

Benton Lynch and Miss Jane Elizabeth Firesheets engaged in some additional therapy on the west bank of Yates Pond the evening following their initial appointment during the course of which Miss Firesheets had brought her considerable talents to bear upon Benton Lynch's troublesome stiffness and had eradicated and relieved it with measurable success. Consequently, Benton Lynch saw it clear to carry with him on the second night a fairly pure rigidity so as to test Miss Jane Elizabeth Firesheets's power of eradication and relief and Miss Jane Elizabeth Firesheets welcomed the challenge and rose to it some herself. This time they spread a quilt out on the grass on account of how Jane Elizabeth had laid down on a slugtrail the night before and straightaway she slipped herself out of her print dress and out of her brassiere and out of her gauzy red panties and lay naked and unabashed in the dewy night beside Benton Lynch who had not even taken his shoes off. She was in fact milky white all over just like the wiry tattooed white boy had figured and the breasts which had kept her out of toeshoes did have some plum-colored features, two ample and erect plum-colored features the likes of which Benton Lynch had never seen except possibly in the backside of his cousin Jerome Lynch's four of diamonds, so understandably Benton Lynch paid some profound attention to Jane Elizabeth Firesheets's bosoms, especially to the plum-colored pointy parts of them, and when he talked he talked at them and when he listened he listened towards them and when he felt inclined to reach over and touch some part of Jane Elizabeth Firesheets his hand chiefly ended up on a plum-colored portion of her.

She was full of news about Chalybeate Springs and about her daddy's brother and her daddy's brother's tobacco farm all on account of a phone call her daddy had gotten in the afternoon from a land speculator who was buying up property around the reservoir which was not even a reservoir yet. They had geed and hawed and generally chewed over the matter and the one had rose up some off his price while the other had dropped down some off his and it seemed to Jane Elizabeth Firesheets they might reach some sort of agreement once that part of her daddy that loved to haggle got itself satisfied. So she was commencing to anticipate life in Chalybeate Springs on a tobacco farm and she was commencing to speculate as to when Benton Lynch might join her there and naturally she asked him outright what he considered a favorable month for it and naturally Benton Lynch told the pointy parts of her breasts he didn't know what month might be favorable for it, so she assisted his decision some by naming off the twelve months in succession and allowing Benton Lynch to indicate yes or indicate no and twelve times to the pointy parts of her breasts Benton Lynch indicated no so naturally Jane Elizabeth Firesheets drew on her red gauzy paties and ran her arms through her brassiere straps and had got so much as a solitary foot and ankle into her print dress when Benton Lynch said, "July," which slowed Jane Elizabeth Firesheets some but did not stop her entirely so he tried, "June," instead and she left off dressing but did not set about undressing until he had said, "May," until he had said it twice actually and with some appreciable conviction, conviction enough anyway to bring Jane Elizabeth Firesheets back out of her dress and her brassiere and her gauzy red panties and she rolled her naked self atop Benton Lynch, laid her open hand full upon his stark rigidity, and said to him, "Tell me where it hurts, sweetness."

By the middle of the third day they had dug up and set aside all the Gilchrists and the Parkers and the Currins and the Suggs and the Sapps and the entire allotment of extraneous in-laws, so there was nobody left in the cemetery proper but for the Gilchrists and the Parkers and the Currins and the Suggs and the Sapps who had not ever been buried there, including the Parker with the broken nose and the split lip and the Currin with the broken nose and the bloody scalp who shared the same end of a Gilchrist mausoleum and seemed to have developed a fondness for each other. The fat negro and the paltry negro and the wiry tattooed white boy and the critter and Benton Lynch and Emmet loaded the caskets and bagged-up corpses into the back of the truck and rode on the tailgate to the high ground where they unloaded the caskets and the bagged-up corpses at a level and designated place that had been a homestead once and a cowpasture most recently. Mr. Overhill and the two negroes returned to the riverbottom for a fresh lot while the wiry tattooed white boy and the critter and Benton Lynch and Emmet dug out the snug, shallow holes. They were seventeen dollar holes nonetheless, and they deposited and covered over the bagged-up and boxed-up Gilchrists and Parkers and Currins and Suggs and Sapps under the casual scrutiny of no one much, nobody whatsoever really, especially not any living and breathing Gilchrists and Parkers and Currins and Suggs and Sapps who had decided against traveling the mile and a quarter out of the riverbottom to the cowpasture mostly because they were not your uphill sort of people.

By evening they were completely done with the transporting of the bodies and half done with the burying of them and as the paltry negro collected and gathered up the picks and the shovels and hunted a thicket to deposit them in Benton Lynch changed into a rinsed-out shirt and departed for Yates Pond where he had been invited to a regular sit-down supper which he took in the kitchen of the Firesheetses' red brick house with Jane Elizabeth Firesheets at his left elbow and the granddaddy Firesheets at his right elbow. The momma Firesheets had cooked up a potful of chicken and slickers and a batch of biscuits and Jane Elizabeth Firesheets herself had made up a bowlful of her own special potato salad which her brother, Raymond, found a long strand of wheatstraw hair in and got most disgusted and sour on account of. The granddaddy Firesheets recollected one by one every Lynch he'd ever met up with in every place he'd ever been to and quizzed Benton Lynch on his relation to them, which there generally was not any of, and whenever the opportunity presented itself the daddy Firesheets probed and sounded out Benton Lynch's knowledge of tobacco and tobacco farming which there generally was not any of either. The momma Firesheets had bought a cherry cobbler in an aluminum tin for dessert and once she had heated it in the oven she served it up all around and the daddy Firesheets and the granddaddy Firesheets said it tasted good as homemade and Benton Lynch threw in with a yes it did and the brother Firesheets said he didn't give a shit what it tasted like long as there weren't any hair in it and the sister Firesheets told him he was lucky they saw it clear to feed an asshole like him and the brother Firesheets said it weren't ever nothing but slop anyhow and the sister Firesheets got indignant and humphed and huffed and exclaimed, "Stupid little cocksucker," and the brother Firesheets told her, "Cunt," and the momma Firesheets asked the daddy Firesheets was he finished with his plate and the granddaddy Firesheets recollected a whole load of Lynches in Zebulon.

After supper the sister Firesheets took Benton Lynch around the house and showed him the bric-a-brac, especially her own personal and private collection of it in her own personal and private bedroom and in addition she reclined herself full across the bed, laid her tongue out one corner of her mouth, and showed Benton Lynch a thing or two that was not specifically in the line of bric-a-brac but proved interesting nonetheless. They retired to the pondbank with the coming of darkness and tumbled around on the quilt until Benton Lynch's stark rigidity had declined way past troublesome stiffness down to a flaccid and thoroughly invertebrate indifference that not even a gyrating Jane Elizabeth Firesheets in all of her milky and plum-colored splendor could do the least little thing about, so they talked some instead, exchanged addresses, and anticipated May in Chalybeate Springs with Jane Elizabeth Firesheets doing the primary and vocal part of

the anticipating and Benton Lynch doing the secondary and silent part of it, and in time Benton Lynch
worked up sufficient spine to distract Jane Elizabeth
Firesheets and shut her up very nearly completely except for the moaning and the boisterous exhalations
which mixed and harmonized somewhat with the
crickets and the bullfrogs and the rest of the wildlife
roundabout.

They had redeposited the remainder of the
Gilchrists and the Parkers and the Currins and the
Sapps and the Suggs by the afternoon of the following
day and the paltry negro packed up the picks and the
shovels in the truckbed and spread out the blanket and
Mr. Overhill laid his roadmap across the open tailgate
and indicated a route down to one place in Mississippi
and down further still to two places in Alabama and
then westward into Texas, and the fat negro said,
"Sandy dirt," and the paltry negro said, "Easy
money," and Emmet said, "Hot damn, hot diggity
damn," and the wiry tattooed white boy said, "I'll
fucking kill you in Alabama. They won't do nothing to
me there. It ain't a civilized place yet. I'll fucking kill
you in Alabama for sure." And then they shut themselves up in the truckbed partly atop the blanket and
partly atop the pick and shovel handles and Mr. Overhill brought his red Dodge out on the Falls of the
Neuse Road heading south away from the Harricanes
towards Raleigh. He circled the city on the bypass and
exited onto what appeared to be a proper and suitable
highway to get him where he was going but which
turned out to run more westerly than easterly or
southerly and so wasn't nearly so proper and wasn't
nearly so suitable as Mr. Overhill had first figured, and
consequently he stopped off at a Grocery Boy Jr. for
directions and candied corn and while he was still inside jawing with the cashier Benton Lynch caught up
his tissuey paper sack in his hands and climbed over
the tailgate to the pavement. "Hey!" the wiry tattooed

white boy hollered to him, "I'm going to fucking kill you and you ain't running off till I do it, so get back in here," but Benton Lynch just spun his angular, pointy, hollowed out self around and proceeded across the lot and the wiry tattooed white boy hollered, "Hey!" again with about as much effect as previously and then "Hey!" a third time prior to turning to the fat negro and asking him, "Where's he think he's going?" And the fat negro sat up on his elbow and replied, "Who gives a happy shit," and him and the wiry tattooed white boy and the paltry negro and Emmet and the critter too watched Benton Lynch flag down a red Mustang which took him so far as Durham where he caught a ride to Greensboro and then hitched onto a produce truck straight into downtown Neely or to the back alley at the Big Apple anyway and he walked from there north past the square and down by the icehouse and on out the Danville Road to Oregon Hill. He arrived in the darkness and stood for a time on the rise above his momma and daddy's chickenhouse and his momma and daddy's trailer not listening to anything in particular or looking at anything in particular but just standing on the rise in the darkness listening to and looking at everything in general which was nothing really but ruin and dilapidation and squalor and a little slip of moon that at last lit his way down the slope and direct up to the metal trailer door which he did not tap or knock or beat on but merely opened before himself and shut behind himself and he sat down on the Mediterranean sofa beside his daddy who dropped his mouth open and said, "You're back."

Three

THEY WERE yellowheaded thumbtacks and Sheriff Burton said that all together they described a corridor of wanton destruction or if not a corridor of wanton destruction then maybe just an alley of it though at times he did not feel inclined towards a corridor or alley either of destruction wanton or otherwise and instead saw in the trail of tacks a graphic geographical and, in this case, yellowheaded gash in the very fabric of our society, a gash running north to south and then east to west and then sort of south to north and kind of west to east which made it fairly much a rectangular yellowheaded gash though not truly and purely a rectangular yellowheaded gash on account of the stomped in northwest corner in the vicinity of Wentworth. But it was all truly and purely square and geographical enough to suggest to the sheriff some sort of pattern and premeditated design which was why he set aside a portion of his every day to ponder the map on his office wall and especially to ponder the previously thumbtacked parts of it so as to formulate, figure, and speculate as to just what might be the subsequently thumbtacked parts of it.

The accumulation of all the pondering and formulating and figuring and speculating had rendered the sheriff capable of rattling off the placenames and the peoplenames too like a litany and he would sit at his desk with his feet atop one corner of it and his back to the map on his wall and tell himself, "Busick in

Draper, McIver in Harrison Crossroads, Barnard in
Bethel, Grissom in Locust Hill, Stem in Union Ridge,
Troutman in Altamahaw, Ross in Hillsdale, Spencer in
Midway," and then he would pinch his bottom lip between his right thumb and forefinger, which was Sheriff Burton's ordinary ponderous and speculative
gesture, and he would rattle off the money too telling
himself, "$147.00 and $189.00 and $123.00 and $155.00
and $78.00 and $230.00 and $112.00 and $150.00
even," and he would go ahead and ponder and speculate over the money some since he was in the proper
posture of it prior to letting loose of his lip, picking
himself up out of his chair, and studying the map on
the wall outright paying some little attention to the
yellowheaded rectangular gash in the very fabric of our
society and expending the bulk of his energies on a
newly plotted silverheaded gash in the very fabric of
our society which was southeast of the yellowheaded
gash and not nearly so linear and rectangular but more
in the form of a clustery bunch so as to suggest more
likely a boil on the buttocks on the very fabric of our
society than any sort of gash on it, and since it was in
fact a fairly recent boil the sheriff had to look at it as
he told himself, "Corinth and Duncan and Wilbon and
Angier and Holly Springs and Kipling and Fuquay-
Varina," and then off by itself way to the west not like
a gash or a boil either but most nearly resembling a
wart or maybe a mole or just some slight and almost
negligible imperfection in the fabric of our society lay
the domed, silvery head of the lone and solitary Lemly
tack which even with its detachment and considerable
remoteness from the gash and the boil too had some
logic to it on account of how the Stem in Union Ridge
had not been a Mr. like the Busick and the McIver and
the Barnard and the Grissom and the Troutman and
the Ross and the Spencer had all been Mr.s but had
instead been a Mrs. and so could not have her testicles
blown to anywhere that the gentlemen could have

their testicles blown to which got her a variant threat
to a further region, and the sheriff left off with the boil
and the wart together and turned his attention to a
scrap of paper he had attached with tape to the top
edge of the map, or more precisely to the single word
written in blue ink on the scrap of paper attached to
the top edge of the map, and twice he mouthed it si-
lently to himself trying out the accent on the frontend
of it and on the backend of it, which seemed the more
fitting location, and finally drawing off a breath and
telling himself out loud, "Poontang," saying it deliber-
ately and with gravity since it seemed somehow extraordinarily significant to him.

Trouble was they weren't any of them his. Trouble
was they were all somebody else's—Draper and Harrison Crossroads and Bethel and Locust Hill and Union
Ridge and Altamahaw and Hillsdale and Midway. So
while he could advise and hypothesize and theorize
and formulate and figure and speculate and tend to his
map and his gasp and his boil and his wart, he couldn't
do anything much in the way of examining witnesses
and questioning victims and pursuing culprits because
they weren't any of them his. They were all somebody
else's. But he was not long in coming once the yellowheaded rectangular gash closed in roundabout Neely
leaving the sheriff and his territory ringed round with
the corridor of destruction which the sheriff wanted
just a little piece of for himself and which he figured he
was entitled to on account of the general meanness of
the times and which he did in fact get some of not two
weeks after Altamahaw had collected a little piece of it
for itself.

However, the sheriff did not get his in Neely proper
but got it instead on the bypass at Mr. Musselwhite's
Citgo station which had not been a Citgo station for
any considerable spell and had been previously Mr.
Musselwhite's general grocery and before that Mr.
Musselwhite's fruit, vegetable, and snake oil stand and

before that the shed Mr. Musselwhite had kept his
mule in. But once the division of roads and highways
bought up the right-of-way and cut the bypass through
and paved it and opened it Mr. Musselwhite's muleshed was sitting near about on the northbound lane
and showed some entrepreneurial possibilities which
was what got the mule evicted and which was what got
the dung shoveled out and which was what got the
melons and the cantaloupes and the peaches and the
tomatoes away from the Big Apple, where Mr. Musselwhite paid something slightly above wholesale, and
out to the bypass where people from all over the place
paid something that did not even resemble retail. And
at first it was just the melons and the cantaloupes and
the peaches and the tomatoes but after a bit it was the
melons and the cantaloupes and the peaches and the
tomatoes and the bottled snake oil which Mr. Musselwhite manufactured himself from melted shortening
mostly, and later still it was the melons and the cantaloupes and the peaches and the tomatoes and the bottled snake oil along with various grocery items such as
loafbread and crackers and Coca-Colas and cornmeal
and sack flour and cigarettes to which were added pullet eggs and sausage and smoked ham and tenderloin
and pickle and pimento loaf thereby ushering into the
muleshed the age of electric refrigeration which called
for some general renovation and expansion on the part
of Mr. Musselwhite who was not your general renovat-
ing and expanding sort and so who himself fashioned
an addition from plywood primarily which did not so
much improve the muleshed as increase and com-
pound it.

Of course once the pullet eggs and the sausage and
the smoked ham and the tenderloin and the pickle and
pimento loaf caught on with the people from all over
the place just like the melons and the cantaloupes and
the peaches and the tomatoes and the snake oil had
caught on with them, Mr. Musselwhite felt obliged to

introduce a new line of products into his business and decided upon leisurewear, more specifically sunglasses and floppy hats and rubber sandals and flowerey shirts, so he fashioned yet another primarily plywood addition on the opposite end from the previous one and thereby increased and compounded the shed still further while maintaining its thoroughly ramshackle and unimproved state which local people did in fact recognize as unimproved and thoroughly ramshackle but which people from all over the place figured for quaint, and once Mr. Musselwhite found out he had a quaint place on his hands he considered there might be some profit for him in antique items on top of the melons and the cantaloupes and the peaches and the tomatoes and the snake oil and the pullet eggs and the sausage and the smoked ham and the tenderloin since antique items generally did turn up in quaint establishments and since, as Mr. Musselwhite understood it, most people—especially people from all over the place—would pay good money for nearly any trifling and incomprehensible geegaw as long as it looked older than they were, and what with two barnfuls and a cellar heaped near about to the floor joists Mr. Musselwhite had no end of geegaws, most particularly crusted and mildewed geegaws which he did not bother to decrust and unmildew but simply transported to the store once he had built a primarily plywood wing for them.

At length the muleshed got purely swallowed up in the additions and though everybody knew it was in there somewhere nobody could tell just where, not even Mr. Musselwhite who had kept track of it for a time but lost it eventually and never could manage to find it again. The geegaws proved extraordinarily successful for Mr. Musselwhite and he expanded into whatnots and bric-a-brac and rustic dohickeys and carried large, truly perplexing pieces when he could get them, and though the leisurewear and the fruits and vegetables and the pullet eggs and the pork and the pickle and pimento loaf continued to sell briskly Mr. Musselwhite did not believe he was realizing quite the profit he could realize considering what a prodigious lot of bypassing went on around Neely day in and day out. So as Mr. Musselwhite sat on his metal stool behind his cash register and in front of his cigarette rack he studied the range of goods in his inventory and he speculated as to what other retail services he might successfully expand into, and though he considered soft icecream and hot dogs and ladies' cosmetics and hardware he did not do any actual expanding until the notion of gasoline came to him there between his cash register and his cigarettes, gasoline and diesel fuel too, he figured, so as to draw in the truckdrivers who generally would not leave the road for melons and geegaws and assorted pork cuts.

He struck a deal with Citgo and they buried the tanks for him and brought in the pumps and the big orange sign and they assisted and advised Mr. Musselwhite in some thoroughgoing improvements to his quaint structure which they were not nearly so taken with as most everybody else from all over the place, and consequently the thoroughgoing improvements did not get done in plywood but got done in real and actual brick and real and actual mortar by real and actual carpenters and masons who fairly much encased Mr. Musselwhite's quaint structure without closing him down for even a part of a day, and when they got done laying the bricks and hanging the doors and snugging up the windows Mr. Musselwhite could not discover a trace of his plywood wings and nowhere could he detect any degree of palpable quaintness which had pretty much gone the way of his muleshed. So he sat in his new building on his metal stool between his cigarettes and his cash register and sold his fruits and his vegetables and his assorted pork pieces and his leisurewear and his geegaws and his gasoline now too and he

opened earlier and closed later and realized near about
as much profit as he had previously.

Now Mr. Musselwhite had never been robbed in the
true and verifiable and legal sense of the thing though
he had once got beat out of some money by a Mrs.
Rouse from Lynchburg who had bought from him an
old crusted and mildewed porcelain figurine at his
usual unreasonable price and had turned and sold it to
a collector in Virginia so as to get back her money and
then some which seemed to Mr. Musselwhite as good
as thievery, or maybe worse really and appreciably
more aggravated than normal thievery on account of
the gloating Mrs. Rouse had stopped in to partake of
later. But he had never been robbed and threatened
and endangered like he got robbed and threatened and
endangered on that Thursday morning in late October
which would be the October after the summer we lost
the bald Jeeter when robbery and threats and endan-
germent were more prevalent than they had been at
any time before. Mr. Musselwhite was alone in the
store or very nearly alone anyway with the exception
of Mrs. Evander Buffaloe whose company anymore
was the same thing as solitude though it had not been
so prior to Mr. Evander Buffaloe's departure and
probably would not have continued to be if Mr.
Evander Buffaloe had simply run off with a woman
like the deacon Furches ran off with a woman, which
was the sort of thing a wife could recover from and
resent eventually, but Mr. Evander Buffaloe had not
simply run off with a woman, had not simply run off at
all, but had instead departed primarily and there
wasn't anything simple about that.

Mr. Evander Buffaloe had kept the books at the
Brownlee brothers' slaughterhouse for going on thirty
years and him and his wife and his two boys and one
girl lived three blocks off the boulevard in what the
ladies of the Neely Flower Society called the stately
Tucker home though there had not been any Tuckers

in it for a full century. They were both from local people, Richardson Road Buffaloes on the one side and Lawsonville Avenue Johnstons on the other, and had got married in the First Baptist Church, which was her persuasion, prior to taking allegiance with the Methodists, which was his. Their boys came near about one right after the other, first Evander Clark Buffaloe II in 1952 and then Vance Johnston Buffaloe in 1953. Martha Porter Buffaloe did not arrive until the winter of 1957 which was after the Buffaloes had vacated their modest brick house behind the grade school and moved into the stately Tucker home that they had bought from some Smiths who had bought it from a Crawford who had bought it from a Moore who had bought it from a Kornegay who might have bought it from a Tucker though possibly not. Mrs. Evander Buffaloe was active in the Women's Christian Circle and worked at the Bargain Box Tuesday afternoons. She was widely well thought of though pitied somewhat on account of her homeliness which is one of the chief features passed from Johnston to Johnston aside from dainty feet. However, Mrs. Evander Buffaloe had learned to dress and carry herself so as to distract from the fullness of her ears and the fleshiness of her nose and the general chinlessness of her chin none of which Mr. Evander Buffaloe had been particularly put off by during their courtship, partially on account of Mrs. Evander Buffaloe's talents and partially on account of the astigmatism Buffaloes pass from one generation to the next instead of homeliness or dainty feet. Otherwise Buffaloes are usually just plain and lean and balding except for the Buffaloe women who are usually not lean, and somehow or another when Mr. Buffaloe coupled his plainness and his leanness and his receding hairline with Mrs. Buffaloe's dainty feet and clandestine homeliness the pair of them together made for what people called a handsome couple and produced between them what people called three handsome children who got some of their momma and some of their daddy in fairly equal shares with the notable exception of Martha Porter Buffaloe who did not get anything from her daddy except his astigmatism and got everything from her momma except her dainty feet and so went around homely and clumsy and thoroughly farsighted until she turned thirteen when she got fat too.

By and large they were your ordinary and normal sort of people. They spent a week every summer at Kitty Hawk and laid flowers at the cemetery every Easter and every Mother's Day. In 1963 Evander Clark II and Vance Johnston played Tiny Tot football in the Wallace E. Abernathy league, or got uniforms anyway and blocked on some kickoffs and blocked on some punts and mostly stood on the sidelines and yelled and chewed their fingernails and spat on ants. In the winter of 1964 Mr. Evander Buffaloe joined a bridge club so as to get out of the house some and in the winter of 1965 Mrs. Evander Buffaloe registered for a political awareness seminar at the Y.W.C.A. so as to get out of the house some without having to play bridge. Throughout the spring of 1966 Mrs. Evander Buffaloe developed some inordinately liberal tendencies, primarily on account of the Y.W.C.A., and in April in the spirit of fairmindedness she purchased from a negro door-to-door salesman a set of encyclopedias which she paid cash money for and which she received twelve volumes of in July, all of them consonants. She did not ever get the vowels, did not ever get the rest of the consonants for that matter, and was forced to withdraw from a summer-long personal introspection workshop at the request of Mr. Evander Buffaloe who found he objected to liberal tendencies. In 1973 Miss Martha Porter Buffaloe became a vegetarian, partly from a sense of pure outrage at the vicious cruelty perpetrated on helpless innocent animals and partly in an attempt to clear up her skin which *Woman's Day* had suggested vegetables might do. In 1974 Miss Martha Porter Buffaloe became a carnivore again and commenced to use a medicated swab in conjunction with vitamin E.

As to their schooling, the Buffaloe children all completed the twelfth grade and Evander Clark II enrolled at the state university in Raleigh where he intended to pursue a business degree but got sidetracked straightaway and set about pursuing the fine art of dissipation instead. He developed a taste for Philip Morris Ovals and Dutch beer and he caught from a girl from Pine Level a wholly unextraordinary and domestic strain of venereal disease which he attempted to make a gift of to a young woman from New Brunswick New Jersey and to her sister also and to her sister's best friend but which he had to keep to himself at last and take a treatment for in the end. He participated in demonstrations against the Asian war and got himself arrested twice, once for failing to disperse and once for setting fire to a sofa in the lobby of the library which the police determined had not been an act of conscience but had instead resulted from the combination of one live and fiery hot Philip Morris Oval, countless Dutch beers, and two little white tablets the size of fertilizer pellets. After two years of steady and earnest extravagance and turpitude Evander Clark II got discharged from the university without any credits to speak of and he returned to the stately Tucker home where he laid around for awhile and complained of ennui which Mrs. Evander Buffaloe took him to Dr. Shackleford to get some medication for but which Dr. Shackleford could not even begin to medicate away and so Evander Clark II continued to lay around and continued to languish and ever increasingly believed that in his two years of college he had done everything there was to do and seen everything there was to see, except maybe for the inside of a barbershop. He felt weary and unmotivated and was in fact tiresome and useless which prompted his daddy to arrange employment for him at the slaughterhouse but Evander Clark II declined to be employed in a bourgeois institution run by philistines, and when his momma attempted to explain to him that the Brownlee brothers had only come from Moncure, Evander Clark II laid his head back and laughed in a most vicious and merciless way. Consequently Mr. Buffaloe cut off his son's association with the Brownlee brothers' philistine meat along with Mr. Wyatt Big Apple Benbow's fruits and vegetables and canned and bottled goods and so provided Evander Clark II the opportunity to lay around and languish straight through the day without any worrisome meals to interrupt him, and on the Sunday the fasting commenced he found it novel and measurably heightening to his awareness, but the novelty wore off some on Monday and by midmorning Tuesday Evander Clark II's awareness, though still heightened, had turned its attention primarily to his stomach cavity. Wednesday he found a quarter in the bottom of a hutch drawer and bought himself a Three Musketeers bar. Thursday he got strapped into a battery-charged prod and encouraged cattle along a chute with it.

Vance Johnston Buffaloe did not prove nearly so unruly and troublesome as his brother. He did not get dissipated or arrested or venereal disease and successfully earned a certificate in electrical wiring at the Rockingham Technical Institute. He failed to fast any or measurably heighten his awareness but instead took a job straight off with Purdy Electric and bored holes and pulled wire and slid around on his backside under houses. Martha Porter Buffaloe did not pursue a formal education after high school and did not pursue any technical training either but went directly to work at the Rexall in cosmetics which she was not nearly so artful with as her mother but which she could manipulate nonetheless so as to reduce her nose and increase her chin and hide her blemishes and disguise her ears

which left only the feet and the fatness for people to
openly regard, lament to each other about, and be
genuinely sorry for. Like her brother Vance Johnston
the electrician and her brother Evander Clark II the
cattle prodder, Martha Porter Buffaloe did not trouble
herself to move out of the stately Tucker home into
her own residence once she had earned and accumulated the money to do so, and consequently the Buffaloes lived fairly much as they had lived previously
except they were bigger now, or at least three of them
were anyway, and did not like each other near as much
as they had before, especially at supper when the sheer
proximity of Buffaloe to Buffaloe made for some noticeable friction.

In the Buffaloe household, time was when opinions
had been a thing peculiar to Mr. Buffaloe like his high
forehead or his brown front tooth, and when he would
lay the tines of his fork on the lip of his plate and dab
at his mouth with his napkin and then deliver himself
of a viewpoint, Mrs. Buffaloe generally agreed with
him straight off and the children, who likely had not
been listening anyhow, would not comment and so
there was an end to the matter. But when the children
grew up their mouths grew up with the rest of them,
and their attention span drew out some and they became opinionated, or what Mr. Buffaloe considered
counter-opinionated since he did not seem to look at
anything from one side that they did not see from the
other. Of course Evander Clark II was the worst of the
bunch because he had been to a university, had actually attended several classes, and so considered himself
educated, or worse than educated really, considered
himself naturally intuitive and highly intelligent and
figured Neely for a vast stagnant pool of ignorance and
wrongheadedness that he had miraculously sprung out
of and risen above. He had been sufficiently intolerable in his laying around and languishing stage but got
worse once he commenced to prod cattle, got actively

political and attempted to organize his fellow stock-yard employees into a socialist workers' party but they were not much intrigued with socialism and instead chased Evander Clark II throughout the corral and singed and jolted his backside with their own battery-charged prods which was the leading amusement at the slaughterhouse.

Vance Johnston Buffaloe, who had not ever possessed much of a personality in the course of his youth, had begun to become somebody in particular under the guidance and instruction of his fellow electricians and their carpenter friends and mason friends and Sheetrocker friends and painter friends who had reduced their primary needs in life to beer and money and snatch, only the other way around, and most every evening they all collected at the integrated club and pool hall out the Burlington road past the cemetery where the beer got drunk and the money got spent and the snatch got talked about, and if there was anything Vance Johnston Buffaloe and his friends liked better than getting snatch it was talking about getting snatch and if there was anything they liked better than talking about getting snatch it was fighting over what snatch they had gotten, or what snatch they had said they'd gotten anyway, and they would knock each other out of their chairs and beat each other and kick each other and brawl all throughout the pool hall for the sake of some young woman none of them were truly acquainted with and who probably would not have given a happy shit for the whole bunch of them together. Consequently, Vance Johnston Buffaloe, who had not been anybody much prior to his course of study at Rockingham Technical Institute and his subsequent employment at Purdy Electric, developed into a fairly rough and vulgar individual and where he had not possessed much of any opinion on any matter previously he now believed every dilemma could be suitably and satisfyingly resolved if him or one of his friends or somebody like him or one of his friends could get his hands on the responsible individual and whipass, he called it.

Understandably, Martha Porter Buffaloe could not abide either of her brothers on account of how the one bored her and the other offended her, and for less understandable but equally acute reasons, Martha Porter Buffaloe could not abide her parents either. They criticized her weight and criticized her hair and criticized her makeup and criticized her clothes and criticized her friends and just generally picked at her and persecuted her and did not even begin to comprehend her, or that's how she saw it anyhow. She did not venture out in public with them when she could help it on account of how dull and ordinary they were, and though she had attempted on innumerable occasions to instruct them in the ways of stylishness and inform them as to the most burning issues of the modern day, they seemed reluctant to be improved upon if not outright opposed to it, and so Martha Porter Buffaloe eventually washed her hands of her momma and her daddy and decided she would just have to be stylish and informed on her own. Consequently, she wore what clothes she wanted to wear, had her hair cut just precisely how she wanted to have it cut, spread the rouge to her cheeks and the shadow to her eyelids exactly how she wanted to spread the rouge and the shadow, and generally packaged and presented herself to the world like she felt she should be packaged and presented notwithstanding the strident objections of her momma and her daddy who picked at her and persecuted her and did not even begin to comprehend her.

There was not much pleasing talk around the Buffaloe supper table any longer. Every human utterance came under fire from somewhere and so there was not much plain human utterance around the Buffaloe supper table any longer either with the exception of regular utilitarian requests for the meat and the vegetables and the biscuits and whatnot and even they got nasty sometimes on account of Evander Clark II primarily who had completely ceased to refer to Martha Porter Buffaloe as Martha Porter Buffaloe but had commenced instead to call her you and yours, the you being the most of herself and the yours being her thighs which were threatening to become the most of herself. Naturally, Martha Porter Buffaloe did not appreciate the title much and always objected to it straightaway and violently insisted she was on a diet, and she was on a diet though it was one of your superficial mealtime diets that did not have anything to do with losing weight, and insisting as well she was big-boned and possibly suffering from a glandular affliction to all of which her brother would smirk, and he was quite an accomplished and effective smirker, and so Martha Porter Buffaloe would call on her momma and her daddy for support and her daddy would lay the tines of his fork on the lip of his plate and dab at his mouth with his napkin and tell her it appeared to him she could stand to whittle herself down some and her momma would suggest a change in clothes or hairstyle to disguise the fullness of her figure which was usually when Martha Porter Buffaloe departed from the table in exasperation and retired to her bedroom where she took consolation in her record player and her assortment of 45's and soothed herself with the sheer racket and volume the two of them made together.

Undoubtedly the 1970's were strenuous and troublesome years for Mr. Buffaloe in particular on account of how his life had changed so little on the one hand but so greatly on the other. The one child that left home had come back and the two children that hadn't left home still didn't, and though Mrs. Buffaloe told Mr. Buffaloe it was nice to have the family all together it wasn't nice really and he knew it and she knew it too which did not prevent her from expressing the contrary but full well kept her from believing it. Obviously there was not anything at all nice about five fullgrown Buffaloes under the roof of the stately Tucker home, especially since not any of the five fullgrown Buffaloes liked each other, including the Mr. and Mrs. who had liked each other once, had liked each other well enough anyway to concoct the remaining three Buffaloes, but who did not seem to share a special fondness any longer, only a bed and a bathroom and a clothescloset and the general habit of each other roundabout the house. So life inside the stately Tucker home had soured noticeably for Mr. Buffaloe, and commencing with April, 1971, life outside the stately Tucker home soured noticeably for him as well because it was in April of 1971 that Mr. Buffaloe lost his mother who had been laid up and disoriented since November of 1969 and who Mr. Buffaloe had considered all along would be better off dead until she died when he changed his mind. And he had not completely forgiven himself for wishing his mother away and had not completely forgiven his mother for leaving when the United States of America proceeded to withdraw from southeast Asia which Mr. Buffaloe considered to be a pure moral cataclysm, and he was just getting to the point where he could live down his little part of it when the honorable Governor George Corley Wallace was shot to pieces by a crazed white man at some yankee gathering where he should have known better than to go anyway. So there was Mr. Buffaloe with his grief and his disgrace and his solitary vote which torture and the threat of death could not induce him to squander upon a Republican but which he did not much care to spend on an incomprehensible and farfetched Democrat either, and consequently he did not use it at all and got accused of apathy on national television by Dr. Eric Sevareid and he could hardly bear up under the humiliation of it. Then when it did not seem things could become worse they became worse: Mr. Buffaloe's Pontiac stock fell off to nothing, Evander Clark II bought a pair of sneakers, a Coca-Cola, and two hot dogs with Mr. Buffaloe's entire collection of Kennedy half dollars, and on the first Sunday in August of 1977 the Neely *Chronicle* ran a graphic and utterly devastating photograph on the bottom front page of the fashion section—Elizabeth Taylor had gotten fat.

It was all Mr. Buffaloe could do to carry on. He had no measurable will or desire remaining to him and of a morning could barely muster the velocity and momentum sufficient to propel him through the day. He took little interest in national events and left off watching the 6:30 news once talk got out of Walter Cronkite's retirement. Anymore he read only the frivolous parts of the *Chronicle,* which was the bulk of it, and rarely did that once the editors dropped Gasoline Alley and Gil Thorp to make room for encapsulated soap opera plots. He could not devote himself to his work because he had always been and surely would always be quite thoroughly indifferent to the Brownlee brothers' debits and credits and general expenses and anymore he could not ignore his work either and meditate with any success on account of his son who was ever getting pursued and electrocuted and so kept the slaughterhouse in an ongoing uproar. Plain and simple, Mr. Buffaloe could not find anything to live for and could not work up the courage and passion to do himself in and so just went along with the flow of the day and the flow of the week and the flow of the month and the flow of the year and did not experience but the usual unpleasantness and disappointment for such a long spell that his attitude ceased to decline and actually leveled off some. He had even laid down his fork and dabbed at his mouth and ventured an opinion or two as late as February of 1979 and he might have been all right, might have stayed leveled off and undeclining if not for the moral degeneration inherent in a capitalistic society, Evander Clark II called it, and his daddy could not find reason to disagree with him.

The deacon Furches ran off with a woman, a Lamont Circle Bailey or actually a Stout by birth who had married a Lamont Circle Bailey and who lived with him for twenty-six years and shared her bed with him and raised his children and who had even appeared and made out to like him some right up until the first Saturday in March of 1979 when the Lamont Circle Bailey himself drove his wife, the Lamont Circle Stout Bailey, to the depot so as to put her on the train for Rocky Mount where her sister lived but where she was not truly going so far as, and the Lamont Circle Stout Bailey gave her cheek to her husband and he kissed it and the Lamont Circle Bailey gave his cheek to his wife and she kissed it and they held each other's fingers briefly and then departed, the Bailey for Lamont Circle and the Stout Bailey for Greensboro where she was met at the station by the deacon Furches who had packed his things and had left his house in the early morning and driven his blue Le Sabre out of Neely and down 29 south. There was not a Mrs. Furches except for the one in the cemetery, so while the Stout Bailey had given up her home and her husband and her two daughters along with, of course, the primary part of her respectability, the deacon Furches had chiefly surrendered his sofabed, his daddy's General Electric floor circulator, and his $175.00 cleaning deposit, not to mention the good graces of the Baptist church which he lost also but which he was not much concerned over on account of what scant few worldly items the Baptist church held in its good graces anyhow and as the deacon Furches figured it, with such a considerable lot of reviling and disparaging to do the church would likely not be inclined to squander any severe damnation on the solitary escapade of a solitary deacon.

Nobody suspected the deacon Furches and the Lamont Circle Stout Bailey had run off together, though everybody knew they had left on the same morning and had gone off in the same direction, but nobody actually suspected they had been in romantic collusion each with the other because did not either of them seem the passionate and scheming type. The deacon Furches had turned sixty-four and retired from the cigarette plant in November of 1978 and since then had passed his time sitting around at the coalyard and sitting around at the Gulf station and sitting around in the basement of the armory where him and Emmett Dabb and Dennis Tuttle and Colonel J. Richmond Morrison ret. talked about most every bland and unprovocative thing they could think of and they could think of plenty between them. The deacon Furches was a tall man, well over six feet, and he wore his trousers near about up to his mammaries and had coarse black hair growing out the ridge of his nose. He was not at all comely and did not possess one of your scintillating wits and dynamic personalities that most uncomely people develop so as to offset their uncomeliness, and he appeared to merely expect that his life would wind out in its own bland and unprovocative and uncomely way until his friends would find him one day stretched out on his sofabed expired and they would collect around him and wonder if he was.

However, the Lamont Circle Stout Bailey changed all that for the deacon Furches even though she was just as bland and unprovocative and uncomely as he was, maybe even more bland and unprovocative and probably a degree or two less comely. She did not have a figure any longer just some drooping places and some bulging places which she covered up but could not disguise with stretch pants and stretch blouses and stretch jackets and plain flat shoes. She had brown hair that was cut to swirl around close to her head and she had brown eyes too and thin lips and a long pointy chin and a regular stalk of a neck all of which together had worked to remind the deacon Furches of General Douglas MacArthur and so he never could help but get

patriotic urges in her presence. However, it is unlikely
that the Stout Bailey primarily suggested General
MacArthur to the deacon Furches since the most of his
urges did not have much of a nationalistic tendency to
them and instead were more along the lines of your
fiery and savagely passionate urges though probably
not your full fiery and savagely passionate urges but
more likely just your partly fiery and moderately savagely passionate urges since it is difficult to imagine
pure fire and thoroughgoing savagery in a man who
buckles his belt across his ribcage. But nonetheless
somehow or another her exceedingly inert qualities
and his exceedingly inert qualities mixed and mingled
together to form a combustible entity, the whole business probably commencing with a few furtive glances
from the deacon's pew followed by several warm
handshakes at the sanctuary door and complicated further with some apparently accidental encounters along
the boulevard and on the square before picking up in
fiery and passionate earnest, if even just partly fiery
and somewhat passionate earnest, with a series of entirely secret and unaccidental encounters where the affections got announced and the plans got made and the
urges got exercised.

  They had intended to go as far as Pago Pago which
the deacon Furches had measured out and figured to
be sufficiently removed from Neely to prevent the primary Lamont Street Bailey or any of his Lamont Bailey relations from coming to fetch back the runaway
Lamont Street Stout Bailey since as the deacon
Furches had calculated it there was surely no man alive
who would travel full across a continent and partway
across an ocean to hunt up a frumpy, middleaged bagging and bulging woman, especially one that favored a
four star general. But in actuality they did not get so
far as Pago Pago on account of the deacon Furches's
blue Le Sabre which became ill and troubled in
Scottsbluff Nebraska and expired in Pocatello Idaho

where it would not even have been if the deacon
Furches had not got on the wrong road in Salina
Kansas, and when the deacon Furches wired for his
pension money and provided his Idaho address he was
to a degree fearful and concerned that a Lamont Street
Bailey that would not travel full across a continent and
partway across an ocean to fetch back a woman that
looked like a four star general might travel merely to
Idaho to fetch one back, but the deacon Furches and
the Lamont Street Stout Bailey stayed on at the Pocatello Motor Hotel for a month and a half apparently
undiscovered and unsoughtafter and when they had
relocated to a rental house just beyond the city limits
the Lamont Street Stout Bailey wrote to her husband a
dear Lamont Street Bailey kiss-off letter on pilfered
Pocatello Motor Hotel stationery and sent along two
insured and registered silver potato pendants for her
daughters but still not the primary Lamont Street Bailey or any of his relations either came looking even
once they knew precisely where to look.

The news did not break in Neely all at once but
broke slowly and in snatches commencing with the
destination of the deacon Furches's pension check followed by an announcement of the disappearance of
the Lamont Street Stout Bailey who was not in Rocky
Mount and was not in Neely and could not be discovered anywhere in between. Then there followed a pe-
riod of several weeks with no additional news and so
most everybody occupied themselves in speculating as
to just what the deacon Furches might be doing in
Idaho and just what brand of mischief might have be-
fallen the Lamont Street Stout Bailey, and nobody
really worked up or even flirted with the theory that
the Lamont Street Stout Bailey might be in Idaho herself and that the deacon Furches himself might be her
brand of mischief so everybody was equally shocked
and surprised when the gist of the dear Lamont Street
Bailey kiss-off letter got printed up in the *Chronicle*

where not the gist or any other part of it was supposed
to get printed up and where not the gist or any other
part of it would have gotten printed up if not for the
Lamont Street Bailey's sister, a Loop Road Bailey
Myrick, who got called in by her distraught brother to
read the letter and soon thereafter let out the contents
of it to the senior editor of the *Chronicle,* the full-
blooded Loop Road Myrick's sister's husband, who felt
an especially acute obligation to print the matter at
hand, partly on account of the matter itself and partly
on account of Mr. Zeno Stiers who was supposed to
have passed away and so had been eulogized and tributized for roundabout a quarter page but who continued to linger at the hospital despite his doctor's
assurances that he would not. So there was the full-
blooded Loop Road Myrick's sister's husband with a
quarter page of *Chronicle* to fill and there was the
Loop Road Bailey Myrick with the majority of poi-
gnant kiss-off letter committed to memory and the rest
of it fabricated straight out and naturally the two of
them got together so as to broadcast the Lamont Street
Bailey's misfortune throughout the county.

Now Mr. Evander Buffaloe, as was the way of
things in the stately Tucker home, got a hold of this
particular *Chronicle* after work of a Wednesday once
Evander Clark II and Vance Johnston had finished
taking it apart and turning it all inside out prior to
putting it back together anyhow they could. It was Mr.
Buffaloe's habit to check on his Pontiac stock at the
outset followed by a quick perusal of the boxscores
when the season called for it and then a look at the
television listings and the weather and Ira Corn on
bridge after which he generally read and ingested an
actual news item or two, and on this particular
Wednesday that Mr. Zoo Stiers lingered at the hospital
and so did not get eulogized and tributized Mr. Buffaloe found his attention fully captured by the headline
"Deacon Absconds with Local Woman" which was a

most strange extraordinary thing to see in the *Chroni-cle* since year in and year out there was usually not much local absconding, not even any regional absconding to speak of. Consequently, Mr. Buffaloe read the article with the greatest of care and then read it through a second time with near about the greatest of care then too after which he folded the paper ever so carefully, laid it across his lap, and ruminated in profound silence right up until suppertime.

He was likely still ruminating over the deacon and the woman and the absconding at the supper table but not any of the Buffaloes could tell really on account of how Mr. Buffaloe seemed naturally disposed towards ponderous silence whether for the cause of legitimate rumination or not, and he did not partake of the general talk and speculation which was concerned chiefly with the deacon and the woman and the absconding and was concerned slightly with the husband and the daughters and the sister and the lingering Mr. Zeno Stiers for whom little could be expressed except grief and considerable wonderment. Martha Porter Buffaloe could not understand exactly why a woman would desert her husband and her children and go off to Idaho in the company of a man with coarse black hairs growing out of the ridge of his nose, and her mother attempted to explain to her how such a thing could come about but decided midway through her explanation that she did not exactly understand why a woman would desert her husband and her children and go off to Idaho in the company of a man with coarse black hairs growing out of the ridge of his nose either. As Vance Johnston Buffaloe saw it the deacon and the woman too should both have some of the shit kicked out of him for being so spineless as to let his wife get away in the first place, but Evander Clark II insisted it was not a matter of coarse black noseridge hairs or shitkicking either but was instead purely an atrocity symptomatic of the moral degeneration inherent in a capitalistic society and he crossed his arms over himself and let his observation lay there on the table with the meatloaf and the potatoes and the butterbeans and not Mrs. Evander Buffaloe or Martha Porter Buffaloe or Vance Johnston Buffaloe either attempted any sort of reply to lay and wallow there with it so Evander Clark II availed himself of the opportunity to expand some on the degenerative qualities inherent in a capitalistic society of which this particular atrocity was merely symptomatic and when he had blown and expanded so as to render himself sufficiently tiresome he drew off a breath and showed every sign of soaring to new and untried heights of tediousness when his daddy, who had not appeared even remotely interested in the nosehairs or the shitkicking or any little pompous fragment of the moral degeneration, did not lay down his fork on the lip of his plate and did not dab at his mouth with his napkin but opened it anyway and said, "I do wish I could find somebody somewhere worth a great big goddamn," and Mrs. Buffaloe dropped her chin some and got herself all set to agree with him until she heard what she was all so set to agree with and then she dropped her chin some more and exclaimed, "Why Evander!" and Martha Porter Buffaloe and Evander Clark II pondered Mr. Buffaloe with some Why Evander! looks of their own but left the additional commenting to their brother, Vance Johnston Buffaloe, who left off grazing on his hunk of meatloaf, picked up his head, and said, "Fucking A, Daddy."

He was not a profane man, not a blasphemous or violent natured man, simply not a man who regularly traded in great big goddamns and so at the introduction of one, especially in the middle of a wholesome meal, Mrs. Evander Buffaloe grew concerned and somewhat agitated and once she had reproved Vance Johnston for his fucking A she turned her entire attention to the great big goddamn and had commenced to

cast around for a gentle reproach to Mr. Buffaloe
when Mr. Buffaloe himself interrupted her direct in
the middle of her hemming and her hawing and said,
"There must be somebody somewhere, somewhere out
of the way maybe, but somewhere anyhow," and then
he dabbed at his mouth and laid his fork against the lip
of his plate and gazed out over Mrs. Buffaloe's head to
the far dining room wall and Mrs. Buffaloe attempted
to reproach him and attempted to reprove him and
attempted to make him sorry and apologetic for having
uttered a vulgarism at the supper table, but Mr. Buffaloe would not be suitably reproached and reproved or
sorry and apologetic either and persisted in gazing out
over Mrs. Buffaloe's head to the far dining room wall
which he pondered with the hollow and near about
haunted expression of a man who fully understands
just how exceedingly rare and elusive a great big goddamn might be.

Some people said later it was the woman but it was
not the woman because he had not even met the
woman yet, and some people said later it was the
menopause and the deacon Furches in combination
that brought it on but it was not the menopause and
was only some little part of the deacon Furches.
Mostly it was everything, everything maybe ending
with and touched off by the local absconding but
everything anyway and not just one or two or three
things but all of it accumulated and heaped together.
The middle block and mortar McKinney said the footings and foundations of Mr. Buffaloe's existence had
given way beneath him which was just the sort of comment the middle block and mortar McKinney made
about most every affair and happenstance there was to
make a comment about but which he was direct on
target with this time on account of how the footings
and foundations of Mr. Buffaloe's existence had given
way beneath him or anyway had sunk and settled appreciably. It seems nothing much had turned out quite

like Mr. Buffaloe had figured it would. He had figured
his children would grow up and move somewhere else,
which they didn't, and he had figured his momma
could not make him feel lowly and disappointing once
she was dead, which she could, and he had figured
American democracy would handily persuade and
overcome a negligible assortment of misguided savage
orientals, which it wasn't able to, and he had figured
the honorable Governor George Corley Wallace for
the thirty-eighth president of these United States,
which he never was, and he figured Pontiac for a
shrewd and perceptive investment, which it did not
turn out to be, and he had figured Elizabeth Taylor
would somehow avoid getting plump and girthsome,
which she eventually got, and he had figured he would
become contented and satisfied with employment at
the slaughterhouse, which he hadn't yet, and he had
figured the Baptist church and its clergy and laymen
and the most of its regular associates and attachments
to be at least near about as stiffly and earnestly forth-
right and upstanding as they claimed to be, which they
weren't not locally anyway any longer, and so now at
last after all his previous figuring and all his subsequent thwarted expectations Mr. Buffaloe went ahead
and decided there was not much left in the world
worth a great big goddamn except maybe for somebody somewhere.

Mrs. Buffaloe gave it out as a vacation, gave it out
as a fishing trip up on the Blue Ridge but when he
departed from the depot he was not in the company of
a pole, was not in fact in the company of any identifi-
able fishing paraphernalia but just a little canvas grip
and ten navel oranges in a plastic mesh bag. Mrs. Buffaloe went with him to the station, went with him right
up onto the bus, mostly because he could not keep her
from it, and she pleaded with him and begged him not
to go or if he had to go to come home in a week or if
he would not come home in a week to come home in

two weeks anyhow and then she laughed ever so lightly and smiled some for the benefit of everybody else who was not to know she was pleading and begging and distraught and finally at length she got run off the bus by the driver and from the pavement waved at Mr. Buffaloe who did not even raise his fingers. And so he was gone and though most everybody knew he had departed nobody knew he was gone really, not even Mrs. Buffaloe who only feared he might be gone and who had in fact been fearing he might up and make off to somewhere ever since the vulgarism at the supper table which seemed to mark Mr. Buffaloe's precipitous abandonment of healthful psychological attitude, or anyway that's what Mrs. Buffaloe's analyst in Greensboro called it once Evander Clark II had persuaded her to visit an analyst in Greensboro on account of her general bafflement and disorientation in the wake of Mr. Buffaloe's fishing trip which nobody much in Neely believed to be a fishing trip any longer and which most everybody had developed ideas and theories about, ideas and theories which covered nearly the entire range of possibilities for a trip on a bus with a grip and a mesh bag full of navel oranges, and wherever people collected and talked they generally set aside some portion of the conversation for serious Buffaloe speculation and while there were those that believed Mr. Buffaloe had run off with a woman or had left to dodge a dark and maybe unlawful past or had embezzled funds from the slaughterhouse or was away taking the cure for tuberculosis or alcoholism or drug addiction not any small group together or even any one person by himself ventured to suppose that Mr. Buffaloe had gone aquesting for that somebody somewhere worth a great big goddamn. That was simply not the sort of thing people figured on from Mr. Buffaloe, not the sort of thing people figured on from anybody really.

Mrs. Buffaloe certainly had not figured on it, had

not expected or anticipated it and with some reason since Mr. Buffaloe, along with not being profane and not being blasphemous and not being violent natured, had never been impetuous either, but the supper table vulgarism had apparently changed all that because Mr. Buffaloe had surely uttered it and had just as surely up and gone on account of it, and they did not hear from him for one week and then two weeks and then three weeks and the fourth week was near about spent when at last there arrived at the Buffaloe household a post-card from Winston-Salem with the picture of a Moravian on it, but there was not any message except for the printed message which told what a Moravian was doing on the front of the postcard anyway, so there was not any indication if Mr. Buffaloe was fine or if he was not fine except for the handwritten address which itself was not much any indication really. Then three weeks later the Buffaloes received a second postcard from Statesville, this one with a picture of a Quality Inn on the front of it and still no message on the back of it, and on the basis of the pair of postcards alone Evander Clark II applied his refined powers of reasoning and perception and announced that his father was heading on a direct line towards the westering sun which struck Evander Clark II as highly metaphorical, and he speculated that a third postcard would arrive from somewhere along about Marion or maybe even Asheville and a third postcard did arrive but from Carowinds instead which was a little left of the westering sun and so deflated the metaphor somewhat.

The postcards did not soothe Mrs. Buffaloe much and after the fourth one had come from Spartanburg South Carolina and the fifth one had arrived from Dahlonega Georgia she went ahead and became distracted and disoriented and most mornings and afternoons too retired to her tiny sewing room up near the peak of the mansard and her wailing and sobbing and moaning carried through the gable window and down to the street where people heard her and so figured they could entirely rule out fishing as a possibility. Of course it was the distraction and the disorientation, manifested primarily in the wailing and the sobbing and the moaning, that prompted Evander Clark II to carry his momma to the analyst in Greensboro and the analyst listened to her and nodded at her and though he could not cure and relieve Mrs. Buffaloe he did impoverish her successfully which returned her to the sewing room to wail and sob and moan without the professional listening and without the professional nodding, and after a spell it seemed to curious pedestrians and to neighbors roundabout the stately Tucker home that the noisome laments had diminished appreciably but this was primarily a false impression due to chill weather which had caused the sewing room window to get shut. The actual distraction and disorientation, not to mention the wailing and the sobbing and the moaning, did not fall off any because Mrs. Buffaloe found she grew increasingly fond of Mr. Buffaloe the longer he stayed gone to wherever it was he was gone to and nobody knew where he was gone to any longer or even where he'd been to lately on account of how the postcards stopped coming seven months after they'd started coming, so Mrs. Buffaloe could not ask herself why Mr. Buffaloe was in Winston-Salem or Statesville or at Carowinds or in Spartanburg or Dahlonega but instead had to settle for some general, un-directed blubbering which she had a talent for and carried out in a most successful and pathetic sort of way and thereby struck up considerable sympathy and pity among her neighbors and acquaintances who by that time had ruled out tuberculosis and alcoholism and drug addiction along with the fishing.

The Buffaloes got by a little more than passably well on the income from the Rexall and the income from Purdy Electric and the income from the slaughterhouse which had been a paltry income but got elevated to a respectable income once Evander Clark II assumed his daddy's bookkeeping position which he assured the Brownlee brothers he was entirely capable of since he had in fact resided upon a college campus for the best part of two years and had in fact received several documented hours of college credit. So the majority of the Buffaloes got by after Mr. Buffaloe's departure just about like they had gotten by before it except for the absence of the mouthdabbing and the forklaying and the opiniongiving which they had not ever paid much attention to anyhow, and it was only the solitary Buffaloe that remained affected and even she left off the wailing and the sobbing and the moaning and the most of the undirected blubbering after Mr. Buffaloe had been gone for a year and she got numb instead and suffered spells of catatonia which was still affliction enough but wasn't nearly so noisome and aggravating as the wailing and the sobbing and the moaning had been.

They did not any of them ever hear direct from Mr. Buffaloe again after the postcard from Dahlonega, and they did not any of them hear indirect from Mr. Buffaloe either for nearly two years and probably would not have ever heard tell of him anymore if Mr. Phillip J. King had not gone off in the fall of the year to visit his sister's son in Copperhill Tennessee and there in the broadest part of the afternoon direct in front of the Copperhill Legion hall, or actually direct in front of the iron cannon and pile of welded cannonballs in front of the Copperhill Legion hall, Mr. Phillip J. King met on the sidewalk Mr. Evander Buffaloe in the company of a large yellowhaired woman in a clingy, silky sort of dress who had ahold of Mr. Buffaloe's right bicep, and Mr. Phillip J. King said he did not openly greet Mr. Buffaloe but did incline his head some and Mr. Buffaloe parted his lips and showed his brown tooth. "Bottled blonde," Mr. Phillip J. King told it, and told it to Mr. Emmet Dabb and Tiny Aaron and

Mr. Wyatt Benbow and Mr. Louis Benfield and Coley Britt, "and Lord God Almighty pure melons out to here and I do mean pure melons," and Tiny Aaron spat and said, "Shitfire," and everybody else agreed with the spirit of the observation. They decided to tell a Buffaloe, decided it was their obligation to tell a Buffaloe, and they selected Vance Johnston on account of how a yellowhaired, purely meloned woman was right in his line and he answered the news with some sort of shitfire of his own, though not precisely a shitfire exactly, and then went off to the stately Tucker home where Mr. Phillip J. King and Mr. Emmet Dabb and Tiny Aaron and Mr. Wyatt Benbow and Mr. Louis Benfield and Coley Britt all figured he would disperse and distribute the news, and maybe he did disperse and distribute it to his brother and sister who never let on that they knew though likely they did know, but his momma remained numb and silent and so probably did not ever get told and did not ever find out that Mr. Evander Buffaloe had eventually and actually hunted up somebody somewhere worth a great big goddamn or some little piece of one anyway.

Of course come the October after the summer we lost the bald Jeeter Mrs. Evander Buffaloe was still relatively numb and still relatively silent and prior to gassing up the car Evander Clark II had turned her loose in Mr. Musselwhite's converted muleshed at the chance she might find some pleasure and distraction in the snake oil or the leisurewear or the fruits and vegetables or the assorted pork cuts or the crusted and mildewed geegaws or any of the other accumulated refuse Mr. Musselwhite called his inventory, but Mrs. Evander Buffaloe did not seem to find any pleasure and did not seem to find any distraction, did not even seem to look for any really, and stayed precisely where Evander Clark II had put her there direct in front of Mr. Musselwhite and his cigarette rack. Being relatively numb and relatively silent, Mrs. Evander Buffaloe had not lately produced much in the way of conversation but Mr. Musselwhite talked at length with her anyhow because she was upright and drew breath which was about all he ever required. He told her most everything he told everybody else commencing with a comment on the general seasonableness of the weather which happened to be the case on that particular day of that particular October after the summer we lost the bald Jeeter, but Mr. Musselwhite was certainly as capable and adept with observations on the unseasonableness of the weather also if conditions called for them. Being a man of methodical and organized faculties, Mr. Musselwhite followed up his specific comments with a rambling local history of the annual rainfall, or more truly a rambling local history of the lack of appreciable annual rainfall which was the general and ordinary case roundabout, but even talk of the rain that did not fall prompted Mr. Musselwhite to a word or two on the ache that set into his joints when the rain that did not usually fall actually fell and the topic of aching joints regularly put Mr. Musselwhite in mind of Mrs. Musselwhite's hernia which she would not go under the knife for on account of her fear of modern medicine, and Mr. Musselwhite said he did not think much of modern medicine himself and he asked Mrs. Buffaloe had she ever gotten operated on to which she did not reply but simply looked at Mr. Musselwhite precisely how she'd looked at him all along and if Mr. Musselwhite had known what a lobotomy was he might have figured she'd had one.

Mr. Musselwhite was just getting onto the topic of healthful eating habits which would lead him to a comment or two on the virtues of fruits and fresh vegetables which would in turn put him onto the subject of gardening and so carry him back at last to the local annual rainfall, but he was only partway through his disquisition on chewing when the glass doors swung open, and a tall, lean, pointy, hollowed out, angular,

and otherwise unremarkable figure passed in through
them and did not go to the drinkbox or the Nab and
peanut rack and did not even attempt to appear interested in the great glut of merchandise all around him
but straightaway stepped up abreast of Mrs. Buffaloe
and asked Mr. Musselwhite across the counter, "You
know who I am?" to which Mr. Musselwhite did not
have a suitable reply on account of how the chewing
disquisition had at the moment monopolized his
powers of thought, which is just the sort of thing a
disquisition will do, so Mr. Musselwhite got shown
barrelfirst a Harrington and Richardson Buntline revolver of extraordinarily high caliber and almost simultaneously had his testicles threatened with a place
called Merry Oaks which they were not in the vicinity
of at the present moment but which Mr. Musselwhite
was made to understand they could readily be dispatched to.

Now Mr. Musselwhite had been waiting to get
robbed ever since the actual muleshed, had been anticipating and preparing for it, and so once the demand
for the contents of the cash drawer was made outright
Mr. Musselwhite immediately reached his arm in the
general direction of the register but not to the register
precisely and instead more directly to a shelf underneath the register where Mr. Musselwhite kept his
single-action .22-caliber Savage revolver loaded with six
long rifle hollowpoint shells which he figured would be
near about as thoroughly damaging and destructive as
any solid high caliber bullet, even an extraordinarily
high caliber one, and which in fact turned out to be as
thoroughly damaging and destructive judging from the
hole Mr. Musselwhite made in the cash register which
was the first thing he shot. It was probably the adrena-
line part of it and the frightening part of it and the
double-thumbed cocking action part of it along with
the anticipation of the ducking and squatting part of it

which caused Mr. Musselwhite to neglect the aiming
part of it and consequently he hit direct between the
three dollar button and the thirty cent button prior to
dropping into a pile on the floor and he had both
thumbs on the hammer and was commencing to draw
it back again when the tall, lean, pointy, hollowed out,
angular, and otherwise unremarkable culprit squeezed
off a retaliatory round and the Harrington and Richardson Buntline revolver of extraordinarily high caliber discharged like a thunderclap while the bullet
which had been intended for Mr. Musselwhite's testicles flew high and wide into a flint display. Mr. Musselwhite answered with a shot of his own which he
managed to put past the cash register and send clean
across the store into a Pepsi-Cola wall clock and he
had just successfully piled up on the floor again when
the Harrington and Richardson Buntline revolver ex-
ploded a second time and opened up a large jagged
hole in a one pound can of Flying Dutchman aromatic
tobacco which was just above the cigarette rack which
was just beyond Mrs. Evander Buffaloe who had
blinked three times now on account of the pistol reports but had not gone anywhere really, had not even
drawn herself in noticeably so as to make a smaller
target and in the heat of the moment Mr. Musselwhite
decided he would use her for cover and so rose up
behind Mrs. Evander Buffaloe to squeeze off his third
round which hit dead onto an assortment of carnival
glass and got answered straightaway by an additional
thunderclap from the Buntline revolver and an additional jagged hole in the one pound can of Flying
Dutchman aromatic tobacco. Rounds four and five
from Mr. Musselwhite's .22-caliber single-action Savage found out a two liter Truade and a slab of salt pork
respectively and the Buntline revolver responded with
some wholesale destruction to the cigarette rack which
left two bullets altogether and Mr. Musselwhite squandered his on a cantaloupe while the tall, lean, pointy,

hollowed out, angular, and otherwise unremarkable
culprit fled with his to the door before discharging it
full into Mr. Musselwhite's gasoline pump control box
which did not please Mr. Musselwhite much and he
returned fire with an indelicate and near about searing
obscenity that was the closest thing he had to a bullet.

Evander Clark II had heard the shots but had not
known they were shots since he had not ever been ex-
posed to any real-life gunfire previously, and he had
seen the culprit but had not actually looked at the culprit on account of how he was not in the habit of studying and looking at people but preferred to allow them
to ponder and contemplate him without the worry of
getting caught at it. Consequently Evander Clark II
was vaguely aware of some noise and was vaguely
aware of some activity roundabout the doorway but
had not become truly and clearly aware of anything
really until the gaspump shut down which he went
ahead and noticed outright just as Mr. Musselwhite
stepped out from the converted muleshed in a fit of
wild and frantic profanation directed first around the
left corner of the building and then around the right
front corner and finally on up among the hillocks and
creases of the pasture which the tall, lean, pointy, hollowed out, angular, and otherwise unremarkable culprit apparently had escaped into. Of course Evander
Clark II, who had paid cash money for seventeen dollars' worth of Citgo regular, wanted to know straight
off just precisely why the pump had shut down at only
thirteen dollars and twenty-eight cents and so he set
out around the converted muleshed and hunted up Mr.
Musselwhite who was still venting himself towards the
hillside when Evander Clark II caught up with him and
quizzed him on the gaspump and quizzed him on the
remaining three dollars and seventy-two cents' worth
of Citgo regular and generally made himself suitably
impertinent and intolerable about the entire business
until Mr. Musselwhite turned full around to look at

him and so revealed in his hand the .22-caliber single-action Savage revolver which captured a goodly portion of Evander Clark II's attention.

"You get a look at him?" Mr. Musselwhite wanted to know.

"At who?" Evander Clark II said somewhat to Mr. Musselwhite but primarily to his pistol.

"That shitass come running out the door," Mr. Musselwhite told him. "You saw him didn't you?"

"I saw somebody," Evander Clark II said, "but I wasn't paying much attention."

"Didn't you hear the gunfire, boy?"

"Is that what that was?"

"Christ Almighty son, me and your momma near about got shot to pieces."

"Shot to pieces!" Evander Clark II said and grew somewhat wild and frantic himself.

"Don't worry, she's all right," Mr. Musselwhite told him. "I mean she ain't exactly all right but she's like she was when she come in, don't you know. I mean it weren't no harm but it weren't no cure either."

Mr. Musselwhite called the sheriff's office but the sheriff was out on official business which likely meant parking violations or some such so Mr. Musselwhite left word of the attempted robbery with Miss Hawkes who worked the switchboard and he made a point to tell her, "Shots were fired," which was how they said it on television whenever shots were fired and consequently the sheriff arrived presently, or probably more shortly than presently and maybe even straightaway propelled as he was by the prospect of gunfire and bodily injury, and he came squealing and skidding to a halt before the converted muleshed and rushed on inside where he did not greet anybody exactly but approached Mr. Musselwhite right off and said, "Square teeth? Pointy nose? Sunk-in eyes? Tall?"

"Tall what?" Mr. Musselwhite asked him.

"Just plain tall, six foot something or another."

And Mr. Musselwhite nodded yes sir.

"That's our boy," the sheriff told him and he turned to Mrs. Buffaloe off his right shoulder and said, "I knew he'd show up. I had it all mapped and figured."

And Mrs. Buffaloe blinked her eyes and dropped her chin some and asked him, "Evander?"

And the sheriff took ahold of Evander Clark II by the sleeve and said to him, "Son, do something with this woman."

Sheriff Burton got most of the pertinent facts himself from Mr. Musselwhite and collected a slight bit of trifling and vague information from Evander Clark II prior to turning the scene of the crime over to his deputy Mr. Larson who fished around for some facts himself and dug in the walls with his knife after the bullets and drank a Pepsi and drank a root beer and ate a peach dumpling and then lamented with Mr. Musselwhite on the hole in his cash register and the holes in his tobacco tin and the holes in his cigarette rack and in his cantaloupe and his slab of fatback and together they collected by the milky fragments of carnival glass and tried to make them into the serving bowl that they had been previously but could not. Sheriff Burton rode the perimeters of Mr. Musselwhite's pasture in his patrol car and stopped at whatever houses or solitary individuals he came up on to ask information which he did not get much of any of except from a Carothers who had been grubbing rocks in a potato field the most of the day who had possibly seen somebody, maybe even a square toothed, pointy nosed, sunken eyed, just plain tall somebody though he could not be certain and maybe it was in the pine thicket along the northern border of his field though he could not be certain of that either but the sheriff crept and snuck and generally stepped lightly into the undergrowth anyway with the heel of his right hand on the simulated pearl handle of his nickel-plated .357 service revolver, and when he got into the midst of the pine grove where there was not any undergrowth but just needles and pine treetrunks and some bright and some shadowy places he drew his gun and cocked it which he did not get to do much except in the evenings in Mrs. Messick's upstairs, and once he'd stayed in the pine thicket long enough to satisfy himself that he had stayed in the pine thicket long enough he backed out around the treetrunks and through the undergrowth and into the potato field again convinced that the somebody the Carothers had possibly seen possibly in the pine thicket was not there any longer if he'd ever been there in the first place, and the sheriff rode the perimeters of Mr. Musselwhite's property all over again and rode the perimeters of Mr. Musselwhite's neighbors' property also and struck out in a generally northwest direction for a ways but did not discover anything of significance and so at last returned along the boulevard to the square and to his office and to the map on his back office wall which he stuck a new yellowheaded thumbtack in and a new silverheaded thumbtack in prior to laying back in his office chair, throwing his feet across one corner of his desktop, and telling himself, "Busick in Draper, McIver in Harrison Crossroads, Barnard in Bethel, Grissom in Locust Hill, Stem in Union Ridge, Troutman in Altamahaw, Ross in Hillsdale, Spencer in Midway, Musselwhite in Neely," and then he pinched his bottom lip between his thumb and forefinger and pondered and speculated and eventually told himself, "$147.00 and $189.00 and $123.00 and $155.00 and $78.00 and $230.00 and $112.00 and $150.00 and no dollars at all," and then without setting his feet to the floor or raising himself from his chair on account of he had learned and memorized them too he went ahead and told himself, "Corinth and Duncan and Wilbon and Angier and Holly Springs and Kipling and Fuquay-Varina and Lemly and Merry Oaks," and he let loose of his lip which he had continued to pinch all throughout his pondering and his speculating and he raised his lip holding hand up above his head and then smacked it down on the desktop and told himself, "Hotdamn."

THE FIRST one arrived along about October in a pink envelope and the fat Jeeter carried it from the trailer down to the chickenhouse where she gave it over to Mr. Raeford Lynch who sniffed at it and yipped once or twice and then sniffed at it again prior to giving it over to Benton Lynch who did not sniff at it or even look at it really but put it direct in his jacket pocket over the protests of his momma and the protests of his daddy who wanted to know was it a serious affection and who wanted to know did she come from nice people and who wanted to know when did it start up in the first place and who wanted to know could they meet her sometime presently to all of which Benton Lynch responded with a couple of yeses and a couple of noes and nothing much else of any utility to the fat Jeeter and nothing much else of any utility to Mr. Raeford either who chiefly was desirous to learn did Benton Lynch get some and so asked him straightaway once the fat Jeeter had struck out up the hillside and he was all set to wonder how if it was yes and to wonder why not if it was no, but it was not yes or no, was not anything but the usual vacant expression, and Mr. Raeford grew anxious and restless on account of having pondered the topic in the first place and so spat on a chicken to distract and relieve himself some.

Benton Lynch carried the pink envelope off into the woods to open it and sat down under a sweetgum tree where he extracted the pages but did not study them straight off on account of how Jane Elizabeth Firesheets had enclosed a dose of her personal scent along with them and the aroma took hold of Benton Lynch and caused him to recollect in considerable detail the milky whiteness and the plum-colored parts also, particularly the plum-colored parts, and he remembered the funny little way she had to gyrating and squirming and bouncing about and consequently he had to stand up and adjust himself in his trousers before proceeding with the actual words on the actual pages which did not convey much in the way of new or ordinary information either but took the form of questions primarily, questions about himself and about what he was doing and about who he was doing it with and about what sort of weather they were doing it in. There was some little passing reference to Chalybeate Springs and the daddy Firesheets's prospects as a tobacco farmer and slight scandalous mention of the brother Firesheets, who Jane Elizabeth did not seem to have developed a fondness for, followed by a sweltering conclusion which dealt in rather specific detail with precisely what Jane Elizabeth Firesheets would do to Benton Lynch if she could get her fingers on the parts of him she would do it to, and though Benton Lynch had experienced precisely that sort of therapy on several previous occasions and had seen any number of photographs of the undertaking in progress on the backs of his cousin Jerome Lynch's playing cards, he had never read it in words before and was prompted to stand up all over again and adjust himself once he realized how mighty the pen could be.

Benton Lynch did not write back straightaway mostly because he did not have any idea of exactly what to write since there was not anything he wanted to know and there was not anything he wanted to tell and since there was not anything at all he desired of Jane Elizabeth Firesheets that could be satisfied in a correspondence. And once he did not write back straightaway and once he continued to not write back he received a second pink envelope which contained a heavily scented letter of its own which itself was as thoroughly inquisitive as the previous one though perhaps more pointedly so. Jane Elizabeth Firesheets wanted to know who he was seeing and what he was doing with her and she wished to inform him that if he was in fact doing something with somebody she would go ahead and end it all, meaning herself primarily. Consequently, Benton Lynch decided he'd best sit down and write a letter anyhow even though there still was not anything he wanted to know and not much of anything he wanted to say except for a denial of the something he was accused of doing with somebody and only that so as to keep the milky parts and the plum-colored parts also from any sort of untimely ruin. He did not have much practice at letter writing since he had not ever written but one and that not an actual and verifiable letter really but more towards your note variety to his Aunt Vergie Lynch Newcombe, wife of the jackleg Pentecostal preacher, thanking her for the argyle socks she sent to him on his fourteenth birthday, and the fat Jeeter had dictated the whole business to him so in truth he had not ever conceived and executed even a note which rendered the prospect of an actual and verifiable letter all the more overpowering. He sat down to write it a variety of times and locations, first of a morning in the chickenhouse but his daddy and the chickens would not give him the peace to accomplish much, and then of an afternoon at the dinette but he found himself distracted by the television and the crackle and rattle of the graham cracker wrapper along with the inquiries of the fat Jeeter at the commercials when she'd want to know was it a serious affection and did she come from nice people and when did it start up in the first place and could she meet her sometime presently. He made some slight headway of an evening after supper under the sweetgum tree where he laid his solitary leaf of paper across his thigh and singlehandedly constructed the salutation which was not presently in the spirit of the Dear Sweetheart that came in the pink envelopes but was more along the lines of a plain Dear Jane Elizabeth Firesheets which still had some warmth to it and about as much outright treacle as Benton Lynch could muster. He managed an opening few lines in the how are you I am fine vein of personal correspondence and surprised himself with an extended flurry of weather talk and speculation prior to running dry which gave him the occasion to chew on his pencil and gnaw on a stick and suck on a weed and toss a sweetgum ball in the air.

He finished the letter four days after he'd started the letter and even then it barely surpassed the argyle socks note in overall length and hardly approached it in substance but somehow or another Benton Lynch did manage to suggest and imply while attempting to state outright that he was not doing anything with anybody, that he did not know anybody to do anything with, and that even if he did know somebody who was willing to do something the something they would do likely could not even begin to measure up with the something him and Jane Elizabeth Firesheets had done previously the pleasant recollection of which prevented Benton Lynch from attempting the same something with anybody else, that is if he could find anybody else to attempt the same something with him, on account of how he was satisfied in his own mind that nobody anywhere could do anything the way Jane Elizabeth Firesheets could do it.

Jane Elizabeth Firesheets herself shot back a pink-enveloped reply to Benton Lynch's argyle-socks-note-length letter bearing the news that she had decided not to end it all since Benton Lynch had made his feelings for her more plain and open and as a token of her undying passion and regard she enclosed in a piece of Saran Wrap a lock of wheatstraw hair she'd clipped herself and Benton Lynch held it up between his fingers and studied it all over but could not determine from where exactly. The correspondence proceeded thereafter somewhat briskly on the pink-enveloped end of it and a little less briskly but with considerable regularity on the note-length end of it and carried on throughout the fall of the year and into winter when Benton Lynch received, along with his usual pink envelope, a tin of Christmas cookies which Jane Elizabeth Firesheets had baked herself and which he did not discover even a solitary strand of stray wheatstraw hair in. His momma bought for him at the drugstore a plastic hairclip that he stuck in his subsequent note-length letter and in her reply Jane Elizabeth Firesheets managed to pass into pure raptures over it like maybe Benton Lynch had not merely mailed it but had possibly conceived of a necessity and an application for the thing and so had gone ahead and invented it himself. But not the sight of the pink envelope or the Dear Sweetheart or the pure raptures or even the somewhat sultry and provocative talk at the close, which had become a regular feature of Jane Elizabeth Firesheet's correspondence, stirred Benton Lynch much by the time January came around on account of how his lengthy separation from the milky white contours and the plum-colored features also had caused his affections to fade considerably which he realized foremost in his trousers where there was not much cause for adjustment any longer. When an oversized pink envelope arrived the second weekend in February, Benton Lynch did not bother to open it for two days and when he did bother to open it at last he just read the first of it and the end of it and did not ever read the middle of it since by the second weekend in February there was not cause for any adjustment any longer and Benton Lynch recollected the milky contours and the plum-colored features only dimly when he attempted to recollect them at all.

The first week in March all the Firesheets together picked up and moved to Chalybeate Springs where they took up residence in what Jane Elizabeth Firesheets called a cottage, and she provided in a pink envelope an extended description of the area roundabout that Benton Lynch read half of since by the first week

in March he did not have any affection at all for Jane
Elizabeth Firesheets, at least not any that he could discover, so he did not send off an argyle-socks-note-
length reply to the Chalybeate Springs travelogue
letter, and when the second pink envelope of March
showed up on the dinette with the premium notice and
the pizza coupons Benton Lynch was not excited like
he had been excited previously and was not embarrassed like he had been embarrassed previously but
was just plain annoyed like he had not been annoyed
before. He could not comprehend, could not even
begin to fathom, why he had ever felt at all strongly
about the milky whiteness and the plum-colored parts
also and at a distance of some months he could not say
truly just what had made the pondbank therapeutics so
savory and attractive to him. He had trouble recollect-
ing what Jane Elizabeth Firesheets even looked like
exactly and he did not think of her at all for days at a
time and so had fairly completely returned to his natural pointy, gangly, toothsome, and primarily vacant
state and likely Benton Lynch, who mostly simply was
not previously, would have become entirely unblatant
and completely unoutright all over again if not for
Jimmy, just plain Jimmy, who showed up in the third
pink envelope of March right there at the outset of a
sentence. "Jimmy," it said, "helped Daddy shore up
the porch floor," and since Jimmy was not the brother
Firesheets and was not the granddaddy Firesheets and
was not the uncle Firesheets as far as Benton Lynch
could tell, that left him to be somebody else, somebody else who had not gotten mentioned previously on
the page and did not get explained subsequently on the
page and so was construed to be a mysterious somebody else, maybe a neighbor and perhaps even a relation, but surely a male somebody else and so naturally
equipped for therapeutics and modest acrobatics and
any other activity performable on a pondbank in addition to watching a cork bobber.

In the fourth pink envelope of March, which was the last pink envelope of March, Jimmy cut a dead limb off a hickory tree with his chainsaw and got asked to supper, which was somewhat of an advancement from shoring up porch flooring, but he still did not get explained sufficiently, or not sufficiently anyway to entirely satisfy Benton Lynch who had figured for a while he was entirely satisfied but then discovered that he wasn't, so the fourth pink envelope of March, which was the last pink envelope of March, got answered with a letter that in sheer bulk and magnitude far outstripped anything Benton Lynch had ever before accomplished with a pencil. He made some trifling statements, asked several dull and harmless questions, ventured on a serious observation or two, and threw in a couple of veiled inquiries as to the identity and motives of the Jimmy in question, highly veiled inquiries, so highly veiled in fact as to be senseless and impenetrable, and consequently the first pink envelope of April did not supply Benton Lynch with any satisfying information about the Jimmy in question except that he tarred around the cottage chimney and made the granddaddy Firesheets a walking stick from a portion of rhododendron stalk which was pertinent maybe and illuminating to a degree but not at all satisfying to Benton Lynch who was only just coming to realize how extremely dissatisfied he was.

Mostly he hadn't ever been anything previously, not dissatisfied or satisfied either and certainly not troubled and impassioned on account of a woman, or on account of those parts of a woman that men generally get troubled and impassioned on account of which is not usually the intellect or the sense of humor or any little portion of the rest of the temperament but most generally falls in the category of milky white parts and plum-colored parts also. And in this particular case Benton Lynch had not had the occasion to anticipate and desire and long for free run over Jane Elizabeth

Firesheet's milky white and plum-colored parts since he had gotten it even before he knew he wanted it and so was pressed to work up an appetite after the meal had already commenced which somehow he accomplished with measurable and thoroughgoing success. But ever since January when the recollection of Jane Elizabeth Firesheet's chief attributes—which would be the pointy and prominent portions of her upper torso and the flexible and gyrating portions of her lower torso—had commenced to fade from Benton Lynch's consciousness and from his trousers also he had not been much troubled and impassioned and not much dissatisfied either, and likely he would have remained untroubled and unimpassioned and undissatisfied if not for the Jimmy of Chalybeate Springs who shoored up porch flooring and cut hickory limbs and ate supper and tarred chimneys and made rhododendron walking sticks and who possibly as well got some access to those parts of Jane Elizabeth Firesheets that Benton Lynch himself had touched with his own fingers and who possibly got some access also to those parts that Benton Lynch himself had examined otherwise. Consequently, it was not really his absence from Jane Elizabeth Firesheet's chief attributes that troubled Benton Lynch so but was more truly the likelihood or the suspicion or maybe just the vague and bothersome notion that the milky white and plum-colored parts, which had been his entirely, were not his entirely any longer, so naturally Benton Lynch, who had never been much of anything before, began to be a jackass.

The first week of April he wrote Jane Elizabeth Firesheets the second in what would be a series of fairly massive and magnitudinous letters, and unlike the first of the massive and magnitudinous letters in which Benton Lynch exhausted a sizable piece of being trifling and dull and harmless, he went direct to inquisitive in the second one, or direct to inquisitive following the Dear Sweetheart anyway, and he came straight

out with some questions and some accusations and a
palpable threat or two and then dispatched the thing
and waited in an agitated state for a reply, which was
extraordinary and novel for Benton Lynch since he
had never been in an agitated state previously, but he
did not get soothed much when the first pink envelope
of April did at last arrive on account of how Jane Elizabeth Firesheets failed to confirm much of anything
and failed to deny much of anything and failed to say
much of anything substantial except for "Jimmy" when
she told how he'd clipped the bushes and glazed a window and puttied up a hole in the wall, and even though
clipping and glazing and puttying aren't your usual in-
timate activities the idea of Jimmy in the shrubbery
and Jimmy at the windowlight and Jimmy in the very
bowels of the cottage with his spackling and his knife
seared and agonized Benton Lynch like so many fire-
coals and so it was in a wounded and tormented state
that he sent out the third in the series of fairly massive
and magnitudinous letters, and since he was not accustomed to being wounded and was not accustomed to
being tormented he failed to stir any sympathy to
speak of in Jane Elizabeth Firesheets who did not
reply immediately to the third massive and magnitudinous letter and so got a fourth one straightaway since
Benton Lynch figured the third one had got misplaced
or misrouted or had maybe got read and misinter-
preted, and though he commenced the fourth massive
and magnitudinous letter in the same wounded and
tormented state that had carried him through the third
one he managed to become purely frantic along about
the midway point prior to lapsing into a truly pathetic
lament that culminated in the love and kisses and the
jagged indecipherable scrawl beneath it.

Jane Elizabeth Firesheets did in fact answer the
fourth massive and magnitudinous letter, or actually
did in fact answer the third massive and magnitudinous
letter but not until she'd already received the fourth

one, and in her reply she admitted to harboring an
affection for the Jimmy of Chalybeate Springs, and
though for the sake of Benton Lynch's wounded and
tormented feelings she did not cleanly admit to having
harbored anything else for him, be it on a pondbank or
in a grassy clearing or maybe even in a bed somewhere, Benton Lynch well enough comprehended the
implications and well enough comprehended the open
admission and while he managed to persevere through
Jane Elizabeth Firesheet's explanation of natural juices
and savage passionate urges, he was not comforted by
it much and felt instead like he'd been sliced open with
a handscythe and left to die. The fat Jeeter and Mr.
Raeford Lynch, especially Mr. Raeford Lynch, could
not fully understand how their boy could be hollowed
out and pointy and angular and vacant like usual one
week and then agitated and tormented and wounded
and frantic and pathetic and plainly agonized the next,
and they were beginning to grow concerned, or actually it was the fat Jeeter who was beginning to grow
concerned and who had suggested to Mr. Raeford
Lynch that he'd best begin to grow concerned also,
which he had himself begun to do on account of the
general sway the fat Jeeter's suggestions held with him,
when Benton Lynch up and departed in the first week
of the month of May, which would have been the May
of the spring before the summer we lost the bald
Jeeter, and not even with a sack this time or any shirts
except for the one on him and with hardly any notion
of just where he was going aside from the name of the
place which he told to the man that picked him up on
the highway who threw his car in gear and asked him,
"What?"

Likely he would have arrived at Chalybeate Springs
sooner than he did arrive there if he'd had any idea
where it was, which he didn't, or if anybody that
picked him up had had any idea where it was, which
they didn't either, so he toured several southeastern

counties in an assortment of vehicles and with a great variety of people and almost entirely without incident except for the marine from Fayetteville who desired Benton Lynch to render him a service which Benton Lynch was neither inclined nor oriented to render nor could even accurately imagine for that matter. He did not actually get to the cottage until nightfall and only then after some exhaustive inquiring which Benton Lynch was not much accomplished at since he preferred yeses and noes to all other forms of human communication, and by the time he did arrive at the cottage it had already stopped being a cottage or maybe had not yet become a cottage entirely because it appeared a shack instead that maybe had been a cottage once or maybe would be a cottage presently but would have to stop being a hovel first which it truly was but got flattered and elevated by the darkness.

He did not knock on the door straightaway but lingered under an ivy-laden chinaberry tree in the corner of the frontyard for a while and looked in the windows where he could see the granddaddy Firesheets talking at the daddy Firesheets and on occasion getting talked at back and where he could every now and again get a glimpse of the momma Firesheets and the brother Firesheets and for one fleeting moment a piece of Jane Elizabeth Firesheet's wheatstraw hair which gave him the nervous stomach and so instead of stepping up onto the cottage porch and knocking on the cottage door, Benton Lynch circled round to the backyard and hunted up the outhouse which he got caught making use of by the brother Firesheets who near about sat down on top of him. They were pleased to see him in the majority; even the brother Firesheets himself gave Benton Lynch a suitable greeting once he'd recovered from his own case of the nervous stomach which he had contracted at the outhouse and remedied there also. The momma Firesheets offered him a hunk of spongecake and the daddy Firesheets offered him a chair and the granddaddy Firesheets offered him an opinion as to the perils of hitchhiking in the modern day and the brother Firesheets offered him an apology for having near about sat his bare bottom down on Benton Lynch's bare topside.

As for Jane Elizabeth Firesheets, she hung back noticeably from the conversation in general and hung back noticeably from Benton Lynch's person in particular and could not be encouraged to be sociable by her mother who attempted to encourage her and by her daddy who attempted to encourage her and by her granddaddy who attempted to encourage her and even by her brother who endeavored to badger and insult her into an outburst. She simply would not have anything much to do with Benton Lynch and did not appear at all pleased to see him and exhibited her displeasure in a dark corner of the room where she sulked and brooded and just generally failed to enliven to talk any. The granddaddy Firesheets recollected one by one every Lynch he'd ever met up with in every place he'd ever been to and quizzed Benton Lynch on his relation to them, and when he was able to in between Lynches, the daddy Firesheets probed and sounded out Benton Lynch's knowledge of tobacco and tobacco farming. The momma Firesheets hoped out loud that Benton Lynch was enjoying the spongecake which Benton Lynch told her yes ma'am he was and the brother Firesheets called his sister a twatheaded moron in an attempt to fire her up some which judging from the sudden separation of her bottom lip from her top lip he succeeded at and likely she would have offered up some sort of utterance or another if not for her granddaddy who recollected a whole load of Lynches in Zebulon and wanted to know from Benton Lynch where they his Lynches or not.

They could not offer him a place to sleep in the house on account of it was a cottage-sized house or a shack-sized hovel, depending on the light, and so instead they offered him a place to sleep in the barn which was a regular barn-sized barn with the usual haysmell and manurestink and ammonia pockets, and he stepped off the backporch and struck out across the yard in the company of Jane Elizabeth Firesheets who carried a blanket over one arm and a quilt over the other and who had not been much enthused at the prospect of leading Benton Lynch across the yard to the regular barn-sized barn but had been encouraged to do so by her granddaddy and her momma and flat out directed to do so by her daddy and so did so, or was in the process of doing so anyhow midway between the porch and the barn when Benton Lynch snatched her by the elbow and spun her around to face him and probably would have said some sort of fiery thing to her if he had not used up the best part of his passion and agitation in the snatching and the spinning and so could only ponder her in a helpless and pathetic sort of way and got pondered back briefly prior to getting snapped and hissed at.

"What are you doing here?" Jane Elizabeth Firesheets wanted to know.

"It's May," Benton Lynch told her. "We said May. You said May."

"Well, it's all different now," she said. "That was then and this is now, and it's all different," and she tried to turn around and set back out towards the barn but Benton Lynch snatched her by the elbow again and spun her to him.

"Why's it all different?" he asked her.

"It just is."

And Jane Elizabeth Firesheets did spin around successfully and did set back out towards the barn and would have gone ahead and arrived there if Benton Lynch had not said, "Jimmy?" just plain Jimmy in a flatout spiteful sort of way which stopped Jane Elizabeth Firesheets where she was and very nearly spun her around all over again but not quite, so instead she addressed Benton Lynch with her backside primarily and advised him against any hasty and ill-considered judgments on account of how he would be talking about the man she loved.

"Him?" Benton Lynch said.

"He is my soulmate," Jane Elizabeth Firesheets told him.

"Your soulmate?" Benton Lynch said, openly perplexed.

And regardless of just who she was telling it to, Jane Elizabeth Firesheets turned around with her face all opened up in a grin and said, "He's a regular prince," and she closed up the gap between herself and Benton Lynch that she had only recently opened up and with her mouth still laid full out she told him, "Jimmy says me and him's like gears in a machine, not neither one of us any good without the other. Appears to me he's got the poet in his blood, don't you think?" And though it had not seemed physically possible for Jane Elizabeth Firesheets to grin any more completely than she was grinning already, the points of her mouth went ahead and disappeared around her jawbones.

Benton Lynch could not rein in his agitation and torment straightaway, but that did not matter much on account of how Jane Elizabeth Firesheet's personal euphoria kept her from noticing the agitation and kept her from noticing the torment, near about kept her from noticing any little part of Benton Lynch or big part either, so he had the leisure to collect and gather up his composure and when the fit had passed and he felt reasonably unagitated and untormented again, he said to Jane Elizabeth Firesheets, "I figured me and you was like gears in a machine. I figured we wasn't not neither one of us any good without the other."

"Oh, Benton," Jane Elizabeth Firesheets said and freed her right arm from the blanket so as to touch Benton Lynch with the tipends of her fingers, "we didn't have nothing much but a night or two and now it's all a fond recollection that will fade and dwindle like all recollections do. Jimmy says that," Jane Elizabeth Firesheets added and very gently drew her fingers along Benton Lynch's forearm which did not serve to aid the fading any and certainly not the dwindling. "We should be grateful," she said, "we should be grateful and satisfied that such a lovely thing happened between us."

And Benton Lynch reached out with his hand and laid it on a particular part of Jane Elizabeth Firesheets thereby indicating he'd be even more grateful and more satisfied if the lovely thing that had happened between them previously would happen between them again, at least once anyhow, but Jane Elizabeth Firesheets backed out from under his fingers and out from under his palm and told him it would be a dangerous and most likely lethal activity from Benton Lynch on account of how Jimmy simply adored her and would most undoubtedly commit murder if he only found out Benton Lynch had put his hand where he had put it.

"Well, if he adores you so much, where is he then?" Benton Lynch asked her, and Jane Elizabeth Firesheets said something low and indecipherable so Benton Lynch asked her, "Huh?" and waited with his arms crossed over himself.

"He's occupied," Jane Elizabeth Firesheets told him.

"Occupied where?" Benton Lynch wanted to know.

And Jane Elizabeth Firesheets blew out a breath and said, "Jimmy's thirty days in the lockup. Mr. Merit down the road here, Jimmy hit him with a prybar. Weren't no fault of Jimmy's, they was both drinking and got to bickering about some money Mr. Merit said he'd let out to Jimmy that he never did and Jimmy told him he never did and Mr. Merit said he was a damned liar and well Jimmy just don't have a tolerance when it comes to getting told he's one damned thing or another damned thing and so he hit him with a prybar which was handy at the time but didn't even hit him flush, just kind of bounced the flat part of it off Mr. Merit's left ear and he says he's got damage and his doctor at the clinic, who's likely in with him, says he got damage too and so Jimmy's in the lockup thirty days."

"Don't sound no count to me," Benton Lynch observed.

"He's a saint," Jane Elizabeth Firesheets said and grew huffy of a sudden.

And Benton Lynch told her, "Ha!" which he'd never had the occasion to tell anybody before but which he found gave him a pleasant and satisfying feeling when he told it to Jane Elizabeth Firesheets.

"Well then," she replied, "if you're going to be nasty I just won't have a thing to do with you."

"Don't then," Benton Lynch told her.

"I won't," she said and flailed at Benton Lynch with the blanket just prior to flailing at him with the quilt. "Make your own bed and lie in it your own self," she told him and fired out towards the house in what had all the trappings of a wiry tattooed white boy fit pique, and Benton Lynch hurled a second "Ha!" behind her and then a third one and stood in the middle of the yard and watched the door slam shut and the porchlight go out.

They offered him his sleeping place in the barn and what the granddaddy called three squares and a toddy in exchange for general labor, or anyhow the granddaddy Firesheets and the daddy Firesheets and the momma Firesheets and the brother Firesheets offered him the sleeping place and offered him the three squares and the toddy while Jane Elizabeth Firesheets offered him little of anything or more truly nothing whatsoever except for the hard looks and the exasperated exhalations. Straightoff the general labor turned out to be singular and specific labor at least for a week or two when Benton Lynch and the granddaddy Firesheets and the daddy Firesheets and the brother Fire-

sheets along with the uncle Firesheets, who would be
W. P. Firesheets, and the uncle Firesheets's boy, who
would be W. P. Firesheets also but did not get called
W.P., did not actually get called anything in particular,
all worked together setting out the tobacco by hand on
account of how W.P. Firesheets, the one that got called
it, did not own a mechanized setter, was not about to
rent one out for money, and could not find one to bor-
row either. So they strung gunnysacks over their
shoulders and carried sticks to poke with and bent over
and raised up what seemed five or six hundred times a
day for at least a week or two, or anyhow for as long as
it took to plant the twelve acre patch down in the W.P.
Firesheets rocky bottom and the five acre patch between his house and the hedgerow on the north bound-
ary. Then of course there was the wheatstraw to cut
and bale and get in before the rain came which they
wished on the tobacco but wished off the wheatstraw
at the same time, so the W. P. Firesheets paid actual
rent money for a mower and a baler and his boy towed
the first one and he towed the second one and the
daddy Firesheets followed up the both of them with
the flatbed trailer that the brother Firesheets and Benton Lynch tossed the bales onto where the granddaddy
Firesheets stacked them when he was not pitching
about and falling over from the swells and dips in the
hayfield.

The women cooked the lunch every day and served
it out back of the uncle Firesheets's house on the concrete welltop and every once and again Jane Elizabeth
Firesheets would put together a batch of her potato
salad which Benton Lynch would attempt to praise ex-
travagantly although he had no background to speak
of in extravagant praising or even moderate or negligible praising either, so the ain't this simply delicious
that showed up every time the potato salad did had no
favorable effect on Jane Elizabeth Firesheets who was
preoccupied in counting down the days of the month to

the twenty-seventh when what was in the lockup would
get turned loose on Chalybeate Springs again, and
probably Jane Elizabeth Firesheets would have continued to be preoccupied and would have continued to
shun and ignore Benton Lynch, no matter how much
potato salad he could choke down, if she had not got
sent out with the garbage on the early evening of the
twenty-second which was just a scant five days from
the twenty-seventh or four days really if you went
ahead and counted the evening of the twenty-second
as the twenty-third, which Jane Elizabeth Firesheets
went ahead and did. She was on her way to the garbage can and was not intending to go anywhere after
the garbage can but back to the house. However, in
the normal course of looking around the yard she happened to spy on Benton Lynch between the slats in the
barnwall and it appeared to her he was either taking
off some clothes that he had on or putting on some
clothes that he didn't and naturally she found herself
interested in the proceedings in an idle and curious
sort of way so she stepped on over to the barn, which
was a trifle northeast of the house but not so far northeast of the house as to be out of the way back to it, and
lingered at the middle of the barnwall where the slats
did not meet so well as they met at the corners.

Benton Lynch was just coming out of his underwear
when Jane Elizabeth Firesheets got her eyes focused
sufficiently to see what was what and he threw his
briefs on the floor atop his shirt and his pants and his
socks and stretched and scratched himself prior to
fetching off a nail on the wall the trousers he'd bor-
rowed from the brother Firesheets which he shook the
dust out of and put one foot in before he decided he'd
not quite had his spate of scratching or stretching either but scratching mostly and so he took himself up in
his fingers all over again. Jane Elizabeth Firesheets
watched the whole business with what she told herself
was strictly a clinical fascination and she paid particu-

lar attention to Benton Lynch's equipment which she had never before observed when it was not at least somewhat agitated and astir. She studied the way it hung ever so loosely and flopped and laid about in Benton Lynch's hand and the sad and sorry spectacle of Benton Lynch's virility drooping between his fingers roused up the therapist in her and she slipped along the barnwall to the barndoor and struck her head around the jamb of it and said, "Hey."

Naturally out of reflex Benton Lynch attempted to cover himself with the brother Firesheet's trousers and he succeeded temporarily, succeeded anyway until Jane Elizabeth Firesheets crossed the planking and stopped herself directly in front of where he could smell the smell of her and even in the dimness could see enough of the milky white parts to remind him of the plum-colored parts, and it was likely the recollection of the plum-colored parts in combination with the sight of the milky parts and the smell of the smell that caused what had been hanging ever so loosely and flopping and laying about to raise up and salute and thereby become the kind of animal that a pair of trousers could not hide but certainly could have hung from. Of course once the brother Firesheets's pants commenced to levitate, the merciful and therapeutic side of Jane Elizabeth Firesheets more truly asserted itself since Benton Lynch's equipment had assumed what was to her mind its native condition and she took the trousers in hand prior to taking in hand the equipment itself while Benton Lynch, who had never before fainted or been especially prone to queasiness, got all pale and goose-pimply at the touch of her finger and figured he would surely drop into a pile on the barnfloor. But he managed not to somehow and instead reached out his hand and laid it on a particular part of Jane Elizabeth Firesheets and this time she did not back out from under his fingers and out from under his palm but ooohed a little and aaahed some and exhaled in an entirely unexasperated sort of way.

They laid down side by side on top of the quilt and
on top of the blanket and Benton Lynch helped Jane
Elizabeth Firesheets out of her shirt and out of her
gauzy brassiere and out of her tiny shorts and her scant
red panties and then studied and examined her actual
plum-colored parts with some considerable intensity,
and anyhow studied and examined them until Jane
Elizabeth Firesheets removed herself to the lower
reaches of Benton Lynch's person so as to have a word
with his equipment, and the confab which transpired
probably would have dropped Benton Lynch into a
pile on the floor if he had not been in a pile on the
floor already. At the earnest insistence of Jane Elizabeth Firesheets, Benton Lynch presently took his turn
communicating with her lower reaches, after which she
and him together allowed their lower reaches to min-
gle and chat with each other prior to striking up what
appeared to be a fairly frantic debate with equally
gracious amounts of give and take. Benton Lynch got
satisfied   straightaway,   got   satisfied   entirely   too
straightaway as far as Jane Elizabeth Firesheets was
concerned and she demanded that she have the opportunity to get satisfied herself and consequently Benton
Lynch rolled over and played dead on his backside
while Jane Elizabeth Firesheets bounced and gyrated
on his frontside until she did in fact get satisfied or
anyway until she did in fact hoot once and fall over in a
sweaty heap.

So then they laid there together all hot and winded
with Jane Elizabeth Firesheets stretched out front-
upwards looking at the barnloft and Benton Lynch
stretched out side upwards looking at the plum-
colored parts, which he had not been able to contemplate lately, and the mere sight of the plum-colored
parts all dilated and upright commenced to stir and
agitate Benton Lynch afresh and so put him in favor of
reopening the channels of communication and he was
on his way to becoming truly fossilized all over again

when Jane Elizabeth Firesheets blew out a breath and said she guessed she would have to tell Jimmy just exactly what went on, guessed it would be the fair and proper thing to do, guessed she would not ever rest easy again until he knew all about it. Now this was not the sort of news to aid Benton Lynch's stark rigidity much, or fairly stark rigidity anyway, and it fell off to nothing directly once Benton Lynch had begun to imagine just what it might feel like to get hit with a prybar, even if only the flat side of a prybar bounced off his ear, and he went ahead and wondered out loud why Jane Elizabeth Firesheets felt compelled to mention their little dialogue to her Jimmy in the lockup since he surely would not ever find out about it otherwise.

"Because," she told him, "truth is the very cornerstone of Romance. Jimmy says that."

And Benton Lynch suggested that maybe she could not tell him anything, which would be very much like telling the truth, or anyway would not be same as lying, but Jane Elizabeth Firesheets sat up on her elbow and told him again that truth was the very cornerstone of Romance, "the whole truth and nothing but the truth," she added in a grave and sanctimonious sort of way, and so Benton Lynch suggested that maybe she could go ahead and tell him just what she'd done and just when she'd done it but not exactly who she'd done it with, and Jane Elizabeth Firesheets did not say anything grave or sanctimonious but shook her head ever so slightly from side to side and thereby set Benton Lynch to wondering just what he might get for having laid his equipment where he'd laid it and so he asked Jane Elizabeth Firesheets, "What's gone happen to me?"

"Likely get killed," she told him. "Jimmy takes a hard view of this kind of thing."

"Then what's gone happen to you?" he asked her.

"Well," she said and laid her head back some, "I got

charms can soothe the beast in him," and she dangled her tongue out one side of her mouth and raked her fingers across the flattest whitest part of her stomach prior to wrapping them clean around the noticeably faded and dwindled flower of Benton Lynch's manhood which got rejuvenated somewhat straightoff but not rejuvenated entirely.

"You mean nothing's gone happen to you but I'm gone get my head broke open?" Benton Lynch said.

And Jane Elizabeth Firesheets told him, "Likely he'll purely rip you all to pieces, but that's just his way. I mean Jimmy says you got to take life by the throat, can't just lay back and wait cause nothing comes to him that lays back and him that waits. So Jimmy says you got to take life by the throat and shake it hard, that's what Jimmy says. He says the world's his oyster. Jimmy don't bend to nobody, don't give way to nothing. Jimmy's a regular electrified dynamo, that what he says, and likely he'll purely rip you all to pieces, and likely he'd just as purely rip me all to pieces too except for what I can do for him that you can't hardly do for him, not that you ain't got your own charms sugarbunch," and Jane Elizabeth Firesheets struck in with some vigorous finger exercises which Benton Lynch appreciated but could not bring himself to truly enjoy on account of his predicament, and he told Jane Elizabeth Firesheets, "This ain't no time for that. I'm gone get killed."

And Jane Elizabeth Firesheets told him back, "It's likely," and once he'd rolled over so as to withdraw his participation Jane Elizabeth Firesheets said, "If that's how you want to be," and laid down flush on her backside.

Of course once Benton Lynch had withdrawn his participation and once Jane Elizabeth Firesheets had laid down flush on her backside Benton Lynch decided that if he was going to get ripped all to pieces anyhow he might as well be as guilty as he could manage to be and so he told Jane Elizabeth Firesheets he'd changed his mind and naturally she told him she'd changed hers too and he laid his private parts up next to her private parts and commenced to make some friction but Jane Elizabeth Firesheets told him, "No, this ain't no proper time for it," and Benton Lynch dropped the pointiest part of his face square down on the flattest whitest part of Jane Elizabeth Firesheets's stomach but Jane Elizabeth Firesheets told him, "No, I can't," and Benton Lynch reached out and took up the tipend of a plum-colored part between his thumb and forefinger and Jane Elizabeth Firesheets opened her mouth so as to say no she couldn't once more but nothing ever came out but plain air until the moaning and the hooting set in in earnest.

So they got together on the barnfloor the evening of the twenty-second, which Jane Elizabeth Firesheets was not so eager to count as the twenty-third any longer, and then they went ahead and got together on the evening of the actual twenty-third prior to the evening of the twenty-fourth when Jane Elizabeth Firesheets insisted they try it in the barnloft on account of how the altitude might have a stimulating effect and it did have a stimulating effect as far as Benton Lynch could tell or maybe it was just an exhausting effect due to the climbing up and the climbing down along with the burrowing around in the wheatstraw in between. On the afternoon of the twenty-fifth Jane Elizabeth Firesheets laid her nimble fingers on Benton Lynch's private parts in a blueberry thicket and the two of them got somewhat pricked and scored over in the ensuing scuffle but recovered by nightfall and hauled Benton Lynch's quilt and Benton Lynch's blanket out into the dewy grass under the starlight and whoever happened to be on the bottom at the time studied the constellations and the little sliver of moon in the southeast.

On the afternoon of the twenty-sixth Benton Lynch

moved out of Jane Elizabeth Firesheets's daddy's barn
and moved into Jane Elizabeth Firesheets's daddy's
brother's barn so as to be out from under Jimmy in the
lockup when he got turned out of the lockup at last,
and he got turned out of the lockup at last on the
morning of the twenty-seventh but by the early afternoon Benton Lynch still had not been purely ripped all
to pieces and had not been purely ripped all to pieces
by nightfall either and so half expected to wake up in
little pulpy bits come morningtime but woke up un-
pulpy and unripped-up and fairly regular except for
the apprehension and except for the dread which he
carried around with him throughout the morning, on
into the afternoon, and all the way to twilight when
Jane Elizabeth Firesheets visited him in her daddy's
brother's barn and confessed that maybe the whole
truth and nothing but the truth was not exactly the
cornerstone of romance when the health and well-
being of such an organ as Benton Lynch possessed
hung in the balance, and so she had not told Jimmy
just what went on on the barnfloor and in the barnloft
and in the blueberry thicket and on the dewy grass but
had told him instead all about her pointy and angular
and hollowed out and square toothed momma's sister's
child since she figured Jimmy would not suspect that
cousins would do with each other what Benton Lynch
and Jane Elizabeth Firesheets had been doing with
each other. And Benton Lynch was so excessively
pleased at having the apprehension and the dread
lifted from him that he offered to show Jane Elizabeth
Firesheets the organ he possessed so as to demonstrate
how openly grateful it was, but Jane Elizabeth Firesheets got testy straight off and said she had some scruples and principles if you please and so she settled for
laying her fingers ever so briefly atop Benton Lynch's
pantsleg.

    He got introduced to Jimmy on the afternoon of the
twenty-ninth while he was cutting brush with the

daddy Firesheets and the brother Firesheets and the
daddy Firesheets's brother along with the daddy Firesheets's brother's boy. Jimmy came round from his
momma's house on the Fayetteville highway so as to
lend some assistance, not any actual and helpful assistance really but mainly some verbal and fairly antag-
onizing assistance in the form of a Cut that bush
yonder or Hack it higher or Hack it lower or Don't
that just eat shit which seemed to be Jimmy's favorite
expression probably on account of its far reaching and
general application. He was not as tall as Benton
Lynch, but then hardly anybody was so tall as Benton
Lynch, and he was considerably thicker, but then most
everybody was considerably thicker too. He breathed
through his mouth primarily probably because his nose
was flat where it had got caved in by something or
another and his eyebrows joined together in the middle of his forehead and so ran uninterrupted from temple to temple which lent Jimmy a kind of prehistoric
demeanor especially when he squatted on his heels
which he had a tendency for. The daddy Firesheets
introduced Jimmy to Benton Lynch and introduced
Benton Lynch to Jimmy, and though he did not say
anything in the line of nephew or relation either, it did
not seem to matter any since Jimmy had not paid much
attention to the introduction and had not paid much
attention to Benton Lynch either which was about as
natural and ordinary for him as his eyebrow or his
squat.

Jane Elizabeth Firesheets stopped by on her way to
setting the lunch out on the welltop and she laid her
arm across Jimmy's shoulders and stooped down to
nibble at his ear the sight of which drew Benton
Lynch's stomach up in a little knotty ball and he swung
his bushax somewhat blindly and near about separated
the brother Firesheets from his left foot and the
brother Firesheets grew hot and abusive straightaway
since his left foot was an object of some utility to him.

At lunchtime Jimmy made several pronouncements about life in general, that would be aside from the shiteating which is a sort of pronouncement about life, and he ate three or four shares of everything and smoked a half dozen of the daddy Firesheets's brother's Pall Malls as he had not been what he called on the outside long enough to buy any himself. After lunch Jimmy dragged off a pile of brush, or a piece of a pile of brush anyway, and squatted some more and advised Benton Lynch and the brother Firesheets and the daddy Firesheets's brother's boy on bushax technique without laying his hands or any of his fingers either on a real and actual bushax. Jane Elizabeth Firesheets showed up again as the afternoon commenced to wane and wrapped her arms about Jimmy's shoulders and laid her face up next to his face and Jimmy reached round and grabbed up a handful of her sweet behind right there in front of her daddy in front of her brother and in front of her daddy's brother and her daddy's brother's boy and in front of her momma's sister's child too who watched the handful of sweet behind right when it first got grabbed and held and studied it as it proceeded on down the road towards the daddy Firesheet's cottage and the daddy Firesheets's barnfloor and barnloft also, and then the brother Firesheets backed clear across the stubble as Benton Lynch wound up with the bushax and laid the blade of it into a melon-sized hunk of quartzstone which caused the sparks to fly and did not please any of the Firesheetses much.

Jane Elizabeth Firesheets did not have hardly anything to do with Benton Lynch all throughout the month of June. Of course she said hello to him when he was around to say hello to and she passed the time of day with him when she was so inclined and every once and again of an evening she dropped by the daddy Firesheets's brother's barn and laid her hand on Benton Lynch's pantsleg but would not allow Benton

Lynch to lay his hand on any piece of herself due to her scruples and her principles if you please. Sometimes when he could not help it otherwise Benton Lynch passed near the daddy Firesheets's barn when the hooting and the moaning was in progress, which was where all the hooting and the moaning took place anymore, and the ruckus generally dried his mouth out and tied his stomach up too, and he figured the ruckus itself and the idea of the ruckus would not continue to do that for long but the ruckus itself as well as the idea and recollection of the ruckus did continue to dry his mouth out and did continue to tie his stomach up all throughout the month of June and he discovered that the less of Jane Elizabeth Firesheets he had the more of her he wanted and the more of her he wanted the less of her he got. He found it painful to even imagine Jimmy of the lockup laying his thick self and his flat nose and his solitary eyebrow atop the milky white portions and the plum-colored parts too so as to have his way with them, and it was a matter of pure wonder and bafflement to him that he'd ever grown weary of even the least little insignificant piece of Jane Elizabeth Firesheets who did not seem to him capable of insignificance any longer whenever he took the time to ponder the various parts and portions of her which was the thing he did the most of next to breathing.

Benton Lynch had come to Chalybeate Springs to relieve himself of his torment and his agitation and for a spell in the shank of May he had got shed of the both of them but they had come back, had come back more potent for having departed, and they lingered with him all throughout the brushcutting and the beanpicking and the tobacco-topping but he got to where he could hide them fairly well from most everybody except Jane Elizabeth Firesheets who he could hide them almost completely from partly on account of his pure effort and labor in the matter and partly on account of her indifference. So what little traces of torment and agitation he did display did not get noticed by Jane Elizabeth Firesheets and whenever she had a thing to say about Jimmy and her affection for him she went ahead and said it to Benton Lynch and could not see his stomach knot up or his mouth go dry. Jane Elizabeth Firesheets was desirous that Benton Lynch think highly of her Jimmy and consequently was ever asking him wasn't Jimmy just the wisest thing or wasn't Jimmy just the handsomest thing or wasn't Jimmy just a regular stitch, and all throughout June Benton Lynch told her yes, he guessed so since he figured a yes, he guessed so was his only chance of laying his hands on the milky white parts and plum-colored parts ever again, and partway through July he was still guessing that Jimmy was wise and handsome and lively and was still figuring he'd get rewarded sometime or another with the seeing and the touching and the general partaking of the milky white parts and the plum-colored parts too, but he had not got rewarded all throughout June and had not got rewarded partway through July and so eventually just got fed up with the yesing and the guessing so primarily because Jimmy was not wise and was not handsome and was not at all lively to the least little degree, so finally of an evening outside the daddy Firesheets's brother's barn when Benton Lynch got asked about the wisdom and the good looks and the purely refined sense of humor he up and told Jane Elizabeth Firesheets, "I ain't real taken with him."

"Why Benton Lynch," Jane Elizabeth Firesheets said back, "I do believe you're jealous," and she attempted to lay the tipends of her fingers on Benton Lynch's pantsleg like she had so many times previously, but Benton Lynch knocked her hand away and said, "Ha!" hard and spiteful and this time without any pleasure or satisfaction to speak of.

"No call to get nasty," Jane Elizabeth Firesheets said. "You don't have to like him. I like him good enough for both of us."

"Well that's fine with me," Benton Lynch told her, "cause I got no use for him. He squats all day like a toadfrog and ain't worth a shit for nothing."

"I beg your pardon, sir," Jane Elizabeth Firesheets shot back in her purest scruples and principles if you please tone of voice. "Let's you and me get straight just who it is that's not worth a shit. Look at you, you ain't worth anything and Jimmy, well Jimmy's set to be something sometime but you ain't anything and won't never be."

"Ha!" Benton Lynch said again just as hard and just as spiteful as before.

"Well tell me then, what prospects you got? Just what is it you got a talent for?"

And Benton Lynch, who had never considered he possessed a talent and who did not figure he had much in the way of prospects decided against admitting anything of the sort to Jane Elizabeth Firesheets and so told her instead, "I ain't sorry and I ain't lazy and you don't know I won't be somebody sometime. You can't know it."

"Don't seem likely, Benton," Jane Elizabeth Firesheets said. "You just don't strike me as the sort that'll ever mount up to anything. But Jimmy, now you can look at Jimmy and just know something will come of him. I mean it sort of hangs all over him, don't you know." And Jane Elizabeth Firesheets got all wistful and gazed off into the treetops. "He's the wisest and handsomest thing," she said, "and just a regular stitch."

"Well, I ain't real taken with him," Benton Lynch told her.

"You don't have to be," Jane Elizabeth Firesheets said.

"It's a good thing, cause I ain't, and I ain't real taken with you either," Benton Lynch said and then jabbed his hands into his pockets and stalked off away from Jane Elizabeth Firesheets and away from her daddy's brother's barn and towards nowhere in particular.

"Benton Lynch where are you going?" Jane Elizabeth Firesheets demanded. "I got a right to know." But Benton Lynch did not stop and did not open his mouth either. "You answer me. Benton Lynch where are you going?"

And still Benton Lynch did not stop but he did open his mouth and in his flattest, emptiest, most thoroughly vacant voice he told her, "Somewhere else."

He slept in a ditch outside Apex which was all he could get a ride to, but it was a dry ditch and the evening was not particularly sweltering so he slept well enough when the bugs did not crawl over him, and early on in the morning he caught a ride with a dirt farmer clear to Roxboro where he bought a stack of flapjacks and a cup of coffee in a grill downtown and got talked at by a retired dentist who had given up his office and had given up his patients but had not gone completely shed of his occupation and so still discussed teeth primarily, specifically Benton Lynch's teeth which fairly much got away with him on account of how especially big they were and how especially square they were. Benton Lynch could not seem to get out of Roxboro except by walking and so he did walk west on the 158 highway clear out of the town limits and on into the county before he got picked up by a woman who thought he was a Montague which she explained was why she picked him up in the first place since she generally did not stop for just anybody on the highway and she carried Benton Lynch for a mile or two prior to letting him out at a body shop which she said was where she was turning off but she did not turn off and so Benton Lynch walked a ways further west and got picked up shortly by a half dozen negroes in a 1971 Buick Electra, all of them a little drunk and wild on stump liquor except for the driver who was near about done in with it and so took the load of them clean to Yanceyville on both sides of the road and every now and again in the ditches too. And then it was a truck and a Pinto and he was on the rise once more above his momma and daddy's chickenhouse and his momma and daddy's trailer with the ruin and the dilapidation and the squalor laid out full before him.

Of course there were not any pink envelopes throughout the rest of July and there were not any pink envelopes throughout the entire of August, only the agitation and the torment and then the bald Jeeter stretched out dead on her bedlinen which led to the sofa and atop it Mr. Tiny Aaron who dropped his chin and said revolver and who dropped his chin and said some dollars and some cents too, and it was like life opened up its collar and showed Benton Lynch its throat, or anyway that's what he might have figured if he'd been at all poetical instead of just vacant and just hollowed out aside from somewhat agitated and somewhat tormented too, and so he paid the dollars and paid the cents and carried home the revolver hid in the folds of his jacket and late in the afternoons for a week running while his momma napped on the couch and his daddy napped in the henhouse Benton Lynch stood before the mirror on the back of the bathroom door in his good brown jacket and his good brown trousers and said to himself, "You know who I am?"

FOUR

THE SHERIFF called it mayhem, called it pure and undiluted mayhem once Bambi Kinch had stuck the microphone direct under his nose and asked him what he might call it if he could call it some one thing or another and the sheriff took ahold of his chin for a spell prior to settling on mayhem pure and undiluted which satisfied him sufficiently and near about set Bambi Kinch to tingling since she did not cover much mayhem but generally just your usual violence and savagery. The sheriff had been all for posing in front of his map with its yellowheaded gash to the north and its silverheaded boil to the southeast and its little Lemly fleck off to the west, but Bambi Kinch who held the microphone decided the map did not suit and Larry who pointed the camera agreed that the map did not suit and Bub who had dragged a cable briefly but did not seem to perform a function otherwise failed to object when Miss Bambi Kinch led Sheriff Burton out from his office, down the courthouse steps and partway across the square. They set up so as to put Colonel Blalock off the sheriff's right shoulder and off Bambi Kinch's left one, or rather they set up so as to put Colonel Blalock's bronze scowl and the pointy end of Colonel Blalock's bronze sword direct in between the sheriff and Miss Kinch who had figured and conjectured that the face and the saber too would give her segment what she called local identity and Larry told her it was a sterling notion and the sheriff told her he

227

guessed it was too and Bub, who did not say exactly what sort of notion he figured it to be, left off with the bunch of them at the Action News 5 van where he sat sideways in the driver's seat and ate shelled peanuts out of a sack.

Sheriff Burton told Miss Bambi Kinch ahead of time he would answer pure and undiluted mayhem if she would ask him something he could answer it to, and so together they formulated a question with suggestions from Larry who was near about as thrilled and over-whelmed with the idea of mayhem as anybody on account of what it rendered up for him, or that's what he said it was on account of anyway, and Bambi Kinch said it rendered up a thing or two for her also, and the both of them together congratulated the sheriff for rendering up what it was he rendered up with his pure and undiluted mayhem and Sheriff Burton poked the toe of his right shoe down into the ground and told them it wasn't anything really but they insisted it was evocative, most highly evocative, and the sheriff said he guessed it might be. So Bub sat sideways and ate shelled peanuts and Larry pointed the camera and Miss Bambi Kinch held the microphone as Sheriff Burton told most of the rest of the state what his par-ticular part of the state was in the throes of and he traveled all the way to Leaksville to watch himself tell it on his ladyfriend's color console and his ladyfriend, who was a Sugg, brought home barbecue and coleslaw and hushpuppies and served them on the coffee table. The sheriff spilt hotsauce down his shirtfront during a motor oil commercial and his ladyfriend Sugg licked her napkin and set about cleaning it off him but was only half done when Bambi Kinch showed up on the screen and so got interrupted by Sheriff Burton and together him and her watched the sheriff say mayhem pure and undiluted.

It had not got to be mayhem until the second week in November when it rose up from corridors and

gashes and shots fired all at once and of a sudden and
so did get to be mayhem after all, mayhem pure and
undiluted they said on the television and in the papers,
but it was not actually pure and was hardly undiluted
though likely it was mayhem mostly on account of who
got killed from it which would be Vernon Littlejohn of
Spray first cousin to the coach Littlejohn Littlejohns
and Vernon Littlejohn's condition kept him from getting just plain killed and murdered and fairly much
dictated the mayhem, fairly much insisted on it. Vernon Littlejohn's arteries had commenced to harden
when he reached sixty-seven and he had not been able
to think straight ever since which would be tribulation
enough for most people but was compounded in Vernon Littlejohn's particular instance by the grocery he
had run on the 87 highway for as long as anybody
could recollect and certainly for longer than Vernon
Littlejohn could recollect since he could not recollect
hardly anything anymore that had happened two minutes previous from the point he tried to recollect it, or
anyhow two minutes previous on a good day and more
towards one minute previous those times when his arteries were particularly stiff and rigid which had been
rare times once but had steadily become fairly usual
and ordinary right up to the afternoon Vernon Littlejohn did not have to bother to recollect anything any
longer.

Mrs. Vernon Littlejohn helped out in the grocery
when she could but she suffered from the phlebitis in
both legs and so generally took to her bed early on in
the afternoon for the most of the year and hardly ever
got out of it in the summer of the year due to the heat
and humidity in combination with her rubber stockings
all of which together served to break her legs out in a
rash. Consequently, Mr. Vernon Littlejohn ran his grocery almost entirely by himself for the most of the year
and absolutely entirely by himself for the rest of the
year although Mrs. Littlejohn encouraged him to hire

help which Mr. Littlejohn saw the advantage in but somehow could not ever recollect to do, so it was just him and his arteries all the summer and just him and his arteries the afternoons throughout the winter and he got on well enough as long as it was mostly him and partly his arteries but gradually it slid in the other direction and became mostly his arteries and only partly him and he did not get along so well from there on out. The trouble was primarily that Mr. Vernon Littlejohn could not make change, or rather could not make anything but the wrong change and so not only gave back a lot of money to people who had a little coming and gave back a little money to people who had a lot coming but regularly returned an assortment of bills and silver too to people who had nothing coming whatsoever, and the problem reached a kind of a head when Mrs. Jack Foster's boy, little Jack, bought three Sweet Tarts and a Tic Tac with a dollar and got $238.46 change which seemed considerably fortunate to him and he carried the money to the Western Auto in downtown Spray so as to shop for a bicycle but he could not decide between a red one with a ten speed sprocket and a yellow one with a spider seat and consequently he bought the red one and the yellow one and paid a little colored boy $22.00 to ride the yellow one home for him which was the only one the little colored boy could sit on and pedal.

Fosters being Fosters and Pendergasts, which was what Mrs. Foster had been prior to becoming what she was, being Pendergasts little Jack did not get made to take back but one of the bicycles and did not get made to take that back really but did anyhow on his own which was how he did most everything he ended up doing since he was the one that ran the show and big Jack and Mrs. Pendergast Foster were just the ones that let him. So accordingly Mr. Littlejohn did not get back but what Little Jack decided he should get back which turned out to be the price of the returned bicycle, which would be the red bicycle that little Jack could not hardly reach the pedals on himself, and even then it was not the full and entire price of the bicycle but only that part of the price of the bicycle left over from little Jack's share of it and little Jack took a sizable share of it, as was little Jack's way in most things. However, Mr. Vernon Littlejohn accepted the money as a kind of windfall since he did not recollect that any money was missing although Mrs. Littlejohn had told him it was, and consequently Mrs. Littlejohn was the one to do the majority of the worrying over Mr. Littlejohn's earnings and how they came to go where they went, and just as consequently Mrs. Littlejohn was the one, stretched out there on her bed with her rubber hose draped over the bedstead, to do the devising and the formulating too so as to prevent Mr. Littlejohn's earnings from going where they generally went and channel them instead to where they did not usually end up which turned out to be a Tampa Jewel box once Mrs. Littlejohn had successfully devised and formulated the new Littlejohn method of changemaking.

Mr. Littlejohn kept the Tampa Jewel box on a shelf under the cash register and every morning Mrs. Littlejohn put inside it $50.00 in tens and fives and ones and silver and pennies. The new Littlejohn method of changemaking was intended to keep Mr. Littlejohn out of the register in the majority so as to reduce his losses to just some sizable or middling or maybe even scant portion of the tens and the fives and the ones and the silver and the pennies. So Mr. Littlejohn did not have to make change any better than he had been making change and mostly did not have to make change at all but instead simply snatched the Tampa Jewel box off the shelf and opened it up for the customer to make his own change out of, which Mr. Littlejohn did not have any qualms about since he had always believed that people were basically honest and trustworthy and since he still believed it whenever he could recollect

that he always had. And Mr. Littlejohn's experience
showed him in fact that people were basically honest
and trustworthy since his regular customers who
traded near about daily at his grocery did not ever take
from him but a little more than they were entitled to
while even his irregular customers did not even lift
much in addition to that, so Mr. Littlejohn even accumulated some money in the course of a day and even
realized a profit every once and again and even made
back the $283.46, or had made back the most of it
anyhow by the second week of November when of a
sudden Mr. Littlejohn ceased to accumulate and realize and make back anything any longer.

They printed two pictures of him up towards the top
of the front page of the *Chronicle*, one from Mrs.
Littlejohn's silver frame on the nightstand taken back
when Mr. Littlejohn's arteries had been as soft and
ordinary as everybody else's and another taken about
as late as it could be taken of Mr. Vernon Littlejohn
strapped and buckled onto a gurney under a taut bedsheet that showed off the tip of his nose and the
upright ends of his feet. According to Mr. H. Monroe
Aycock, who wrote the article that filled up the space
all around Mr. Littlejohn with his ordinary arteries and
Mr. Littlejohn with his buckle and his bedsheet, the
events of the day transpired beneath a leaden sky and
in particularly brisk and gusty weather which seemed
somehow notable and significant to Mr. H. Monroe
Aycock who let the sky go to ashen in the bottom of
column one and then to tufted and gray midway
through column two while the wind picked up some
and whipped and tore and screeched and whatnot and
the temperature fell off to bracing or maybe rose up to
it since Mr. Aycock did not clearly explain if bracing
was colder than brisk or brisk was colder than bracing.
He built towards and concluded with a paragraph on
the sheer and general oppressiveness of the afternoon
and seemed to indicate that maybe it had caused some

little piece of the calamity, or actually seemed to indicate that maybe it had caused some major piece of the calamity, but between the leaden sky and leaden bullet public opinion tended to ride with the latter though most everybody agreed that Mr. H. Monroe Aycock was to be congratulated on his vivid and fairly lyrical rendering of what most everybody agreed was in fact a true and verifiable calamity.

However, as Mr. H. Monroe Aycock's passions and sensibilities kept to the lyrical end of things he did not truly get around to the hard facts and circumstances of the calamity and consequently the full-blooded Loop Road Myrick's sister's husband felt compelled to supplement Mr. H. Monroe Aycock's account of the calamity with one of his own devising which was not nearly so stirring and dramatic as Mr. H. Monroe Aycock's but proved to be appreciably more informative. The full-blooded Loop Road Myrick's sister's husband, with the aid of material evidence and eyewitness accounts and the usual guesses and assumptions, reconstructed and reconstituted the crime as best he could which turned out to be accurate in the majority except for the ferocious struggle which the full-blooded Loop Road Myrick's sister's husband decided there had been one of on account of the ointments and pouches of loose chew and cigarette packs that lay strewn all about the stiffening corpse which Mr. Vernon Littlejohn had decided he did not want to get made into just prior to getting made into one, or anyway that was the theory formulated by the full-blooded Loop Road Myrick's sister's husband who judged the evidence and figured there had been a struggle of some considerable ferocity, a wild and frantic battle near about that had caused the ointments and the pouches and the cigarette packs to get strewn like they did get strewn and had caused Mr. Vernon Littlejohn to get shot and murdered and killed like he did get shot and murdered and killed.

But there had not been an actual struggle really, had not been anything much wild and frantic about it except for the dying which Mr. Littlejohn pulled off with appreciable vigor. Otherwise this time was just the same as the other times. He stayed outside off behind a honeysuckle hedgerow until the lady in the green Plymouth came out with her loafbread and her Coca-Colas and the man in the farmtruck got his five gallons of fuel oil and departed. Then he stepped on around the corner and in through the door and looked to see was it just him and was it just the clerk and was it just him and the clerk, or actually just him primarily since the clerk had propped his feet up by the gas heater and dozed off. So he said, "Hey," in his usual flat and vacant voice and when the clerk ran his tongue out his mouth and chewed the air he said, "Hey," again and slapped the counter with the flat of his hand. Of course Mr. Littlejohn, who stayed somewhat perplexed and confused on account of his affliction, generally woke up in a pure quandary and he stretched himself and dragged over to the register and rubbed the top of his head and yawned and was just about to close his mouth when he got asked, "You know who I am?" and so did not close his mouth entirely but replied straightway, "Why surely," and since the Harrington and Richardson Buntline revolver was already too far out from the folds of the jacket to get put back it got brought on out the rest of its length and got aimed and pointed and then the question got asked all over again and Mr. Littlejohn said he guessed he knew though maybe he didn't know after all and so he found himself informed shortly in a most straightforward and demonstrative sort of way and he eyed the pistol barrel afresh and eyed his privates, or rather eyed the part of his trousers where he recollected his privates to be, and he recollected fairly accurately in this instance, and he said, "I guess you'll be wanting this then," and he reached his arm in the general direction of the register but not to the register precisely and instead more directly to a shelf underneath the register.

The bullet did not hit him in the testicles exactly, did not even hit him in the stomach, but entered direct through his chest and exited square between his shoulders and it wasn't even the hole in himself that snared his attention initially but was instead the thundrous bang from the pistol which he jumped from and which he figured was all he jumped from until he saw where the angular, pointy, and hollowed out face was looking and looked there for himself. It was a big ragged pulpy wound and the blood sluiced out from it soaking Mr. Littlejohn's shirtfront and splattering somewhat onto his hands and the top of his Tampa Jewel box, and it had even stung him the least little bit until he saw it when it commenced to ache and burn and torment him and thereby caused him to raise his fingers up and touch it and he drew them away all bloodied over and looked at them with his mouth hanging loose and open. Then he commenced to sink, commenced to sink straight down into the floorboards it appeared like a man in a quagmire and he seemed contented with sinking initially and just watched himself get shorter until he decided he was not contented with sinking after all and so scratched and grabbed at anything he could scratch and grab at which turned out to be ointments and loose chew and cigarettes and they came down all around him and atop him and joined him on the floorboards from where he gazed up at the ceiling primarily, gazed up at the ceiling exclusively really until the angular, pointy, and hollowed out face showed itself over the counter and so he gazed up at it instead and it gazed down at him and watched him blow out the last of his breath and watched his eyelids flutter and go still.

And Sheriff Burton called it mayhem pure and undiluted and called it willful and called it vicious and called it heinous too when he'd had time to think of

heinous which he did not get much occasion to throw
around and so threw around now that he could, and
most everybody else called it heinous once the sheriff
did and called it vicious and willful and called it mayhem pure and undiluted in addition to just plain meanness which the most of them had called it straight off
and continued to call it primarily except for the sheriff
and except of course for the bulk of old ladies roundabout who did not find plain meanness lurid enough to
suit them and so insisted on the heinous and the vicious and the willful and the mayhem pure and undiluted along with most every other thing that would
scare and terrify them and palpitate their hearts at
night, but it got to be mayhem alone, solely mayhem
pure and undiluted once the sheriff said it to Miss
Bambi Kinch, said it there in the middle of town with
the pointy bronze sword and the bronze scowl over his
shoulder and got broadcast and circulated saying it all
across the Piedmont and partway into Virginia, and he
asked his ladyfriend the Leaksville Sugg her true opinion once Bambi Kinch had said it was Bambi Kinch
and had sent things on back to the studio, and the
Leaksville Sugg licked her napkin again and told him
she did not believe it would come out altogether on
account of the vinegar and the tomato juice in combination.

HE FOLDED it up and mailed it in an envelope without even an argyle-socks-length note to explain what it
was since he figured it would explain what it was by
itself and Jane Elizabeth Firesheets took it out from
the envelope and unfolded it and looked for a note or
just some trace of handwriting somewhere but did not
discover any and so looked at the inky headlines and at
the photograph of Mr. Busick, the victim, and at the
photograph of Mr. Winn with his chin dangling alongside Mr. Bobbit with his cigarette and the pieces of his

arms, the witnesses, and at the little square of roadmap that was Raleigh mostly and Wendell and Garner
and Knightdale and Zebulon and down the 401 highway to the south Fuquay-Varina also with a bold black
arrow to indicate and distinguish it, and she sat down
on the front cottage steps with the unfolded paper in
her fingers and she looked away from it and then
looked back at it again and her mouth commenced to
lay out across her face and wrap partly around her
jawbones. He sent her the McIver one too and then
the Barnard one and the Grissom one and the Stem
one also and still not even an argyle-socks-length note
to explain what they were since he figured they would
explain what they were by themselves, and they did
explain what they were by themselves and got pressed
all together in a *Glamour* magazine where they stayed
when they were not getting looked at.

The first pink envelope did not contain anything of
much consequence as far as Benton Lynch was concerned, not anything anyway worth adjusting himself
in his trousers over but just your polite talk and your
general inquiry and some passing mention of Jimmy
who had gotten himself into a difficulty that remained
vague and unspecified but still thrilled Benton Lynch
near about as much as a sweltering conclusion would
have thrilled him though not precisely as much exactly,
and it was not until the second pink envelope that
Benton Lynch learned the true nature of Jimmy's predicament which had something to do with a social se-
curity check and something to do with his endorsement
on the back of it and something to do with the pocketbook he had pilfered it from and considerable to do
with the three to five in Caledonia he was very likely
to get on account of all of it. Of course, Jane Elizabeth
Firesheets could not hide her agitation and her dismay
and wondered out loud along about the bottom of the
back of the first page just what she would do for three
to five years without anybody to see to her needs and

to see to her desires and Benton Lynch, who had been sitting down, stood up as he commenced to wonder about her desires some himself.

She did not get to any purely sultry and provocative talk until the third pink envelope which was shot full of purely sultry and provocative talk from the Dear Sugarbunch straight through to the p.s. and the whole business kept Benton Lynch on his feet for a solid day and likely would have kept him upright for the majority of the day after but he could not stand up on the bus which was what he took out from the depot in Neely south to Greensboro and then east clear to Raleigh where he changed over to a local and made the twenty-seven miles to Chalybeate Springs in just under two hours and at last descended onto the roadside where he stretched and adjusted and scratched himself prior to walking the twenty-eighth mile and the twenty-ninth mile too clear out to the cottage that was still a hovel there in the afternoon light but was preparing to become a shack once the evening set in, was preparing to become a shack with some suggestion of a cottage to it.

Right off he ran up on the granddaddy Firesheets who was in the sideyard tending to the grandmomma Firesheets's marker and he greeted Benton Lynch enthusiastically which was the way the granddaddy Firesheets did most everything he bothered to do and then he led him on into the cottage proper so as to let him get greeted by everybody else and the momma Firesheets said Hey and the daddy Firesheets said Hey and the brother Firesheets asked him where in the hell he'd run off to and on account of what and Benton Lynch said Hey back. Jane Elizabeth Firesheets was out behind the barn throwing seed to the chickens and Benton Lynch excused himself from the momma and the daddy and the brother and the granddaddy Firesheets and slipped out the door, across the backyard, and direct up behind Jane Elizabeth Firesheets who felt his

long pointy fingers on the flattest whitest part of her
stomach and so instinctively yipped and howled and
flung the seed bucket prior to whirling around so as to
discover just whose long pointy fingers it was on the
flattest whitest part of her stomach, though she had
figured they were attached to who they were attached
to, and she put her face up in his face and asked him,
"What are you doing here?" but not much at all like
she had asked him that previously.

They retired to the barnfloor almost straightaway,
or actually as immediately straightaway as they could
encourage their legs to take them, and they rolled
around on the wood planking and grappled with each
other for a spell until Jane Elizabeth Firesheets suggested and then insisted on the hayloft, not so much
for the loft part of it this time but more for the hay
part of it, and naturally Benton Lynch agreed with her
emphatically almost before she could finish suggesting
it as he was in a state which had rendered him acutely
agreeable and thoroughly emphatic, and he laid his
head back and watched Jane Elizabeth Firesheets's
sweet behind ascend towards the barnroof after which
he endeavored to ascend some himself and even succeeded at it but without any grace to speak of. They
rolled around in the hay some and grappled some like
they had rolled around and grappled on the wood
planking and then Jane Elizabeth Firesheets took the
liberty of separating Benton Lynch from his trousers
and from cotton briefs, or anyway she had commenced
to take the liberty of separating Benton Lynch from his
trousers and his briefs when she discovered she had to
separate him as well from his Harrington and Richardson Buntline revolver of extraordinarily high caliber
which she had taken for something long and steely
from the outset but not a gun exactly, and she held it
and looked at it and cocked it and uncocked it and
pointed it and ran her tongue out her mouth and back
in her mouth again and said, "Oooohhh," in a tone

Benton Lynch had never heard used on a revolver before.

He got invited to undo the buttons down Jane Elizabeth Firesheets's blousefront but could not synchronize and coordinate his fingers sufficiently to undo them like they were meant to be undone and so tugged at the buttonhole side of the blouse with one hand and yanked at the button side of it with the other and thereby laid the thing open with the kind of passion and vigor that prompted Jane Elizabeth Firesheets to oooohhh all over again and Benton Lynch could tell it was genuine and legitimate oooohhhing once he'd unhooked and opened Jane Elizabeth Firesheets's brassiere so as to see for himself the plum-colored parts which had blossomed and spread out like they usually did when the oooohhhing was genuine and when the oooohhhing was legitimate. As a token of her gratitude and appreciation for the open display of passion and of vigor, Jane Elizabeth Firesheets undertook to render Benton Lynch unconscious with some lively fingerplay and general therapy and since Benton Lynch was not one of your natural oooohhhers or one of your natural squirmers too, he just breathed heavy and inadvertently whistled through his nose a time or two before lapsing off into what appeared to be a faint once Jane Elizabeth Firesheets stuck the pointy pink tipend of her tongue direct into his bellybutton.

They got all knotted and tangled up together presently though not exactly after any fashion they had got knotted and tangled up before but a little sideways this time and somewhat upside down which Jane Elizabeth Firesheets said she picked up from Jimmy who Benton Lynch of a sudden discovered an appreciation for that he had not previously been aware of. Of course they got knotted and tangled together rightside up too and backwards for a spell and with him on for the ride and her on for the ride and then a little sideways and somewhat upside down again prior to getting unknotted and untangled up and just laying together in the hay so as to recuperate. Jane Elizabeth Firesheets fetched a squashed and flattened pack of cigarettes out from her back pantspocket and rounded one up some and lit it while Benton Lynch engaged himself in the observation of the plum-colored parts which had commenced to shrink in ever so slightly. Jane Elizabeth Firesheets said it was the best she'd had, said it was the best she'd had ever, and she asked Benton Lynch was it the best he'd had ever too and Benton Lynch grunted like he usually grunted when Jane Elizabeth Firesheets asked him was it the best he'd had which she always asked him. But she insisted this time it was really the best she'd had, the best she'd had ever, probably on account of she'd never done it with a true culprit before, hadn't ever had the occasion to get all knotted and tangled up with an actual outlaw, she called it.

"I thought Jimmy was a culprit," Benton Lynch said still eying the plum-colored parts which appeared to contract acutely.

"Jimmy was a hoodlum," Jane Elizabeth Firesheets told him in a sharp and spiteful sort of way. "Oh he had his wit and he had his charm and he had his regular good looks but he didn't ever do nothing but little old piddly mess. I mean he didn't have no class and didn't have no style much and wasn't never anything going to come of him. I guess I just got took in."

"I guess," Benton Lynch said.

And Jane Elizabeth Firesheets rolled onto her side and reached her arm across Benton Lynch's midsection and told him, "But you, you got this," and she ran her fingers down the long slender barrel of the Harrington and Richardson Buntline revolver and wrapped them around the grip of it. "I ain't never seen a gun so big as this one," she said and picked it up and cocked it and uncocked it and held it in front of herself in both her hands. "What do they do when you point it at them? What do they say to you?" she wanted to know.

"They don't say nothing much," Benton Lynch told her, "don't do nothing much either."

"They do what you say do, don't they?"

"I guess," Benton Lynch told her.

"I bet they do just exactly what you say do. I bet they don't hardly breathe or move or nothing less you say breathe or less you say move. I bet they don't never stop looking at this thing here." And Jane Elizabeth Firesheets cocked the hammer with both her thumbs and drew onto the ridge beam overhead. "Lord, don't you know that feels good," she said, "don't you just know it."

"I guess," Benton Lynch told her, addressing almost exclusively her plum-colored parts which had shrunk in and shriveled so as to be only a portion of what they had been previously.

"And I suppose they just throw the money at you," Jane Elizabeth Firesheets said. "I mean I don't figure he'd be anxious to get shot on account of it. Probably ain't even their money anyhow."

"Likely not," Benton Lynch told her.

"And it's a bunch of money, I imagine. I imagine it's a pure load of money, isn't it?"

"What's that?"

"The money, Benton. I said I imagine whenever you make off with some it's a load of it."

"Ain't no regular load," Benton Lynch said, "just whatever's around in the cash drawer and that ain't been no regular load so far."

"But it's something anyhow," Jane Elizabeth Firesheets told him, "and you get the thrill of sticking somebody up for it. I mean it must make you tingly all over."

"I could go to prison," Benton Lynch said.

And Jane Elizabeth Firesheets cocked and pointed the gun all over again. "Yea," she told him, "ain't that exciting."

Jane Elizabeth Firesheets wanted to see firsthand

Benton Lynch's technique and wanted to get stuck up doing it, but Benton Lynch was reluctant and a little embarrassed to show off his technique straightaway and flatout refused to do it until Jane Elizabeth Firesheets suggested that she might flatout refuse to do a few things herself, and so Benton Lynch got up out of the hay and played like the culprit and Jane Elizabeth Firesheets got up out of the hay and played like the clerk. As he did not have any pants to stick his gun into, Benton Lynch held his pistol behind his back and stepped up square in front of Jane Elizabeth Firesheets who was making out to dust the countertop. "May I help you?" she said, and Benton Lynch asked her did she know who he was and she told him of course she did, but Benton Lynch told her back she didn't and explained why and so they started all over again with the May I help you? followed by the You know who I am? which immediately preceded the arrival of the Buntline revolver that got brought into view but did not get aimed at Jane Elizabeth Firesheets exactly, or anyway did not get aimed at Jane Elizabeth Firesheets exactly until Jane Elizabeth Firesheets insisted it get aimed at her exactly and so it did get aimed at her exactly eventually but did not get cocked straightaway until Jane Elizabeth Firesheets insisted it get cocked too if cocking was what Benton Lynch usually did to it once he had aimed it, so it got aimed at Jane Elizabeth Firesheets and got cocked as well after which Jane Elizabeth Firesheets had her testicles threatened with Walnut Cove which was the first place to pop into Benton Lynch's head.

And Jane Elizabeth Firesheets said, "Hold on here. You see any balls to blow to Walnut Cove or anywhere else?"

And since he could not discover any but his own, Benton Lynch shook his head no.

"Well what is it you're going to say if it's a woman?" Jane Elizabeth Firesheets wanted to know.

And as the Stem in Union Ridge already had been a woman unlike the Busick and the McIver and the Barnard and the Grissom, Benton Lynch told Jane Elizabeth Firesheets what it was he would say since he had already said it.

And Jane Elizabeth Firesheets asked him "Poontang?" to which Benton Lynch shook his head yes.

She wanted to take it from the outset one time through and so Benton Lynch uncocked the pistol and stuck it behind his back and Jane Elizabeth Firesheets commenced to dust the countertop and she stayed at it until she got talked to and then aimed and cocked at, and likely it was the sight of the bore along with the threat of the bullet that thrilled and excited her and caused her plum-colored parts to swell and expand appreciably the sight of which distracted Benton Lynch from his thievery and thrilled and excited him to where it was a pure toss up as to which of his weapons would go off first. Naturally when she saw that both barrels were trained on her, Jane Elizabeth Firesheets got even more thrilled and even more excited which led to some additional swelling and some additional expanding and thereby set Benton Lynch into a pure frenzy and he near about threw himself at Jane Elizabeth Firesheets and knocked her down into a haypile where him and her did some serious wrestling and tumbling around and gyrating and oooohhhing and groaning and grunting and nosewhistling and not a shabby lot of perspiring until at last they both gave out almost simultaneously and laid back free of each other panting towards the rafters. Jane Elizabeth Firesheets said it was the best she'd had, said it was the best she'd had ever, and she asked Benton Lynch was it the best he'd had ever too and Benton Lynch told her he believed it actually was.

They planned to make off together, planned to rent out a modest little house off and away somewhere and loot and plunder the countryside roundabout it until they had massed the accumulated sufficient money to buy a ragtop and take it south to Daytona so as to drive it on the beach which Jane Elizabeth Firesheets admitted had always been a particular ambition of hers ever since she gave up the ballet, and though it had not ever been a particular ambition of Benton Lynch's he said he would be pleased to own a ragtop and drive it on the beach, insisted he would be pleased to own a ragtop and drive it on the beach, insisted upon it most strenuously and with considerable passion so as to be permitted to go back to looking at and touching those parts of Jane Elizabeth Firesheets he had been looking at and touching when they got onto the subject of the ragtop in the first place. And it had to be a brick house, Jane Elizabeth Firesheets said, a modest little brick house off and away somewhere to loot and plunder from primarily on account of the insulating qualities of brick which Jane Elizabeth Firesheets had developed a refined appreciation of especially since her move to Chalybeate Springs as your cottages and your shacks and your hovels generally do not display much in the way of insulating qualities, and Jane Elizabeth Firesheets complained that her feet had not known a warm moment since Labor Day which she said was a particular problem in chesty women like herself whose blood did not circulate like it did in everybody else. And Benton Lynch, who appreciated at least half of the dilemma, nodded his head sympathetically.

The momma Firesheets and the daddy Firesheets and the granddady Firesheets and the brother Firesheets all got told it was a visit northwest to the trailer and the dilapidated henhouse so as to acquaint the Jeeter Lynch and the pure Lynch with Miss Jane Elizabeth Firesheets and it was a visit to the northwest and even to the trailer and the dilapidated henhouse eventually, but straightaway it was just a visit to the northwest alone up through Raleigh, west on to Graham, and then north on 87 as far as Altamahaw where Jane Elizabeth Firesheets insisted her and Benton Lynch get off the bus and do some casing around, she called it. Naturally Benton Lynch wanted to know some casing around for what and Jane Elizabeth Firesheets told him Action and Benton Lynch asked her what sort of Action exactly and Jane Elizabeth Firesheets pointed at the front of Benton Lynch's trousers where the pistol was which Benton Lynch had been afraid she would point at. He was not so anxious for Action himself and he followed Jane Elizabeth Firesheets out from the bus station and along the street all the while attempting to convince her that she was not so anxious for Action either, but Jane Elizabeth Firesheets told him she knew what she was anxious for, told him she'd figured he'd be anxious for it too unless of course he was too scared to be anxious, unless of course it hadn't been him doing any of it all along, and then she struck on out ahead of him and Benton Lynch watched her sweet behind ever so briefly prior to blowing out a breath and saying, "Where then?" which spun her around and brought her on back to him. "Out this way," she said and hooked her fingers in the crook of his elbow. "There's bound to be something out this way."

And there was something out that way in the form of big Robroy Troutman's Grocery Boy Jr. on the right side of 87 just past the city limit. It was chiefly operated by big Robroy himself who was known as big Robroy not because there was a little Robroy anywhere but mostly because big Robroy was just too plain big to stay regular Robroy, was too plain tall and too plain wide to be anything else but big Robroy. Mrs. big Robroy, who was not especially dainty herself, generally sat behind the counter with Mr. big Robroy weekday afternoons and Jane Elizabeth Firesheets could see the both of them from the corner of the parking lot, Mrs. big Robroy reading a beauty magazine and Mr. big Robroy cleaning under his fingernails with the edge of a laminated pocket calendar. Jane Elizabeth Firesheets desired to do the casing herself, insisted upon doing the casing actually even though Benton Lynch told her she'd done quite enough with the casing around, told her he usually did not do much casing anyhow but just some sneaking and some lurking and whatnot, and Jane Elizabeth Firesheets wanted to know what in the world he thought casing was if not sneaking and lurking and whatnot, and so Benton Lynch admitted to having cased previously but was still reluctant to let Jane Elizabeth Firesheets partake of the least little bit of the sneaking and the lurking and the whatnot on account of the risks to her person and to those parts of her person which Benton Lynch so adored. However, once Jane Elizabeth Firesheets got so far as desiring and insisting on a thing there ordinarily was not any beating her back from it and consequently she got to case after all once she'd outlined the alternatives for Benton Lynch who developed a new appreciation of her stand on the matter and watched her cross the parking lot past the gaspumps and step on into the store proper where she browsed all throughout the premises, lingered some at the breadrack, and then bought a pack of Winstons from Mr. big Robroy who she chatted with and grinned at and even touched ever so briefly with the tipends of her fingers until Mrs. big Robroy looked up from her beauty magazine and commenced to glare in a venomous sort of way.

Jane Elizabeth Firesheets reported that there weren't nobody but them two and they didn't strike her as troublesome since the man was too fat to get anywhere in a hurry and the woman couldn't kill with her ugly which was what she seemed to have the most of, and though not intending to tell Benton Lynch his business, Jane Elizabeth Firesheets went on to suggest that maybe he ought to squeeze off a round in between the two of them just to get the blood going but Benton

Lynch told her he did not believe he would and Jane Elizabeth Firesheets suggested that maybe he should consider it and Benton Lynch said he would consider it but did not believe the considering would change his mind any and Jane Elizabeth Firesheets asked him what in the world he had the gun for then and Benton Lynch told her to point primarily and Jane Elizabeth Firesheets asked him why didn't he go ahead and shoot it every once in a while just to stir things up a little and Benton Lynch did not say anything directly and so Jane Elizabeth Firesheets asked him again and Benton Lynch did not say anything directly the second time either and so Jane Elizabeth Firesheets demanded to know how come and Benton Lynch told her, "I ain't got no bullets," which seemed to hit Jane Elizabeth Firesheets all wrong and she crossed her arms over herself and exclaimed, "Sweet Jesus Christ!"

Benton Lynch attempted to explain to her the economics of his predicament, attempted to explain to her how the sizable lead bullet and the sizable brass casing and the powder load all together ran into some money not to mention his general reluctance to shoot anybody in the first place, but Jane Elizabeth Firesheets just turned her backside on him and he walked around to her frontside but she just turned her backside on him again and so Benton Lynch told her backside he'd buy some bullets, told her backside he'd buy some bullets first chance he got, but Jane Elizabeth Firesheets said that wouldn't cure it, and said it wasn't even the bullets anyway, it was just that she'd figured he was mean and vicious and she guessed he wasn't after all. Then she exhaled, drew in her shoulders some, and said she supposed she'd get over it. And although Benton Lynch insisted he was mean and insisted he was vicious, Jane Elizabeth Firesheets did not unstoop her shoulders or show him her frontside or generally seem at all convinced that he had any savagery to him, so Benton Lynch stomped on the asphalt and said he'd just let her see for herself exactly what sort of nasty motherfucker he could be and Jane Elizabeth Firesheets stiffened some on account of how talk like that generally had a way with her.

He crossed the parking lot at near about a dead run with his long skinny arms slashing the air, and he did not even pull up at the door but kicked it open and ran straight to the counter where Mr. big Robroy had stood up to see what the commotion was and Mrs. big Robroy had laid down her magazine and turned her lips inside out in utter annoyance. And Jane Elizabeth Firesheets watched Benton Lynch holler something at Mr. big Robroy, holler something she could not hear exactly but could understand well enough, and Jane Elizabeth Firesheets watched Mr. big Robroy shake his head no. So he drew it out from his trousers and cocked it and did not just aim it this time but laid the bore of it flush against Mr. big Robroy's pantsfront and with his free hand grabbed up a portion of Mr. big Robroy's shirt and apparently a portion of Mr. big Robroy's chesthairs as well, and he brought his pointy hollowed out face up tight into Mr. big Robroy's face and he communicated some with Mr. big Robroy who in turn communicated some with Mrs. big Robroy who let her mouth go rightside in and made some considerable use of it as she crossed behind Mr. big Robroy to the cash register, opened the drawer of it, and emptied out what money there was into a brown paper bag which she rolled down the neck of and set on the countertop. With his left hand still full of shirtfront and chesthairs, Benton Lynch raised up his pistol and pushed on the tipend of Mr. big Robroy's nose with it so as to bring home a point he was at the time making to Mr. big Robroy, and when Mr. big Robroy seemed to comprehend just exactly what it was he was meant to comprehend, Benton Lynch opened his mouth and bared his big square teeth first at Mr. big Robroy and then at Mrs. big Robroy who got called something unseemly on top of it.

He recrossed the parking lot at a full and thorough
dead run with his long skinny arms slashing the air and
the rolled up paper sack bulging out from his jacket
pocket, and Jane Elizabeth Firesheets turned her full
frontside to him and set herself to tell him how wrong
and sorry she was, set herself to tell him how mean
and vicious he'd turned out to be after all, but before
she could even get started good she got snatched up
like a mailsack and carried along with some immediate
velocity and Jane Elizabeth Firesheets wanted to know
the why of it, demanded to know the why of it, and
Benton Lynch told her they generally called it making
off which he explained was the prudent thing to do
once you'd separated a man from his money, and Jane
Elizabeth Firesheets admitted she had not considered
the getting away part of it quite as carefully as she
might have. They crossed the road and ducked off
around a brick house but could not pass through the
backyard on account of a Cyclone fence and the dog it
had been put up for, and when they came back out
towards the road again Mrs. big Robroy Troutman
commenced to scream at them from the parking lot of
the Grocery Boy Jr., commenced to scream at them in
a general and hysterical sort of way, and wailed and
waved her arms and pointed every now and again, and
Benton Lynch and Jane Elizabeth Firesheets tore out
to the south towards town and ducked off this time
behind a little white frame house without a fence and
without a dog either but just a green Nova parked beside it and a shriveled up white-haired lady in the
kitchen window, and Jane Elizabeth Firesheets grinned
and said Hey to her and jerked at Benton Lynch's arm
and told him to grin and say Hey to her too, and Benton Lynch wanted to know exactly what for until Jane
Elizabeth Firesheets pinched up some of his armskin
and squeezed it and Benton Lynch grinned and said
Hey.

The shriveled up white-haired lady said Hey back

but did not truly grin in the course of it and Jane Elizabeth Firesheets stepped a little closer to the window
than she had been previously and asked her, "Have
you seen our cat, ma'm?" and Benton Lynch and the
shriveled up white-haired lady near about harmonized
with "Cat?" which got some more armskin pinched up
and squeezed and Jane Elizabeth Firesheets said, "Yes
ma'm. He's a big yellow cat and he run off. Raymond
here thought he seen him come up this way, didn't you
Raymond," and once Jane Elizabeth Firesheets had
showed Benton Lynch her two fingers he said, "Yes
ma'm," and fairly smirked. The shriveled up white-
haired lady could not recollect having seen a big yellow
cat, and could not recollect having seen a cat of any
description roundabout the house anytime lately which
she said suited her just fine on account of her allergy
to cats which caused her eyes to water and her nose to
run and her glands to get puffy, and Jane Elizabeth
Firesheets asked what was it she said as her voice did
not carry especially well through the windowglass, so
the shriveled up white-haired lady stepped on around
to the sidedoor and opened up the six light wooden
one and the aluminum storm one and said she could
not recollect having seen a big yellow cat, could not
recollect having seen a cat of any description roundabout the house lately which suited her just fine on
account of her allergy to cats which caused her eyes to
water and her nose to run and her glands to get puffy.
And Jane Elizabeth Firesheets said, "Yes ma'm," and
stepped up onto the stoop and then pushed her way on
into the house taking with her the shriveled up white-
haired lady who insisted she had not seen a big yellow
cat, insisted she had not seen any cat whatsoever.

"Shut up," Jane Elizabeth Firesheets told her. "We
want the keys to that car yonder."

"He'll turn up on his own," the shriveled up white-
haired lady said. "You needn't go out scouring the
countryside."

"Just you shut up," Jane Elizabeth Firesheets told her and she turned around to Benton Lynch, who was still outside standing where he'd been standing and was still wondering about most everything in general, and she said to him, "Get in here and do something with this woman," and so he stepped on into the house himself and asked her, "What?"

"Show it to her," Jane Elizabeth Firesheets told him. "Go on and show it to her," and she pointed her finger at Benton Lynch's pantsfront and the shriveled up white-haired lady sucked air.

So he went ahead and drew it on out and cocked it and pointed it and Jane Elizabeth Firesheets said, "We want the keys to that car yonder. Now where are they?"

And the shriveled up white-haired lady addressed the bore of the Harrington and Richardson Buntline revolver primarily and told it, "In my pocketbook," and pointed backwards over her shoulder fairly much towards the ceiling.

Jane Elizabeth Firesheets emptied the thing out on the kitchen table and took the keys and the credit cards and what money there was along with a little round tortoiseshell compact that she said she'd always wanted one of, and she searched through the refrigerator after some cheese but there was not any cheese in the refrigerator or anywhere else in the house that she could discover and Jane Elizabeth Firesheets wanted to know why not and the shriveled up white-haired lady told her she could not pass cheese, and Jane Elizabeth Firesheets said that was the sorriest reason she'd ever heard of and she told Benton Lynch, "Knock her on the head."

"What?"

"Knock her on the head," Jane Elizabeth Firesheets insisted. "Go on. They always knock them on the head."

"I don't like cheese much myself," Benton Lynch observed.

And Jane Elizabeth Firesheets said, "Christ Almighty. Gimme that thing," and she took hold of the gun by the handle and swung it for practice once but did not find the grip suited her. "We can't leave this woman running loose," Jane Elizabeth Firesheets said.

"We could tie her up. We could lock her in a closet."

"Nope," Jane Elizabeth Firesheets said. "We gone knock her on the head. They always knock them on the head," and she took the gun by the barrel and made a swing with it that way which proved far more satisfactory and so she backed the shriveled up white-haired lady against the corner cupboard and swung the pistol one time at the crown of her head striking her flush on the topnotch with the buttend of the handle, and the shriveled up white-haired lady said, "Ouch!" and reached her fingers up to touch herself as Jane Elizabeth Firesheets swung the pistol a second time and chiefly struck her fingers but some of her topnotch too and the shriveled up white-haired lady said, "Stop!" and Jane Elizabeth Firesheets swung the gun again and hit pure scalp causing the white-haired lady to slide down the face of the corner cupboard in a shriveled up white-haired heap on the floor, and Jane Elizabeth Firesheets gave the pistol back to Benton Lynch and told him, "Ain't nothing to it."

She drove and he lay curled and knotted up on the floorboard so as to not be seen traveling south through Altamahaw, and he heard the one siren off behind them and they met the other on the highway and Jane Elizabeth Firesheets told him, "State trooper," and asked him wasn't it just thrilling, wasn't it just absolutely thrilling. Once she got to Graham she took the 85 highway to the west but only traveled the little ways to Burlington where she stopped at the outlet mall on account of how she'd always wanted to stop at the outlet mall but had never before had the opportunity to, and Benton Lynch asked her couldn't they come back

to the outlet mall some other time but Jane Elizabeth
Firesheets told him as long as she was there already
she might as well go on ahead and buy a thing or two
and she reached over and helped herself to the rolled
up paper sack in Benton Lynch's jacket pocket and
took out a handful of money from it. Benton Lynch
couldn't judge time with much accuracy on the floorboard on account of how everything seemed to take
forever so he figured Jane Elizabeth Firesheets stayed
gone from twenty minutes to two and a half hours before she came back with two paper bags and a big
Styrofoam cup that did not have any of the Coke left
in it but did have some of the ice which she gave Benton Lynch and then showed him the pair of nylons
she'd bought and the two pair of sheer black underpanties and the shortsleeve pink sweater with padded
shoulders that she was particularly fond of and she
held it up in front of herself and wanted to know from
Benton Lynch did the pink set off the highlights in her
hair and soften up her milky white skintone, and Benton Lynch studied the pink sweater and the milky
white skin and the wheatstraw hair all at once and together and told Jane Elizabeth Firesheets pink was just
the thing for her and she said she thought so too and
decided it would not suit her to do anything but wear
her pink sweater straightaway so she came out of her
blouse right there in the front seat of the Nova and
Benton Lynch watched the new pink sweater go on
overtop the brassiere, or actually watched the brassiere disappear beneath the new pink sweater, and got
agitated there on the floorboard and commenced to
fidget and squirm and slide around until he managed
to wedge himself up under the glove compartment.

They decided to keep west as far as Greensboro, or
anyhow Jane Elizabeth Firesheets decided to keep
west as far as Greensboro and a little bit past it to the
Albert Pick Motor Hotel at the airport exit where she
took a room as Mrs. Roosevelt and parked the Nova

around at the backside of the lot and collected up her nylons and her panties and her discarded blouse and offered some little assistance in the unbending of Benton Lynch's various joints. She wanted to count the money first thing, insisted on counting the money first thing, and spilled it from the sack all over the bed where she spread it out with her hands and picked it up and dropped it and generally threw it around some and guessed it was probably a thousand dollars or probably eight hundred dollars or probably six hundred dollars anyway and then actually counted it and totaled it up and figured it was likely upwards of $230.00 before the nylons and the underpanties and the pink shortsleeve sweater, and she told Benton Lynch it was a right fair haul but Benton Lynch, who had laid himself out on the part of the bed where the money wasn't told her back, "It ain't hardly worth knocking an old lady on the head for."

Naturally that touched off Jane Elizabeth Firesheets as she herself had done what knocking on the head had gotten done and in her best scruples and principles if you please voice she wanted to know from Benton Lynch just why he'd set out in a line of work he didn't have the stomach for.

"It ain't my line of work to beat up on old women," Benton Lynch said.

And Jane Elizabeth Firesheets laid her hands on her hips and told him back, "I didn't see you jump in to keep me from it."

"Well we were in a predicament, we were in a pure fix and wouldn't never been in one if you hadn't wanted some Action."

"It's my fault then is it," Jane Elizabeth Firesheets said, "and here I've run off from home and left my momma and daddy and my brother and my grand-daddy and give up a man that loved me truly, just give up everything for you and you a criminal getting tracked down everywhere. Ain't this some gratitude."

And Benton Lynch crossed his arms over himself and told her, "Nobody made you come and nobody keeping you here."

"That's right, use me up, violate my holy temple, and then just throw me off somewhere. You just a sorry little cocksucker like all the rest of them."

And Benton Lynch, who was not one to usually move in a quick and snakelike sort of way, moved in a quick and snakelike sort of way this time, rising up from the bed and taking Jane Elizabeth Firesheets by the shoulders in one motion and flinging her down onto the mattress in another. "I ain't taking that off you," he told her.

And Jane Elizabeth Firesheets said, "Shitass," and kicked at him and punched at him and tried to get up but he pushed her back down onto the bed and so she tried to get up again but he pushed her back down again and so she held her wrist and moaned until he leaned over to see what the trouble was when she raised up of a sudden and butted him square in the nose with her forehead. Naturally the tears blinded Benton Lynch straightaway and Jane Elizabeth Firesheets slipped off the bed to his right side and punched him in the ear prior to clenching her hands together so as to hammer him in the stomach one time, and even though he was part blinded and part deaf and near about fully stooped over, Benton Lynch managed to hook his fingers into some little piece of Jane Elizabeth Firesheets's new shortsleeve pink sweater and though it was not much of a little piece it was enough of one for Benton Lynch to hurl Jane Elizabeth Firesheets against the headboard with and of course the hooking and the hurling caused the fabric to give and stretch some which Jane Elizabeth Firesheets took notice of immediately and she grabbed up the little stretched and bulging portion between her fingers and shrieked, "You've ruint it! You sorry son-of-bitch you," and then she went fairly berserk and flailed with

her arms and kicked with her legs and hollered and
swore and spat once or twice and was just generally all
over Benton Lynch from everywhere at once and so he
threw himself at her to cover her up and smother her
some and she tried to flail and tried to kick and still
hollered and swore and spat, but with the weight and
bulk of Benton Lynch atop her Jane Elizabeth Firesheets could not draw breath with much effect and so
did not do anything after a spell but lay stretched out
on the bed beneath Benton Lynch's cumbersome
weight and bulk and with her private parts in close
proximity to his private parts, and likely it was somewhat the proximity and somewhat the weight and bulk
and somewhat the agitation and exasperation all mixed
up together with the actual bedstead and the actual
mattress and pillows and the actual bedlinens that
stirred and excited Jane Elizabeth Firesheets who wiggled her hips just enough to get detected at it and got
answered with the best part of a gyration which led to
some true grinding and some oooohhhing and some
groaning and some grunting and some nosewhistling
and directly the articles of clothing were sailing all
about the room except for the pink shortsleeve
sweater, which got folded up and put in a drawer, and
except for the two pair of socks, which did not get
separated from the two pair of feet as the bedsheets
were noticeably chilly.

They had not ever gyrated and oooohhhed and
groaned and grunted and nosewhistled atop a proper
mattress before and so found the whole business novel
and exotic which intensified the gyrating and the
oooohhhing and the groaning and the grunting and
even the nosewhistling too and thereby hastened the
exhaustion some and while they recovered they told
each other how sorry they were about what they had
said and what they had done and then they talked
about the little brick house and the ragtop, or anyhow
Jane Elizabeth Firesheets talked about the little brick

house and the ragtop and Benton Lynch watched her
naked parts and let her until he'd had enough of the
talking and had enough of the recovering and reinsti-
gated the gyrating and the oooohhhing and the groaning and the grunting and the nosewhistling and
persevered with it near about courageously but ultimately gave out all over again. Jane Elizabeth Firesheets suggested they should take a shower to get shed
of the perspiration and the various by-products of the
undertaking, but Benton Lynch, who had never
washed himself in front of a woman before, did not
take to the idea right off and consequently got dragged
into the bathroom and pushed up under the shower-
head and Jane Elizabeth Firesheets unwrapped the
Ivory and lathered Benton Lynch with it prior to
handing the cake over to Benton Lynch who returned
the favor and then they rinsed and dried each other
and got back into their socks and got back into the
bed, but even after all the soaping and the lathering
and the rinsing and the drying off somehow Benton
Lynch did not feel much cleaner than he had previously and laid on his back thinking about the plum-
colored parts and the milky white parts and the
wheatstraw parts until he could not stand to just think
about them any longer and rolled over to find Jane
Elizabeth Firesheets curled up asleep with her mouth
open and her every breath clicking in her throat.

  They continued to the west as far as Winston-Salem
since it was Jane Elizabeth Firesheets's opinion that
they should go to the trailer and the dilapidated henhouse by the most undirect and roundabout way they
could go there, which Jane Elizabeth Firesheets said
was how it always got done everywhere she'd ever seen
it get done. So they did not head north exactly until
the 158 highway and even then they did not proceed
direct to Neely and on to Oregon Hill but instead went
a little west at Stokesdale and then northeast a spell
and then a little west some more and finally pure east

to Pelham and south down 29 to the gravel road that led up and over the rise to the trailer and the henhouse and the general ruin. They had not been expected or anticipated by the fat Jeeter or Mr. Raeford either and so did not get greeted exactly, or anyway did not get greeted perceptibly by the fat Jeeter, who they caught in the middle of her favorite story and partway through a graham cracker, and only got purely leered at by Mr. Raeford who did not see much milky whiteness from day to day except for feathers and except for eggs.

The fat Jeeter thawed out and heated six chicken fried beef patties and served them along with some canned succotash and a dozen Hungry Jack biscuits, and once she'd fixed it all and got it on the table the fat Jeeter ate the primary part of it as well and Benton Lynch watched her and chewed his ice while Mr. Raeford fairly much interviewed Jane Elizabeth Firesheets and patted her near hand some and rubbed her near arm some and pinched her near cheek some and grinned a whole hell of a lot and just generally made a jackass out of himself which he persisted in after supper and on throughout the evening there on the Mediterranean sofa in front of the television where he patted and rubbed and pinched those parts he had patted and rubbed and pinched previously and ventured off into some bold new territory as the evening wore on and the beer cans got crushed and discarded. However, Mr. Raeford did not truly get anything for all his patting and rubbing and pinching except unduly agitated or anyway did not get anything from Jane Elizabeth Firesheets, but later in the night he did manage to slide down the paneling and pile up on the trailer floor a number of times, the first occasion being far and away the most violent one, and Jane Elizabeth Firesheets sat bolt upright in bed and said, "Whut's at?"

"Daddy," Benton Lynch told her.

"Doing what?" Jane Elizabeth Firesheets wanted to know.

"Hardly anything," Benton Lynch told her and he showed his big square teeth which Jane Elizabeth Firesheets could not see in the darkness.

And Jane Elizabeth Firesheets laid back down and clasped her hands under her head. "Your daddy must not ever get none," she said. "Looked at me like he could smell it."

"Momma and him don't get on much," Benton Lynch told her.

"I guess not," she said, "and don't seem to me like he'd want none even if he could get it. Your momma's a hog. I ain't seen her yet when she wasn't chewing something."

"Momma's all right," Benton Lynch told her. "Daddy's all right too. They just don't get on much anymore."

And Jane Elizabeth Firesheets sat up sideways on her elbow and said, "I'll tell you one thing Benton Lynch, they can get on as little as they please but I ain't staying around here to listen to it. Can't hardly turn around in this place, your daddy's done touched every touchable thing I got, and your momma don't care for nothing won't fit in her mouth. I ain't staying around here."

"It ain't so bad as that."

"I'm telling you this thing Benton Lynch, I ain't staying around here. Don't no robber I ever heard tell of live in a trailer with his momma and daddy. This just ain't no way to do it and me and you gone go out and find us a place to rent, gone find us a place tomorrow."

"It ain't so bad as that."

"Tomorrow Benton Lynch," Jane Elizabeth Firesheets said and then she added, "or me and you ain't gone get on at all," and Jane Elizabeth Firesheets rolled over and showed Benton Lynch her backside but not hardly like she'd shown him her backside previous times.

They had not eaten the waffles the fat Jeeter

heated in the toaster and Jane Elizabeth Firesheets
had only been patted on the forearm once when they
left in the Nova to look for a place to live which
Benton Lynch did not feel it proper to tell his parents they were leaving in the Nova to do and so told
them they were just going to drive roundabout for a
spell and they did drive roundabout for a spell but
did not find anything to suit Jane Elizabeth Firesheets, actually did not find anything for rent until
Benton Lynch suggested they buy a *Chronicle* which
they bought and studied the classified section of
where a woman in Stacy had taken out an advertisement for a Christian couple to fill her bungalow, and
Jane Elizabeth Firesheets said she'd always wanted
to live in a bungalow so they called the woman and
did in fact get up with her before midday, but the
woman in Stacy looked at Jane Elizabeth Firesheets
and Benton Lynch one time hard and decided they
were likely not the Christian couple she was after
and she told them as much which prompted Jane
Elizabeth Firesheets to call the woman a snotty old
bag and so she went ahead and decided they were
certainly not the Christian couple she was after.

They looked at two apartments in Neely proper
and a tenant house out the Burlington road which
had been advertised as well ventilated but turned out
near about windy, and as Jane Elizabeth Firesheets
and Benton Lynch could not see that ventilation was
much of an asset they declined the tenant house
partly on account of the draft throughout it and
partly on account of the general look of the place
which Jane Elizabeth Firesheets said was altogether
too niggery for decent white folks, and likely it was
somewhat the draft and somewhat the niggery that
discouraged Jane Elizabeth Firesheets but surely it
was mostly the bungalow or anyhow the idea of the
bungalow that she could not shake loose of since she
had always wanted to live in a bungalow, had de-

cided she had been meant to live in a bungalow ever since earlier in the day when she saw what a bungalow was, but no matter how she held her head or squinted or shaded her eyes she could not see even the least little hint of bungalow in the tenant house and had failed to discover a trace of it in the pair of Neely proper apartments and so was understandably downcast and discouraged since she could not find anything with that bungalow quaintness and that bungalow charm to it except for the actual Stacy bungalow that she had not been Christian enough to move into.

There were not any promising advertisements after the well ventilated tenant house which had not itself truly been a promising advertisement but had got read and taken as one by Jane Elizabeth Firesheets who had figured there might be some hidden charm and might be some hidden quaintness where there had only turned out to be a preponderance of ventilation. So they did not know where they would go to find what it was they were looking to find though Jane Elizabeth Firesheets insisted she knew where they would not go to find what it was she knew they would find if they went back there, and consequently Benton Lynch felt pressed to make something in the way of a suggestion and so he made something in the way of one and directed Jane Elizabeth Firesheets who directed the stolen green Nova down the boulevard to Lawsonville Avenue and then east four blocks to the second Mrs. Cummings's house. Benton Lynch had visited Otway Burns once previously and so let himself and Jane Elizabeth Firesheets in through Mrs. Cummings's side door and up the back stairway to the third floor where Benton Lynch knocked three times hard on what had been Otway Burns Lynch's door but was not Otway Burns Lynch's door any longer and so got answered by Miss Alma Sue Frazier of the Roxboro Fraziers

whose door it had become and who was still in her
housecoat and had not yet tended to herself and so did
not have any face to show them but the one she had
woke up with. Benton Lynch looked at Miss Alma Sue
Frazier like she'd been dredged up off a riverbottom
with a grappling hook and did not offer to speak to her
until she asked him, "What is it?" which prompted him
to ask her back, "Otway Burns Lynch?" and Miss
Alma Sue Frazier pointed at the floor and thereby sent
Benton Lynch and Jane Elizabeth Firesheets down a
flight to the second floor hallway which Otway Burns
Lynch had moved onto once Mr. Etlington had relocated to the first floor after Mrs. Hinton got sent to the
Masonic Eastern Star Home in Greensboro as it was
the way of things among Mrs. Cummings's boarders to
precipitate ever downward and so drop lower and
lower in the house and closer and closer to the kitchen
and to the dining room, or as low and as close as
ground level anyhow but not quite so low as the basement where the Ling brothers lived in a little concrete
room with a lavatory in the corner of it and two tiny
dirty windows near about on the ceiling. They were
very quiet and very clean and extraordinarily yellow
and blinked an awful lot even for Chinamen.

Benton Lynch knocked three times all over again
and did in fact rouse up Otway Burns who was between shifts at the cigarette plant where he had got
promoted from pushing cigarettes around on a cart
and now organized and directed and orchestrated the
general pushing around of cigarettes on carts all
throughout the plant which did not call for any actual pushing on his own part but just the organizing
and directing and orchestrating, and as he did not do
anything to get dirty any longer he had left off wearing the green poplin trousers and the green poplin
shirt and the leather Red Wing boots and instead
wore suits primarily, some that he owned and some

that he'd paid on and every now and again a sport-
coat from the Johnny Miller collection when he felt
lively and bold enough for it. But it was just a plain
gray flannel suit with a plain gray vest overtop and a
powderblue shirt and a skinny maroon tie that he
opened the door in and Benton Lynch said to him,
"Hey," and Otway Burns pondered Jane Elizabeth
Firesheets and pondered Benton Lynch again before
his eyebrows rose up and he said, "Oh," and then
said Hey back.

Benton Lynch made the necessary introduction, or
anyhow pointed at Jane Elizabeth Firesheets and
worked his mouth and pointed at Otway Burns Lynch
and worked his mouth and then stepped aside so Jane
Elizabeth Firesheets and Otway Burns Lynch could introduce themselves to each other which they succeeded at more completely and Otway Burns stuck his
arm out to Jane Elizabeth Firesheets with his hand
hanging off the end of it like a rag on a peg and Jane
Elizabeth Firesheets took ahold of his fingers and near
about curtsied which was not the sort of thing Jane
Elizabeth Firesheets had much history of but her knees
could not seem to help themselves in the presence of
Otway Burns Lynch who was not fat like his momma
or vile like his daddy or pointy and angular and hollowed out like his brother but was fairly regular or
even better than regular really partly on account of his
gray flannel suit that he owned the most of and partly
on account of his broad foreign accent that he had
contrived, cultivated, and mastered on his own. With
one regal sweeping gesture he invited Jane Elizabeth
Firesheets and Benton Lynch on into his room which
he did not call his room but called his quarters when
he was not calling it his digs, and he asked them
wouldn't they like some herbal tea from southeast
Asia and showed them his cupful which was almost
precisely the color of urine and Benton Lynch, who
had said straightaway he would have some herbal tea

before he saw what the herbal tea looked like, decided he would not have some herbal tea after all while Jane Elizabeth Firesheets got purely rapturous over it and clasped her hands together and could not seem to control her delight at the prospect of southeast Asian herbal tea which she said she'd been in the mood for since she didn't know when, and from his little hot-plate by the window Otway Burns observed, "How extraordinary," and Jane Elizabeth Firesheets told him, "Yes, quite."

Otway Burns Lynch asked after his momma and his daddy, who he did not call Momma and Daddy but called Mother and Father instead, as he had not had occasion to drop by the trailer lately, which he did not call the trailer but called the homeplace where he would not drop by to exactly but rather would pop in at, and he said he had been meaning to call, which he did not call call but called telephone, in lieu of popping in, which was what he said precisely, but had not gotten round to it and so was curious to know were his momma and daddy getting along all right, which he called carrying on, and Jane Elizabeth Firesheets, who had not been asked any of it, answered all of it. "I'll say," she told him.

Benton Lynch sat on the couch with the fronts of his knees against the edge of the coffee table, and Jane Elizabeth Firesheets wandered roundabout Otway Burns Lynch's quarters picking up and perusing various of Otway Burns Lynch's personal items when they seemed worth troubling herself to pick up and peruse and eventually she parked in front of a framed picture of a woman dying in an opera and she asked Otway Burns Lynch what she was doing and who was she anyhow and Otway Burns Lynch told her who she was in Italian and said she was dying in an opera and told what it was in Italian, and Jane Elizabeth Firesheets said she'd almost gone into the theater herself, said she'd almost gone into the ballet, and Otway Burns

Lynch bobbed his teaball in his pot of water and said, "Oh?" and Benton Lynch looked at that portion of Jane Elizabeth Firesheets where he knew the plum-colored parts to be. She said she'd always had a natural talent for the dance, she called it, said she'd always had an instinct for rhythms and melodies, and she asked Benton Lynch didn't she have an instinct and Benton Lynch said yes she did. And Otway Burns Lynch asked her why had she not pursued her endemic urges to which Jane Elizabeth Firesheets replied that personal family matters had kept her from it, though she insisted she could still cut a figure with the best of them and of a sudden Jane Elizabeth Firesheets lit out towards the center of the room, leapt into the air, and managed about a quartertwist prior to landing firm on the hardwood causing every loose item in the place to jump up and settle again. "Brava!" Otway Burns Lynch exclaimed, and from the sofa with his knees against the coffee table Benton Lynch said, "Christ," but to himself mostly.

Jane Elizabeth Firesheets told Otway Burns Lynch the southeast Asian herbal tea was simply divine, though that was after Jane Elizabeth Firesheets had spooned in a few sugars and added a touch of honey since the southeast Asian herbal tea in its natural naked yellow state had not struck Jane Elizabeth Firesheets as simply divine exactly, but she insisted the sugar and the honey too brought out the oriental subtleties of the blend and she offered her cup to Otway Burns Lynch who sipped from it and rolled the tea around in his mouth and looked off towards the ceiling. He said he did believe the sugar and the honey noticeably enhanced the tea, he said he believed they enhanced it noticeably, and Jane Elizabeth Firesheets offered her cup to Benton Lynch so as to allow him to taste the oriental subtleties and appreciate the noticeable enhancement for himself, but since the sugar and the honey together had not

rendered the southeast Asian herbal tea any less
urine colored than it had been previously, Benton
Lynch declined to drink any, and so Jane Elizabeth
Firesheets asked him why didn't he take just one tiny
little taste, and Benton Lynch said he did not believe
he wanted a tiny little taste, and so Jane Elizabeth
Firesheets insisted he just sip at it one time, but
Benton Lynch said he did not want to sip at it, and
so Jane Elizabeth Firesheets turned her face so as to
show it to Benton Lynch exclusively and stretched it
and twisted it and just generally worked it up into an
indisputable and fairly ferocious goddamn-well-
better-drink-this-fucking-tea expression and she said
to him, "Please," and Benton Lynch said he guessed
he'd have just one tiny little taste and so sipped at
the tea for himself and got asked wasn't it subtle and
wasn't it enhanced and said Yes, wasn't it.

They got around to the bungalow presently, or
anyhow got around to the bungalow once Otway
Burns Lynch had pointed out a few of his more pre-
cious possessions and had explained what they were
and where they'd come from and how much he'd
given for them, all of which Jane Elizabeth Firesheets announced she was purely intrigued with and
every now and again she'd turn to Benton Lynch and
ask him wasn't he intrigued too, at the same time
indicating to him that he should be, and he would
shake his head Yes he was. But they did in fact get
around to the bungalow presently and Jane Elizabeth
Firesheets told Otway Burns Lynch what had happened to them earlier in the day with the woman
from Stacy, or anyway related to him an episode loosely based on what had happened to them earlier in
the day with the woman from Stacy who Jane Elizabeth Firesheets described as surly once Otway Burns
Lynch told her surly was the word she was looking for,
and she asked Benton Lynch wasn't it surly that the
lady had been after all and Benton Lynch shook

his head yes. She told Otway Burns she was after a
bungalow chiefly but would take most any quaint
and charming place she could come up on and she
said Benton Lynch had suggested, and she pointed at
Benton Lynch for effect, that maybe Otway Burns
Lynch could help them find some quaint and charming place, perhaps even an actual bungalow, on account of his numerous acquaintances and contacts
roundabout, and Otway Burns Lynch set his teacup
down and took his chin in his hand and admitted he
did have numerous acquaintances and numerous contacts too. Then he pondered for a spell and chewed
his bottom lip and at last snapped his fingers one
time and announced he believed he had a line on
just the thing, not a bungalow exactly but the sort of
place that could be construed as quaint and could be
made charming, and Jane Elizabeth Firesheets got all
agitated and excited and wanted to know what was it
and where was it and how much was it, and Otway
Burns told her it belonged to a Mr. Jack Albright
and he said to Benton Lynch, "You know Jack Albright, don't you?" but Benton Lynch, who did not
have numerous acquaintances and numerous contacts, shook his head no.

Otway Burns Lynch said it was a five room painted
block house with a wood before it and a tobacco field
behind it and a hedgerow to the left of it and a garden
plot to the right of it, and he said it had been empty for
a while on account of Mr. Jack Albright could not find
anybody to let it out to that suited him, not that he was
courting Christians—Otway Burns said Mr. Jack Albright did not show any particular enthusiasm for
Christianity—but just that he did not want any niggers
and did not want any trash, though Otway Burns did
not call them niggers and did not call them trash. And
then Otway Burns held his chin again and thoroughly
chewed his lip prior to announcing that he believed he
could get what he called an inside line on the Jack

Albright painted block bungalow if an inside line was what Benton Lynch and Jane Elizabeth Firesheets wanted gotten, and Jane Elizabeth Firesheets said most emphatically Yes it was what she wanted gotten and said most emphatically Yes it was what he wanted gotten too, and then she asked Benton Lynch wasn't it just exactly what he wanted gotten after she'd already said most emphatically it was and Benton Lynch told her he supposed so, and Otway Burns Lynch said, "Done then," and gave his fingers to Jane Elizabeth Firesheets who shook them and said Done then herself after glancing inquiringly at Benton Lynch who did not seem to find the finger shaking in any way objectionable or stirring either.

They slept another night at the trailer even though Jane Elizabeth Firesheets had announced and swore she would not sleep another night at the trailer, and the morning after the night they slept at the trailer that Jane Elizabeth Firesheets had swore she wouldn't she insisted Benton Lynch get up with his brother but Benton Lynch told her Otway Burns would call or Otway Burns would drop by though Jane Elizabeth Firesheets feared he would not telephone and would not pop in either and kept after Benton Lynch until Otway Burns did in fact ring up which was what he told the fat Jeeter he was doing in lieu of popping in which he did not presently have the leisure for, and as the fat Jeeter and Otway Burns exchanged trifles Jane Elizabeth Firesheets fretted by the dinette until at long last the fat Jeeter handed the phone receiver over to Benton Lynch who exchanged a trifle or two himself and then just listened some which did not soothe Jane Elizabeth Firesheets's fretfulness the least little bit and she pulled at Benton Lynch's arm and wanted to know was it done but just got answered with several all rights and a couple of Uh Huhs and so continued to fret and continued to pull and continued to yank until Benton Lynch cradled the receiver, turned full around to Jane

Elizabeth Firesheets, and told her, "Otway Burns says hey."

They moved in directly even though it wasn't exactly what Jane Elizabeth Firesheets had figured it would be and even though Jane Elizabeth Firesheets and Benton Lynch weren't exactly what Mr. Jack Albright had figured they were, but it all got settled and it all got done anyhow and they moved in directly without hardly a grumble from the fat Jeeter and with somewhat of a stifled grumble from Mr. Raeford Lynch who could not grumble outright in front of the fat Jeeter and so rubbed Jane Elizabeth Firesheets's near arm and patted her near cheek and touched another thing or two as a general sendoff. They piled up what clothes they had in the backseat of the Nova along with an iron frypan that the fat Jeeter hadn't any use for ever since her electric skillet and they stopped off at the 7-Eleven for a bottle of Champale which Jane Elizabeth Firesheets intended to break against the front stoop for luck but Benton Lynch convinced her Champale was not lucky but for boats and so they drank it at supper with their eggs that they had to eat off their fingers direct out of the iron pan as they did not have any dishes or any utensils either except for Benton Lynch's pocket knife. There was, however, some furniture roundabout that Mr. Jack Albright had gone ahead and let out with the house, primarily an iron bedstead with iron springs and a mattress and a kitchen table and two kitchen chairs and several curtain rods and a piece of a drapery and a solitary upholstered settee that smelled like old socks, and once Benton Lynch had licked off his fingers and Jane Elizabeth Firesheets had run water in the pan they toured the house together and Benton Lynch got told what the kitchen would look like and what the living room would look like and how bright and airy the den and the bathroom would be and then he got taken on into the bedroom which suited him already and he snatched up Jane Elizabeth Firesheets and fell with her onto the mattress which smelled like old socks itself once you got your nose right up to it.

As Jane Elizabeth Firesheets figured it they needed some general repair and renovation money but Benton Lynch insisted they had about as much general repair and renovation money as they would likely require, or anyhow he insisted it for a spell until Jane Elizabeth Firesheets fetched a state roadmap out from the glovebox of the Nova and commenced to cast around for a favorable spot to draw some funds out of which moved Benton Lynch away from insisting and more towards suggesting and Jane Elizabeth Firesheets struck on and decided upon Hillsdale almost straightaway which prompted a little pleading and pathetic moaning on Benton Lynch's part but Jane Elizabeth Firesheets just smoothed out the wrinkles in the brown jacket with the flat of her hand and preceded Benton Lynch out the door to the driveway. She took the 158 highway southwest and then headed due south along route 135 to Hillsdale where there was no scantling amount of puny grocery and convenience stores and she pulled into a couple of lots and aided Benton Lynch in casing a Pantry and a Li'l General but they were both too busy to suit him and he directed her out the city limits a ways on a backroad where they came up on Ross's Grocery No. 2 which did not have much of a crowd about it, did not even appear open really, and Benton Lynch announced that this was the very place he would knock over, he called it.

Jane Elizabeth Firesheets parked the Nova back a ways behind Ross's Grocery No. 2 just off the blacktop alongside of a curing barn and Benton Lynch glanced at the roadmap and said to himself, "Duncan," prior to getting a goodluck kiss on the cheek and a therapeutic flurry somewhere else so as to remind him what he had to live for, and then he excused himself to go off and plunder and he did go off and plunder, plundered direct from the proprietary Ross who did not have a No. 1 grocery any longer and so stayed permanent at the No. 2 and who as well had cultivated an endearment for his private parts and did not want them going anywhere without him and so gave up the extent of his riches which Jane Elizabeth Firesheets said, "Shit," at once Benton Lynch had counted it out on the seat. She did not see as $112.00 would go hardly anywhere, did not see as how she could be expected to set up house with $112.00 and she bitched some and moaned some partly out the window and partly at Benton Lynch who had retired to the floorboard and consequently could not see where it was they had stopped until Jane Elizabeth Firesheets told him, "Get out and do something," and he peeked up over the dashboard at the gaspumps and the glassy storefront and before he could even say, "Uh Uh," before he could even work up the spit to say Uh Uh, Jane Elizabeth Firesheets unfolded the map herself and told him, "Corinth. Now get on out," and she opened the door for him since he did not seem disposed to open the door and she pushed him with her foot since he did not seem disposed to get on out the door once she'd gone to the trouble to open it and she did not give him a kiss or a flurry or a goodluck even but drove on around the store out of sight.

Jane Elizabeth Firesheets said $262.00 would likely be quite a plenty. Jane Elizabeth Firesheets said $262.00 would likely be a suitable and fitting amount and she reached down underneath the dash and patted Benton Lynch atop his head. Jane Elizabeth Firesheets said she was going to buy some pots and some pans and a knife and a fork and spoon set and some bedlinens and pillows and plastic windowshades and bathtowels and a shower curtain and two or three of those plastic endtables that stack up on each other. Jane Elizabeth Firesheets said she had to have a radio too, maybe even a record player, and one of those tiny Japanese televisions that you can put on your stomach which she told Benton Lynch she'd had a particular yearning for since she'd never looked at anything but a Motorola, and she said she wanted a half dozen houseplants and a doormat with some ducks on it and a hatrack and a picture for over the sofa and a picture for over the bed, and once she had steered into the K-Mart plaza west of Neely and parked the Nova in the lot she asked Benton Lynch was there anything he had a particular yearning for and he laid his head back against the door panel and told her, "Uh Uh."

She got it all but for the television which she did not have the money to get as tiny Japanese stomach-top models were at a premium, so instead she bought a Ricky Skaggs record album for her new radio/phonograph and pushed it all outside in a cart which she left beside the Nova for Benton Lynch to unload while she went in the Food Lion next to the K-Mart and bought potatoes and a pork roast and applesauce in a jar and white wine and lime sherbet and toilet paper and something potent and sweet-smelling for the old socks aroma all of which she carted outside too and all of which she piled into what of the backseat Benton Lynch had not already piled things into. And Jane Elizabeth Firesheets said she guessed they'd live like royalty for a spell, said she guessed they'd live like a duke and a princess, and she asked Benton Lynch didn't he guess that was the truth of it and Benton Lynch said he guessed it was, and so she talked about dukes and she talked about princesses all the way back to the bungalow which Jane Elizabeth Firesheets had decided was not one of your pure and absolute bungalows but had some measurable cottage to it and maybe a touch of hideaway seeing as how it was tucked off behind the hedgerow and the general undergrowth and she stopped just short of the driveway and told Benton Lynch to raise up and look see didn't it have some cottage and some hideaway to it and Benton Lynch brought his face up over the door panel to the windowglass and told her, "Uh Huh."

Jane Elizabeth Firesheets situated her pots and her pans and her flatware and arranged the plastic tables and set out the plants and instructed Benton Lynch to hang the windowshades but Jane Elizabeth Firesheets neglected to buy any windowshade hardware and so Benton Lynch did not have anything to hang the windowshades from and decided he would hang the shower curtain instead but Jane Elizabeth Firesheets had neglected to buy any shower curtain hooks too and so Benton Lynch figured he would treat the sofa with the potent sweet-smelling disinfectant and so he treated the sofa with the potent sweet-smelling disinfectant and then sat down on it and sniffed for the old sock aroma which was just about when Jane Elizabeth Firesheets came out from the bedroom and up the hallway towards the kitchen and she spied Benton Lynch on the sofa where he was midway through his sniffing but she did not truly notice the sniffing and was taken primarily with the sitting instead and she laid her hands on her hips and asked Benton Lynch why in the shit didn't he do something useful for a change and he attempted to explain to her the sniffing part of it that went along with the sitting part of it but Jane Elizabeth Firesheets just turned around and stomped back into the bedroom since she had not asked her question so as to get an answer to it.

Benton Lynch made himself especially useful thereafter and insisted on hanging the picture over the sofa and hanging the picture over the bed and demanded the privilege of connecting the record

player and then would not hear of resting himself
until he had moved and adjusted most every piece of
furniture to Jane Elizabeth Firesheets's satisfaction
after which he offered to cook supper and Jane Elizabeth Firesheets told him No, thank you, so he offered to help cook supper and Jane Elizabeth
Firesheets told him No, thank you again, and so he
offered to set out the dishes and the silverware on
the table and Jane Elizabeth Firesheets told him
plain No, and so he insisted on setting out the dishes
and the silverware on the table and Jane Elizabeth
Firesheets asked him why in the shit didn't he get
out from under her feet anyhow.

She barbecued the pork roast in the oven and boiled
the potatoes and opened the applesauce and as she had
not recollected to buy any proper dinner candles she
hunted up a pink birthday candle and a white birthday
candle in the back of the utensil drawer and stuck
them on a shoebox top and set them on the table.
Then she got herself done up somewhat for supper,
piled her hair up onto the point of her head, slipped
into a lacy white dress, and put some color to her
cheeks out of the compact she had got in Altamahaw
instead of the cheese after which she lit the birthday
candles and called Benton Lynch off the sofa where he
had been just sitting and hardly sniffing at all. Benton
Lynch had not expected birthday candles and so was
somewhat surprised by them and had not expected the
pile of hair and the lacy white dress and the rouge
either and so was somewhat surprised by them and had
not truly expected a pork roast but was not very astounded and dumbstruck by it like he was verily astounded and dumbstruck by the shimmer and glisten
of the milky white skin and the wheatstraw hair in the
birthday candlelight. He lost his appetite almost
straightaway but she made him sit down at the table
anyhow and she made him unscrew the top off the
wine and pour out a portion for herself and a portion

for himself and she made him raise up his glass and knock it together with hers in a toast. "Luck," she said.

She had a present for him, told him she had a present for him and brought it up from her lap where she'd kept it hid away. It was near about the slightest of boxes wrapped in a piece of bag and tied up with string and he loosed the string and tore the paper and read the box which he found to contain fifty Remington .45-caliber hollow point cartridges with brass casings and copper tips, and Benton Lynch said, "Oh," and Jane Elizabeth Firesheets told him, "Dump some out," and he dumped some out and they laid there on the tabletop bigger around than a twenty-penny spike and generally meaner looking, or anyhow they laid there on the tabletop but for the one Jane Elizabeth Firesheets took up between her fingers and held in the birthday-candle-light and the sight of it there with the orange glow dancing roundabout the casing made Jane Elizabeth Firesheets all tingly and she told Benton Lynch as much and showed him a scant piece of her tongue which straightaway rendered Benton Lynch a little worse than tingly himself and he came near about direct across the tabletop after Jane Elizabeth Firesheets and reached around behind her and commenced to take her dress off right there in the kitchen and the idea of getting her dress took off her in the kitchen made Jane Elizabeth Firesheets even more tingly than she'd been at the outset and once her dress had dropped off her to the floor she helped Benton Lynch out of his shirt and loosened his pants for him and they both slipped down onto the linoleum and rolled around until they got chilled enough to retire to the bedroom. Jane Elizabeth Firesheets sat up high and gyrated and laid down low and let Benton Lynch gyrate some and then the both of them slammed together for a while and Benton

Lynch panted hard and grunted once and Jane Elizabeth Firesheets groaned prior to whimpering prior to passing out what looked like dead away. She did not revive for a considerable while, but naturally when she did revive she told Benton Lynch it was the best she'd had ever and asked him wasn't it the best he'd had ever too and he made some kind of affirmative noise or another and laid his head on the soft fleshy part of Jane Elizabeth Firesheets's frontside. She raked her fingers through his hair and asked him was he happy and asked him was he contented and he told her Yes and she told him back she was happy and she was contented too. "But," she said and then played with Benton Lynch's hair momentarily until she said again, "But," and then proceeded with, "me and you we've shared our passion and our love and the very roof over our heads and you've met all my people and I've told you all about them and all about me and I've met your people but you ain't never told me anything about anybody, especially not anything about you. I wish you would tell me something, Benton."

"Ain't nothing to tell," Benton Lynch said.

"Bound to be," Jane Elizabeth Firesheets insisted.

"Ain't," Benton Lynch said.

And Jane Elizabeth Firesheets told him, "All right then," and lifted her fingers up from Benton Lynch's scalp and removed the fleshy part of her frontside out from under Benton Lynch's right ear and once his face hit the bedlinen he decided there was likely something to tell after all and he said, "Hold it."

"What for?" Jane Elizabeth Firesheets asked him.

"I thought of something," Benton Lynch said. "I thought of something about me." And he lifted his head so as to make room for the fleshy part of Jane Elizabeth Firesheets's frontside which got put back where it had been. "Go on," she told him and he adjusted himself until his ear was just where he wanted his ear to be and was as unfolded and as uncrimped as he could get it and he waited to feel the fingertips on his scalp after which he did in fact open his mouth and begin to speak. "We stepped in some shit," he said, "stepped in some big, big shit."

*T*HEY DIDN'T none of them want to end up like Mr. Vernon Littlejohn had ended up all stretched out dead in his own puddle, didn't none of them want to get even the least little piece of what Mr. Vernon Littlejohn had got the whole of and so they did not struggle, did not breathe hardly, especially Mr. Radford whose store it was anyhow but not Mr. Burke or Mr. Mountcastle either who had only stopped in to jaw and then got reason to wish they never had. They said he did not seem anything but agitated and agitated was the last thing in the world they wanted him to seem what with his right hand wrapped around what it was wrapped around and his foremost finger flush up against what it was flush up against. And straightaway the sheriff wanted to know, "Square teeth?" and Mr. Radford and Mr. Burke and Mr. Mountcastle told him, "Yes sir." And the sheriff wanted to know, "Pointy nose?" and Mr. Radford and Mr. Burke and Mr. Mountcastle told him, "Yes sir" again. And the sheriff wanted to know, "Tall of stature?" and Mr. Radford and Mr. Burke told him plain "Yes sir" a third time while Mr. Mountcastle of Eden told him just exactly and precisely how tall of stature right down to the quarter inch.

The sheriff asked after the manner of dress and got a jacket from Mr. Radford and some trousers from Mr. Burke and the entire ensemble from the Eden Mountcastle who recollected a missing button on the top jacketpocket and a greasy smudge on the left trouserknee and seemed to recall that one of the brown brogans had a black shoelace and one of them didn't but he could not recollect which was what and apologized for it. The sheriff wanted to know were there distinguishing marks, scars and moles and warts and such, and Mr. Radford took up his chin in his hand and Mr. Burke crossed his arms over himself and together they considered the matter and decided there had not been any detectable scars or moles or warts and such, except for the scar on his left thumbjoint, Mr. Mountcastle said, and the mole on his forehead and the piece of wart just at the hairline on the back of his neck. And the sheriff asked them did he cock the gun and did he point it and if he did cock it and point it what did he cock it and point it at, and Mr. Radford said it was his jewels which the Burke did not object to and the Mountcastle did not elaborate upon, and the sheriff asked Mr. Radford, "Where was it this time?" and Mr. Radford told him, "Lillington," and Mr. Burke agreed, "Lillington," and Mr. Mountcastle said, "Down 401 south, don't you know, twenty-six, maybe twenty-seven miles outside Raleigh."

The sheriff was anxious to identify the weapon precisely and he asked Mr. Radford if he could precisely identify the weapon and Mr. Radford told him, "Sure enough. It was a pistol," and he looked at Mr. Burke who agreed with him that most definitely it was a pistol, and Mr. Radford held his hands apart in front of him what he judged to be the length of the barrel and then looked to Mr. Burke again who said, "Longer," and then looked to Mr. Mountcastle who said, "Whatever's nine inches."

"Nine inches?" the sheriff asked him.

And Mr. Mountcastle said, "Yes sir. Standard bore length on a Harrington and Richardson Buntline revolver."

"A Harrington and Richardson Buntline revolver?" the sheriff asked him.

"Yes sir," Mr. Mountcastle said. "Forty-five caliber."

"You're certain?" the sheriff asked him.

"Yes sir," Mr. Mountcastle said.

"It had a wood grip," Mr. Radford added.

"Surely did," Mr. Burke said.

And Mr. Mountcastle told the sheriff, "Walnut."

Sheriff Burton had rode to Greensboro with his eye-witness account from Mr. Musselwhite and had got the police artist there to draw him a picture which he took out from his front shirtpocket, unfolded, and showed to Mr. Radford. "This the man that robbed you?" he wanted to know, and Mr. Radford told him, "Well I do guess it is," and the picture got stuck in the face of Mr. Burke who said, "Yes sir, the very one," and then got shown to Mr. Mountcastle who asked could he hold it and carried it direct under an incandescent bulb where he found himself in possession of a rude line drawing of a face that, except for the freckles, was the very image of Mortimer Snerd. And the sheriff asked Mr. Mountcastle, "That the man?" and got told, "Lord no."

"Ain't nobody looks like that," Mr. Mountcastle said. "I mean the teeth was big but they wasn't sit-ting out in the horizontal and the nose was pointy but you couldn't hardly bore a hole with it and if a man's eyes was that far back in his head he could see out his ears. That ain't him, favors him some but it just ain't him."

"All right then," the sheriff told him, "we gone make it him, you and me," and he took Mr. Mount-castle in what appeared to be custody and drove him off in the squad car not so far as Greensboro since Mr. Mountcastle flatout refused to ride so far as Greens-boro but so far anyhow as Mrs. Alice Covington's house on Russell Avenue. Mrs. Alice Covington painted snow scenes on rocks at Christmas and bun-nies on rocks at Easter and turkeys on rocks at Thanksgiving and just sundry items on rocks the rest of the time, and though it was just rocks and just Santas and bunnies and turkeys and flowers and butterflies and whatnot Mrs. Alice Covington was considered quite the artist roundabout and was measurably pleased and gratified to find herself called upon by the sheriff and the Mountcastle, was measurably pleased and gratified to find herself privy to even some little piece of the mayhem pure and undiluted and she studied the police artist's rough drawing of Mortimer Snerd and aired out her appreciation for the general texture of the thing. She told the sheriff she found it a primitive piece but moving and satisfying nonetheless and she asked him didn't he think it had a dash of the Fauves to it and the sheriff told her it was a plain Beasley, like some strain of Beasley indigenous to Greensboro, and the sheriff said it might be primitive and it might be moving and satisfying too but it wasn't who they wanted it to be, and Mrs. Covington chewed on her top lip ever so briefly prior to suggesting to the sheriff, "Matisse?" and the sheriff told her, "No ma'm. Beasley."

Mr. Mountcastle said the teeth were what was wrong primarily but the nose was what was wrong too and the eyes were what was wrong on top of it and he took in hand the primitive and moving and satisfying Beasley and pointed out to Mrs. Covington what she might do to the teeth and what she might do to the nose and the eyes as well but Mrs. Covington would not lay her pencil point to any part of the Greensboro Beasley's paper on account of the pure sanctity of the artistic endeavor, she called it, and so she fetched a broad hunk of shale out from under her worktable and set to sketching on it with the assistance of the Eden Mountcastle who suggested how she might draw one thing and indicated how she might draw another, and once she'd sketched out the face to suit the Mountcastle she touched it up here and there so as to suit herself and then set about the painting of it with acrylic paint and tiny little pig

bristle brushes and when she got done she held the
thing away from herself and eyed it at arm's length
prior to turning it around to Sheriff Burton and the
Eden Mountcastle who found themselves perusing
what looked to be Howdy Doody but for the
checked shirt and neckerchief, and though Howdy
Doody was closer than Mortimer Snerd Howdy
Doody was not right on it exactly and the Eden
Mountcastle suggested and indicated that Mrs.
Covington hollow out the eyes some and get shed of
the freckles and get shed of the grin all of which Mrs.
Coviwngton obliged him in prior to turning the thing
roundabout to the sheriff and the Eden Mountcastle
all over again and the sheriff said, "Well?" and the
Eden Mountcastle told him, "Yes sir, the very one."

The full-blooded Loop Road Myrick's sister's husband had not ever reproduced a picture from a rock
before but said he would attempt to, and the sheriff
asked him would he keep Mr. H. Monroe Aycock otherwise occupied and write the copy himself on account
of how it was the sort of thing which called for a fact or
two to leak in with the general palaver, and the full-
blooded Loop Road Myrick's sister's husband nodded
and then studied the hunk of shale and said, "Alice
Covington?" and the sheriff nodded and the Loop
Road Myrick's sister's husband said he had one of her
Christmas rocks holding his backhall door open.

They printed the picture in color at the top of the
front page of the morning *Chronicle* which did not
from year to year come out with much but your seasonal color picture of a pumpkin in autumn and a
flower in springtime and such as that, so an unseasonal
color picture especially an unseasonal color picture of
a man painted on a rock captured the attention of most
everybody in general and captured the attention of Mr.
Tiny Aaron quite specifically. He had got up in the
dark when he usually got up and had put on his striped

robe and his socks and had dunked his head in the sink and plugged in the percolator and then had got the paper in and carried it to the breakfast room with the rubberband still on it. He did not open it up to look at it until he'd poured himself a cup of coffee and creamed it and sugared it and dumped a little of it in the saucer so as to blow on it and slurp it out, but when he did unroll the paper at last he got attracted straightaway to the color photograph and he looked at it with his mouth open a little and then read the print all roundabout it with his mouth moving a little and then looked at it again with his lips still parted and swallowed once and slurped some coffee and finally told himself aloud, "Uh Oh."

FIVE

Mr. Raeford Lynch said it weren't him, said it weren't no way it could be him, said it just plain weren't him and kicked at the ground and swore and spat a time or two. The fat Jeeter said it weren't him too but without the enthusiasm that Mr. Raeford said it weren't him and then she put something in her mouth and chewed it and swallowed it. Mr. Raeford said it weren't in a Lynch to kill and pilfer, said it weren't in a Lynch to do but the decent and righteous thing and he swore and spat and kicked at the ground all over again. "It weren't him," Mr. Raeford said. "That boy's good as gold," and the fat Jeeter said it weren't him too and put something in her mouth and chewed it and swallowed it.

The full-blooded Loop Road Myrick's sister's husband ran the picture of the rock once in the morning of a Thursday and once in the evening of a Thursday and it was not until Saturday late that he got ahold of an actual snapshot which Mr. Raeford and the fat Jeeter had to be excised from along with a piece of the trailer and assorted chickens. It was a grainy black and white picture that Otway Burns had taken with his Instamatic the summer he had decided a photographer was what he intended to be which was the summer he wore the skyblue seersucker jacket, even in August, and tied the silk handkerchief around his neck. He had posed the fat Jeeter and had posed Mr. Raeford and Benton, had even posed the chickens to the extent that the chickens would let themselves get posed, and had turned the Instamatic at a tilt for effect which the full-blooded Loop Road Myrick's sister's husband did not seem to appreciate much, which nobody at the *Chronicle* seemed to appreciate much really except for Mr. H. Monroe Aycock who could see the art in the thing who could sense the aura of the latent creative juices he called them, and who objected to the razor blade and the general excising because of the art and because of the juices, and consequently so as to shut Mr. H. Monroe Aycock up the full-blooded Loop Road Myrick's sister's husband let him write the accompanying copy, and Mr. H. Monroe Aycock said it would be a contemplative piece with ramifications and got asked i maybe he couldn't throw in a fact or two every now and again when the mood hit him.

Mr. H. Monroe Aycock followed his usual method of composition which called for several feverish bursts of torrid scribbling interrupted by spells of pure and unproductive reflection when he would mostly marvel at what he had been torrid over just previously and then anticipate just what he might say once he got to feeling torrid again, but he was not torrid much in the afternoon at the office and did not get truly frantic until after supper when he retired to his study, which was the paymaster's desk in the northwest corner of the dining room, where he worked himself up into a contemplative fit with ramifications and then reflected and marveled and even doodled some in the margin of the page. He was awfully pleased and awfully satisfied once he got done scribbling and marveling and doodling and so as to share and distribute his pleasure and his satisfaction he stepped into the living room and read aloud his contemplative piece with ramifications to Mr. H. Monroe Aycock while she quilted a pillow cover and watched The Love Boat on television which she would not let Mr. H. Monroe Aycock turn off which she would not let Mr. H. Monroe Aycock even turn down entirely on account of how the girl off The Brady Bunch and the girl off Petticoat Junction had both gotten themselves infatuated over the boy off The Partridge Family who had a romantic fondness for Betty White as he did not know she was his aunt. Mr. H. Monroe Aycock read the contemplative parts and read the ramifications too in a loud theatrical voice that fairly completely drowned out the television except when Captain Steuben and Gopher got into a heated discussion over Gopher's mother, as played by Ethel Merman, and except when the man from Burlington came on to sell his Datsuns. Otherwise Mr. H. Monroe Aycock made himself heard almost exclusively and he finished out with a boisterous flourish followed by a lingering poetical silence after which he asked Mrs. H. Monroe Aycock, "Well?" and Mrs. H. Monroe Aycock told him, "That's very nice dear," and Mr. H. Monroe Aycock told her back he had figured it was.

Most people found it even more inspiring and even more vivid and lyrical than the ode to Vernon Littlejohn or anyhow that was the general consensus among the guests at Mrs. Estelle Singletary's annual autumn harvest brunch which everybody with an opinion worth airing usually attended. Mrs. Estelle Singletary herself was particularly fond of the part about breaking the bonds of degradation and the shackles of penury. She said it stirred her, said it stirred her profoundly, and while Miss Bernice Fay Frazier found herself stirred by the bonds and the shackles as well she argued that the part about striking out at the myriad inequities of this our existence was likely the most moving and agitating piece of prose she had ever had the pleasure to peruse, and the widow Mrs. Jennings W. Hayes wanted to know just how many was a myriad anyhow but she never did find out as Miss Bernice Fay Frazier got short and peevish straightaway and insulted the widow Mrs. Jennings W. Hayes's poetical sensibilities. Mr. H.

Monroe Aycock himself arrived shortly thereafter and accepted the congratulations of the hostess and of the hostess's sister and of the general assortment of guests as well and he got asked almost right off did he have a favorite part and what was it and as he liked so very much of the thing he had to think a minute before he could decide and at last he selected the part where the chickenhouse and the chickens served as a metaphor for the hectic, troubled, and fateful lives we lead on our speck of swirling dust in the vast darkness of space, and he repeated the speck-of-swirling-dust-in-the-vast-darkness-of-space part of it as he found that phrase particularly apt, he called it.

Mrs. Estelle Singletary directed Mr. H. Monroe Aycock to the only comfortable chair in the house and assorted guests collected roundabout him once he had sat himself down so as to congratulate him all over again on the article as a whole and especially on the swirling-speck-of-dust portion since the particular aptness of it had hit most everybody once Mr. H. Monroe Aycock had pointed it out to them. Mrs. Estelle Singletary brought him his coffee with his cream and his sugar already in it and as she handed it to him she happened to mention how profoundly stirred she'd been by the bonds and the shackles which Miss Bernice Fay Frazier got wind of and so felt compelled to say a word or two on the myriad inequities of this our existence and felt compelled to tell how she'd been moved and how she'd been agitated which the widow Mrs. Jennings W. Hayes happened to be near enough to hear and so got reminded of what it was she wanted to find out and she slipped up on Mr. H. Monroe Aycock when he was otherwise unengaged and asked him just how many was a myriad anyhow.

"Scores and scores," he told her.

"How many's that?" she wanted to know.

"Very many," he said.

And the widow Mrs. Jennings W. Hayes told him back, "Ah."

The widow Mrs. Askew, who had been strangely silent and reflective all throughout the proceedings, set her untouched Waldorf salad and her nibbled at sliver of breakfast steak down on the coffee table and wondered out loud how it was that a man who would plunder and kill could have risen out of Jeeter stock and Mr. H. Monroe Aycock commenced to put forth his theory and his hypothesis on the influences of deviant brain cells in conjunction with socio-economic considerations but the widow Mrs. Askew had not wondered what she had wondered so as to get a theory and a hypothesis but had instead wondered what she had wondered so as to proceed on to wondering something else which she did in fact wonder once Mr. H. Monroe Aycock had played out on his brain cells and his considerations and she asked out loud why it was that the bald Jeeter had not seemed larcenous or murderous or even a little criminal which she had not asked out loud so as to get answered out loud but which did get answered out loud by Mr. H. Monroe Aycock who had a theory and a hypothesis on that part of the thing too as he had studied the whole business from every end and the middle also, and the widow Mrs. Askew heard the theory and heard the hypothesis and once Mr. H. Monroe Aycock had spent himself on them and closed his mouth at last the widow Mrs. Askew recollected aloud the peculiar way the bald Jeeter had of stooping over so as not to dump her wig off and she dabbed at the underside of her nose with her napkin and said, "Three months, almost three months to the very day."

"Hardly seems it," Miss Bernice Fay Frazier observed.

"Surely doesn't," the widow Mrs. Jennings W. Hayes added.

"We were near about sisters," Mrs. Askew said, "near about kin," and began to blubber genuinely. "We were like this."

And Miss Bernice Fay Frazier said, "So were we."

"We were too," the widow Mrs. Jennings W. Hayes added, "we surely were," and she raised her fingers up into the air and joined in the general waving.

They could not hunt him up anywhere, not Sheriff Burton or his fulltime deputy Mr. Larson or his parttime deputy Mr. Warner, they did not even know where to start to look as they could not get anything out of the fat Jeeter but for the chewing and the swallowing or out of Mr. Raeford Lynch either but for the swearing and the spitting and the stomping around. So they did not find him straight off as they did not know where to look to find him exactly though they had thought they had found him a week to the very day after Mrs. Alice Covington's picture on the shalestone when Mr. Newsome ran up the courthouse steps and direct into the sheriff's office all blanched and winded. "I seen him," he wheezed. "I seen him just now," and the sheriff got especially stern and earnest of a sudden and leapt to his feet in that purposeful sort of way people will leap to their feet when they are stern and earnest and he asked Mr. Newsome, "Where?"

"Out 29 a ways on the roadside," Mr. Newsome told him.

"Doing what?"

"Just sitting," Mr. Newsome said.

"Just sitting on the roadside?"

"In a truck," Mr. Newsome said, "in that pickup truck of his."

"Alone?" the sheriff wanted to know.

"Naw. Had that crew in the back."

"Lynch ain't got no crew," the sheriff said.

And Mr. Newsome studied the sheriff like maybe part of his face had puffed up and turned colors of a sudden. "Lynch?" he said.

"Lynch ain't got no crew," the sheriff told him.

"Overhill," Mr. Newsome said back.

"Overhill who?" the sheriff asked him.

"Overhill the gravedigger," Mr. Newsome said. "Overhill the gravedigger what Benton Lynch used to work for."

"Sometime lately?" the sheriff wanted to know.

"Not real lately," Mr. Newsome told him, "but sometime."

"Well what is it you want me to do with him?"

"Round him up," Mr. Newsome said. "Round him up and ask him a thing or two."

"Such as?"

"Well how in the hell should I know. You the law and if you can't see a hot tip when it comes up and slaps you in the face then ain't nothing I can tell you." And Mr. Newsome whirled around and attempted to storm on out the door but he had whirled around a little too vigorously and overshot the door and stormed off towards the wall instead and so had to stop and adjust his course some which gave Sheriff Burton the opportunity to catch up with him and lay his thick mealy hand on Mr. Newsome's shoulder and tell Mr. Newsome, "All right now, no call to get hot. Take me to him," and he followed Mr. Newsome out the office door and into the hallway where he attempted to tell the mayor's secretary, who was his secretary too sometimes, just where he was going and just why he was going there but the mayor's secretary was not behind her desk in her little alcove and there was no sign of her anywhere in the hallway but for the remote clack clack clacking of her heels on the courthouse steps as she descended towards the square on her way to the offices of the *Chronicle* so as to tell whoever might listen about the Overhill and about the truck and about the crew in the back of it.

They were right where Mr. Newsome had said they would be and they were doing just precisely what Mr. Newsome had said they were doing which was not anything really or not much of anything really as most of the boys in the back were poking and kicking and gen-

erally beating up on one of the boys in the back while
Mr. Overhill laid up against the cab door sucking on
the neck of his Ancient Age bottle. The poking and
the kicking and the general beating along with the
sucking too did not even let up any when the sheriff
and Mr. Newsome eased off the pavement in the squad
car and as the sheriff situated in the ring on his belt the
long black club he fetched out from under the carseat
some variant form of humanity crawled out from the
bed onto the tailgate and attempted to urinate over the
edge of it which he very nearly succeeded at. Sheriff
Burton asked for Mr. Overhill's registration and asked
for Mr. Overhill's license, and though Mr. Overhill
scratched around in the glove compartment and come
up with the registration soon enough he could not find
his license straightaway on account of how it was in his
wallet and on account of how his wallet was in his gray
pants and he did not have any idea where his gray
pants were and commenced to cast around for them
underneath the maps and the general rubbish in the
truck cab and continued to cast around for them until
Mr. Newsome pointed out to him that he was wearing
his gray pants which, after some gaping and some
gawking, Mr. Overhill learned to be the truth of the
thing and he did in fact fish his wallet out from the
right back pocket of his gray pants where he said it had
been all along.

Sheriff Burton studied the license just like he had
studied the registration and asked Mr. Overhill if he
was in fact Mr. Claude Elwyn Overhill of Altoona
Pennsylvania, and the poking and the kicking and the
general beating up broke off of a sudden in the
truckbed and five or six voices raised up at once saying, "Claude Elwyn!" and Mr. Overhill said, "Shit,"
and snatched back his license and snatched back his
registration. "C.E." he told the sheriff and then turned
around and told "C.E." to the back cab window and
got answered with "Right, Claude," from two people

at once followed by some florid profanity of which a solitary motherfucker was the only truly distinguishable item.

The sheriff wanted to know from Mr. Claude Elwyn Overhill just why he'd come to park himself and his truck and his crew out 29 on the roadside and Mr. Claude Elwyn Overhill told him, "We just come straight up from Louisiana and we're recuperating from it afore continuing on through Virginia and into Ohio."

"Recuperating?" the sheriff said.

"That's right."

"Seems to me you're just plain drunk," the sheriff said.

"Well that's a part of the cure," Mr. Overhill told him, "and anyhow I ain't doing nothing in this truck but sitting."

"Just sitting," the sheriff said.

"That's right."

"You not here to meet anybody?"

"Now who would I meet in this shithole?" Mr. Overhill wanted to know.

"A Lynch maybe," the sheriff told him.

"A Lynch what?"

And Mr. Newsome piped in with, "Benton Lynch, Benton Lynch. You picked him up in my store, put your stinking feet all over my chairseat."

"Who's he?" Mr. Overhill asked Sheriff Burton, "and what's his trouble?"

"Mr. Newsome here says you picked up Benton Lynch at his store a while back and carried him off with you wherever it was you went."

"Gangly?" Mr. Overhill said. "Horsefaced?"

"That's the one."

"Well hell," Mr. Overhill said, "I ain't see him since, I ain't seen him since uh. Hey," and he turned around to the back cab window, "where is it we ain't seen Benton Lynch since?"

"Benton Lynch!" the wiry tattoed white boy said back and stuck his face between two of the side louvers. "I'll fucking kill him. Where is he?"

"That's what I said, I said where is it we ain't seen Benton Lynch since?"

And the wiry tattooed white boy with his face still between the side louvers told Mr. Newsome primarily, "I will, I'll fucking kill him."

And Mr. Overhill laughed some and shook his head some and told Sheriff Burton primarily, "He don't mean nothing by it."

"You got no love for Benton Lynch then," the sheriff said to the wiry tattooed white boy and got told back, "Hell no."

"So you'd tell me where to find him if you knew where he was."

"I'd hunt him up my own self and I'd fucking kill him," the wiry tattooed white boy said between the louvers, "but I ain't got no idea where to look."

"We ain't seen him," Mr. Overhill said, "we ain't none of us seen him since somewhere or another. What is it he done anyway?"

"Well," the sheriff said and hooked his thumbs behind his belt so as to show off his paraphernalia some, "we figure he's robbed some people, we figure he's shot at one man, we figure he's killed another one. We figure he's armed and dangerous and likely a little desperate round about now."

"Benton Lynch?" Mr. Overhill said.

"That's the one," the sheriff told him.

And Mr. Overhill exclaimed, "Well I'll be goddamned!" and when the crew in the back heard Mr. Overhill being goddamned so enthusiastically they decided they would be goddamned too and so they were all goddamned together, were all moved and astounded, and did not say anything aside from the sporadic goddamns until the paltry negro piped in with "that ugly motherfucker" in a warm and affectionate sort of way.

The shock and amazement had not worn off but partly when Mr. H. Monroe Aycock eased up behind the sheriff's patrol car in his green Ford Galaxy and he got out the door with his pad and his pencil and his plastic camera and beat it on up to the truckcab like there might be some advantage gained from beating it on up to the truckcab but he did not get anything aside from a pair of hard looks and a "Who's he?" which was not even directed at him anyhow, and Sheriff Burton attempted to explain Mr. H. Monroe Aycock to Mr. Overhill but as there was really no explaining Mr. H. Monroe Aycock the sheriff let Mr. Aycock ask his questions and make his observations and air out his theories and thereby exhibit his various characteristics and his various qualities all of which Mr. Overhill paid some appreciable attention to right up until Mr. H. Monroe Aycock paused to draw breath when Mr. Overhill asked the sheriff, "Who is this asshole anyhow," which seemed to indicate to Sheriff Burton that Mr. H. Monroe Aycock had fairly well given himself away and so he went ahead and said, "Mr. H. Monroe Aycock," to Mr. Overhill and went ahead and said, "Mr. C. E. Overhill," to Mr. Aycock and did not further embellish the introduction himself though it got a Claude Elwyn or two added to it from the truckbed.

Mr. H. Monroe Aycock generally conducted curious interviews in that he usually did the primary part of the talking and wrote down the most of what he said and only every now and again asked a question, ordinarily a question that could be answered with a plain yes or a plain no, but the trouble was that Mr. H. Monroe Aycock, aside from doing the primary part of the talking, ordinarily did the primary part of the listening too since there was nobody much that cared to follow him where it was he seemed to regularly go, so when Mr. Overhill said his plain yeses and said his plain noes he never truly knew what he was saying plain yes or plain no to but just said one or the other

anyhow and then rested his ears for a spell. Mr. Overhill did manage to squeeze in an actual and solitary
comment just prior to the picture taking and did manage to get his own picture taken separate from the
crew, even managed to get it taken twice as he was
sure his eyes had been closed the first time, after which
he got the fat negro and the paltry negro and the wiry
tattooed white boy and Emmett and the critter along
with somebody else they had picked up somewhere out
onto the tailgate together and Mr. H. Monroe Aycock
backed up with his plastic camera until he could get
everybody just where he wanted to get them and he
snapped one picture and was set to snap a second one
when Mr. Overhill said to him, "Hey buddy, your camera's a little cattywumpus," and Mr. H. Monroe Aycock looked at him in that cold steely way he had
practiced looking at people and let loose with a plain
yes himself.

They did not run the picture cattywumpus exactly,
actually they did not run the picture cattywumpus at all
on account of the full-blooded Loop Road Myrick's
sister's husband who was not the sort to tolerate much
foolishness and looked just once at the photograph all
crooked and sideways and then looked just once at Mr.
H. Monroe Aycock and told him, "This ain't Bat-
man," and so they ran the picture of the crew all
square and proper and ran the picture of Mr. Overhill,
the one with his eyes open, right next to it and filled up
the rest of the top of the page with the story of the
thing which was a dense and highly intricate piece of
journalistic writing that had some plain yeses and some
plain noes to it along with an ample dose of your speck
-of-swirling-dust-in the-vast-darkness-of-space
talk which Mr. Overhill seemed to agree with, seemed
to even have said some of, though he had not actually
listened to much of it and had not uttered any of it
except for the yeses and except for the noes and except
for the "fine sort" which got printed underneath his
name and underneath his picture.

S. A. Knox picked it up off the sheriff's desk and unfolded it and looked at the picture of Mr. Overhill and at the picture of Mr. Overhill's crew and ran the tipend of his tongue up and down the grooves in his teeth as he looked at some of the words and some of the paragraphs though did not truly read any of them prior to refolding the *Chronicle* and handing it over to S. A. Billingham who unfolded it and looked at the picture of Mr. Overhill and at the picture of Mr. Overhill's crew and did not even bother with the words and the paragraphs at all but went ahead and announced, "Raggedy-assed bunch," which S. A. Knox said, "Surenough," to and Sheriff Burton nodded at. They had come in from Raleigh at the request of no one in particular but had just got wind of things, they called it, had just got wind of things at the bureau and so had dropped on by to aid in the apprehension of the suspect, they called it, though Sheriff Burton insisted he was just before apprehending the suspect entirely unaided and he suggested that maybe S. A. Knox and S. A. Billingham ought to get on back to entrapping public officials or whatever it was they'd been up to, and S. A. Billingham ha!ed one time loud and sharp and S. A. Knox honked in his throat and said to Sheriff Burton, "I like you," and S. A. Billingham said he did too. The sheriff, however, did not have much use for either one of them and decided it straightaway, had decided it primarily on account of how S. A. Knox was ever drawing back his coatflaps so as to show off his oiled leather shoulder holster and the buttend of his automatic revolver, drawing them back even in public places or actually especially in public places, and even going as far as to take his entire coat off in Mr. Castleberry's Gold Leaf Dinette where Mr. Castleberry's girl, June, wanted to touch the shank of the thing and was allowed to. The sheriff simply did not hold with that sort of behavior in an enforcement officer and so did not have much regard for S. A. Knox from the outset and went ahead and did not have much regard for S. A. Billingham either as he was in with him and the sheriff told them to go on back to wherever it was they'd come from and get on back to whatever it was they'd been doing but they just ha!ed at him and honked at him and went most everywhere he went so as to be available for consultation and advice though they did not ever get consulted and did not ever get advised.

It seemed to the sheriff they did not ever do anything fruitful and constructive really except for once and it was the sort of fruitful and constructive thing he was getting around to himself but just had not gotten around to yet and S. A. Billingham simply beat him to it when he got up from the Mediterranean sofa and commenced to wander roundabout the tiny paneled living room as Mr. Raeford Lynch swore and spewed on account of one thing or on account of another and the fat Jeeter chewed something and swallowed it. S. A. Billingham looked at the pictures on the walls and looked at the geegaws on the tabletops and flipped through a magazine or two prior to snatching up a photograph off the t.v. and asking the fat Jeeter, "What one's this?" and asking the fat Jeeter, "Well where is he then?" And the sheriff said he had been getting around to it himself but just had not gotten around to it yet, insisted he had been getting around to it himself, said it was the very next thing he was going to do anyhow, and S. A. Billingham held the sidedoor open for him and said, "Uh Huh," to him as the sheriff passed on into the hallway and commenced to climb the stairs with the two S. A.'s just behind him, and he knocked on the door on account of how he was local and they weren't which indicated to him that he should do the knocking and they should just do the standing around and they did just the standing around until a voice from inside asked, "Who is it?" to which the sheriff answered, "Sheriff Burton," and to which the

S.A.'s answered, "Billingham, S.B.I." and "Knox, S.B.I." and then fetched their badges and their picture identification cards out from their inside jacket pockets and showed them to the door panels initially though eventually showed them to Miss Alma Sue Frazier who got told what it was once she asked, "What is it?" and then pointed to the floorboards in reply.

*J*ANE *E*LIZABETH *F*IRESHEETS bought four pink aza-leas that did not look much in the cans and did not look much along the front banister either but got planted there anyhow by Benton Lynch who dug the holes and fertilized the dirt and set the bushes while Jane Elizabeth Firesheets looked on from the ditch so as to get the wide view of the thing, she called it, so as to coordinate the various components into their proper spatial relationships which she had been told she could do best from the ditch by the nurseryman Mr. Jimmy Oakley's only boy, little Jimmy Oakley, who'd at-tended horticulture school and so had a grasp of coor-dinated spatial relationships and such though he could not grow azaleas worth a piddle. She'd brought home a half dozen hydrangeas for the sideyard and had to back on up into the hedgerow to get the wide view of them and as she was not much taken with standing in the hedgerow she asked Benton Lynch would he stop dragging ass if you please and plant the goddamn things and Benton Lynch grunted a little louder than he had been grunting and waggled his elbows a little faster than he had been waggling his elbows and so created the illusion of accelerated labor which satisfied Jane Elizabeth Firesheets for near about five full min-utes after which she asked Benton Lynch would he stop dragging ass if you please and plant the goddamn things.

She decided she wanted to root some ivy around the

trunk of the chinaberry tree in the sideyard and she figured a camellia bush would suit the front right corner of the house as well as anything and so she went after the ivy and went after the camellia bush in the green Nova but had got only partway to Mr. Oakley's nursery when the engine commenced to rumble and sputter and at last cut off altogether leaving Jane Elizabeth Firesheets just halfway where she was going and just halfway from where she'd come and not near anything really but for a solitary house down off the roadbank a ways with a kidney shaped pond before it and some shrubs and bushes and ornamental plant beds and such all throughout the grounds. She admired the general prospect some from up along the pavement and paid particular attention to the various spatial relationships which clearly exhibited themselves even though autumn had set in in earnest and the most of the leaves had dropped off the bushes and the shrubs and the willow trees and were getting themselves raked into a pile by Mr. Lamont Graham's least son, Jules Henry, who had his pipe going and had his rake going and had turned his thoughts loose as well and so did not hear Jane Elizabeth Firesheets call to him and whistle at him and did not see her until she was close enough to him to reach out and touch his sleeve with the tipends of her fingers which she did in fact reach out and touch his sleeve with and Mr. Jules Henry lurched backwards and snatched his pipe from his mouth and said, "Ain't no fishing here," and Jane Elizabeth Firesheets told him, "All right," and reached out all over again with the tipends of her fingers so as to soothe Mr. Jules Henry whose agitation was quite apparent and undisguised.

Of course he settled down presently as Mr. Jules Henry appreciated milky whiteness as much as the next fellow and Jane Elizabeth Firesheets asked him all about his spatial relationships prior to quizzing him on his flora in general, and Mr. Jules Henry offered up

his elbow and squired Jane Elizabeth Firesheets along
the kidney shaped pondbank indicating what was what
and just why it had ended up where it had ended up.
Jane Elizabeth Firesheets said it was plain to her that
Mr. Jules Henry had a way with spatial relationships
and Mr. Jules Henry admitted he had always figured
he did, and they were approaching the bulbous northwest end of the pond admiring Mr. Jules Henry's azaleas and the dying stalks of Mr. Jules Henry's trumpet
flowers along with Mr. Jules Henry's nandinas, or anyway admiring how the azaleas did not cramp and stifle
the trumpet flowers which did not cramp and stifle the
nandinas, when Jane Elizabeth Firesheets shrieked
and let loose of Mr. Jules Henry's elbow so as to dash
over to one of Mr. Jules Henry's concrete benches and
sit herself down on it. "Oh I do like this," she said and
rubbed the benchtop with the flat of both hands and
Mr. Jules Henry, who had got caught up in the dashing
and the activity it had generated all about Jane Elizabeth Firesheets's person, found himself struck speech-
less temporarily and so could not tell her straight off
just where he'd got the concrete bench from and just
how much he'd given for it though he did tell her presently as Jane Elizabeth Firesheets insisted she had to
know on account of how she had to have one just precisely exactly like it.

Naturally it was only once Jane Elizabeth Firesheets
decided she had to have a concrete bench just precisely
exactly like Mr. Jules Henry's concrete bench that she
recollected how the backseat of the green Nova could
not possibly accommodate one which led her to recollect how the backseat and the frontseat and all the rest
of the Nova too was dead and broken on the roadside
and so she got pitiful straightaway and explained her
predicament to Mr. Jules Henry with her lips turned
inside out. Fortunately Mr. Jules Henry possessed a
fair degree of mechanical aptitude along with a hammer and some wrenches and screwdrivers and a drill

press and he fetched his socket set and a flathead and a phillipshead and accompanied Jane Elizabeth Firesheets up the roadbank where he listened to her turn the key and listened to the starter click and peered in the brake fluid container and then proceeded to take various parts of the Nova engine all to pieces prior to blowing on them and putting them back together again which was Mr. Jules Henry's chief talent where automobiles were concerned. And after he'd gotten sufficiently greasy from the ratcheting and the screwing and unscrewing and after he'd gotten noticeably dizzy and lightheaded from all the blowing, Mr. Jules Henry determined and decided that Jane Elizabeth Firesheets's green Nova was dead and broken and so he told her it was dead and told her it was broken and suggested she get it towed off to a proper garage and Jane Elizabeth Firesheets got pitiful all over again. She turned her lips inside out and sucked up air through her nose a time or two and said she did not know what she would do, did not know anybody who would carry her where she needed to be carried as she was from somewhere else altogether and did not make friends easy like some people made friends easy and she dropped her head and commenced to snort and shake at the shoulders and Mr. Jules Henry said, "Now darling," and reached out with the tipends of his fingers.

He called the garage up the road and arranged for the towing and then started his gold Chevrolet pickup and let it run in the sideyard while him and Mrs. Jules Henry and Jane Elizabeth Firesheets drank hot tea in the breakfast room and talked about the ballet and told what ailments they'd suffered through and strayed off on spatial relationships ever so briefly prior to concluding with a catalog of the terminal cases roundabout as rendered by Mrs. Jules Henry who had the sort of flare for gravity that Jane Elizabeth Firesheets said she'd never seen the likes of previously and Mrs. Jules Henry told her back, "Well thank you." Mr. Jules

Henry drove Jane Elizabeth Firesheets out to Mr.
Oakley's straight off where she got her ivy, which was
green and hardy, and where she got her camellia bush,
which was primarily just sticks in a pot, and then they
proceeded northwest a spell to the place where Mr.
Jules Henry had bought his concrete bench, which was
not exclusively a concrete bench outlet but sold ce-
ramic flowerpots too and flagstones and birdbaths and
a general assortment of yard ornaments. They did not
have but two benches to pick from as there had been a
kind of a run on benches, or anyhow as they had sold
the other two in the course of the summer, and Mr.
Jules Henry and an old colored man who could not
raise the bench between them but could drag it well
enough did drag it across the lot to Mr. Jules Henry's
truckbed and then stood together at the tailgate and
speculated as to how they might get it from the ground
up into the truck without actually lifting the thing
while Jane Elizabeth Firesheets for her part wandered
in amongst the ornaments and selected two cement
babies to carry home with her, one of them a cupid for
the ivy bed and the other just a regular cement baby
which showed a remarkable resemblance to Jane Elizabeth Firesheets's daddy's brother's boy except for the
baby part of it. She carried one under each arm and
secured them behind the fender wells of Mr. Jules
Henry's truckbed which Mr. Jules Henry and the old
colored man had not managed to speculate and hypothesize and just plain wish the bench up into yet and
likely they would have left off with the speculating and
the hypothesizing and the wishing too and thereby quit
the whole business if Jane Elizabeth Firesheets had not
picked up one end of the thing herself and so shamed
the two of them into picking up the other end.

Benton Lynch slipped around the house and in
through the backdoor when he heard the truck coming
and he peeked out the little square window in the
frontdoor and watched the gold pickup pull on into the

yard and stop there and he watched Jane Elizabeth
Firesheets get out one side of it and Mr. Jules Henry
get out the other side of it, who he did not know was
Mr. Jules Henry, and he listened to Jane Elizabeth
Firesheets call out for him in the pleasant way she had
of calling out for him when there was somebody aside
from just him and just her to hear it, and then he listened to Jane Elizabeth Firesheets call out for him in
the way she called out for him when it was just him
and when it was just her, and then he listened to Jane
Elizabeth Firesheets call out for him in that if-you-
ever-want-to-see-any-naked-part-of-me-again way she
had of calling out for him, and Benton Lynch opened
the door just enough to stick his head outside and said,
"What is it?"

Mr. Jules Henry wanted to know just what sort of
Lynch he was since Mr. Jules Henry himself was ac-
quainted with an assortment of Lynches, and Benton
Lynch told him he was just a regular Lynch. "Tobacco
Lynch or Chickenhouse Lynch?" Mr. Jules Henry
asked.

"Chickenhouse," Benton Lynch told him.

"I know your daddy," Mr. Jules Henry said. "Been
knowing him for years. Never seen a man could quite
spit to match him."

And Benton Lynch could not recollect ever seeing a
man that could quite spit to match him either.

Jane Elizabeth Firesheets got the ivy and the camellia bush out from the truckbed and removed the cement babies from behind the wheel wells one at a time
commencing with the plain cement baby which she
held up to Benton Lynch as she asked him, "Now who
does this look just exactly like?"

"Nobody I ever seen," Benton Lynch told her.

"Ain't I got a cousin it favors?"

And Benton Lynch said, "Maybe. Somewhere."

"Ain't I got a cousin you seen it favors?" Jane Elizabeth Firesheets asked him.

"I didn't ever see him when he was little," Benton Lynch said.

And Jane Elizabeth Firesheets let the cement baby down some so as to put her own face up into Benton Lynch's face and tell him, "Christ AllMighty!"

She did not pick up either end of the bench this time but let Mr. Jules Henry and Benton Lynch struggle with it their own selves while she directed and orchestrated them to the pear tree in the sideyard straightoff but decided she did not much care for the bench beneath the pear tree once it was beneath it as there would ever be the threat of shock and discomfort from falling pears so she directed and orchestrated the thing around the house to the chinaberry tree which the ivy would get planted at the base of and so make for a suitable backdrop and Jane Elizabeth Firesheets sat down on the flat concrete top and surveyed the vista, she called it, which was only a moderate success as far as vistas go, and she decided maybe the vista would be improved from under the dogwood tree in the frontyard but once she sat beneath it she discovered the vista was not improved much, likely was not improved any, so it was back to the chinaberry tree where Mr. Jules Henry finally dropped his end of the bench and clutched at his shirtfront some and panted prior to making a wry and altogether pointed comment about women as a general form of humanity and though Benton Lynch did not laugh at it outright and did not agree with it outright Jane Elizabeth Firesheets sensed he approved of it anyhow and so she showed him one of her faces which did not seem to mean any solitary sharp and sour thing in particular but just all of them in general.

Once Mr. Jules Henry had wiped his forehead and regulated his breathing he sat himself down on the concrete bench beside Jane Elizabeth Firesheets and surveyed the vista with her. She told him it was not the best vista she'd ever seen but she guessed it would

have to do, and Mr. Jules Henry told her back the
vista did not matter much anyway. "A man don't so
much look out from a bench," he said, "as he looks in
from it," and Jane Elizabeth Firesheets slapped her
hands together and told Mr. Jules Henry that was the
finest and truest thing she'd heard anytime lately and
she asked Benton Lynch wasn't it the finest and truest
thing he'd heard anytime lately too but Benton Lynch
had not been listening exactly and so said, "What's
that?" instead of Yes and instead of No, and Jane Elizabeth Firesheets told Mr. Jules Henry, "Don't matter.
Ain't nothing for him to see." And Benton Lynch said,
"What's that?" all over again.

After Mr. Jules Henry had got thanked and departed Jane Elizabeth Firesheets told Benton Lynch all
about the green Nova like maybe he'd been responsible for it somehow, and she told him it would cost
money to get it back and she told him they did not
have any money much on account of the shrubbery
and the bench and the cement babies and whatnot and
that seemed to be fairly much his fault too. So they
had to make a withdrawal, Jane Elizabeth Firesheets
said, had to make a sizable one, and Benton Lynch
wanted to know how exactly with no green Nova to get
a place in and no green Nova to get away from it in
either and she told him he'd do it like he done it at the
outset, do it like he done it at the start. Naturally Benton Lynch resisted for a spell as he was not particularly
fond of plundering any longer, and Jane Elizabeth
Firesheets put the bullets in the gun and fetched the
brown jacket out from the closet but Benton Lynch
would not take the jacket and would not take the gun
straightaway and attempted to have an opinion on the
matter but Jane Elizabeth Firesheets showed him a
face he could decipher well enough and so the gun got
stuck in his pants and the jacket got buttoned across
his stomach and Jane Elizabeth Firesheets laid her
mouth right up alongside Benton Lynch's head and

told him, "Merry Oaks," prior to nibbling on his ear-lobe.

He decided on the bypass, which was not so remote as other places, and he crossed the gravel road and struck out through the underbrush and on into the woods which was an oak and hickory woods primarily and then a pine grove and then a power company right-of-way and then a pine grove again and then the north border of a potato field which Benton Lynch at last spilled out into and crossed direct through the middle of prior to resting himself atop a rise at the far end where he could look down across the hillocks and creases of a pasture to the bypass and to the Citgo station alongside it which did not seem to have much in the way of business except for a Pontiac at the pumps. He ran most all the way back, sprinted actually, sprinted up the hillocks and along the creases and then due north into the pine thicket and across the right-of-way and into the pine thicket again and straight through to the oak and hickory woods where sprinting became somewhat of a treacherous undertaking but got persisted in nonetheless. He even sprinted through the underbrush and tore his trousers and his kneecaps and fairly darted across the gravel road and around the house to the backdoor which he opened with his shoulder primarily and shut with his entire backside. He could not get a breath straight off, could not swallow either, and tried to grab his knees but could not bend over on account of the pistol barrel, so he just leaned against the door and panted while Jane Elizabeth Firesheets asked him, "Well?" and then asked him, "Well?" again and then patted his left jacket pocket with her hand and his right jacket pocket with her hand prior to crossing her arms over her chest and asking him, "Well?" a third time, but he still could not get up spit or get up air either and so instead drew the Harrington and Richardson Buntline revolver out from his pants, tilted it barrel upwards, and rotated the chamber so as to drop the empty casings one after another onto the linoleum.

She said it was like riding a horse, or anyhow at first she said it was like riding a horse and then she changed it to falling off a horse since she could not seem to make riding a horse work for her like she wanted it to work for her, and she insisted he had to strike out again as straightaway as he could manage to strike out again, but even after she'd soothed him and held him and laid his ear against the fleshy part of her frontside he would not commit himself to striking out anytime soon, would not commit himself to striking out anytime later, would not do anything really but watch the ceiling and blow long forlorn breaths out his mouth and so she continued to soothe him and continued to talk at him and desired to know chiefly just what it was like to shoot at somebody and Benton Lynch set out to tell her but realized early on that he could not tell her really since it was not the shooting but the getting shot at part of it that had made the most serious impression upon him and so she asked what was it like to get shot at anyhow and he set out to tell her but realized early on it was not the sort of thing he could render into words so he did not tell her anything afterall but just watched the ceiling and blew long forlorn breaths out his mouth.

She stayed on him, stayed right atop him maybe not every hour of the twenty-four but in a pure and pervasive sort of way, and she told him to pick himself up off the ground and get back on that thing, told him there weren't no other way to it and likely he'd get put off again but he'd just have to pick himself up one more time as that was how things operated in a general way, but Benton Lynch just watched the ceilings and watched the walls some and ventilated himself and every once and again got soothed though Jane Elizabeth Firesheets gave out of sympathy and compassion a goodly while before Benton Lynch had exhausted his forlorn exhalations so he just laid around breathing hard and Jane Elizabeth Firesheets attempted to impress upon him how food cost money and rent cost money and electricity cost money and how the green Nova would cost a few dollars itself, and though Benton Lynch persisted in watching the ceilings and watching the walls too his forlorn exhalations gradually got transformed into resigned ones.

Jane Elizabeth Firesheets put the bullets in the gun and fetched the brown jacket out from the closet and Benton Lynch did not venture an opinion on the matter this time but just stuck the pistol in his pants and just buttoned the jacket shut over it and got his ear nibbled and got his privates caressed prior to getting shown out the front door. He walked a ways, walked a considerable ways west primarily but south some too and did not ever attempt to get a lift but got one anyhow from a Ruffin Jasper who was out with his brother-in-law and stopped in the road long enough to direct Benton Lynch on up into the truckbed with the Ruffin Jasper's hound which was pleased at the company and stuck its nose direct into Benton Lynch's crotch like dogs will usually insist on doing in a public place. He did not know where he would end up but just sat on the Ruffin Jasper's toolbox and took the air and watched the scenery down 14 to the south and then north on 87 towards Stacy and when he spied the frame grocery and the gaspumps just shy of the town limits he figured he knew where he'd end up after all and slapped the cabroof twice prior to jumping out onto the roadside. And he did not come back and did not come back and Jane Elizabeth Firesheets fretted straightoff and then lapsed into some peevishness which itself turned into a thoroughgoing surly fit and the surliness persisted and even got pitched up some when he still did not come back and did not come back and things had rose up to a wild and venomous head by the time Benton Lynch finally tapped on the front doorglass with his pointy first knuckle.

"Where in the shit you been that's what I'd like to know?" Jane Elizabeth Firesheets asked him once she had succeeded in opening the frontdoor which she had wanted to jerk and yank open for the effect of the thing and which she attempted to jerk and yank open but got thwarted at on account of the chainlatch and so only managed the jerking and the yanking but could not manage the actual opening part of it until she'd shut the door and unfastened the chain but by then the most of her anger had dwindled away to pure exasperation which did not lend itself to anything but hysteria really and so she blubbered and screeched and attempted to say an intelligible thing or two but couldn't seem to until Benton Lynch had stepped into the house and had shut the door behind him when Jane Elizabeth Firesheets caught a glimpse of the Tampa Jewel box under his arm and snatched it away for herself, and she prized open the top with her fingernail and found the two twenties and the singles and the dimes and quarters which was actually more than it looked like though not much more, anyhow not hardly enough to suit Jane Elizabeth Firesheets who slapped the boxtop shut and said she would just be goddamned, just be purely goddamned, and she shook the box at Benton Lynch and defied him to tell her what would buy the groceries and pay the rent and pay the lights and get the green Nova back.

He could not tell her even after she'd asked him three or four times could he tell her. He did not even attempt to work his mouth but just leaned against the front door and at length drew the Harrington and Richardson Buntline revolver out from his trousers, tilted it barrel upwards, and let drop a lone empty casing onto the planking. "I killed a man," he said.

And Jane Elizabeth Firesheets, who had finally got surly all over again, deflated straightaway and asked him, "What for?"

"That."

"This ain't hardly nothing," Jane Elizabeth Firesheets told him and shook the box so as to demonstrate how close to nothing it truly was.

"I figured," Benton Lynch began. "I mean he just stooped over and well I figured that, I mean I just shot him."

"Dead?"

"Lord," Benton Lynch said, "stone dead," and he laid the pistol on the stacked up plastic tabletop and dropped himself onto the sofa without any grace or restraint to speak of.

"In the balls?" Jane Elizabeth Firesheets wanted to know, "killed a man in his balls? Don't seem likely somehow."

And Benton Lynch laid his first finger direct across the center of his chest. "Near about here," he said.

"Well I guess that did punch his ticket," Jane Elizabeth Firesheets observed. "I mean this thing don't shoot peas."

And Benton Lynch told her, "Yea," which was a yea it punched his ticket primarily but somewhat of a yea this thing don't shoot peas as well.

"And I guess he dropped over dead straightaway," Jane Elizabeth Firesheets said, "I mean I don't guess he lurched and stumbled around much, did he?"

"Some," Benton Lynch told her, "sort of spun and pitched off backwards a little."

"And I don't guess they was blood all over," Jane Elizabeth Firesheets said, "I mean I don't guess they was blood all over like at the movie show."

"Come out a foot seemed like."

"A pure foot?"

"Seemed like."

And Jane Elizabeth Firesheets said, "Christ Almighty," and set herself next to Benton Lynch on the sofa with some grace and some restraint too. "It ain't like it's your fault," she said. "I mean there's some things people shouldn't never do when they're getting robbed and stooping and reaching is one of them. So it ain't truly like it's your fault, I mean you did the shooting and the killing but he did the stooping and the reaching and so there's some blame for you but there's some blame for him too."

"Hell, I just killed him," Benton Lynch said, "ain't hardly his fault."

"But he did something," Jane Elizabeth Firesheets told him.

"Not nothing but get shot," Benton Lynch said, "and it don't matter no how."

"Does matter," Jane Elizabeth Firesheets insisted, "does matter too on account of you can't go round feeling like the blame's all to be laid on you cause that ain't the kind of thing a man can bear up under."

"It don't matter," Benton Lynch said. "It don't feel like anything anyhow."

"Not anything?" Jane Elizabeth Firesheets asked him.

"Nothing."

"Might feel like something tomorrow," Jane Elizabeth Firesheets said, "might feel like something altogether entirely different tomorrow," and she drew Benton Lynch's head down to her and set about dragging her fingers across his scalp.

"Maybe," Benton Lynch told her and uncrimped his ear so as to let it lie flat.

And Jane Elizabeth Firesheets said aloud but not to Benton Lynch exactly, "A killer, a mean and vicious killer. Well Jesus Christ."

Jane Elizabeth Firesheets liked it best in the morning as it tended to get her blood going and rouse up her various senses while Benton Lynch generally liked it best most anytime and so was usually ready to accommodate Jane Elizabeth Firesheets once he'd got the crust out of his eyes, but the morning following the afternoon Benton Lynch had shot Mr. Vernon Littlejohn stone dead Jane Elizabeth Firesheets could not seem to muster him into a thoroughgoing rigidity no matter where she laid her fingers and no matter what she probed with the pointy pink tip of her tongue and naturally it was an item of some concern with her that she could near about double it over well into the gyrating and the grinding which did not get contributed to by even the slightest little snatch of nosewhistling. She knew it wasn't the best she'd had ever, knew it wasn't the best he'd had ever either and so did not bother to tell him it was for her and ask him if it was for him but instead she sat up on her elbow and wanted to know was it altogether entirely different in the daylight like she said it might be. Benton Lynch did not answer right off but just studied Jane Elizabeth Firesheets's frontside for a spell commencing with the wheatstraw part and working his way up past the milky white part to the plum-colored parts which were somewhat swelled out but somewhat shrunk in too and drooping and sagging as well off to the low side, and there in the morning sunlight he studied how they drooped and sagged and considered the freckles and the moles on them and the place the bedspread had made along with the hairs that sprouted all roundabout the plum-colored parts, most of them tiny little hairs but some of them not and none of them anything he'd ever bothered to notice much before.

"I bet it's worrisome," Jane Elizabeth Firesheets said. "I bet it's worrisome this morning when it wasn't any worrisome last night. That's it. That's it right there, ain't it?"

And Benton Lynch told her, "Uh Huh," told her he supposed it was.

"Well the blame ain't hardly all yours," Jane Elizabeth Firesheets said and she commenced to refresh him on the stooping and the reaching aspect of the thing and reminded him just how the blame was to get portioned out after which she had a thing or two to say on horses and the riding of them, or actually the falling off of them primarily along with the getting back up on them again, but as Benton Lynch had heard all about the falling off them and the getting back up on them previously he got up from the bed and went out the bedroom door and down the hallway to the bathroom and Jane Elizabeth Firesheets continued to talk about the blame and continued to talk about the guilt and the impact of the whole business only louder now, loud enough to be heard over the watertaps anyway, and Benton Lynch splashed his face and looked at himself in the mirror, looked at the pointy places some and the hollowed out and angular places too, but looked at the two vacant and sunk-in places primarily, and heard the talking from the bedroom, persistent and steady and concluding with a pair of isn't its that did not get answered straightaway and so got contributed to once Jane Elizabeth Firesheets had sat up in the bed so as to increase her volume some. "Isn't it?" she said a third time and Benton Lynch, who figured it probably was or likely could be, splashed his face and told her, "All right."

She counted it out and totaled it up two times over and got somewhere around $64.00 the first time and somewhere around $67.00 the second and so figured it at just about $65.50 which was not enough to pay the rent or the lights and the fuel oil together but was just barely enough to get the green Nova back from the garage on 29 where the engine of it had got taken to pieces and blown on by a certified mechanic who knew just where to be windy and so had got the thing running again. Of course they did not have any way to fetch it back but to walk over and get it and Benton Lynch volunteered to do the walking over and fetching back as the garage was such an appreciable ways from the hideaway-bungalow and as Benton Lynch wanted to get out and wanted to walk anyhow, but Jane Elizabeth Firesheets seemed to feel that he did not have much business out in public since he had if he would pardon her for mentioning it, killed a man just the day before which was precisely the sort of thing to stir up people, and so she walked the appreciable ways to the garage on 29 or anyhow set out with the intention of walking the entire appreciable ways but had only walked a small portion of it when she got a ride with a passing Dunleavy who had been quite taken with her backside and so stopped for her. She bought some eggs on the way home and bought some milk and bought some Champale and picked up a *Chronicle* as well which she opened in her lap in the green Nova and studied the front page of, especially the part all roundabout the photographs of Mr. Vernon Littlejohn with his ordinary arteries and Mr. Vernon Littlejohn with his buckle and his bedsheet, and she took in the leaden sky portion of it and the brisk and gusty portion of it along with the ashen and the tufted and gray and the bracing portions too and of a sudden she found herself altogether struck with the lyrical beauty of the thing, taken with the poetry and the drama of it, and somewhat caught up in the tragedy though not caught up in the tragedy entirely. Mostly she just felt significant, significant primarily on account of Benton Lynch who had been significant himself for a spell but had cocked his hammer and pulled his trigger and thereby had become something beyond significant, something bigger than significant really, something rare and desperate and utterly fearful which naturally enhanced the angularity and the pointiness and the vacancy to a considerable degree, and so Jane Elizabeth Firesheets felt not only significant but began to feel a little sweltery too and she got herself home in a ferocious hurry and burst on in through the front-door with her eggs and her milk and her Champale and her *Chronicle* as well.

Benton Lynch had not moved from the sofa, or anyhow was on it when she got back just like he'd been on when she left, and she deposited the eggs and the

milk and the Champale on the stacked up plastic table
and threw herself down beside him without much
grace or restraint to speak of. "You're famous," she
said, "top of the front page where all the big news
goes," and she dropped the open *Chronicle* onto his
lap for him to peruse and study it but he did not peruse
and study it really, did not hardly glance at it, so she
took it back up and commenced to read it out loud to
him leaving one hand free to gesture with when she got
to the dramatic and the lyrical and the poetical parts of
the thing, and she did wave her hand and move her
fingers and change her voice up and down and generally performed the entire article in a sterling and im-
peccable sort of way but Benton Lynch did not appear
much moved by any part of the business and just sat
like he'd been sitting and watched the wall before him
some and the ceiling above him some. As for Jane
Elizabeth Firesheets, however, she was considerably
moved by the dramatic and the lyrical and the poetical
parts of the thing and she got sweltery all over again
and took her gesturing hand and set it to rubbing and
massaging herself about the neck and shoulders prior
to migrating south a ways, and she told Benton Lynch
there was something about a famous, something about
a dangerous and mean and vicious man that set her
blood to boiling, and Benton Lynch left off watching
the wall and watching the ceiling too and got a little
interested in the workout Jane Elizabeth Firesheets
was inflicting upon herself, and she opened up her
shirtfront and maneuvered her fingers even more vigorously still and Benton Lynch stuck his pointy nose
between the shirtflaps so as to see the process up close
and once Jane Elizabeth Firesheets had detected the
first little piece of whistling she grabbed Benton
Lynch's head from behind and mashed his face direc
into her frontside.

It was all considerably savage and brutal even if i
did take place on a sofa mostly. The clothes got tor

some and balled up and thrown all roundabout the
room and in the throes of passion Benton Lynch
bucked up of a sudden and loosened Jane Elizabeth
Firesheet's front teeth with the back of his head. But
there was not much lasting harm done otherwise and
they banged together and gyrated and even fell off the
sofa and onto the hardwood without missing a beat,
and for a spell Benton Lynch nosewhistled like he had
not nosewhistled anytime lately and Jane Elizabeth
Firesheets oooohhhed and squealed and bounced and
jiggled and generally made such a spectacle of herself
that Benton Lynch began to figure maybe the gyrating
and the oooohhhing and the nosewhistling and the
milky white parts and the plum-colored parts too were
all in fact the best things to partake of and have in this
life, were maybe even the only things worth partaking
of and worth having, but before he could decide and
conclude outright that there was not anything better,
that there was not anything more really, he commenced to tingle and commenced to pant and flush
and felt himself surge and discharge and knew of a
sudden that there was actually not anything worth partaking of and worth having, especially not the milky
white parts and the plum-colored parts and the wheatstraw parts too. And Jane Elizabeth Firesheets exhaled most profoundly and laid the back of her hand
across her forehead and said it was the best she'd had
ever, and she asked him wasn't it the best he'd had
ever too, wasn't it just absolutely the best he'd ever
had and Benton Lynch grunted prior to blowing out a
breath himself and contemplating the ceiling.

   She said she would not ask him to but for the rent
money and the light money and the fuel oil money as
well as the grocery money which she hated to even
bother him with as he'd shot at one clerk lately and
killed another, but it did not seem to Jane Elizabeth
Firesheets that the time was right for them to get
evicted or disconnected or frozen or go hungry either

and so she had to suggest and felt compelled to insist that Benton Lynch do what it was he generally did when things got tight and do it just like he generally did it so as to maintain the rhythm and habit of things and keep his nerve up where he usually kept it, and though he was not perceptibly enthusiastic Benton Lynch didn't object or argue and instead just sat around on or about the sofa and laid around on or about the bed and watched all the walls and watched all the ceilings for three or four days which Jane Elizabeth Firesheets called cooling off but which did not seem to be anything really to Benton Lynch. And when they did at last go out Jane Elizabeth Firesheets decided when and decided where and fetched the map out from the glove compartment and decided that too. For his part Benton Lynch only did the actual plundering while Jane Elizabeth Firesheets parked off a ways and left the engine to run, and he felt fairly usual and fairly normal when he asked his question and when he showed his revolver and when he gave his answer too, but once Mr. Radford lowered his arms some so as to reach for the cash drawer Benton Lynch got agitated of a sudden and commenced to feel all tight and quivery inside and he shook his gun close by Mr. Radford's upper lip and threatened him afresh and turned part way around to Mr. Burke and Mr. Mountcastle and made some overtures to them as well prior to returning his attention to Mr. Radford and addressing him all over again with the breech of the revolver mostly, so Mr. Radford reached down to the cash drawer without seeming to move his hand or his arm either and brought out just regular money which he put into sack.

Jane Elizabeth Firesheets said it was a pure haul said she could tell just by the bulk of the thing, and she lifted the sack up off the carseat and set it down again and said she figured it for $400.00 anyway and maybe $450.00 and even after she'd spilled it out on the bed spread she still figured it for $375.00 and thought it might hit $300.00 while she was partway through the counting of it, but it did not ever approach $300.00 really, did not ever get past $238.00 which it did not even get up to until the third time through, but Jane Elizabeth Firesheets still insisted it was a pure haul coming as it did just after the $65.50 which had not struck her as any sort of haul at all. And she commenced to spend it straightaway like maybe it was $400.00 after all, and she paid the rent and paid the lights and paid the fuel oil and took the Nova out to the K-Mart Plaza where she went into the Food Lion straightoff and bought a family pack of ribeye steaks and chopped mushrooms in a jar and large grade A eggs instead of the medium ones and real butter and a bottle of sparkling water and beer imported from Canada and spinach quiche in a milk carton and the pie shells to go with it along with four rolls of the powderblue toilet paper that smelled so sweet and she figured she was done once she got to the checkout but she decided she'd have herself a magazine and as she could not choose between the *People* and the *Us* and the *Star* and the *Life* and the *Cosmopolitan* and the *Glamour* and the *Enquirer* and the *Family Circle* and the diet book and the horoscope book and the word puzzles she went ahead and bought one of just about everything but the almanac and she said, "Cash," in a loud high voice when they asked how would she pay for it all and she showed off the twenties and the tens and the fives and the ones too. There was not hardly any left after that but there was enough anyhow to carry into the K-Mart where she could not buy outright what she had intended to buy outright but where she could lay it away and did lay away a little Japanese radio/television that would sit on your stomach if you had the muscles for it and she figured she did.

As for Benton Lynch, he just cooled off some on the sofa and cooled off some on the bed and cooled off some at the kitchen table and watched the walls and watched the ceiling and looked at the woman on the *Cosmopolitan* and at the woman on the *Glamour* and tried to work a word puzzle, even wrote down some letters in the boxes, but did not get any of it right and so went back to the walls and the ceiling and the women on the magazines until the Thursday he got to see himself on a rock and he looked at that for a spell. He sat around for near about ten or twelve days altogether and looked at and watched most every item in the house and anything he could spy out the window too, and every morning Jane Elizabeth Firesheets drove down the road to the Easy-Go Mart and brought back a *Chronicle* and she would read the parts about Benton Lynch out loud to him when there were parts about Benton Lynch to read and she read the one about Mr. Overhill with special relish and vigor, the first time through with the vigor so as to get the facts of it and so as to, ever so briefly, vilify the wiry tattooed white boy, and the second time through with the relish so as to savor Mr. H. Monroe Aycock's style and poetical grace which Jane Elizabeth Firesheets did the most of the savoring of though she encouraged Benton Lynch to savor it some himself.

He laid around a week before she even hinted that maybe he would finish cooling off sometime and go out and get hot all over again and it was not until ten days that she said outright he would surely plunder somebody somewhere sometime soon and it was not until twelve days that she told him where and told him when and attempted to persuade him to agree with it, attempted to persuade him with her plum-colored parts primarily which she brought out from her nightgown into the morning light, and as it was a Sunday the plum-colored parts struck Benton Lynch as particularly forbidden and so naturally all the more worth having and he endeavored to have them straightoff and lunged at them nose foremost but got intercepted and interfered with and just generally thwarted until he agreed to the where and agreed to the when after which he was given the free run he had been burning to get until he got it when he decided he did not want it much after all. She did what she did to him like she usually did it and he did what he normally did to her and they got tangled and locked up together like they most always got tangled and locked up and in the regular sequence and then there was some oooohhhing and groaning on her part followed by a smattering of nose-whistling on his, all of it concluding and terminating in a general disengagement and she laid on her side of the bed and whimpered some and perspired and he laid on his side of the bed and sweated and just laid still and just sweated until he got up of a sudden and carried himself off to the bathroom where he splashed his face and looked in the mirror at his pointy places and at his angular and hollowed out places prior to glaring down between his legs at something else entirely and he said, "You," which came out loud and firm and primarily in the way of an accusation, and from the bed Jane Elizabeth was just set to ask him, "You who?" had her mouth all open and ready for it but did not get to ask it after all on account of the squealing and the screeching and the brief spell of honking that came from outside somewhere, somewhere close by, and Jane Elizabeth Firesheets said, "What in the shit is that?" instead which was not what she had opened and readied her mouth to say but which seemed to suit better to the moment.

THE SHERIFF beat the bullhorn one time with the fleshy part of his palm, which was the most of his palm, and said, "Goddamn this thing," without pulling the trigger as that was not what he had a mind to broadcast. But once he did in fact pull the trigger after the solitary click the bullhorn honked again and

squealed again and about half screeched and so Sheriff
Burton beat it one more time with his open hand and
pummeled it with some additional abuse. Deputy Larson told him it was the batteries likely but the sheriff
snapped back that he had put in new ones just lately
and he wondered out loud why it was Deputy Larson
couldn't watch the crowd like he'd been instructed to
do and Deputy Larson said, "Yes sir," and hung his
head and turned back around to the crowd which was
not much of a crowd really but just Mr. H. Monroe
Aycock and Mr. Jack Albright and Mr. Jack Albright's
negro tenant who was a Stone and Mr. Jack Albright's
negro tenant's dog who was a plain assortment of most
everything possible.

   S. A. Knox said he had his mouth too close to it and
S. A. Billingham said he had the trigger pulled in too
far and so he drew his mouth back some and let the
trigger out some and it did not screech and did not
squeal and did not honk but a little and so the sheriff
went ahead and drew a breath and said, "We know
you're in there," which the sheriff had always wanted
to say, especially through a bullhorn, and it came out
and filled the air almost exactly like he'd imagined it
would except for the squealing which punctuated it.
"Don't make any trouble now," he added. "You'd best
give yourself up," and that came out plain and clear
without any squealing whatsoever but without any volume much either as the sheriff had inadvertently let
loose of the trigger. So he squeezed the trigger again
and the bullhorn screeched and honked and squealed
and he beat it twice this time prior to throwing it onto
the ground and using just his cupped hands and just his
lungs instead. "Don't make any trouble now," he hollered. "You'd best give yourself up," and him and
S. A. Knox and S. A. Billingham and the crowd and
Deputy Larson over his shoulder studied the frontdoor
of the hideaway-bungalow, which was the only door
they could see of it, but nobody saw it swing open

nobody saw it get set ajar even the least little bit as it did not get swung open or set ajar either but just got looked out ever so briefly by Benton Lynch and by Benton Lynch only as Jane Elizabeth Firesheets was not tall enough to see out the little square windows.

S. A. Billingham picked the bullhorn up off the ground and laid his mouth next to the little end of it and squeezed the trigger and identified himself and identified his partner and identified their agency and did not get preceded by any squealing or screeching or honking, did not get interrupted by any, and did not get punctuated by any either which prompted Deputy Larson to wonder if maybe it wasn't the batteries after all, to wonder if maybe throwing it on the ground hadn't done it some good, and he asked Sheriff Burton if maybe he didn't figure that was the case of it and while Sheriff Burton had a few things to say to Deputy Larson in reply they did not any of them have much at all to do with the bullhorn or the batteries either. S. A. Billingham said he knew they were in there and he said they'd be smart not to make any trouble and go ahead and give themselves up, and when the sheriff told S. A. Billingham he'd just finished saying the same thing himself, S. A. Billingham told him it was the sort of thing that bore repeating especially without the squealing and the screeching and the honking to distract from it, and Deputy Larson figured it was a bad connection, a bad connection that maybe the impact had healed up, and he set out to tell how he'd beat his lawnmower with a stick of redoak once but got sent around to the back of the house by Sheriff Burton who was not much interested in the deputy's mechanical aptitude.

The mayor's secretary had been fairly much touring the city ever since she heard where they were going and why which she found out from Mrs. Deputy Larson who did not get occasion to tell the mayor's secretary hardly anything she did not know already, and as it was a Sunday morning people did not have much to do but worship and since a desperate criminal holed up in a farmhouse and surrounded by the law seemed a degree or two more inviting than an oak pew most people figured they'd worship later. So the crowd, which had started out as two white men, a negro, and a dog, expanded in size and complexity and came to encompass all manner of people who were as a group anxious to see justice done and a little bloodthirsty too. Naturally Sheriff Burton recognized the bloodthirstiness right off as he was trained to and so he called on the radio for his auxiliary deputies which was the loan officer at the First Union, Mr. Fontain, along with Mr. Demitt the pharmacist, but he had not needed a radio really since Mr. Fontain and Mr. Demitt were as bloodthirsty as the next fellow and came out from the crowd so as to control it and marshal it as best they could, and they did control it and did marshal it on their own for a while but got assisted eventually by Miss Bambi Kinch who stepped out from the Action News 5 van and marshaled and controlled the crowd herself without even attempting to.

She offered Sheriff Burton her fingers and Sheriff Burton took ahold of them and shook them ever so slightly and got told what a pleasure it was to be seen again and said near about the same thing himself and was set to make a comment or two on the general predicament when S. A. Knox S.B.I. stuck out his fingers to Bambi Kinch and told her, "S. A. Knox S.B.I." prior to pondering Bambi Kinch's yellow hair which was S. A. Knox's favorite kind of hair to find on a woman. Bambi Kinch shook S. A. Billingham's finger too and Mr. Fontain and Mr. Demitt wanted their fingers shook as well but had a crowd to control and marshal and so had to settle for nods and grins and such. Larry got the camera out from the back of the van and carried it over to where Bambi Kinch wanted it which was four different places altogether before he struck on one with a backdrop to suit her, and Bub switched on the switches and plugged in the plugs and set up the antenna and then carried the camera cable over to Larry when he was good and ready to. She talked to the sheriff first and was careful to put the bungalow door just between him and her, and the sheriff told her this and told her that and speculated and wondered and then got cut off while he still had some theorizing left to do and he told Bambi Kinch he had some theorizing left but she told him back she wanted a few words from an S.A. on account of their general credibility, she called it, and S. A. Knox volunteered to give her whatever few words she wanted and he told her armed robbery and told her attempted armed robbery and told her assault and told her murder one and then he rattled off the names near about as fluently as the sheriff himself, commencing with the Busick and concluding not with the Radford exactly but with a widowwoman Smallwood instead, a widowwoman Smallwood from Altamahaw who had got all fractured and scrambled and could not recall how. And Bambi Kinch said, "Him?" and S. A. Knox directed her attention around to the green Nova and told her, "Him for sure," and then laid his hands on his hips so as to show off his straps and his holster and pistolbutt which launched Sheriff Burton into a regular paroxysm but not extended regular paroxysm on account of the scream that came out from the bungalow-hideaway or anyhow came out from the entrails of it, Bambi Kinch called it, and she asked S. A. Knox what it was anyhow and S. A. Knox told her, "Duress likely," which satisfied Bambi Kinch well enough and satisfied S. A. Knox too but did not much suit the sheriff who wondered out loud, "What in the hell was hat?" and Jane Elizabeth Firesheets said it had been ntended for a plaintive cry.

"Well what's the good of it?" Benton Lynch wanted o know, and Jane Elizabeth Firesheets explained how they would not storm a place that had a threatened woman in it and it seemed to her she could not suggest and hint at a threatened woman any better than with a plaintive cry so she cut loose with a second one and then peeked out from behind the front windowshade to see the effect of it which was not entirely apparent straightaway as Jane Elizabeth Firesheets could not read Duress off S. A. Knox's lips though Sheriff Burton's sentiments seemed plain enough. And Jane Elizabeth Firesheets said, "I knew it, I knew it right off. Come here, Benton, come here and look and see if it's not that woman off the t.v. I figured it was, I'd know that yellow hair anyplace. Come here. Come here." But Benton Lynch did not go anywhere really and just stayed on the sofa with his pistol in his hands and his arms dangling down between his knees and when he was not watching the ceiling and watching the walls he watched Jane Elizabeth Firesheets's backside ever so briefly and blew out a forlorn exhalation.

Sheriff Burton said he did not give a happy shit what they called it as long as they did something on account of it, and then he pardoned himself to Bambi Kinch who excused him.

"Like what?" S. A. Knox wanted to know, and Sheriff Burton told him as he was the S.A. seemed he could come up with something on his own, or anyhow him and S. A. Billingham together might be able to generate a solitary idea between them, just some tiny little useful notion, which Sheriff Burton said it seemed to him they should be able to do somehow.

"All right then," S. A. Knox said, and S. A. Billingham said, "All right then," for himself, and they did get together and did discuss the matter and at length did decide on some tiny little useful notion which S. A. Knox got the privilege of announcing as he was the most maligned S. A. of the two. "We'll far out," he said.

"What for?" the sheriff asked him.

"So as to surround the place," S. A. Billingham told him.

"And then?"

"Why then we'll tell him to come out," S. A. Knox said.

"And he'll come out?" the sheriff wanted to know.

"That's right."

"The boy's killed one man, shot at another, cracked an old woman's head open, and plundered near about the entire countryside and he's gone come out just because you tell him he'd better?"

"That's right."

"What about the girl?" the sheriff said. "What about the DURESS?"

"Might be she's in with him," S. A. Knox said back. "Might be she's in with him and he's just gone mean on her."

"Might be she's not."

"Well, she likely was once anyhow and maybe still is. I got my suspicions."

"Oh you do?"

"Yes sir."

"Well what's it gone be then?" the sheriff wanted to know.

"We'll fan out." S. A. Knox told him. "We'll fan out and take him when he comes to us."

And Sheriff Burton said, "All right," and S. A. Billingham said, "Agreed," and S. A. Knox said, "Agreed," too just to finish the thing.

The sheriff circled off to the right and the S. A.'s circled off to the left which put the sheriff in the backyard and the S. A.'s in the frontyard and forced Deputy Larson over into the sideyard, and as they had not agreed beforehand just who would do the shouting, Sheriff Burton and the two S. A.'s together commenced to shout almost in unison very nearly the same request but not the same request exactly and so they all three decided independently they would shout again and thereby clear up any lingering confusion as to the coming out and the surrendering, and they all three did shout again, almost harmoniously this time.

Jane Elizabeth Firesheets said she'd never been so worked up over a thing before, said she'd never felt the blood pump and surge in her like it was pumping and like it was surging and she stepped round from window to window and snuck a look out at the crowd and at the S.A.'s and at the deputy and at the sheriff himself and her blood pumped and surged and got her generally worked up like she'd never been worked up over a thing before. She told Benton Lynch they'd insist on a helicopter and insist on a jet and insist on getting carried wherever it was they wanted to get carried like Daytona or maybe even so far as Miami where they had brick houses too, and she said they'd hide and lay low for a spell and Benton Lynch would grow a mustache and she'd have her hair trimmed away and maybe they'd get some legitimate work somewhere after a bit and so just blend in and mesh and whatnot, and she asked Benton Lynch wasn't that the way it should go, wasn't that the way it could happen, but from his place on the sofa Benton Lynch just breathed hard and watched the ceiling and watched the walls and said he couldn't grow a mustache, said he didn't have the follicles for it.

Sheriff Burton told Deputy Larson, "Pssssst," and Deputy Larson thought it was a groundsnake and jerked his feet out from under himself and jigged briefly prior to getting Psssssted at again and then just plain called to and so he left his post in the sideyard and held a brief confab in the back of the house with Sheriff Burton who sent him off to the trunk of the squad car after the gun and after the tear gas which he had not consulted the S.A.'s on but which he figured would be a little more persuasive than all the hollering and yelling he could muster. And though Jane Elizabeth Firesheets did not know what the deputy was off

to fetch exactly she saw for herself he was off to fetch
something anyhow and she called to Benton Lynch
from the backdoor and told him to come look how the
deputy was off to fetch something and Benton Lynch
came to the backdoor to look out the windows of it
and see for himself but the deputy was already gone
from sight by the time he got there and the sheriff
moved around to the sideyard and so got gone from
sight presently himself which left nothing to look at
really, or nothing anyhow to hold Jane Elizabeth Firesheets's attention and she hurried off to the frontwin-
dow so as to see what it was the deputy had gone off to
fetch while Benton Lynch lingered at the backdoor
and looked out the little square windows of it across
the yard to the tobacco field, where the stalks had
been cut and plowed under, and on beyond that to the
pine grove and the water hole amidst it and the scantling dogwoods that had managed to take root and
flourish somehow or another and above it all to the sky
which was not especially tufted or gray but plain blue
mostly clear out to where it disappeared over the pine
tree tops which was where Benton Lynch looked primarily once he had looked most everywhere else and
which was what he exhaled and sighed at prior to
throwing the barrel bolt and turning the knob.

Jane Elizabeth Firesheets did not hear the bolt and
did not hear the knob and did not hear the thing open
but heard it shut plain enough and so ran to it and
looked out the little square windows of it at Benton
Lynch's backside as it receded from her across the yard
and on into the field, and while Sheriff Burton did not
hear the bolt or the knob and did not hear the thing
open either he heard it shut plain enough his own self
and ducked around the corner of the house in time to
see the profile of the pointy nose and one hollowed out
cheek and a solitary vacant eye along with the Harrington and Richardson Buntline revolver dangling at
the end of the near arm. He cocked his own nickel-

plated pistol and hollered, "Hold it, buddy," with
about as much authority as he could manage but the
nose and the cheek and the eye and the gun along with
everything else beat it on out of the backyard and into
the dirt field where the feet went from furrow to furrow and generated some velocity. The sheriff hollered,
"Hold it, buddy," a second time as loud and earnestly
as before and fired a shot into the air but the feet did
not stop or even slow any and so he aimed this time
and hollered with his arms out before him and his left
eye shut and then he squeezed off the first one and the
whole angular pointy and hollowed out body flinched
but proceeded nonetheless, or anyhow proceeded until
he squeezed off the next one which took the feet away
and put Benton Lynch on his knees atop a furrow
where he bobbed back and forth until the third one hit
him and knocked him over on his face. And Sheriff
Burton opened his left eye and trotted some himself
out across the backyard and into the field while Jane
Elizabeth Firesheets took up a dishtowel off the
kitchen countertop and commenced to rip it into long
slender pieces.

They all came round the house presently, the S. A.'s
in somewhat of a squat and with their guns drawn, but
everybody else stark upright and at a dead run with
Deputy Larson in the front followed hard up by Mr.
Fontain and Mr. Demitt and the unmarshaled and uncontrolled crowd behind them, or anyhow that part of
the unmarshaled and uncontrolled crowd that still had
some run in them which included Bambi Kinch who
always wore her flats just in case and had included the
cameraman Larry until his cable got wrapped around a
treestump and stopped him of a sudden. The sheriff
had come up cautious and ready but there had not
been anything to be cautious and ready about really as
did not anything move but the plume of dust his nostril
stirred up and then there was not that even, so he
loosed the pistol from the fingers and eyed the empty

chambers of it and then got run up on and surrounded and just generally washed over by the S.A.'s and the deputies and Miss Bambi Kinch and everybody else too who all wanted to see a dead man up close and saw one. And Sheriff Burton said to S. A. Knox and S. A. Billingham, "He wouldn't stop," and he said to Deputy Larson and Deputies Fontain and Demitt and Bambi Kinch and everybody else too, "He wouldn't stop," and S. A. Billingham poked the pointy tip of his shoe into Benton Lynch's ribcage and thereby satisfied himself that the culprit was in fact deceased before stepping across the body so as to grab up a piece of Sheriff Burton's shoulder with his fingers and tell him, "Outstanding," which was followed by what congratulations and salutations seemed appropriate to the moment and the sheriff got his hand shook and got his back pounded and even took ahold of Bambi Kinch's fingers for the second time in an hour before anybody recollected Jane Elizabeth Firesheets who Deputy Larson recollected first off and he said to the sheriff, "What about her?" and jerked his head at the house which reminded the S.A.'s primarily and they both exclaimed, "Her!" all at once and to each other prior to making off in a squat with their guns drawn.

They took up positions on either side of the backdoor and S. A. Billingham kicked the thing in with his left foot as somehow that seemed to him more expedient than turning the knob and S. A. Knox plunged on into the kitchen with S. A. Billingham right up tight behind him. They snuck up the hallway to the front room where S. A. Knox peeked behind the sofa and S. A. Billingham yanked open the coat closet door without discovering anything between them really except for an ever so insubstantial stale sock aroma, and then they snuck back down the hallway into the bathroom and S. A. Billingham snatched up a handful of shower curtain and jerked the thing down off the hooks but did not find anything in the tub except for

the green spot the drip had made, and as it was S. A.
Knox that went into the bedroom first it was S. A.
Knox that truly found her when she was at last found
though S. A. Billingham came in just behind him and
found her himself and together they stood fairly much
in the doorway and holstered their pistols and dropped
their chins some and just generally contemplated Jane
Elizabeth Firesheets who lay all naked and goose
pimply atop the mattress with her ankles tied to the
iron bedposts on one end and her wrists tied to the
iron bedposts on the other. She humphed and har-
umphed and attempted to speak but she had a pair of
gauzy underpanties stuffed in her mouth and so could
not make much in the way of conversation and instead
she jerked and squirmed and rolled on the bedlinen
revealing the back of her milky whiteness as well as the
front of it and setting her plum-colored parts into fairly
violent motion and they accelerated to a constant and
near about mesmerizing speed and maintained it until
S. A. Knox sat himself down on the mattress and relieved Jane Elizabeth Firesheets of the balled up gauzy
underpanties while S. A. Billingham loosed the rags
from her ankles and the rags from her wrists. "Praise
God!" she wailed. "Praise God!" and as S. A. Knox
endeavored to wrap his coat around her she laid her
bare frontside against him and whimpered.

*M*R. *EMMETT DABB* had mixed the punch in a bucket
and would not tell what it was but for the gingerale
that the Leaksville Lassiter deciphered and arrived at
once she'd separated the various components in her
mouth and smacked them between her lips, and
though Mrs. Estelle Singletary insisted it was Hi-C too
Mr. Dabb would not admit to anything but the gingerale and thereby touched off and peeved Mrs. Estelle
Singletary who had a great native capacity for irrita-
tion and she snapped at and bickered with Miss Ber-

nice Fay Frazier for a spell to relieve herself some. The
food got put all roundabout the trailer on most everything that had a top to it, and as there was not any
considerable room inside, the men got to stand outside
chiefly except to get the chicken and the deviled eggs
and the bean salad and the sponge cake when they felt
a need to. The fat Jeeter and little Ivy Jeeter Throckmorton Lanier sat together on the Mediterranean sofa
and held each other in their arms and every now and
again the fat Jeeter would dab at her eyes with Mr.
Raeford Lynch's yellow bandanna and wonder aloud,
"Why, oh why?" and when his mouth and his throat
were otherwise unoccupied the Reverend Mr. Lynwood Wilkerson would attempt to tell her straightoff
just exactly precisely why, oh why, but mostly he would
hold up his open hand and chew fast for a spell. For his
part Mr. Raeford Lynch was intensely profane and
made some extraordinarily vile comments on the outside of the trailer and every now and again stepped
through the doorway and made a vile comment or two
on the inside as well prior to excusing himself to the
reverend and to the ladies and especially to Miss Jane
Elizabeth Firesheets who was in the care of the widow
Mrs. Askew and the widow Mrs. Hayes in the far
corner of the den and who found herself from time to
time in the care of Mr. Raeford too which got her knee
touched and her arm rubbed and her general self
leered at. And it was while Mr. Raeford was touching
and rubbing and leering that the men on the outside
did their most earnest conversing under the guidance
of Mr. H. Monroe Aycock who had come as just a
regular human being and did not take notes or snap-
shots but nonetheless could not help but observe how
apt it all was, dramatically speaking, and the consensus
among the men fell with Mr. H. Monroe Aycock who
let his left foot up on the trailer step, laid his forearm
across his knee and said dramatically it was likely the
aptest thing he'd ever seen.

Commander Avery selected the casket himself as not the fat Jeeter or Mr. Raeford or Otway Burns either were much disposed to pick one, and he decided upon the plain box with the iron fittings which seemed to him to make an altogether appropriate statement and he said as much to the fat Jeeter and Mr. Raeford and Otway Burns too but did not any of them seem taken with the aura of the thing except maybe for Jane Elizabeth Firesheets who had not got consulted exactly but went ahead and observed that the pine casket was rough and rugged like he'd been rough and rugged, and she attempted to observe an additional something but her lips turned all inside out on her and she put her face against Otway Burns's coatfront and touched his arm with the tipends of her fingers. The people who viewed him were most generally the people who had gorged themselves in his honor the night previous, or not in his honor exactly but somewhat in his honor anyhow, and they arrived at the Heavenly Rest curious to see what he looked like up close since not anybody of them had known him much but for his likeness on a rock. The fat Jeeter received sympathy on the Duncan Phyfe couch with little Ivy Jeeter Throckmorton Lanier on her left side and Mr. Raeford's sister Vergie on her right side and with Jane Elizabeth Firesheets off just a slight ways in a chair where she got some sympathy too and hard looks every now and again on top of it. But sympathy was not primarily what people had come on account of and instead they gathered all roundabout Benton Lynch's half-open casket and viewed him with noticeable intensity as he had been mean and vicious and savage and considerably sought after and finally shot to pieces though he did not look it really, did not look anything really but pointy and sunk in and hollowed out and just generally deceased.

The men malingered outside in the cold on Commander Avery's frontporch and smoked and spat and listened to Mr. Fontain and Mr. Demitt who raised up their arms like the sheriff had raised up his arms and said, "Hold it, buddy," like the sheriff had said Hold it, buddy, and closed their left eyes like the sheriff had closed his left eye and made pistol shots with their breath, and then they talked about the sheriff, not just Mr. Fontain and Mr. Demitt, but all of them talked about the sheriff in a way he'd have been pleased to hear if he'd been there to do it, but he was not there to do it as it had not seemed the fitting and just place for him to be and so he took supper with Mrs. Messick and got talked at and congratulated and fawned over and was even offered seconds once but not in a voice that seemed at all sincere and he wasn't hungry anyhow and just drank his water and picked at his greenbeans and tore his piece of loafbread in half.

He led the procession himself though Deputy Larson said he'd do it, insisted he'd be pleased to, and he used the lights primarily but let loose with the siren every now and again at crossings and he took the route by the hospital and then left across the boulevard to the Burlington road and out to the cemetery. The afternoon was cold and likely tufted and gray to the trained eye though just cloudy to most everybody else and sunless and windy too out in the memorial park part of the cemetery where they had bulldozed the trees but only breezy every now and again up on the hillside where there were some elms and some oaks and some cedars of Lebanon and even some shrubbery here and there to break the monotony of pure headstones. Mr. Raeford's brothers Benton, Jip, and Harland Lynch carried one side of the casket and Mr. Raeford himself along with Otway Burns and William Petworth carried the other side of it and they set the whole business down over the hole atop the belts of the commander's shiny chrome casket lowering contraption which freed Mr. Raeford to fetch the fat Jeeter out from one side of the limousine and freed Otway Burns to fetch Jane Elizabeth Firesheets out from the other. And all the Lynches and the Jeeter-Lynch and the Firesheetses sat in the folding metal chairs under the canopy, that is it was only Lynches and the Jeeter-Lynch and the Firesheetses until Mrs. Phillip J. King fell over a guy wire and got put in Mr. Harland Lynch's chair to collect and tend to herself.

The Reverend Wilkerson said pretty much what he usually said but with some embellishments as it was a special case, and the tenor Mr. Tupperman sang The Lord's Prayer without any accompaniment or much success to speak of, after which the proceedings got benedicted by the reverend and at last finalized by Mrs. Jack Vestal who did not sound out with her "Farewell, brave soul" all shrill and firm like usual but said it anyhow and flung her good linen handkerchief which settled on the very lip of the grave and got kicked on in by Mr. Raeford. And that was fairly much the end of it though people loitered and smoked like people will and the widow Mrs. Askew and Mrs. Hayes corralled little Ivy Jeeter Throckmorton Lanier's husband down the hillside and waved their fingers at him for a spell. And then there was not anybody left but for the pair of men from the vault company, who sealed up the casket and covered it over, and but for Sheriff Burton, who stood off a ways and watched the canopy come down and the chairs get folded and the grave get filled up, and then there was not anybody but him and he still stood off a ways and still watched until a gust of wind came ripping down from the hillcrest and blew the solitary wreath over backwards when Sheriff Burton turned of a sudden and very nearly fled.

Mrs. Messick had prepared an actual beefroast and dirt grown chunked potatoes with butter in them as opposed to the flaked and reconstituted variety she was usually partial to, and she called up the stairway and hollered up the stairway and screeched up the stairway and then dialed the phone but she did not get an answer and did not get an explanation and did not get an apology, did not get anything but agitated and disgusted and so called and hollered and screeched up the stairway to tell Sheriff Burton as much and when he did not answer and did not explain and did not apologize again she got more agitated and more disgusted. He had not turned on the lights when he came in as it had not been dark when he came in but just gray and murky and he sat in the bedroom with the table and the straight chair in it chewing his foremost finger and watching the afternoon give way to the evening, and though he heard the calling and the hollering and the screeching and the ringing of the telephone he just sat in the darkness and breathed in and breathed out and figured and pondered and wondered until late in the night.

Fuquay-Varina
1983

About the Author

T. R. Pearson was born in Winston-Salem, North Carolina, in 1956 and now lives in Fuquay-Varina, North Carolina. *A Short History of a Small Place* was his first novel.

SOME
OF THE
BEST
IN
SOUTHERN
FICTION
by
Lee Smith